PRAISE FOR *Over Tumbled Graves:*

"Riveting. . . . Walter's omniscient narrative explores the inner hopes, fears, and motivations of all [his] people, bringing depth and tenderness of emotion to every portrait . . . with setting and dialogue so real that the reader feels as if he or she were sitting in a corner of the squad room."

—*Washington Post Book World*

"[A] powerful fiction debut. . . . The book stands out from run-of-the-mill serial killer novels, thanks to the full-bodied characterizations of its protagonists. . . . Walter writes dialogue that actually sounds like real people talking."

—*Seattle Times*

"[A] disquieting first novel. . . . Walter doesn't stint on the procedural details that give his novel the conviction of authenticity. But his novelist's instincts also provide the plot setbacks and corrosive humor. . . . Walter applies the same incisive sensitivity to the victims, their stalker, and the city itself."

—*New York Times Book Review*

"Exceptional. . . . As Jess Walter probes the nature of evil and its impact, he challenges his readers to reconsider their own complexity."

—Ursula Hegi

"Stunning. . . .Works on deeper levels to leave us thoughtful as well as breathless. . . . Crisply told and filled with heart-stopping moments."

—*Portland Oregonian*

OVER
TUMBLED
GRAVES

OVER
TUMBLED
GRAVES

JESS WALTER

10 ReganBooks
Celebrating Ten Bestselling Years
*An Imprint of HarperCollins*Publishers*

A hardcover edition of this book was published in 2001 by ReganBooks, an imprint of HarperCollins Publishers.

First paperback edition published 2005

Designed by Elliott Beard

The Library of Congress has cataloged the hardcover edition as follows:
Walter, Jess, 1969–
    Over tumbled graves / Jess Walter
      p. cm.
    ISBN 0-06-039386-6
    1. Police—Washington (State)—Spokane—Fiction. 2. Spokane (Wash.)—Fiction. 3. Serial murders—Fiction. I. Title.
PS3573.A4722834 O94 2001
813'.54—dc21
                                      00-045826

ISBN 0-06-098867-3 (pbk.)

06 07 08 09 ❖/RRD 10 9 8 7 6 5 4 3

In the faint moonlight, the grass is singing
Over the tumbled graves.

—T. S. ELIOT, *THE WASTE LAND*

ACKNOWLEDGMENTS

These pages were puzzled over by some fellow writers and friends, chiefly Dan Butterworth, whose enthusiasm was inspiring, his criticism invaluable. Jim Lynch shared pages as well as angst, and Terry Morehouse researched my cop questions and took me skiing once.

My deep thanks and respect to Cal Morgan, the kind of incisive, insightful editor I'd heard doesn't exist anymore, and of course to Judith Regan, for her energy, her vision, and her patience with flaky writers from remote corners.

Finally, I have the great fortune of being married to my favorite editor. Like everything I do, this book is dedicated to Anne, and to my children, Brooklyn, Ava, and Alec.

PART I

A P R I L

Burial of the Dead

1

Caroline Mabry was transfixed by falling water. For her, the river had other currents, pulling her to its banks when she was upset or distracted, when she wanted to lose herself. She did this most often at the falls—the dramatic series of rocky, churning rapids at the center of her city. Determined upstream, even languid and eddied in places, the Spokane River began to tumble here, to froth and roil, and eventually to fall.

Sometimes the river's pull surprised Caroline. She would be running errands or jogging or riding her bike and suddenly find herself here, on the footbridge between the upper falls and the Monroe Street Dam. She was amazed by this place, by what it meant for a city to have at its heart a tumbling, roaring waterfall. Here, overwhelmed by scale, she could drift into epiphanies of scope and flow and believe that a river has a purpose more vital than transportation or power. The river cleansed the city, carried away its debris, its sump and its suicides. The river irrigated the long, gray wound of civilization. Over time she'd begun to bring her own chronic infections to the river, her random loneliness and cyclic despair, her isolation. And if she wasn't cured by the falls, her jagged anxieties were at least dispersed, drowned out by white water, dwarfed by boulders that jutted like broken bones from the river's skin.

Caroline paused on a footbridge over the falls, checked her watch, and finished crossing, pushing the baby stroller deeper into the park, over an embankment covered with people and blankets, Frisbees and Hacky Sacks, to a still arm of the river, dammed off from the rocky channel across the park as a place for ducks and park benches, for lovers and quiet contemplation. The Spokane River was steel and steady here, gray, moving like molten metal between its banks. Caroline wondered what it meant to be more comfortable with the airy roar of the falls than with this pleasant meandering, this stillness. But she blinked away her doubts and concentrated, wheeling her stroller along the sidewalk, finding her place. Waiting.

At thirty-six, Caroline Mabry looked ten years younger and felt ten years older, with round green eyes and short brown hair that softened her tall, athletic build. She stood next to the stroller at the base of a wide footbridge and leaned against a piling to tie her new running shoes. Looking up, she made eye contact across the bridge with a transient who had been in the park all day, a transient in new running shoes. Then, as if operating from a checklist, Caroline stretched, bent at the waist in her nylon running suit, pushed away from the piling, checked on her baby, put on her sunglasses, and surveyed the park.

The park that day had a strange but familiar feel, very much like a map on a wall, with pins marking the major players. But it was also tinged with a fleeting déjà vu, a sensation Caroline had always imagined was akin to losing one's mind, attaching meaning to every movement. Looking around the park, she allowed herself to believe that *none of it* was real—not the Frisbees, not the dogs, not even the river, and certainly not herself, a young mother out for a walk on a sunny day in the park.

Across the bridge, a businessman on a park bench paused to look up from his two-day-old *Wall Street Journal*, caught her eye, and smiled. Her own thoughts seemed deafening, as if everyone would know what she was thinking, and wonder how she knew the businessman had been there all day and that he was wearing the same brand of ninety-dollar running shoes as the transient, the same as she was.

The three—Caroline with her baby, the transient with his pack, the businessman with his newspaper—made a sort of triangle around the wide footbridge, Caroline on one side, the other two across the bridge. In the middle of the triangle, just over the bridge on the side of the businessman and the transient, was a sinewy black kid in baggy carpenter pants, a white T-shirt, untied cross-trainers, and a New York Giants football cap. His name was Kevin Hatch, but he went by the street name Burn, a fact that Caroline knew as well. If someone did share her thoughts, that person would be amazed at the things she knew, the nearsighted omniscience she had in the park that day, like a god who knows everything except what will happen next.

A voice crackled in Caroline's ear: *"We're good. Go on the next buy."*

Caroline sat down against a bridge piling with a paperback book and turned the page every minute or so. After five pages, she stood and checked her baby, then sat back down and turned more pages. Within ten minutes, a man had approached Burn, a man about forty, with shoulder-length hair, wearing khaki pants and a plain black T-shirt. He wore sunglasses, and Caroline was taken by the fact that she knew nothing about him. She watched Burn greet the man, first suspiciously, then warmly, as if the man had mentioned a mutual acquaintance to gain Burn's confidence. The man spoke and Burn listened, nodding a couple of times.

Nearby, conversations rose and blended—a couple's charmed declarations, teenage pleas, some hushed conspiracy from men in suits. On the other side of the bridge, the transient eased up from the ground and began moving forward as the sun edged away from thin cloud cover, lighting the park and river as if a curtain were being drawn.

They waited for Burn to reach out with a cupped hand to the man in khaki pants, a move repeated dozens of times each day— drugs going out in one handshake, cash coming back in the next. But it didn't happen. They just talked, the man in khaki doing most of the talking, Burn adding a word here or there. Still, they watched, waiting for the deal. Finally, Burn put his hand in his pocket. Thirty feet away, the businessman folded up his old newspaper, stood, and reached into his jacket.

Caroline stood too, ready, but she was stopped by the nearby jangle of a cell phone, familiar but muffled. Had she left her phone on? It was in the stroller. She paused, looked around, then bent forward to turn the phone off. She wedged her hand beneath the bundle and grabbed the phone, but snagged the blanket too. She stood quickly and the blanket—tucked under the baby into the side of the stroller—went taut, like a slingshot. Or a rebounding trampoline.

It was an image she would have to compose later, because in that moment Caroline lost track of the sequence and sense of things. Disparate images crashed together, straining against the time required to process each event.

People screamed. The baby was launched into the air. A man reached out, but too late. The baby flew over the railing. People began rushing toward the bridge, to watch or to help, perhaps only sorting out their own motives later. The baby hit the water, barely breaking the surface, floating on its back in its swaddling blanket, pulled along by the slow gray mass as it eased through the downtown park. Like Moses.

Startled by the screaming, the drug dealer Burn and his potential customer in khaki pants looked up from their conversation in time to see two undercover cops, dressed as a transient and a businessman, handguns drawn, coming toward them, but momentarily caught up in the crowd coming toward the bridge to help the baby, or to watch it drown.

Caroline saw all of this from the other side of the river, frozen in place next to her stroller, and before she could form a full sentence—"No! It's just—" a man in jeans and a sweatshirt had leaped over the footbridge and into the water.

"—a doll!" Caroline finished. As if for punctuation, her cell phone rang again.

"*Suspects on the move!*" someone yelled over the radio.

Caroline turned away from the river. Both men were coming toward her, the two detectives fifteen feet back and falling away in a crowd of gawkers. She reached behind her back for her gun, but there was too much commotion over the bundled doll floating downstream—people pulling at Caroline's arms, pointing, trying to comfort her. Burn and the other man raced by, and she could only grab at their shirts. She managed to get a hand on the older man in khaki, but he swung wildly and hit her in the neck. She fell away.

Sergeant Lane, still dressed as a businessman, was there immediately, crouching to see if she was okay.

"I'm fine." Caroline rubbed her neck and nodded in the direction the two suspects had gone, and Sergeant Lane ran after them, much to her relief. There was a ringing then, and Caroline realized the phone was still in her hand. She stared at it. Dumbfounded, she stood, brushed herself off, pressed the button, and held the phone to her ear.

"Hello."

"Hey, babe."

Joel.

"How'd the bust go?"

She turned the phone off.

Two other drug detectives came from the van, but they were too late and were coming from the wrong direction. Caroline couldn't watch the thing unravel anymore and so she turned back to the water. In the calm stretch of river, the hero had reached the doll Caroline was planning to give to her niece, but he could do nothing except swim with it to shore and hold it up by a plastic arm. The people on the bridge applauded anyway and he shrugged, embarrassed.

As Caroline stood along the river, she thought she knew how the man must feel, crawling from the dark water. Was he still a hero, even if the baby wasn't real? For herself the question seemed even more pointed: If the trappings weren't real—the baby, the stroller, the jogging suit—then what about the feelings? The disconnection and the longing for something more. Were those things real?

2

Riverfront Park covered a hundred acres surrounding Spokane Falls, spread over both banks of the river and a hilly island in the middle of the rocky channel. A onetime rail yard, the park had been transformed during the city's 1974 World's Fair into the centerpiece of a downtown that was forever failing to revitalize itself, a drunk constantly falling off the wagon. It was a safe, busy park with walking trails and footbridges, gazebos and carnival rides, a gondola, a clock tower, and a vintage carousel. There was so little crime in the park and it was such an open, public place that when a drug dealer set up shop near one of the footbridges, the narcotics detectives in the Special Investigations Unit figured a day of surveillance would be enough to arrest him.

But when the bust went to shit, the park became a liability. Hilly and covered with trees and brush, it could be entered or exited from at least a dozen places, and so the search for the drug dealer and his customer was scattered and maybe halfhearted. After an hour, the Special Investigations sergeant, Daryl Lane, called off the search, but he stalked around the park for another hour, still in the tight business suit he'd worn for the sting. Caroline was afraid to meet his eyes. The uniformed patrol officers were the first to leave the park, then the support detectives from other units, until it was just Sergeant Lane in his sweaty business suit and the homeless Gerraghty. And Caroline. Sitting on the steps below the carousel, she watched old people feed the ducks until Lane and Gerraghty came shuffling by, on their way to their cars.

"It's not your fault," Sergeant Lane said in a way that implied that it was. He stared at a spot just to her left, then snapped out of it. "We're headed back," he said. "I decided against using the dogs." He and Gerraghty took a step away from her, leaning, as if whatever she had was contagious. Lane hesitated, though. "Look," he said, "it was nothing. A day of planning. A few hours. Nothing."

Caroline didn't answer, and after a moment the sergeant turned again and walked away, joined in mid-stride by Gerraghty, who shuffled in his greasy pants and shirt. Gerraghty loved his undercover street-person outfit. His personality changed when he put on the filthy jeans and black T-shirt, when he let his hair out of its tight ponytail and pulled the loaded pack onto his shoulders. She supposed that was the biggest difference between herself and the other Special Investigations detectives. They loved dressing up, going undercover, fooling people. They liked the change in themselves.

She had thought she would like it too, although after two years in property crimes, anything had sounded more interesting than chasing down stolen car stereos. But she was simply wired differently than Gerraghty. Drug detectives were as sneaky and duplicitous as the desperate junkies they hounded; it was the reason more than a few lapsed into drug use themselves. Caroline could manage desperate, but she didn't like the sneakiness, the pretending. More to the point, she didn't like whatever might be the truth behind the pretending. The baby, for instance: She'd bought the doll for her niece in San Francisco and found the stroller in the property room. Caroline knew it was a bad cover, that it would have an emotional hitch that could distract her from what she was supposed to do. She had figured it would only be an internal ache, though, not this public slapstick.

Below her, on the steps, the baby stroller sat with its wheels pointed out, like a kid waiting to be scolded. Caroline gave it a nudge with her foot and the carriage turned over and spilled out

9

onto the steps, the doll falling out for the second time today, this time coming up short of the river.

"Do I arrest you for littering or child abuse?"

Caroline turned slowly at the sound of his voice and squinted into the sun, which silhouetted Dupree in a way that made Caroline marvel at his impeccable sense of bad timing. "Hello, Sergeant Dupree."

He stepped out of the sun and sat on the steps next to her, unable to contain his smile. It was especially jarring, that smile. He was so thin and wiry, his face was so angular, so *vertical*, that when he smiled, all those anxious, down-turned lines stopped and softened and his lagoon-blue eyes leaped out and she found herself wishing for things she didn't believe she really wanted.

"Go ahead," she said. "I know you've got something to say. Or didn't you hear?"

"Oh, I heard. It's probably in the guild newsletter by now. Pollard wet his pants when he heard."

"Oh, good. That makes it all worthwhile," Caroline said, "providing some entertainment for the lazy asses in Major Crimes."

He leaned forward and looked at her over the rims of his small rectangular glasses. "You know," he said, "only crazy people blame themselves for stuff like this. Guys who talk to themselves. People with Christ complexes."

"I'm not blaming myself. I just feel stupid."

"Yeah? You should. It was stupid." He leaned back and stared out at the still river in front of them. "So forget it." She glanced up at his profile, knowing that he was aware of her watching him. He had been her first patrol shift supervisor, in David Sector, downtown. Six years earlier, he'd been the first one on the scene the only time she ever fired her gun, when she reported to a domestic and shot and killed a man who was attempting to carve up his wife. There was a shooting review and Caroline had been cleared of any wrongdoing, but she had taken it hard anyway and might even have quit if it hadn't been for Alan Dupree. Personally, his effect on her made her angry and unsettled because of the irrationality of her attraction. He had an awkward ropiness, was sinewy and balding, like an old movie cowhand. He was flippant in a way that irritated other cops and horrified civilians. He was constantly making inappropriate jokes to cover his anxiety. He didn't know when to just be quiet. And there were plenty of other reasons that she shouldn't be attracted to him. He had the tiniest damn feet. She had never trusted men with small feet. And he was married. There was that, too.

"What I didn't hear," he said, "was who called you."

"Joel."

He paused and she could feel the joke bubble up in him. She waited. Perhaps something about his penchant for working out. Dupree sometimes called Joel "Chippendale," or simply "Meat." But more likely, it would be about his age. Joel was twenty-four, twelve years younger than Caroline.

"He need a ride home from school?"

Caroline smiled. "That was actually funny. That's unlike you."

He stood then, picked up the doll, and put it back in the stroller, which he righted for her. "In a week," he said, "patrol will pick up your little drug dealer sniffing glue in a park somewhere. Guys like that always float to the surface."

"I suppose."

"No supposing. It'll happen." Dupree looked over toward the carousel, and for the first time Caroline realized someone was waiting for him. She looked back and saw a guy wearing Dockers, a tie, and a ten-year-old sports coat—the uniform of newspaper reporters, community college professors, and new homicide detectives.

"Is that Spivey?" Caroline said grimly, forcing herself to smile and wave back. "Tell me that's not Spivey."

"They got me partnered with him for a while. Training him."

"Chris Spivey made homicide detective?"

He shrugged again. "They make monkeys into astronauts."

"Actually, I don't think they do that anymore." Caroline had requested a transfer to Major Crimes six months earlier and had been told that the only open position was going to be kept dark for at least a year. But apparently it had been given to Spivey.

"I just train 'em," Dupree said. "I don't pick 'em."

She turned back to the river.

"Hey . . ." He reached out and squeezed her forearm, just above the wrist. "So how's your mom doing, anyhow?"

"Fine."

"Good." He let go of her arm, nodded, and began walking back toward Spivey.

Caroline watched him go, then called out. "Say hello to Debbie."

Dupree stopped and turned back. "Okay. Say hi to Joel." He walked away, muttering just loud enough for her to hear, "You know, when he finishes his paper route."

When he was gone, Caroline turned back to the river. She picked up the doll and turned it over in her hands. Fifty percent of babies are boys, but most dolls are girls. Ornaments and playthings. Caroline dumped the doll back in the stroller and began pushing it through the park. She checked her watch—almost five—and gave the stroller a big push, then walked to catch up with it, pausing alongside the steady river to replay the blown sting in her mind. Why hadn't she just let the phone ring? She followed a walking trail up away from the falls and was about to leave the park when she stopped to look back over her shoulder at a stand of thick bushes. A woman in a tight dress and tennis shoes, a secretary walking home, stopped and bent over the stroller.

"Can I peek?" the woman asked.

Caroline couldn't look away from the thick bushes. "No," she said flatly.

"Why? Is she asleep?"

"No," Caroline said. "Plastic."

She left the woman with the stroller and walked toward the thicket, thinking about the second suspect's khaki pants. She brushed aside the bushes with her arm and then all at once the world exploded around her, Burn and the man in khaki bursting forth from the stand of bushes like birds being flushed. Something, either the force or the surprise, knocked her back, and by the time she regained her balance the two suspects were ten yards away and moving quickly, the man in khaki pulling Burn by the arm.

Caroline ran after them, grabbing her cell phone off her hip and trying to punch in the numbers as she ran through the park. She followed the two men past the carousel and along the river, conscious of them pulling away. Caroline dropped her phone, but didn't turn back for it, just kept running after the men, who crossed a wide footbridge over the still arm of the river and ran deeper into the park.

Caroline chased them across a parking lot, through an empty daycare playground and down a grass embankment, toward the thundering falls. Caroline knew this part of the park, and she cut behind them through a stand of trees, bursting down the hill as they did, now just a few steps behind. She dropped to a crouch and had her nine-millimeter out smoothly and quickly.

"Stop! Police!"

They were on the narrow, cable-suspended footbridge, the falls on their right—water blasting over and around boulders—and the dam downstream on their left. The two men stood smack in the middle of the bridge, too far to make a run to the other shore. They turned slowly. Mist from the waterfall lapped up against their legs as they stood before her, their shoulders heaving from the run. Caroline looked from one to the other and began edging toward them. Her eyes locked with the older man's sly face and dead eyes. Without moving his head, the man's eyes shifted to Burn.

"Lie down! On your stomachs!" Her voice sounded tinny in the crash of the falls and, two hundred yards downstream, the deep rumble of the dam and power plant that marked the end of the upper falls.

Slowly, Burn lifted his hands in the air. But the older man didn't budge, didn't even acknowledge her gun, just stood with his arms at his sides, his jaw set forward, his black eyes boring into hers.

Caroline stopped walking toward them. There was something eerily familiar in this man's stare, like some desperate question she remembered hearing before: *Is this where we are, you and me?* She had the sense that something here was beyond her understanding, that there was more to this situation than these three figures on this narrow bridge. The air was heavy with mist and potential, and Caroline was surprised to hear her own chopped breathing within the roar of the falls.

"Get! Down!" she yelled again, gesturing at the ground with the gun. Burn nodded and began to lean forward.

That's when the older man turned and, without changing his flat expression, put two hands on Burn's shoulder, and Caroline realized what he was going to do just before he pushed Burn, which he did swiftly and seemingly without thought. Caroline cried out, the sound lost in the howling water as the young man tumbled, arms cartwheeling, over the bridge railing and into the river.

Caroline ran to the railing. The water beneath the falls was deep and churned with currents and undertows from the white roiling foam. Caroline found herself holding her breath while Burn was under, and when, finally, he surfaced in the darker water, she let out a gasping sigh. In the river, Burn was immediately pulled by the current toward the Monroe Street Dam. The man in khaki began to edge sideways, casually, without hurrying, like someone leaving a picnic. He watched her, his eyes placid and cold. She stared at him in horror and he stopped, turned slowly to the river, seeming to know that her eyes would follow his. He seemed curious to see what she would do with the terrible choice he'd just given her: Arrest the suspect on the bridge or try to save the one in the water.

There are moments as a cop, Dupree always said, that are sheer paradox, the world upside down. It was one of his many "theories," the job punctuated by moments that are ludicrous on their face and to which any response is wrong; any reaction to an irrational event is bound to be irrational. Laughing at funerals. Crying at weddings. If you'd been a cop for long, you were always mixing up your laughing and your crying.

Caroline looked once more at the man in khaki and then went after Burn. She jumped the bridge railing and landed on the high bank, but it was too steep and rocky to negotiate. She watched Burn struggle against the surging flow and tried to gauge the angle he was swimming and the distance to the concrete spillway. He might make it if he didn't panic. The trick would be to pull himself out of swiftly moving water onto the rocky bank. That, and not looking ahead. Caroline imagined what it would look like from the boy's vantage point: A hundred yards from where he thrashed, water crested the concrete face of the dam and dropped into nothing. She looked back over her shoulder once, but the man in khaki was gone.

She climbed the embankment and sprinted through traffic across the busy street and around the old downtown power plant, leaving the riverbank and the boy for a moment. As she ran, she pictured Burn's file from that morning's strategy meeting, when they'd planned the simple, one-day undercover sting, part of a larger operation. Short surveillance, watch the kid make a few sales, bring him down during a deal. Suspect's name: Kevin C. Hatch. Street name: Burn. Nineteen years old. A dealer and pimp with a long juvie sheet: burglary, assault, drugs. Nineteen.

When she could see down into the river again, Burn was gone. She ran her eyes back and forth over the river and the dam, and finally saw him just upstream, on the same bank she was on, gripping the rock wall that lined the river. Caroline ran down the riverbank, on concrete steps carved into the steep hillside, sprinting them two at a time.

Lungs aching, she reached the yard of the power plant next to the dam. Fifty yards upstream Burn was clinging to sheer rock, struggling to keep a handhold. The current pulled him away from the bank two or three times before he managed to haul himself up against the jagged river channel; his legs dangled in the water.

"Wait there!" Caroline called, but her voice was drowned out again, this time by the turbines and the endless sound of water slapping the spillway's concrete face. She moved toward him, but Burn wouldn't wait. He was trying to climb the rock wall and had pulled himself completely from the cold river.

"I'll get a rope!" Caroline waved her arms and sprinted toward him, but the kid ignored her and continued climbing the rock wall, made slick by the mist from the falls. "Please! Wait there!"

Three feet above the water, his left foot slipped. He stepped desperately, like kick-starting a motorcycle. For a moment he seemed to right himself, then he was scratching at the wall with one of his hands and he fell back. Caroline watched helplessly as he bumped down the rock wall and into the river, slipping for a moment beneath its surface. He got another handhold briefly, but the water seemed to reach up and grab him by the legs, pulling him away from the rocky shore and into the current.

Caroline looked desperately around the yard of the power plant for a rope, or even a long stick, but found nothing.

She jumped a chain-link fence and stepped out onto the deck of the dam's housing, the turbines rumbling beneath her. Six feet from the concrete spillway, a metal catwalk extended out over the water—four feet above the surging flow. Caroline crept to the end of the catwalk, which extended out over the river like a fire escape. She got down on her hands and knees and reached between the railings. But the catwalk was too high above the river and so she sat, wrapped her legs around the railing, took a breath, and dropped, hanging upside down like a kid on monkey bars, dangling by her knees above the raging flow.

Dizzied by the speed of the water, stung by its spray, Caroline swung from the catwalk. She fought the urge to pull herself back up. Upstream, just thirty yards away, Burn struggled against the increasing current. He looked over his shoulder and for a moment they made something like eye contact, only more desperate. She nodded once, encouraging, and as he was swept toward her he seemed to understand her ridiculous plan and kicked so that he was almost in line with her, Caroline holding her breath and concentrating on the tentative hold her legs had on the wet catwalk. Below her, the water rose in stinging, white fingers. Hanging there like a trapeze artist, she extended her arms downward, so that her own fingertips dangled just above the rough water.

Caught in the current and flying toward her, he reached up with his own hands, and for the second time that day, Caroline felt the world move faster than she could comprehend, felt herself as the only clarity at the center of a great whirling blur.

His left hand hit hers, a quick slap. She closed her hand and was snapped toward the dam with him, one of her legs coming off the catwalk. And then he was gone, sucked over the face of the dam and ground onto the concrete fifty feet below.

Caroline cried out, but couldn't hear herself over the roar of the falls and the dam. She felt the thrum in her hand and tried to figure out if she'd ever had him. The force of his passing caused her to swing from the catwalk by one leg, and even when she stopped swinging Caroline hung there, in the place where the river momentarily flew and was bent and curled by gravity, where the water fell.

3

"You know what awful means?" Dupree squinted into the sun.

Spivey considered for a minute. "Bad?"

Dupree rolled his eyes and held out a cup for a senior volunteer, who was pouring coffee for the officers searching for Kevin Hatch's body. "Listen to the word. Awe. And full. Awful. Full of awe. Okay, how about wonderful?"

Spivey considered again. "Full of wonder?"

"Right. Full of wonder. Full of awe. You tell me, what's the difference?" Dupree sipped his coffee and wrinkled his nose. "Awful and wonderful. You see what I'm getting at? It's a theory of mine. We're all just fixed points on a circle." He dumped his coffee in the weeds alongside the road.

"Give you an example. Guy steps onto his porch and gets shot in the foot by a gangbanger doing a drive-by. He's a victim, right? Next day, he goes and shoots the guy who shot him. Now he's a criminal. Next day, the gangbanger's friend shoots the guy again and kills him. Now he's a victim again. Victim, criminal, victim. Fixed point on a wheel. Bet no one taught you *that* in college."

They started back toward the remote stretch of riverbank again, where patrol officers, firefighters, senior volunteers, a troop of Explorers, and some Eagle Scouts with scanners were all trudging through the deep brush, searching for the body in the river. Dupree thought it was a waste of time to search for floaters below the falls. Kevin Hatch's body would show up eventually at one of the dams farther downstream or snag somewhere on a branch or a rock. Of course, if it didn't, the body could theoretically float all the way to the Columbia and—if it somehow made it through a dozen or so dams—all the way to the Pacific. Dupree thought it would be all right sometimes to let bodies float, an experiment to see how far they might go.

After he'd slipped through Caroline's hands, Kevin Hatch—Burn—slid over the spillway, was bashed against the face of the dam, pulled under the water, then spit out into the last rapids, the water in his body joining the surge around it, flowing over and between rocks, then spilling out in the cool, calm water downstream, beyond the streets of downtown to a floodplain of old houses, vacant fields, and thick brush, where the river resumed its more gradual drift to the north and the west.

Since Burn had been pushed, his death was classified as a homicide, and assigned to Dupree and Spivey, who hacked through weeds and bushes and came into a clearing around an eddy where transients had recently camped, unmistakable because of the campfire, the cigarette butts, and the orderly piles of shit on the fringes of the campsite.

"The thing about a floater is that if you don't find 'em right away, they can get right disgusting," Dupree said. He turned to make sure Spivey wasn't taking notes. It was one of the more irritating things about this kid. Dupree could be telling him which bathroom at Denny's had the best toilet paper and Spivey would be making those tiny marks in one of his notebooks, like he had no memory of his own and could only process information he wrote down.

"Worst thing about a floater that's been in the water a few days is the smell. That and the bloat. You don't wanna see that bloat. Trust me. Takes away any respect you might have for the human body."

Spivey hummed the same response to every one of Dupree's bits of dispensed wisdom. "Mmm-hmm," he said.

Dupree rubbed his thin hairline and looked downstream. Then he turned to Spivey. "Why don't I look upstream. You check the Pacific Ocean."

Spivey nodded and began walking west.

"That was a joke," he said, but Spivey was already gone. He couldn't figure out why the lieutenant was so high on this kid. When Spivey was out of sight, Dupree pulled out his cell phone and hit Caroline's cell number. It rang four times before her voice mail came on.

When he heard the beep Dupree began talking quickly, nervously. "Hey, just wanted to see if you were all right." He looked over his shoulder at the calm river. "By the way, the kid you"—he paused—"tried to save, you know, I talked to him six months ago on an assault. He was a shit." He rolled his eyes at himself. That wouldn't make her feel better. "I just wanted to tell you . . . you know . . . it's amazing what you did . . . I mean . . ." He bit his lip. He was no good at this sort of thing, at making people *feel better*. Especially her. Too many feelings too close to the surface.

"Any idea what kind of bait a guy uses to catch a drowned drug dealer? You know, maybe a Cool Ranch Dorito? A '78 Monte Carlo?" He had the sense that this message was going on too long. "All right. I just wanted to see if you could tell me anything else about the guy who pushed him. Looks like it's my case. So call me later. When you get a chance."

He tried her home number, got no answer, then turned the phone off and stared at it for a moment. Caroline had given her story to patrol officers and then had gone home, according to the patrol sergeant on duty. He could imagine how upset she was. He didn't like her taking things so hard. A person had to find a way to disconnect, to find a buffer between himself and the world. How many times had he told her that?

Dupree walked for several hundred yards, through more transient camps and teenage hideaways. It occurred to him that people only came to this part of the river to get drunk, get high, or have sex with someone they weren't supposed to have sex with. It was as if everything shameful about Spokane seeped down the valley, over the falls, and into this riverbed.

Someone screamed and Dupree spun around.

It came from farther upstream, just below the dam and the last part of the falls. At first he thought someone had found Kevin Hatch's body, but the scream was harrowing, and he didn't figure the kid's body to be in a state to inspire that kind of scream. Not yet.

He loped along the riverbed, reaching back for his handgun, and came into a clearing where a young Explorer stood, pointing at something pressed up against the riverbank, partly covered with branches. There was no mistaking what it was, but Dupree had trouble seeing the whole, focusing instead on a single point, a dull white shining, not like a coin or a beer can, but something flat, barely reflecting the light at all.

Bone.

Dupree stepped past the young volunteer, who couldn't put her arm down, and began pulling the branches away. The bone was part of a forearm, the forearm part of a decomposing human body. The smell was strong, but fading.

He felt a rising in his chest and pulled more branches away, then brushed off a thin layer of dirt. At the shoulder, darkened, leathery skin hung in place, shrink-wrapped around the bone, the flesh drying away. There was some skin attached still lower too, at the breast. He keyed his mike, but nothing came out of his mouth, and he knew he should stop, shouldn't disrupt any more evidence, but he couldn't stop, just kept pulling branches away, filled with the irrational fear that he might know who this was.

More branches came away, revealing a small head, already shrinking in on itself, features wearing away, patches of wiry hair. Female, her lips pulled tight over her teeth, as if she had eaten something sour, her eyes darkly socketed, drawn in on themselves. Dupree felt his mouth go dry. The things men do to women. He pulled the branches away, further disrupting the crime scene because even though he knew it wasn't possible, he had to know this wasn't his daughter or his niece or his wife. Or Caroline.

That night, another detective would tell him the body was that of a hooker and methamphetamine user named Rebecca Bennett, whom no one could recall having seen alive since April 1, four weeks earlier. No report had been filed, because it was assumed she'd gone back to Seattle or perhaps down to L.A., or perhaps had gotten married, or maybe had been abducted by aliens, or, more likely, no one cared enough to notice she'd gone missing. A disappearing hooker was not much of a magic trick, as it turned out. Her file could've had a hundred different names on it, the details were so basic: victim of a sexual abuse at eleven, drug charge at thirteen, runaway at fourteen, theft at fifteen, foster care, runaway again, another drug charge, another theft. When she was killed—strangled and then shot in the head—Rebecca Bennett was twenty-two.

As he crouched in front of her, Dupree couldn't stop thinking of her as one of the women he cared for, especially Caroline. "I'm sorry," he whispered, staring into the face of the decomposing young girl. It took far more strength than it probably should have for him not to reach up and brush the hair from the dead girl's eyes. Instead he pulled a few more branches away until the girl's other arm emerged, bones with patches of dried skin, and then a hand, still clutched around the thing that had drawn his eye: two folded, twenty-dollar bills.

4

Caroline had gone back to the office, turned off her phone, and looked through a book of mug shots for the man in khaki pants. When she had looked through pages of mugs of forty-ish white men, she sat staring out a window. Time passed without any gauge. She took a shower in the locker room, letting the water pool in her long, narrow fingers, then changed into dry clothes. When she came out into the SIU offices, Sergeant Lane was standing at her cubicle, holding a picture of her niece that he quickly put back on her desk.

"They find the kid's body?" Caroline asked.

"No. Not yet." He sat down, overweight and blanched, still wearing the suit from the sting. After a moment, she sat across from him. "Dupree just called, though. They found a body, a young woman, probably been there a couple weeks."

"Jesus. What a day."

"You taking tomorrow off?" he asked.

"I wasn't planning to. Aren't we doing the house on Sixth?"

"Caroline," he began, and already she flinched. He never used her first name, always called her "Mabry." "I want you to see someone in professional services."

She smiled at the department's euphemism for its psychiatrist—professional services. She knew who went to see the dour woman in professional services: drunks just before they were put on disability leave; drug users just before they were fired; wife beaters, attitude problems, and burnouts, the guys who beat the shit out of people at routine traffic stops. "Sarge, I don't need this." Caroline lifted a hand to rub her jaw, but became self-conscious and dropped it back in her lap.

"After the day you had, Caroline . . . "

"I fucked up a bust. I know that."

"It isn't about that."

Reflexively, she turned steady and cool, cleared her head of the fog, allowed her anger to dissipate, and stared at him through calm eyes.

"You work sixty-hour weeks," he was saying. "I get my ass chewed for carrying your comp time and sick days over from the year before . . . at this rate, you'll be able to retire at forty."

"No one asked you to carry my comp days over."

"That's not the point." He took a breath and covered his mouth, looking to come from a different direction. "It's my responsibility to watch out for anything that might have an effect on the way my detectives do their jobs."

Caroline just stared at him.

"If you were getting divorced, I would be concerned. I might suggest you talk to a counselor. If you had been involved in a shooting, if you had some personal crisis . . ." He gestured with an open hand, as if he'd made his case already.

Caroline started at the words "personal crisis." She thought about her mother. "But those things aren't happening to me," she said quietly, not exactly convincingly.

"No," he said. "No. But we both know what happens if you don't deal with the stress of this job. It can't be easy being the only woman in SIU. And I understand your mother is ill. I just thought it might help to have someone to confide in."

Caroline stood and paced away from her desk. "So is this an order? Do I need my guild rep in here?"

"No." He stood and took a step back, smaller than he'd been. "No, there's no need for that." He smiled. "I'm not the enemy, Caroline."

He backed out of her cubicle and retreated to his office. Caroline ran her eyes along the metal-lined cubicles of the SIU office. Thankfully, there were no other detectives in the room. At least he had the sense to wait until the room was empty. She shook as she packed her briefcase, then started for the door.

Outside, she stood in front of the cop shop for a few minutes, breathing the cool April air and watching the light traffic in front of the courthouse. A patrolman bringing in a drunk driver gave her a little wave and she nodded back. She watched the patrol car pull into the cul-de-sac in front of the jail and then she walked to her own car and climbed in, but didn't start it right away.

She didn't want to go home yet, to sit there all by herself waiting for Joel to get off work, wondering which granola-fed college students were throwing themselves at him tonight. She didn't want to go to the bar where he worked either; he would think something was wrong.

And maybe something was wrong. Caroline thought about what Sergeant Lane had said. The kid in the river was horrible, the stuff of nightmares. There was a time, when she first started on the force, when Caroline would've needed a couple of days off to sort through what had happened. Like the shooting.

After the shooting, she'd cried on Dupree's shoulder like a scared kid—and even that wasn't enough. She took a week off and probably could've used two. She'd had trouble sleeping and had a case of the shakes that came and went for months, as if the reverberations from her nine-millimeter had followed her home. The next two months were consumed by shooting reviews, and in every question Caroline heard the accusation that a male officer wouldn't have needed "deadly force" to subdue a drunk man. She had to answer questions about whether she was the victim of abuse herself (she wasn't), or had witnessed abuse as a child (she hadn't). The man had been arrested twice before for beating his wife and had a couple of other minor felony charges on his record. That night he'd come home drunk, found that dinner had been put away, and had gone after his wife with a dull bread knife. Caroline was the first officer on the scene and found the man standing over his wife, beating and stabbing her on the kitchen floor. She yelled at the man through the back door and he turned on her, screaming and moving toward her. Twice she told him to stop, but he stalked out the door, Caroline backing down the steps, into the yard. Finally he lunged at her, and she fired when he was twenty feet away, within what police called the "kill zone," that space in which a police officer's life was in danger, though maybe not from a drunk with a dull bread knife. Alone at night, Caroline sat up staring at the walls, trying to remember if she'd made a conscious effort to shoot the man. In the end, it was Dupree's insistence that she had done the right thing that kept her from quitting. The other officers said all the right things and were overtly supportive, but she could feel their doubt. The best attribute a police officer had was the knack for defusing potential trouble. She had made a situation worse, possibly even panicked, and shot a drunk man who was too far away to really do her any harm. No cop would ever say as much, but she knew what they were thinking.

Caroline started the car and began driving, figuring she'd know where to go once she got there. She started with the Longbotham Pub, where Joel worked. The bar covered the main floor of an old miners' hotel in downtown Spokane, converted into the kind of young professionals' pub that serves micros and Guinness black-and-tans to junior law partners and sweet martini derivations to fifth-year college students.

And cops. Younger cops found their way to the Longbotham, and that was how she'd met Joel. He was tending bar when she'd come in with some other detectives after a particularly adrenaline-filled drug raid eighteen months ago.

For her, the attraction had been simple, basic. He was twelve years younger, six feet three inches tall, with the round, muscular shoulders and flat stomach of a swimmer, short black hair, and green eyes with black borders. When she was insecure about his fidelity, which was more often lately, it was those eyes that scared her.

On their first date, they talked about leaving Spokane; she was waiting to hear from law school, he from an Alaskan fishing boat. That conversation had taken place on almost every date Caroline had in Spokane. Everyone was either in the process of leaving or apologizing for not leaving yet. Caroline found herself hoping it was the same in other mid-sized cities, that there were some places that could only be left, cities just barely boldfaced on road maps—Dayton, Des Moines, and Decatur; Springfield, Stockton, and any city with "Fort" in its name—places that spark none of that romantic quality that young people believe will keep them from growing old.

It wore on Caroline. Everyone dragged around heavy suitcases filled with excuses for staying in Spokane, and her own sounded no more convincing than any others she'd heard. "I was planning to leave, but I met this guy . . . " "I would've left months ago, but my mother is ill." She was thirty-six. What was her excuse before she met Joel? Before her mother got sick? Before she shot the wife beater? Before Dupree?

She stood outside the Longbotham, which was fronted on the street by big picture windows. She watched from outside as Joel pulled the taps and served up beers to a couple of young men in baseball caps. She ran her eyes along the bar until she found the girl who worried her: thin, blond, faded jeans cinched around a rubber-band waist. The girl leaned across the bar and yelled over the music into Joel's ear as Caroline tried to imagine a drink that took that long to order.

From the street, Caroline watched the college girl shrug demurely. Joel began mixing her a margarita, never looking away from the girl, drawing her in, making her think stupid thoughts. Caroline thought about warning her: Get out of town while you still can. It's not real, the thing you see in those eyes.

She stepped away from the window, looked up and down the street, and then started back for her car.

She drove through downtown and up the first crest of the South Hill, parked in the lot of Sacred Heart Hospital, and walked inside. She showed her badge to the security guard, who waved her inside. She took the elevator to the seventh floor oncology unit and chatted with the nurses for a few minutes. They seemed uncomfortable with her being there and had trouble making small talk.

"She was awake for about an hour tonight," a nurse said. "She ate some pudding."

They walked to the end of the hall, Caroline keeping her eyes straight ahead, avoiding eye contact with the patients in the other rooms. The door swung open silently, and even in the dark Caroline could see that her mother was in the same position as she had been the day before, on her left side, airing out the bedsores on her right. At 6 A.M., the nurses would turn her again. At 6 P.M., they would turn her again. And on and on, perfect in their symmetry. It struck her that the only thing her mother's doctors treated with any certainty at all was bedsores.

Caroline bent over her mother's face and kissed her dry cheek, rattling the plastic IV lines. The room hummed with the motorized morphine drip and the grinding oxygen machine and the whir behind every wall of the hospital. Caroline leaned over to read the setting on the morphine.

"You upped her dosage?"

"The doctor did, yes," the nurse said. "Earlier today."

"How's she supposed to be conscious if she's all doped up?"

The nurse stiffened. "She's in a lot of pain."

"I know. I'm sorry. I didn't mean—" Caroline pushed her hair out of her eyes and set her face.

"You really should talk to the doctor about this."

Caroline turned back and took her mother's hand. Her bottom lip curled over her teeth. Her skin was bunched up beneath her eyes, dark and dry, leathery, the skin of a woman seventy-eight, not fifty-eight. Caroline tried to remember her mother at the small kitchen table, wry and lean and tough, the ever-present cup of coffee in her hand, legs folded in front of her, like someone waiting for the world to play itself out chiefly for her amusement.

But maybe that woman was gone and all that was left was this husk, these bedsores, this pain. All Caroline wanted to do was talk about her day with her mother, tell her about the bust and the bridge. What she wouldn't give for one more conversation, one more reassurance in that easy kitchen-table voice that her mother used. "Baby, all you can do is the best you can do."

Caroline spoke to the nurse without looking up. "It's going to be soon, isn't it?"

The nurse didn't say anything.

"Her hands are so cold."

The nurse said, "I wish you'd talk to Dr. Beldick."

"Please."

The nurse shifted her weight. "Her bowels have stopped working. Sometimes, the body has its own order of shutting down . . ."

Caroline nodded, soaked up this bit of information as she always did, feeling it diffuse inside her, dispersed along rivers of blood, and could almost feel it tingling in her arms and legs until she felt the rawness of it dissipating, until she believed the information could do no more harm. "Thank you," she said.

She waited for the nurse to leave, then sat down and took her mother's cool hand, pressed it to her mouth, and whispered, "I'm here."

5

After witnessing a couple of them firsthand, Alan Dupree had come to recognize a kind of season, a certain dark streak that a city endures—when every knife fight seems to end with someone bleeding to death and every domestic violence call carries a comic threat of disaster, when all the really bad guys seem to finish their probation and start work again all at once. Some guys on the job made themselves feel better by blaming full moons or hot weather or the disbursement of government checks. The guys in crime analysis studied changing patterns of crime like weather charts. The brass looked for the evil in funding deficiencies. Patrol cops became religious. Detectives became cynics.

But Alan Dupree had seen his share of these bleak seasons and they seemed to him almost organic, at least self-sustaining, capable of creating their own energy and spinning off into endless replication. The only thing he could equate it with was sports—a hitting streak or a series of errors or missed baskets. A streak. A slump. A run in which cause becomes effect which becomes cause and then effect again, bad fortune causing more bad fortune, until the thing just plays itself out, until the ill wind dies down. From a distance, such periods could look like simple statistical spikes and valleys, evening out the averages so you got four murders in one month and none the next and still hit Spokane's monthly average of two. But try telling a baseball player that he's not on a streak, or a basketball player, or a guy at a craps table. Try telling him some unseen force isn't at work against (or for) him, that one botched grounder doesn't lead to another, that one murder doesn't spawn another, that it's just the numbers evening out.

The distinction occurred to Dupree at 11 P.M., as he was climbing into the car with Spivey, preparing to drive to the third apparent homicide of the day. For a mid-sized city like Spokane, which might get twenty murders in a bad year, three bodies in one day was incredible, something like a 150-pound shortstop belting three homers in one game. Although, to be accurate, the hooker they'd found that afternoon along the riverbank had been murdered at least two weeks earlier.

Dupree thought about talking to Spivey about his theory of streaks; it was the kind of thing he used to share with Caroline. He loved sharing his vast criminal epistemology. And if the other detectives mocked him when they called him "Officer Philosopher," well, Dupree thought it was important not only to train but also to educate rookies like Spivey.

"Any questions?" Dupree asked.

"Yeah. Do I ever get to drive?"

Dupree stared at him for a moment before starting the car. They drove in silence until Dupree turned onto Monroe Street and crossed the bridge above the dam where the drug dealer had gone over earlier in the day. What would he have done in Caroline's position? Try to help the kid who got pushed in the river, or keep his gun on the guy who pushed him? He wondered if it would have been possible to shoot the older guy in the leg or something. That's what a TV cop would do. But in twenty-six years he'd only had to pull his gun maybe thirty times and he'd never had to fire it, let alone been confronted with the kind of situation where he had to shoot someone in the leg. How would you go about shooting someone in the leg? First of all, it was against policy to shoot a guy in the leg. For better or worse, if you shot someone, it was to "stop" him, to fire until he no longer posed a threat, which was, of course, when the subject was dead. Still, he wished the decision had been his and not Caroline's, because whatever he would have done, he could live with the wrong choice. He wasn't as sure about her.

He got on the Interstate heading east, flashed his grille lights at a car in his way, and quickly had the car up to ninety, Spivey fidgeting like a dog in the passenger seat. Dupree got off at the second exit and wound his way into a familiar neighborhood; they were all familiar if you'd been on the job any time at all. He'd imagined starting a guided tour with retired cops, with starred maps of murder, theft, and perversion. His own map was no different from any other cop's: a rape in that house, a two-car fatal accident in front of that convenience store, a house where a biker had fenced stolen auto parts.

The house that was about to be added to his own tour was a simple one-story, surrounded by shrubs that needed trimming, a flower pot at each corner of the driveway, and a tidy, kidney-shaped flower garden carved into the yard. Uniforms stretched police tape around the block while the public information officer kept the news trucks at bay.

Dupree parked, crossed the street, and climbed the steps, bumping a macramé pot on the porch of the small house. The smell of cigarette smoke hit him like a slap, and he was reminded of the power of dormant urges.

"Long day, huh?" asked a patrol cop on the porch. He wrote Dupree's and Spivey's names on the crime scene log and stepped out of the way so they could enter.

Inside, Dupree and Spivey found the other detectives and evidence technicians, who stretched white rubber gloves onto their hands and talked and pointed and gestured in the cool, detached way that almost hid the fact that bodies were the best part of the job: a completed story with no secrets, all the evidence right there for them to read, blood spatters and puncture wounds and the darkening of flesh that told where the blood left first, very important when you've got a guy who has given up the best of three quarts, when what little blood he has left has settled in his back.

Best of all, dead ones didn't lie or forget or protect the people who beat them. They cooperated, in their way. With carpet fibers, DNA testing, and computerized fingerprint databases, you could make the argument that a guy like this was more helpful dead than alive. This particular guy in front of Dupree, for instance—a guy in his sixties with a criminal record—how could they know if he was telling the truth? What kind of witness would this old shit make, with his felony record and his alcoholism? But if they got prints, DNA from the dead guy's fingernails, footprints in the carpet, they might as well have videotape and a confession from the guy who did it.

There were two other detectives, two evidence techs, and a deputy coroner in the house, and they all smiled the minute Dupree entered the room.

"Guy gives this much blood," he said to no one in particular, "he should at least get a donut and a glass of juice."

Dupree bent down and looked at the body. He was in his sixties, with a ring of wild graying hair. He was fat, wearing coveralls, lying in a pond of thickening blood. "You're gonna need a lot of club soda to get the blood out of this rug."

Polaroid flashes lit the house as evidence techs pulled small brown paper sacks down over the victim's hands in case he got a scratch in before being killed. This turned out to be especially helpful for hookers, like the one Dupree had found earlier, who often got scratches in, and who seemed to become dead as easily as other people get caught in traffic. Dupree flicked one of the paper bags. "Jesus. Bastards even took his hands."

Small, orange, numbered evidence flags—eighteen of them so far—were laid out on the coffee table and the floor around the body, each one marking a potential piece of evidence for the corporal taking photographs: a blood spatter, a deep indentation in the carpet, a bloody fingerprint on the coffee table, a pipe wrench.

Dupree grabbed an orange-flagged pylon. "It's clear to me now, Mrs. Stanhouse." He held it up. "Your husband was killed by a very tiny slalom skier."

It was too much for Spivey, who had been fighting every one of Dupree's inappropriate jokes and now laughed so hard his gum fell out. Dupree liked it when someone finally laughed. It seemed to let the air out of the room, and he usually found himself getting quiet after that. The young detective pushed his way to the door, covering his mouth and nose as if he were about to vomit. He squeezed past the lead on the case, Pollard, dark-rimmed glasses beneath slick, black hair, like some early 1960s hipster. As he edged past the gagging Spivey into the crowded house, Pollard looked up at Dupree for an explanation. Dupree shrugged.

Dupree and Pollard stood next to each other, staring at the body like two men admiring a car, speaking without looking away from it.

"Hear about that shit at the dam?" Pollard asked.

"Yeah."

"I wonder how Caroline's doin' with that?"

"I tried calling her. Boyfriend said she was sleeping."

"That same guy she was seeing at Christmas?"

"Yeah."

"How old is that guy?"

"I don't know. Twenty-two. Nine. Somewhere in there."

"Good for her. If I was a woman, that's what I'd do."

Dupree looked away from the body to Pollard.

"No," he said, "I just mean, if I was attracted to guys, that's what I'd do . . . Men do it all the time, you know, go out with someone a lot younger. You know what I mean."

"You're attracted to younger guys?"

"No, I mean . . ." He shifted his weight and looked to change the subject. "That's a tough call she had to make. Poor kid."

"She'll be all right. She had good training."

"Oh, that's right. She worked for you. As if that wasn't enough bad luck for one lifetime."

Dupree nudged the dead man's foot with his own. "Neighbors know anything?"

"Yeah. The guy's nephew stops by earlier today for a visit. Some screaming. About nine P.M., neighbor sees the nephew leave in the victim's car."

"Get a plate on the car?"

"Yep. Plate, make, model. I got it all. The reason I called you was that one of the neighbors said the nephew was wearing khaki pants."

"No shit?" Dupree looked more closely at the dead body on the rug.

"Don't know if it's Caroline's guy from the park, but the description's close."

"What about the rest of Uncle Stiffy's family? Any of 'em know the nephew?"

"We're lookin'. Wife's got Alzheimer's, lives in a home. I guess he's got a sister in the Bay Area we're trying to track down."

Dupree picked up a photo album and began leafing through it. "I forgot to ask, who won the pool?"

Pollard motioned to the huge pipe wrench lying in a corner, marked with one of the small evidence flags. A technician crouched to dust it.

Dupree shook his head. "You're kidding. A pipe wrench? God-damn Spivey."

Every December at their Christmas party, the Major Crimes detectives picked a weapon—everything from a baseball bat to a .38 to an Uzi to different kinds of knives—and whenever there was a murder the next year, each of the eight detectives tossed in twenty bucks. The guy with the right weapon won the pot. Some guys bought two or three weapons and so the pot was usually more than two hundred dollars.

They went by seniority, the newest detective choosing last each time, and since all the likely weapons were chosen by the time Spivey came aboard, he stared at the list and then said, in perfect Efrem Zimbalist Jr. inflection, "miscellaneous blunt objects." Now, here it was only the end of April, and already they had a murder committed with a shovel and now this—a pipe wrench. Unbelievable. Nine murders this year and already Spivey wins two.

"So, what do we do? Arrest Spivey?"

"No shit," Pollard said.

The assistant chief, James Tucker, came in then. With the chief a year away from retirement, at the most two, Tucker showed up at every crime scene where there might be reporters. It was taken for granted that he was in line for the job, even though many of the older cops didn't like him because he had come from San Diego instead of the insular world of Spokane cops.

"What've we got?" Tucker asked.

"Miscellaneous blunt," Pollard said.

"Goddamn Spivey," Tucker said.

Dupree turned his back and looked through the photo album for a picture of the nephew, knowing it was a long shot. But that was the thing about streaks and runs. If the guy who pushed Caroline's drug dealer off the bridge also beat this old man to death, then the string was already playing out, each movement taking the thing out a little further, the coincidences piling up, just waiting to be revealed.

So he wasn't surprised when he saw, in one picture, the dead guy leaning against a pier in San Francisco with a stump of a woman, her husband, an attractive young girl with black hair, and a guy who looked about thirty-five, a guy with a cocky smirk and the kind of simple, colorless tattoo on his forearm that a person usually acquires in prison. Dupree slid the photo out of the album and put it in his pocket.

Outside, a spring wind had picked up. Dupree found Spivey talking to a cute television reporter, his foot up on the bumper of Dupree's car, speaking under his breath.

"You having a press conference?"

Spivey brought his foot down and shifted his weight. "We were just talkin'."

"You tell her about the neo-Nazis?"

Spivey tried to smile nonchalantly. "He's kidding. He always jokes around."

"Oh, shoot. You're right," Dupree said. "We're not supposed to talk about that. Thanks for keeping me out of trouble, partner."

The TV reporter glanced at her notebook, and Dupree leaned over to read what she'd been writing.

"I can neither confirm nor deny rumors of castration," he said. "You'll have to ask the chief about that."

She opened her mouth to say something, but nothing came out.

"And don't quote me saying they cut his heart out. I'll deny having told you that."

"Don't listen to him," Spivey said. "He's just messing around."

Dupree opened the car door and motioned at Spivey, who reluctantly climbed in. They drove quietly for a block before Spivey spoke. "That was mean."

"I told you, don't talk to reporters unless you ask me first," Dupree said. "And when you ask me, I'll always say no."

Spivey stared out the passenger window as Dupree drove, the car almost moving itself, its driver deep in thought. They crossed the river to the north side of the city.

He rolled his window down and turned into the quiet neighborhood around Corbin Park, porch lights twinkling through front-yard shade trees, sprinklers raining water like shattered glass on the sidewalks. He drove slowly, taking in the smell from the flower beds and lilac bushes. He'd always liked the neighborhood along this park, in part because he'd never been to a serious crime here. It was late and he should just do this in the morning, but he wanted at least to drive by her house to see if she was up. At the end of the park he turned, and his headlights ran across her car in the driveway. He parked in front of the small one-story house. A light was on in the back of the house, where he guessed the bedroom would be. He reached in his pocket and pulled out the photograph he'd taken from the dead guy's album, held it against the steering wheel, and imagined her behind the dark picture window.

"Whose house?" Spivey asked.

Dupree didn't respond at first. "Hmm? Oh . . . nobody's."

Inside, Caroline had started when the headlights rolled across the picture window in front of her house. She sat in the dark on the couch. She watched out the window, waiting for the car to leave. She knew who it was. Joel finished his shower and Caroline heard the creak of footsteps behind her and knew again without turning that Joel would be in the doorway, wearing a pair of flannel boxer shorts, drying his hair with a towel.

She envied the way men could date younger women without any self-consciousness. She'd heard men say stupid things like, "As we get older, we're getting closer in age." She longed for that kind of self-deception, but her mind played the opposite game, constantly imagining him as a little boy—six when she graduated from high school; four when she had sex the first time. There was something especially troubling in realizing that she began having her period the year he was born.

"I really am sorry, Caroline."

She turned and smiled. "I told you, it's not your fault. I shouldn't have left my phone on."

"It was stupid of me to call."

She turned back to the window and could still see the sliver of headlight on the curb, could still hear Dupree's car idling outside.

Joel took a step into the room. "Someone out there?"

"I don't think so."

They'd already made love, when Caroline had come home from the hospital. She had initiated it, in part because she wanted to distract herself, to fall away, to lose herself in the tumble and flow.

The other part was that she didn't want to talk to him about the things that had happened that day. Anyway, the sex had been nice, tender and slow, and she hadn't felt caged, the way she sometimes felt when his thick arms surrounded her.

In the doorway, he shuffled his feet. "I'm going to bed."

She smiled. "Go ahead. I just need to sit here a minute."

He hesitated. "You never told me, how was your mom today?"

"Fine."

"She doing any better?"

"Yeah."

"Great," he said and edged along the wall to the bedroom. Caroline turned back to the window and hugged her knees as the car outside shifted into gear.

Dupree looked over his shoulder once more at the house, then at the photograph in his hand. The man with the tattoos was still smirking, still staring out at Dupree as if he were unafraid and knew the secrets that Dupree knew about the capricious nature of death, about the vulnerability of women, about how easy it was to kill someone. He imagined the guy coming face-to-face with Caroline on the footbridge over the falls, and it made Dupree want to kill him.

Spivey leaned over to look at the picture in Dupree's hand. "So is that the guy we're lookin' for?"

Dupree set the photo on the dashboard, shifted into gear, and spoke quietly to the smirking man looking out from the picture in front of him. "Hmm? That you? You the guy we're lookin' for?"

6

Lenny was sitting in his uncle's car across the street from the
pawnshop when the fat pawnbroker pulled up in his pickup,
unlocked the gate, and pushed it back. The guy was wearing Sea-
hawks sweatpants and a filthy white T-shirt with a shiny frog on
it. Lenny couldn't understand why people wore dirty clothes like
that. Drove him nuts. Shelly used to do that, when she wasn't
hooking, used to lounge around in whatever clothes happened to
be close. Lenny even did her laundry sometimes and still she'd
grab some tiny pair of shorts that she'd worn the day before
rather than put on clean clothes. It was one of the things Lenny
counted on never understanding about her.

The shop was called Nickel Plate Pawn, but Lenny had been
disappointed in the selection of handguns. He'd pick one up anyway, though that wasn't why he was here. He was here because the
thing in the park had changed everything, cut short his time.

Lenny climbed out of the Pontiac and crossed the street, hands
deep in the pockets of his khaki pants. The pawnshop owner had
pulled the cyclone fence back and unlocked the door and was enter-

ing when Lenny came up behind him, grabbing the door before the shop owner could close it.

The man jumped, turned, and looked at Lenny, his hand on his chest.

"Jesus, man! I almost shit my pants. You shouldn't sneak up on people."

"Sorry," Lenny said, moving past him into the shop.

"You'll have to come back," the man said, "I don't open till eight-thirty."

Lenny ignored him and walked up and down the glass cases, looking at hunting knives. Maybe that would be better.

The pawnshop owner looked at his watch. "Eight-thirty. That's not for another twenty minutes."

"Oh," Lenny said. "Right."

The pawnshop owner cocked his head and grinned a little bit as Lenny leaned over a glass case, peering in at an elaborate hunting knife with a bone-white handle.

"What are you, some kinda retard?"

"No," Lenny said, and like a flash, he raised his left arm and brought his elbow down on the glass case, sending a deep crack along the length of it. Before the pawnshop owner could say anything, Lenny brought his elbow down again, this time shattering the glass in a circle around where his elbow had gone in. As the pawnshop owner stood there, dumbstruck, Lenny pushed the broken glass from the frame, reached in, and grabbed the hunting knife.

When he turned, the man recognized him. "You were in yesterday . . . askin' about a . . . what was it?"

"Bracelet." Lenny walked over, calmly took the keys from the man's hand, and locked the front door. He walked back just as slowly and showed the pawnshop owner a claim check for the bracelet, then turned back to the items under the glass.

"Yeah," the pawnshop owner said, trying to pretend nothing was wrong. "A bracelet. That's right. Some chick you knew sold it."

"Yeah. You wouldn't give it to me."

"Well, like I told you, after a certain time . . . I can't sell it back at the pawn price . . . except to the person who pawned it." He looked at the hunting knife in Lenny's hand. "But you know what, for you I'll make an exception."

"Thanks," Lenny said.

Relieved, the pawnshop owner edged behind the counter, Lenny following. He opened a drawer of jewelry and flipped through it. He looked up and forced a smile. "I think I retagged it. I'm trying to remember . . ."

"It's gold."

"Oh, right, right." The man opened another drawer.

"You gave her ten bucks. It was worth two hundred. She needed the money."

The pawnbroker looked up again, nervous. "Yeah, sorry about that. She didn't make a big deal about it, I guess." He held up a gold chain and Lenny winced when he saw it. He handed it to Lenny, who stared hard at it.

The pawnshop owner backed toward the wall. "Yeah," he said, "I remember you now. We talked about prison. Your tattoos. You just got out."

"Couple months ago," Lenny said, still staring at Shelly's bracelet.

"Yeah," the man said, "I asked if you liked being out and you said you'd never go back and I said, 'Yeah, no shit.' Remember?"

Lenny stared at the bracelet, and its slightness made him angry. He wondered how they curled those little gold rings around each other, wondered at the grace and delicacy of some people's hands, at the bluntness of his own.

"Yeah, it's coming back now," the pawnshop owner said. "You asked about . . . uh . . . who was it? The girl who sold this thing . . . she was a hooker, right? Worked with that black kid who runs dope in the park. Did you find him?"

"Yeah." Lenny moved away from him to the glass case filled with handguns.

The pawnshop owner kept talking nervously, hoping. "So, did he hook you up? The kid in the park?"

"Mmm-hmm."

The man was pleased. "You get some good shit? Maybe mellow you out?"

Lenny pointed at a nine-millimeter in the case. "You got ammo for this?"

"Uh, I don't sell ammunition."

Lenny turned his left arm over and noticed that his elbow was bleeding where he'd broken the glass case, that the blood was dampening his long-sleeved black T-shirt. He made a face more of irritation than of pain, took two quick steps, and flicked the knife at the pawnbroker, who put his hands up to protect himself and was cut across the palm.

"Ah, Jesus! Okay!" he said. "There's ammo in the bottom drawer." He unlocked the drawer and handed Lenny a loaded clip and two boxes of nine-millimeter ammunition.

"Unlock the case too."

The pawnshop owner hesitated, wiped his brow with his good hand, and unlocked the case. Lenny reached in, took the handgun, hefted it, pointed it at the front window, and then turned it over in his hand.

The pawnshop owner clenched his bleeding hand as Lenny loaded the handgun. When he was done, he looked up at the pawnbroker with something approaching pity.

"Why don't you wash that shirt before you wear it?" Lenny asked.

"Huh?"

"That shirt. It's dirty."

The pawnshop owner looked down at his shirt and swallowed hard. "I got it out of the hamper. I like this shirt."

Lenny scooped up the bracelet. The bright lights under the jewelry case glistened off the gold links.

"I've been robbed before," the pawnshop owner said. "You don't have to worry about me. I never say nothin'. I did six months myself, man. Fraud and some business with checks. So I understand. You don't have to worry about me."

Lenny looked up from the bracelet, his face flushed, cheeks red. "Why'd you give her such a bad deal? Why weren't you fair with her?"

The pawnshop owner just stood there with his mouth open.

"What else did you do?" Lenny said. "What did you make her do?"

"I don't—" But no other words came out of his mouth.

"Get down on your knees."

The man was crestfallen. "I thought we got along good before. I thought everything was cool."

"Get on your knees."

"Hey, I'm sorry about your friend."

Lenny motioned with the handgun and the man slowly dropped to his knees, looking around the room once, as if there might be some reset button, or a trapdoor, or someone to help him. Lenny stared at the man, shaking in his sweatpants and dirty T-shirt, so small like this, on his knees, and felt a shudder go through his arms. Maybe he didn't have to do this. He could scare the man and then stop. He saw the pawn ticket in his hand still. The man seemed unaware of the fact that his jaw was quivering. Lenny tried to imagine what the man was thinking, what Shelly would've been feeling. There were people he wanted to talk to, no doubt, and things he wished he'd done differently. But those were adult thoughts and Lenny guessed the pawnshop owner was thinking little-kid thoughts, wishing he could curl up somewhere in the safety of his momma or hide under his bed. When an animal died, people said it was out of its misery. There was something to that, he supposed. All the scratching and fucking around makes up a life. And finally, what difference does it make, you do it right or you do it wrong. Every life comes to an end.

The man began to cry as Lenny raised the handgun.

"Jesus." The pawnshop owner squinted and covered his face. "What happened to you yesterday?"

7

"That's him."

Dupree put his hand on Caroline's shoulder and gestured to the stack of six-packs in front of her, five sheets of photographs, each with a half-dozen mug shots. "Take one more look," he said. "I want you to be sure."

"I don't need another look. That's him."

Dupree smiled. "Humor me."

Caroline flipped through the stack and settled again on the second sheet, her eyes moving from left to right across the photos. When she was done, she tapped the print and pushed back away from the table. "I'm sure. Number four."

"That's right," Spivey said.

Dupree said over his shoulder to Spivey, "This isn't a test."

Caroline turned and looked up at Dupree. "Number four."

Standing behind them in the interview room, Spivey spoke into his newest toy, a microcassette recorder that had recently replaced his ever-present notebook. "Twenty-nine April. Officer Mabry has identified suspect number four from a photographic lineup as the man she saw on twenty-eight April push Kevin Hatch, AKA . . ."

Dupree put his hand over Spivey's and used the younger man's fingers to squeeze the stop button on the tape player. "Don't do that," he said. "It's embarrassing."

Spivey walked outside, mumbling into the tape as he left.

"Sorry about that." Dupree gathered the photos and sat on the table, a few feet from where Caroline was staring a hole into the tabletop. "I guess there was a reason they stopped using monkeys in the space program."

Caroline took the photos from Dupree. "His hair is a little longer," she said, "but it's him. The eyes . . . What's his name?"

"Lenny Ryan. Just finished a nickel at Lompoc in California. Assault, theft, possession with intent—simple shit. Got out a couple months ago. Skipped on his parole in Oakland. No one knew he was here until he taught your guy to dive."

Caroline stared at the picture. "So he has family here?"

"Far as we know, just Uncle Pipe Wrench. But we only got the name an hour ago from the guy's mother. She hasn't seen him since he got out of prison."

"So he comes here to buy a dime bag and steal his uncle's twelve-year-old Pontiac? That makes no sense." Caroline held the photo in front of her, staring into the man's eyes. "So why's he here?"

"Who knows," Dupree said. "Maybe no reason, a guy like that."

"A guy like what?"

"Like a top," Dupree said.

"A top?"

"You're too young to remember tops. Had a big round end and a pointy end. Wrap a string on the round end, pull, and it spins on the pointy end." Dupree couldn't believe there was a theory he hadn't shared with her, this top theory. After four weeks with Spivey, he was excited to be teaching again. "A guy like this, you yank on his string and he's gonna spin around for a while, bump into things, careen off, till he just spins off the table or hits something that stops him. You can't apply the rules of reason and logic to a thing spinning in circles."

She grinned. "So you think I pulled his string?"

"No." Dupree was sorry he'd brought it up. "Not you. The bust. Guy gets out of prison and now he's gonna be arrested for a hand-to-hand dope deal? He doesn't want to go back, so he pushes your guy into the river to get away. Bang. You got a top."

"He doesn't want to be arrested for a misdemeanor drug deal, so he commits felony murder? How much sense does that make?"

"My point exactly. A top doesn't make sense. Just spins."

"And so, what, we just wait for the top to stop spinning?"

Dupree considered the question half as hard as he considered the lines above her eyes. "How's your mom?" he asked after a moment.

"Fine," Caroline said.

"She feeling better?"

"Yeah."

"Good. I'm glad."

Caroline looked once more at the photo, and it seemed to Dupree that she was memorizing every detail of Lenny Ryan's face, his blockish head and thick sandy hair, his dark eyebrows and cocked mouth. Then she handed the photo back to Dupree. "You need anything else from me?"

"No. I think that's it. What've you got today?"

"We're raiding a house over in East Central at ten. Burn's supplier."

"Undercover?"

Caroline laughed. "Not me. I'm in the truck. I don't think they're gonna let me play dress-up with the fellas for a while."

"I suppose." Dupree shifted, still trying to figure out how to approach the things he had so much trouble talking about. "You seem a little . . . how are you?"

"Lane wants me to see someone in professional services. I made some noise about talking to my guild rep and he turned and ran like he was on fire."

Dupree nodded, then stood and stuck his hands in his pockets, thinking that maybe he could strike a pose that would say the things he couldn't, express his feelings for her in a way that wasn't creepy, because creepiness seemed a definite possibility, given the things he was thinking just then. "There'd be no shame in seeing someone. You know that, right? Might even help."

"You know, you're right," she said. "You really ought to go."

He smiled at her sharpness and felt a pride and a responsibility that were different from the other thing he felt around her, the shortened breath, the gentle tug and taunt of her proximity. Sometimes he would stare at a hand-sized place on her body, the notch above her hip, the curve of her calf, the groove at the back of her neck, and he worried about the loyalty of his hands, daydreamed about their betrayal. And he wished that putting a hand on her side would be enough, even though he knew it couldn't be.

The interview room was narrow and long, with a table at its center and no windows, no two-way mirror from the movies, just a door and walls that pressed against Dupree, that hummed with the promise and threat of intimacy. He cleared his throat and looked at the photo of Lenny Ryan again.

"Hey, this is my kids' swimming instructor."

She smiled and, having felt the tug too, shifted in her chair away from him, telling herself the usual dodges: He's married and flippant and skinny and cynical and too old. This last made her smile at her own hypocrisy. Dupree was twelve years older than she; she was twelve years older than Joel. She had dated only one other man significantly older than she was, fifteen years ago, in college. He was a graduate-level instructor in the English department, almost as thin as Dupree, and it made her smile to think how old he seemed at thirty, when she was now six years older than that. He had seduced her by the book, if such a book existed for that kind of man, the kind who quotes Neruda after sex on the mattress on his bookstrewn floor, who pretends to listen to her every word, who has a boy's fumbling zeal when making love. Since she was a criminal justice major, the Neruda poetry was a nice diversion—*So I pass across your burning form*—but it was a bottle of wine and a Wallace Stevens poem that first did her in, "The Emperor of Ice-Cream," its refrain still rattling around amid the guilt and waterfalls and elegies of the job: *Let be be finale of seem. The only emperor is the emperor of ice-cream.* The graduate instructor had begun to explain the poem, the existential insistence of letting "be be finale of seem," the triumph of a moment over its potential, tangible over abstract, ice cream over death, but by then Caroline had already decided to sleep with the man and get a double major in poetry and criminal justice.

She thought about that attraction and about this one. Such an attraction said certain things about a girl whose father had left the family. An attraction to a man older and in a position of authority was inherently unhealthy, the blending of father figure and lover, and was fraught with disappointing glimpses of the future, at least the male version of it—love handles and graying hair, an increasing knack for self-delusion, and, in Dupree's case, the shell he'd built over the years to protect himself.

Noise outside the interview room yanked them both from their thoughts, and Caroline stood. "Well, I suppose . . ."

"Yeah," he said. "You've got a drug house to raid."

They left the interview room and returned to the Major Crimes office, both looking around furtively, like people returning from a lunchtime affair. There was a general rush of movement in the Major Crimes office, Pollard putting on his jacket and grabbing a notebook and pen from his desk, beginning to move toward the door. Dupree stood at the long filing cabinet at the front of the room, Caroline at his side.

"What's going on?" he asked.

Pollard answered. "Guy robbed a pawnshop and shot the owner."

"Jesus." Dupree shook his head. "What's that, four in twenty-four hours? That's gotta be a record."

"Not yet," Pollard said. "The guy's alive."

"No shit?"

Pollard shook his head appreciatively. "Don't ask me how. The guy gets popped in the face and sits there for an hour before anyone finds him."

Caroline walked toward the door, and Dupree turned from Pollard to her. "I'll see you later, then."

"Yeah," she said. "See ya."

He waited until she was gone before taking a deep breath and rubbing his face. The attraction and tension between them grew in periods of trouble like this; it was an undeniable fact. It was probably true of cops everywhere. No occupation promoted infidelity like police work, especially after women began joining police forces in the seventies and eighties. The worse things got, the longer the hours, the more adrenaline coursed through their bodies, the more they were likely to wind up on the floor somewhere, wrapped up in each other like they could provide some distraction, or cure. And he couldn't remember a time when things were worse than they were now, couldn't remember a streak that felt blacker than this one.

"You know," Pollard said, "if the guy kicks, you win the pot."

Dupree turned to face him. "Hmm?"

At the door, Pollard smiled on the left side of his mouth, the left eyebrow rising at the same pace as the corner of his mouth. "The pawnshop guy. Shooter used a nine. That's your weapon, right?"

Dupree thought back to the Christmas party and his surprise that a common weapon like the nine-millimeter was still available when he chose. The other guys howled and giggled and joked that he was going to shoot people himself—detectives carried nines—but in truth it hadn't seemed funny to him; he could never get drunk enough at the Christmas party to make the drawing seem anything but what it was.

Pollard was still standing there, apparently waiting for Dupree to say something funny. But nothing came.

8

Thick Jay was in his underwear and a once-white T-shirt, bent over the coffee table, inflating himself with smoke from the glass bong, his back arching as he inhaled. When the hit had gone on a few seconds, he pulled the webbed filter from the end of the bong and sucked the rest of the smoke from the glass tube into his lungs. He set the bowl in the bong and fell back against the couch, letting loose a cloud of smoke. "Up at noon, stoned by one. Nothin' like a little wake-and-bake, my friend."

Chase looked up from his cereal. "Why you still use that thing, man?"

"I don't know," said Thick Jay. "Nostalgia." He pushed a pizza box onto the trash-strewn floor to give himself more room.

Katrina came around the corner then, her hair already coming out of the braids she'd been building. "Jesus, Jay, you gonna take care of him or what?"

Jay cocked his head at the raspy whimpering from the back bedroom. "Yeah, I'm a little busy right now. You think you could . . . "

"No way, Jay. It's your responsibility. I'm gonna get some cigarettes." She went outside. Jay watched her go, then rolled his eyes at Chase.

Through the open front door another man leaned in, a guy in his thirties with long, scraggly hair, faded jeans, a black tank top, a backpack, and new running shoes. He gave a short wave. "Hey, man. What's the special today?"

Thick Jay and Chase looked up together. Jay smiled. "You back already?"

"Yeah," the guy said. "Whatcha got for me?"

"You smoke all that rock you got yesterday? What are you, fuckin' iron lung?"

"Hey, I had a party."

Thick Jay and Chase exchanged glances. "You get your invitation, Chase?"

Chase shook his head solemnly.

"Maybe we oughta go check," Thick Jay said.

"Yeah," Chase said. "I better go home and check my mail for an invitation."

"Aw, man." The guy with the backpack threw his arms up.

"Don't get all shitty with me, man," Thick Jay said. "You're the one had a party with my rock and didn't invite me. That's fucked, my friend."

In the surveillance van, Caroline rechecked the clip in her handgun as she listened to Gerraghty on the wire: *"I got so fucked up I thought you were there."*

Sergeant Lane winced and looked over at Caroline and the other four detectives. Caroline shrugged. It was a good line. There was a brief pause on the other end of the wire and then the two suspects burst into laughter. Usually the wire was closed, with just one officer listening, but it drove Lane crazy wondering when to go in, so he began opening it up, having them all listen.

"No shit?" asked the older suspect, whom Gerraghty's confidential informant had identified as "Thick Jay" Pringle, a Portland biker who dealt crack and methamphetamine from the house. The meth wasn't a surprise; bikers had been dealing it in some form for forty years. Spokane was a meth town. But the rock cocaine was a bit surprising. Gerraghty was convinced that Thick Jay had been Burn's source, and they had hoped to squeeze Burn to get to Jay,

then squeeze again to get Jay's source. With everyone dealing meth, crack was still pretty easy to trace, and Thick Jay seemed to be the only person with any sort of quantity.

"No shit, huh?" Jay's voice came over the radio, *"I told you, that's primo stuff, man. Fuck you up, yeah?"*

In the background, Caroline heard the hoarse whimpering of a dog. Crouched on the floor of the van, she shifted her weight, wishing this would go faster, so they could get in the house and cuff these idiots, and she could get back to the hospital to see her mother. What had the nurse said? A body has a way of shutting down.

"So you got anything else?"

Listening to wires drove Sergeant Lane almost as crazy as not listening. Caroline wished, for his sake, that this would go faster. After each exchange Lane looked around the van, trying to gauge their reaction, to figure out how it was going.

"Damn, man! You a fuckin' smokestack!"

The other suspect, for whom Gerraghty had only gotten a first name, Chase, laughed appreciatively and repeated the line. *". . . fuckin' smokestack."*

In the van, they waited impatiently, every scrape and cough that came over the wire putting them more on edge, punctuated by the faint, rhythmic whimpering.

"Christ," said Solaita, who sat in the front seat of the van with binoculars, watching the house, "would someone let the fuckin' dog out."

They heard the screen door open. From the front seat, Solaita held up one finger and touched his chest, the sign that the woman who'd left earlier had returned.

"What's goin' on, Jay?" the woman asked.

"What do you think is goin' on? A little commerce."

It was quiet in the house for a moment and then the woman laughed nervously. *"So can I talk to you a minute, Jay?"*

Inside the van, they recognized the tone, and Sergeant Lane ran his eyes across the other SIU detectives, dressed all in black and body armor. Four cars of patrol officers were on standby, and Lane spoke quietly into his headset to move them into place.

"I wish you could talk for only a minute," Jay was saying.

The girl was losing her temper. *"You're so fuckin' stupid, Jay. He's a cop."*

"Shit!" Sergeant Lane stood in a crouch and pointed at the driver, who shifted into gear and ripped across the parking lot.

Going by the book, Gerraghty tried incredulity. *"You think I'm a fuckin' cop?"*

The girl laughed. *"You arrested me six months ago. What, you quit since then?"*

"Get down!" Gerraghty yelled. *"Get on the ground!"*

The van veered down an alley, turned, and jumped onto the dead grass in front of the house, a house that Caroline saw and knew immediately with a precision drawn from so many other busts: They would find a couch on the porch, bedsheets on the windows, chipped-paint and primer-shake walls, gray roof shingles dissolving into dirt.

The back door of the van flew open and the detectives burst out, spreading across the lawn and up the porch. Caroline took the porch steps two at a time and was the third cop in the house, Gerraghty already having wrestled Jay to his substantial stomach, a knee in his back, screaming at him—"Hands out at your sides! Hands at your sides!"—as Solaita began the same process with Chase, who had the dumbest look Caroline had ever seen, as if he were contemplating his first tool.

A veteran of this kind of raid, the woman was on the floor with her hands on the back of her head, so Caroline passed her on to one of the other detectives and kept moving through the disgusting house, stepping around garbage into a hallway and then a bathroom in which the water apparently had been turned off. Caroline had seen bathrooms like this before, the occupants taking to shitting in the bathtub when the toilet was full. She covered her mouth and backed out of the room. "Bathroom's clear," she said into her microphone and kept moving through the house.

Beneath the yelling and wrestling from the living room, Caroline could hear the whimpering more clearly. The dog was in a back bedroom.

Caroline moved through the kitchen, a pan of cold macaroni and cheese on the table along with parts of countless other meals, sandwiches and bags of potato chips and beer cans. A diaper. "Kitchen's clear," Caroline said into the radio.

The back bedroom was off the kitchen and had been at one time a back porch or eating nook. Even before she turned the loose door handle, Caroline had a terrible feeling. The crying was clearer here, the smell precise, and before she stepped through the door, Caroline knew what she would find.

He was maybe six months old, lying on his side, running his fingers over the bars of his crib, his voice nearly gone from crying. He was naked, and Caroline could smell before she could see that he had been lying in his own waste for some time now. Someone had taped a pacifier onto his mouth but he had gotten it partway off and it hung from his cheek by a square of duct tape. His crying was steady and throbbing, like a record that's finished playing, but keeps spinning under the needle. Caroline doubted the cry was for attention anymore. This baby didn't know what other sound to make.

She grabbed a flannel shirt off a chair in the kitchen and returned to the crib, wrapped it around the boy, and lifted him from the soaked and soiled bed. He weighed as much as her purse. He didn't seem to notice that he was in someone's arms.

Caroline carefully took the taped pacifier off his cheek.

She held him beneath her chin and rocked back and forth, but he just kept crying. Through the kitchen and down the hallway, she could see the Kevlar-vested detectives wrestling with Thick Jay, Chase, and the woman. She opened her mouth to let someone know what she'd found, but nothing came. The baby lay limp against her shoulder, not hugging or resisting, just lying there. Caroline could hear her own breath in her head.

Sergeant Lane stepped through the kitchen, covering his mouth because of the stench. It took a moment for the flannel lump on Caroline's shoulder to register, but when it did, the sergeant removed his glasses and rubbed the bridge of his nose. Her hand shaking, Caroline held out the tape and the pacifier. "I'll call CPS," he whispered.

While Sergeant Lane called Child Protective Services, Caroline looked for a bottle. There seemed to be no rhyme or reason to the cupboards—half-eaten chips and two black bananas in this one, a box of rice and a photo album in that one. No baby supplies anywhere. She finally found a bottle in the refrigerator, but it was empty, just stained with old milk, the rubber on the nipple old and flaking.

The whimpering hadn't changed and so Caroline stuck her pinkie in the boy's mouth, the way she'd seen her sister-in-law do when Chelsea was crying. He began suckling her finger, pausing every few seconds to rest, then starting in again on her finger. After a few tugs at this he stopped crying, and after a few more was asleep.

She walked gingerly through the house, trying not to wake the baby. The other detectives slumped when they saw what she held, when they recalled the whimpering dog. Caroline moved into the living room, where the suspects were laid out on their stomachs, being questioned. She pushed the clothes and garbage aside and set the baby down on the couch, taking the ratty flannel shirt away and replacing it with a T-shirt that would be softer on his little body. But without the feel of her, the baby began crying, more softly this time, reaching out with clawed fingers for her.

On the floor across the room, Thick Jay lifted his head at the sound. "Hey, what are you doing with my kid?"

Caroline didn't even realize she had crossed the room. She grabbed one handcuffed arm, and with her other hand grabbed Thick Jay's hair. She pulled equally on them and he screamed as he was lifted by the shoulder and the hair to a standing position. Detectives and uniformed cops came into the room and saw Thick Jay balanced on the balls of his feet, his face wrenched in pain. Caroline cranked on his arm and hair. She slammed his face into the fireplace. Jay's knees buckled and he fell away from her. Caroline stood above him, still holding a patch of his curly brown hair.

Sergeant Lane and a uniformed officer grabbed Caroline and pulled her away, then shoved her in the direction of the front door. She lurched to a stop and stared at the clump of hair in her hand. The baby was whimpering again on the couch, as loudly as he had in the back bedroom. Finally, she dropped the hair and looked at Jay, whose nose was bleeding, but who otherwise appeared fine.

Another pair of hands pushed her in the back again, out the door, and Caroline found herself on the porch steps. She slumped down against the side of the house and listened to the rusty squeak of the baby inside the house.

9

Dupree's first thought when he was called to the river that afternoon was that a fishing boat had finally bumped into the bloated body of Kevin Hatch. But as he drove downstream from the dam into Peaceful Valley, listening to Lieutenant Branch explain the situation over the cell phone, he realized this was something else, a thing he had theorized but never encountered before, a rare, natural phenomenon—the criminal equivalent of a black hole, a thing that at once proved and dwarfed his roundabout conclusion that violence was contained in self-sustaining streaks, in seasons of dark and light.

"In my professional opinion?" Lieutenant Branch was saying on the other end of the phone, "I think we got us a bad guy."

The new body had been found in the same wash where Rebecca Bennett's body was discovered the day before. The evidence technicians had spent most of the night processing that crime scene and had gone away after midnight, leaving the area marked by police tape stretched around the trees and guarded only by the routine patrols of uniformed officers. But when the lead detective on the case, Chris Laird, returned the next afternoon, he found another woman's body in the same position, in the same clearing, under the same cover of branches where Rebecca Bennett had been found. It was as if her killer had been angry that the police had disturbed the grave and had restocked it. The man's brazenness struck Dupree dumb. This was a killer so cocky, so adept at killing, that he returned to an active crime scene to dump a second body.

"I just don't know about this week—" Dupree began.

"—amazing," Lieutenant Branch finished his thought. "We've racked up so much comp time, I ain't gonna have anyone to work, come fall."

But Dupree had been contemplating something else, the unfathomable four homicides in two days—five if the pawnshop owner died. Dupree was thinking of critical mass, of black holes, areas with so much density and gravity they cave in on themselves, warp time and space, alter physical laws, create their own energy. People tend to look at violence as an aberration, as something wrong, unnatural. But what could be more natural than violence? And like any law of nature, couldn't violence be factored out to its extreme, a state in which it was capable of sustaining itself, increasing in weight and density and speed, spinning off into itself?

Dupree had left Spivey at the cop shop, ostensibly to work on a teletype describing Lenny Ryan. But the other reason was that the kid was driving him crazy. Dupree knew some dense cops, but he'd never met one with less understanding of irony and complexity. As he parked his car above the riverbank, next to Laird's car, Dupree thought about talking to Branch about his black hole theory, but it would be pointless.

"All right," Dupree said into his phone. "I'm here. What do you want me to do?"

"I need you to run this thing."

As he spoke into the phone, Dupree rubbed Vicks VapoRub on his upper lip to prepare for the smell. "I thought this was Laird's case."

Dupree could hear Branch search for a delicate way to talk about Laird's generally acknowledged incompetence. "This might end up being everyone's case," he finally said.

"Okay." Dupree hung up and walked over the roadside into the thick brush, branches and twigs cracking beneath his feet, until he reached the clearing where the Explorer had found Rebecca Bennett's body yesterday.

Today was even hotter, almost eighty, ridiculous for the Pacific Northwest in April. Bloated spring runoff bulged the riverbank and flushed the channel behind him, the current tugging at trees that had been fooled into believing they were safely on shore.

More police tape marked the perimeter of the clearing, inside which detectives and evidence techs pored over every stick and piece of bark, taking photographs from every angle, sifting through sand and dirt. The clearing had been gridded with string, laid out like a checkerboard so that each piece of evidence could be graphed and traced to the exact place where it had been found. Since it was a transient camp, there was garbage everywhere, empty bottles and food containers. Each piece was photographed, catalogued, and then lifted with gloved hands into separate bags, sealed and stapled with a brief explanation and location. The garbage would prove to be a logistic tangle of its own, Dupree knew. Each piece would be fingerprinted and traced and they'd come up with seeming leads on all kinds of bums, none of whom had the courage or resources to replace a body after the police took one away. No, this was someone else, someone with a car and access to hookers, someone who'd seen the discovery on the TV news and had simply gotten another victim, killed her, and dumped her.

The killer had access to hookers. He had mobility and knew that the police were no longer guarding the crime scene. Could be a resident of Peaceful Valley, just upstream, who saw the police leave. Could be a cabdriver. Could be a cop.

Laird loped across the clearing, angular and unsteady, weighted to his hips, a six-foot bowling pin. He stepped carefully over the stringed gridwork toward Dupree.

"How many times have I told you," Dupree said, "you don't get the roots, these damn bodies just grow back."

Dupree slid under the police tape into the edge of the grid, the strings laid three feet apart at knee level across the clearing, the entire crime scene photographed from above, each quadrant photographed, each square yard dissected, garbage removed, twigs and branches checked for fresh breaks, ground cover checked for impressions and footprints, the very dirt itself sifted. The local FBI guys, a couple of former military types whom Dupree called Gomer and Pyle, were arrogantly and casually offering lasers and computer databases, like rich cousins at a family reunion.

Laird pulled Dupree away from the FBI agents. "This is bad," he said. For the first time, Dupree looked at the body. She was blond; the other girl had been dark-haired. And it was clear by the clusters of maggots that she'd been killed more recently. Other than that, it was eerily similar to Rebecca Bennett's murder. The body was nestled in the same dugout, covered by the same branches. Dupree felt a twitch along his right arm and turned to the river, pretending to look for the direction the killer might have come. He let his breath out in little skips, then cleared his throat and felt the familiar urge to sweep up Debbie and the kids, protect and hide them in the same motion.

His voice came out raspy and light. "Where was patrol?"

"A car came by once an hour," Laird said. "He must've snuck her in."

Dupree nodded and looked around the clearing again, trying to avoid eye contact with the FBI assholes, who were walking around giving orders to the evidence techs and looking every bit like guys trying to take over an investigation. But there was something else going on with the federales, something even more irritating than usual.

"FeeBIes giving you any trouble?" Dupree asked.

"Nah, they're just a little keyed up. I guess there's a profiler coming."

"Oh, good. A hindsight expert." Still avoiding the body, Dupree turned back toward the road. "You check for tire tracks along the roadside?"

Laird squeezed his eyes shut. "Goddamn it. I forgot."

"Don't worry about it," Dupree said, catching his breath and taking a moment to look around the perimeter. "I'll go back up."

Laird turned again toward the body. "You think it might be a copycat?"

Dupree steeled himself and turned to face the young woman's corpse, which lay curled against the bank. Only the top of her head and her bare feet were visible, the rest of her partly covered by sticks and brush. He pulled a glove onto his right hand, bent down, and began to pull some branches away.

"Alan, maybe you should wait for the techs to clear this—"

Dupree carefully pulled one twig at a time, revealing the right arm and wrist and, finally, what he was looking for, the hand. He stood and backed away. Two twenty-dollar bills had been pressed into the girl's palm, curled in her hand like paper flowers. Just like Rebecca Bennett. Dupree and Laird stood quietly, as if in a museum, turning their heads this way and that, viewing the work, the simplicity and the daring. Dupree made a noise between a peep and a sigh, and Laird nodded. "Goddamn," he said.

The local FBI agents came up, stepped gingerly over the string grid, and took their places next to Laird and Dupree, barely able to contain themselves.

"We got a guy coming in from Quantico, happened to be in the area," said the taller agent, whom Dupree called Pyle. "A profiler."

"And you think this guy did it?"

He ignored Dupree. "Your lieutenant asked us to run it through the database." The FBI operated a database at its Behavioral Science Unit in Quantico that kept track of serial killings all over the country and could be searched for similarities in motive or evidence. For a moment, none of the men looked away from the body, just stared at it as if they were waiting for the woman to do something.

Finally, the agent Dupree called Gomer turned away. "Unreal. City's goin' nuts."

Dupree thought about the last two days, imagining a thing that traveled like a wave or a current, invisible until it rolled across your path, when it raised the hair on your neck or made you shiver, its wind pooling with other winds, drawing into streams into branches into rivers that bulged and ran over their banks. He imagined the thing picking up momentum and curling back on itself, doubling and tripling its density and gravity as it spun faster and faster around itself. A whirlpool. A black hole. Fly into a black hole, the theory went, and you emerged on the other side of the universe. Dupree imagined he was standing at the point of a great funnel that could spew dead people forever.

He walked away to search beyond the clearing for more evidence, spreading out away from the river and exploring every dugout, depression, and stand of pines. Despite being just a couple of miles downstream from Riverfront Park and downtown, this stretch of riverbank remained lightly traveled. A natural floodplain, it had escaped development after the dam went in and had become the place high school kids went for keggers, where transients went to camp, where aging hippies went to sunbathe. Garbage was the only sign that Dupree was actually in the city, and it was garbage he investigated, bottles, boxes, and cigarette butts, carefully sealing bits of promising refuse into sandwich bags.

Back in the clearing the FBI guys positively beamed as they waited for their expert to arrive. This was so much more glamorous than the usual fare of speed-whacked bank robbers and jughead neo-Nazis. They leaned over their field computer and high-tech evidence kits and used lasers to grid off the fields that earlier the Spokane police, like some Neanderthal investigatory agency, had covered with string. Gomer and Pyle took turns narrating into cell phones, their faces betraying the rush that sickened Dupree because he understood it so well—the humiliating excitement of a murder investigation.

In contrast to the buzzing FBI agents, Dupree faded as the day went on. He supervised the K-9 officers with their dogs as they searched the riverbank for more evidence. Or more bodies. It stood to reason that if the killer was so attached to this place, he might have dumped other bodies here too.

Still, Dupree felt unprepared when he rounded a bend in the river, three hundred yards from the first clearing, and was hit with that familiar sweet, rotting smell. One of the cadaver dogs was sniffing at a mound of brush and dirt, so much like the other mound that Dupree heard himself groan. The officer holding the dog was a decent, dull guy named Farley, who scratched the dog's ears but wouldn't meet Dupree's eyes, both of them sharing the horrible and exhilarating flash of guilt at having discovered this.

Dupree came closer, pulled away a few branches and some of the dirt, and saw just enough dried, darkened skin to know. He stepped back and called the lieutenant on his cell phone to tell him what he'd found and to get an evidence team down there. When Dupree turned back, Farley was staring off into space, the dog still scratching at the mound. Dupree was surprised by the sharpness of his own voice.

"Get the goddamn dog out of here!"

Farley pulled the dog toward the river without a word, the dog's head jittering from side to side as he sniffed for more bodies. Farley looked over his shoulder to make one last eye contact with Dupree, who shrugged a kind of apology.

Dupree stood in front of the mound, which didn't so much hide the body as mark it. This was someone who needed a marker to help him return to the body, to see it again. Suddenly, he wished he knew more, and he envied the FBI agents. This was a discipline unto itself, the search for serial killers, separate from routine detective work. Dupree had attended countless evidence and investigative conferences and seminars, though he had chosen to ignore the FBI agents talking about profiling and signatures and sex-offender models and the other aspects of serial murder investigation. It seemed too much like voodoo, like something completely removed from the intuitive common sense he relied on as a police officer. Now he found himself wishing he'd paid more attention.

The sun was dipping behind the hillside and patrol officers were carrying in floodlights and a generator to keep the riverbank lit. Evidence techs and other detectives drifted into the second clearing and Dupree helped them put tape around the perimeter. When the mound had been photographed and measured, Dupree knelt and began pulling branches, one at a time, away from the girl's right side. Finally, Dupree stepped back and nodded to the corporal with the video camera to come closer. Two twenties lay flat in the girl's decomposing hand, held in place this time by a rubber band.

Dupree backed up and dropped to a crouch. The girl was tiny. He thought immediately of his daughter. Dupree felt his stomach curl and he turned away, put his head between his knees, and stared at the ground, a carpet of stinkweed and field grass.

Spivey put a hand on Dupree's back. "You okay?"

Dupree was relieved when the hand was removed. He took another deep breath, nodded, and stood. "Allergies."

Spivey headed back upstream. Still lightheaded, Dupree felt a tightness like claustrophobia as he pushed through the thick bushes toward the roadside. He got into deep cover, the branches poking him, tugging at his clothes, his discomfort bleeding into desperation and panic, until finally he burst into the open along the road. Downstream, patrol was setting up a perimeter that would reach two miles of riverfront.

Looking upstream, Dupree could see the command post; the assistant chief would be there with Branch, who'd been getting regular briefings from Dupree. He began making his way back, his breath evening out, nerves settling. He wiped the perspiration from his upper lip but it returned immediately. Behind the command post, TV news satellite trucks were lined up, their dishes pointed back toward the heart of the city.

The command post was a blur, the awkward grab and grapple of competing jurisdictions—the FBI and Spokane police both "volunteering" to handle certain aspects of the case, while the county sheriff stood by, pointing out sections of riverbank that were outside the city limits. With the discovery of the third body, new cops arrived all the time, both uniforms and detectives. Dupree looked for Caroline and felt a mixed sense of relief and disappointment that he didn't see her—relief because this was the last thing she needed. There was no denying it, though; he wanted to see her.

With the sun down, a chill seeped from the ground, as if April's warmth had been merely a taunt. In the cordoned-off command post, detectives grabbed for slices of pizza and clutched Styrofoam cups of coffee beneath floodlights that lent a surreal cast to the cars and vans parked alongside the road. Dupree met beneath the tarp of the command post with Lieutenant Branch and Assistant Chief Tucker. They huddled over a map and pointed out the areas where evidence had been processed. They had just decided to keep a presence at the crime scene all night when a tall, muscular white man in a tight, ribbed sweater marched into the command post, his FeeBIe credentials swinging from his neck like bells. Dupree recognized him from somewhere. TV, maybe.

Tucker lunged forward and shook the man's hand. "Jeff. Thanks for coming." Then he turned to Dupree. "Alan. This is FBI Special Supervisory Agent Jeffrey McDaniel . . . with the Investigative Support Unit."

McDaniel was older than Dupree's first impression of him, hair graying at the temples, stomach held in. He champed on a piece of gum and stared hard at Dupree without actually meeting his eyes. When Dupree didn't say anything, McDaniel extended a hand and offered a choking handshake. "From Quantico," he said.

"Right," Dupree said, "the Australian airline."

McDaniel didn't even flinch. "Quantico, Virginia. The Behavioral Science Unit."

"Well, that makes more sense."

McDaniel dropped Dupree's hand and strode off toward the first body. After a moment, the cops fell in behind, like junior officers at a battlefield inspection.

"We lucked out," the assistant chief whispered over his shoulder to Dupree. "Jeff was working on a Portland case and agreed to fly in and give us a quick consultation at the crime scene. This is very rare."

"Lucky us," Dupree said.

McDaniel stood over the body, running his eyes from one end to the other, as if he were measuring a deck. He asked a series of one-word questions—"Time?" "ID?"—but gave back no information, pacing around the body, staring at it from different angles, then turning toward the vacant fields and blocking with his hands, moving them in shadowy patterns like he was re-creating movements. The effect was of an actor preparing to speak, and everyone, including Dupree, stopped to watch him, to listen.

"This victim was killed elsewhere," McDaniel said. "Dragged down here. Gunshots are secondary, overkill. Fingernails broken off, through struggle maybe, but more likely to conceal evidence." The FBI agent finished speaking and crouched on a hillside. He chewed a piece of grass.

Dupree looked from Laird to the lieutenant. Was that it? Was that what they'd been waiting for all day? Broken fingernails? After a moment, Spivey came up to McDaniel sheepishly. It looked like he might ask for an autograph. "You think the money is to let us know these are hookers?"

McDaniel nodded without looking up. "He's telling us they deserved to die."

"Right, right," Spivey said. "That's what I think too. Wow. That's great." Spivey kicked at the ground with his feet and continued. "I have to tell you, I read your book, like, ten times."

This, finally, caught McDaniel's attention, and he looked up.

"That case in Detroit—"

"The Kitchen Killer," McDaniel said, and Dupree thought he detected a smile on the man's face.

"That was amazing. His fascination with handcuffs and everything. Oh, and the guy in Fort Worth. And the Pacific Coast Killer. Oh, man!"

McDaniel stood and shot Spivey a glare. "That's Blanton's book."

Spivey looked sick. "What?"

"The Pacific Coast Killer. That was from Curtis Blanton's book. Asshole leaves the bureau and makes a fortune talking about *our* old cases, consulting on every goddamn cop show in Hollywood." Then McDaniel turned to the river. "And I get to come here." Spivey stood with his hands at his sides crestfallen.

It was too much for Dupree, who climbed the riverbank and walked east toward Peaceful Valley. Here the houses ran along three streets parallel to the river and residents had come outside to lean across backyard fences, meeting in the strips alongside their clapboard houses, exchanging rumor for fear, finding new significance in strange cars that had trolled past and the "retard" who used to deliver papers, recalling the recent backfire of cars and the old guy who'd enticed the neighborhood kids into his house with promises of candy.

The more aggressive gawkers made their way to the edge of the police tape on tiptoes, like the gallery at a golf tournament. Dupree found himself listening to detached voices as the crowd compared other crimes they'd seen, relayed TV shows that made them experts on serial murder, and spun dramatic tales of hearing the sirens.

"At least he's just killing hookers," Dupree heard one woman say. He spun to face the crowd, arms shaking with anger. He couldn't find the woman who'd said it, and he wondered if he'd heard right; perhaps the sentence was a product of his own fatigue and edginess. Or perhaps it was his opinion. Staring at the expectant faces made him feel exposed and alone, this occasional feeling that the general population was made up entirely of criminals and that it was him against all of *them*.

Dupree scanned the faces on the other side of the barrier, but saw nothing out of the ordinary. Still, he found Corporal Galatta and instructed him to get some photographs of the crowd, just in case the killer had come down to watch.

Dupree was starting to feel wasted, too tired to concentrate. He checked his watch. Just before midnight. He didn't want to go back and watch the arrogant FBI profiler anymore. He called Lieutenant Branch on his cell phone and said he was going to take his first break of the day, head home for a quick shower and change of clothes.

He fought sleep as he drove up the hill south of the river, and sat for a moment in his driveway before climbing out of the car. He lingered on the T-ball set in the front yard, picked up Marc's glove, and opened the unlocked door. He wondered if Debbie did that on purpose, leaving the door unlocked when he wasn't home, just to piss him off.

He came in and found her sitting at a bar stool in the dining room, reading a magazine. She removed her glasses and gave him a sad smile that he returned. Her long black hair was ponytailed, draped over her shoulder, and he still could see the girl behind her widened and lined face.

"You left the door unlocked," he said.

She nodded. "You missed the session." They'd begun going to a marriage counselor two months earlier. She'd been in therapy herself for two years, hoping to avoid the depression that had swallowed her mother, and decided they needed to do something about the creeping discontent in their marriage. But Dupree had missed two of the three sessions, and if there was one thing he felt from her right now, it was discontent.

"It was a crazy day," he said.

She shrugged. "I saw the news. Nothing you could do."

Somehow that made it worse. "Whatcha reading?" he asked. He didn't like reading himself, but he loved hearing about what she read.

She flopped the magazine over so he could see the title—something about Victorian houses. She'd always wanted one, instead of this rancher. "You all right?"

"Tired." He slumped against the wall. "Debbie, I'm really sorry—"

"It's fine, Alan." The way she said his name, it felt like a low, flat kick.

He walked toward the bedroom, undressing. "How was Staci's conference?"

"There's some stuff on the table."

Dupree peeked in first on eleven-year-old Marc, balled up in his NFL covers, his hair a tumble of straw. Staci, who was six, slept with her mouth open, a flowered jumper and white sandals carefully laid out at the foot of the bed for tomorrow. Dupree stood in the doorway for some time before moving toward the bathroom.

He leaned against the shower wall and let cool water cascade down his back. He closed his eyes and saw the bodies, hands and feet, the darkening of flesh, the branches spread over most of the corpse but not all, as if whoever killed those girls *wanted* to leave a little bit of them showing, *wanted* him to see the money in their hands.

The riverbank was etched into his eyelids. He opened his mouth in the shower to try to get rid of the taste and the smell—of chokeweed and transient camps, of rotting flesh. He leaned against the wall, letting the water roll over him, and woke with a jolt, like snapping awake behind the wheel or at his desk, every muscle tensing after a disconcerting split second of sleep. He shook the water from his head like a dog and turned the shower off. When he left the bathroom a few minutes later, he wasn't surprised to find Debbie gone from her bar stool, the light out in their bedroom.

10

Caroline expected more from death. Whether it came from some soaring movie soundtrack or the reverie of some childhood funeral Mass or just the tangled anxieties of her own subconscious, she had always imagined dying would at least offer some substance, some tangible feeling she could share with others who witnessed a long, slow death—"Ah, sure, I remember death." The sense of a spirit passing on, perhaps, a lightening, a change in the atmosphere of the room, a kick to the head—however it came, she expected it to feel like *something*.

She had been in Sergeant Lane's office, enduring a lecture and suspension about bashing Thick Jay's head into the fireplace, when she was paged by the hospital. She called on the lieutenant's phone and reached her mother's doctor, who began explaining the same thing that the nurse already had explained. Caroline's mother's body had had enough and was shutting down.

The sergeant was grim and understanding; he had no idea her mother's condition was so serious. He told her he'd talk to the chief, explain her behavior in the context of her mother's illness. Caroline just nodded. When Sergeant Lane offered to have someone drive her to the hospital, she surprised herself by accepting.

In her mother's hospital room the doctor spoke into his fist, concentrating on a spot a few feet from Caroline and choosing his words as if they might pick locks. "I talked with your mother about . . . what sort of . . . measures she wanted . . . employed . . . at this stage . . ."

"I know," Caroline said. "She didn't want you to do anything."

The doctor nodded and continued speaking with great care. "If you would like . . . we could still try . . . moving her home . . . and have hospice . . . attend."

"Is there time for that?"

"She's made a . . . drastic decline the last two days . . ." For the first time, he met her eyes. "I don't think so . . . no." She looked back over at her still mother. The doctor patted her on the hand and left the room.

Caroline leaned back in the chair and took in the sterile sanctity of her mother's hospital room, lights dimmed, door closed. The nurses had put Caroline's mother on her back again, no longer worrying about the bedsores they'd battled for the last month. They'd unhooked the oxygen machine as well, and even the morphine IV drip. For the first time that spring it was just Caroline's mother lying there, her breathing irregular and raspy, as if she were drowning in dust. Caroline leaned across the bed and held her mother's face in her hands, pressed their foreheads together and felt her mother's weak breath on her own face. When she had drifted out of consciousness four days before—for the last time, it was clear now—Caroline had been flooded with all the things she wanted to say. Now all the words seemed dried up, and all she wanted to do was lean across the woman's bed and hold her, feel the mix of things that made up her mother—bone and flesh, humor and cunning, the warmth of her mother's lap. During the last part of the illness Caroline hadn't had time to feel sorry for herself, only empathy for her mother, the desire to somehow lessen her mother's pain. But now she imagined life without this person; for the first time Caroline felt worse for herself than for her mother.

Maybe her mother was gone already, leaving behind only reflexive breath and smoldering synapse. Or maybe she was still in there, dreaming her front porch, a cup of coffee, a romance book, Caroline stretched out on the porch steps beneath her, scolding her about this bit of gossip, that bit of cattiness, even as she covered her own half smile.

Caroline whispered, "I love you, Mom," her voice quavering, and then let go of her mother's face and fell back in the chair next to her bed. She supposed all the other things had been said. What good are faded compliments and moments of understanding, the things between people? Did they have some weight? Or were they gone the moment they were uttered, lost in the moment of conception, the finale of seem?

The doctor had told her it might be twenty-four hours, even thirty-six. Habit could prop up even the frailest human body. Fifty-eight years of breathing and circulating and thinking didn't turn off like a toggle switch. She could last days, her body recollecting itself and taking one more charge up the hill. Or it could be hours. No matter; Caroline had decided she wasn't going to leave the hospital until it was over. She curled up in the hospital chair, holding her mother's hand and rocking slowly.

Caroline was shocked when she realized that she was asleep, in a dreamy haze somewhere, unsure if her eyes were open now or closed, wondering if the awareness of sleep meant she was awake. She couldn't hear or see anything, but maybe there was nothing to hear or see. She felt for her mother's hand and that's when her eyes snapped open, when she saw her mother's fingers drooped, wrist curled over the edge of the bed, and knew that her mother was gone.

She felt cheated by the moment; no rising, no change in the atmosphere of the room, no brush with transparency. Her mother was just gone. Caroline walked into the hall. She checked her watch. Two-thirty in the morning. Exhausted, Caroline had slept six hours. The nurse wasn't at her station so Caroline picked up the phone and tapped in a long-distance number.

A woman answered sleepily. "Mmm. Hello." Caroline's step-mother.

"Ramona? Is my dad there?"

"Caroline?"

"Is my dad there? I told him I'd call."

"Sure. Just a minute."

She heard whispering, the shuffle of covers, her father clearing his throat. "Caroline?"

"She's gone, Daddy." And with that the tears burst forth in gasping sobs that shook her violently, that echoed up and down the carpeted hallways and brought a nurse from another room.

"Caroline?" Her father's voice was small on the dangling phone. "Caroline, are you there?" Caroline handed the phone to the nurse and slumped to the floor of the nurses' station, her arms over her head, eyes closed, rocking with every sob. The nurse talked to her father for a moment and then hung up the phone, helping Caroline to her feet. They walked to the end of the hall and to a patio overlooking the city. They stood until Caroline felt the control returning, stopped crying and took a breath.

"I need to call my brother," Caroline said.

"Not now. There'll be time."

Caroline nodded.

"I'm going to go in and have the doctor look at your mother," the nurse said.

"Can I stay out here?" The nurse said yes and when she was gone Caroline walked to the edge of the balcony and leaned out over the railing into the blackness, feeling the cool wind on her face, stinging where her tears were left to dry in the creases of her eyes. A few cars trickled along the freeway and the streets of downtown, people going home from bars, trudging off with strangers, going to bay at the windows of old flames. Traffic at two-thirty in the morning is the flow of desperation.

Beyond the freeway was the river, a seam through the city, coming straight into downtown, then splitting and curling around Canada Island and Riverfront Park, through the falls and the dam, then beginning its slow meander west. Caroline thought about Burn, still out there somewhere, and remembered the way their hands had connected in the split second before he died. She opened and closed her hand, stared at it. She felt more connected to the young drug dealer, and wondered if she'd done as much to save her mother. The tears came again, silently this time, curling over her cheeks and falling.

And then Caroline understood that death did have a specific feeling and why she hadn't recognized it before. It was actually familiar, something revealed every day in glimpses of strangers, in solitary walks along the river, in moments of quiet, the realization that, for all the people we surround ourselves with, in the end, we go over alone.

11

In Loving Memory
Theresa Marie Mabry

Born: August 9, 1942
Passed on: April 30, 2001
Beloved Mother and Friend

"Behold, I show you a mystery;
We shall not all sleep,
but we shall all be changed,
In a moment, in the twinkling of an eye . . .
and the dead shall be raised
incorruptible,
and we shall be changed."

—I Corinthians 15:51–52

Private graveside service to follow. No reception.

PART II

MAY
A Game of Chess

12

The chair she sat in was a throne of leather and dark-stained oak, more imposing than the person encased by it, a plump, dark-haired white woman who tapped a pen on the frame of her bifocals as she peered at the form Caroline had filled out. At the end of each page Vicki Ewing looked over her glasses, and then back to the next page.

"You left the emergency contact line blank."

Caroline had stared at that line and thought about her mother. Dupree flashed in her mind too. But she said, "I have a boyfriend. Joel Belanger. Same address."

Dr. Ewing scribbled in the line and then removed her glasses and looked up at Caroline. "You left this whole section blank, too. Where you were supposed to describe the problem . . . your anxiety . . ."

Caroline stood and removed a paperback medical textbook from the bookcase near the door. She checked the worn spine, then held it up. "Looks like you've read some of these."

"Some of them. We were talking about your problem."

"I don't think I have one."

"Oh, good. Makes it an easy day for me, then. But, since we've got another forty minutes, why don't we talk about why you're here."

Caroline thought a moment. "I'm here because my sergeant doesn't think a woman can handle the pressure of being a detective."

"Can you?"

"I smacked a guy's face into his fireplace. I guess that was uncalled for."

"And that was last month? The day your mother died?"

Caroline nodded. "Three weeks ago. What's with that chair?"

Dr. Ewing turned slightly in the huge leather chair. "My father was excited to have a doctor in the family. I'd get rid of it but I'm always afraid he'll just drop in."

Caroline looked down at the textbook in her hand, which was open to a page on kleptomania. She looked around the office and smiled. "Professional services. That's funny. Anyone ever come in to get their taxes done? Or to get a wart removed?"

Dr. Ewing smiled. "No."

"So the only service you provide is brain repair. That's just one service. Shouldn't it be called professional *service*?"

"I consult with various law enforcement agencies on criminal behavior and victim anxiety . . . and I repair a brain or two on the side. I think that qualifies as plural. Now, please. Sit down."

Caroline did, and the session went faster than she would have guessed, the doctor more easygoing and funnier than she expected. They talked about Caroline's terrible month of April. Thick Jay was becoming a minor pain in the ass, claiming he'd had vision problems and dizziness ever since "the attack." In the newspaper, the police chief characterized what happened as "a suspect becoming entangled with a detective," but Jay's lawyer was talking about filing a claim against the city. The prosecutor was hoping to package a light plea bargain of his drug-dealing charge with the dropping of any potential claim. Thankfully for Caroline, the prosecutor was refusing to deal on the child abuse charge at all, so even if Thick Jay got a deal on the drug case he'd still do time.

Caroline had been suspended for a week—time she used to mourn her mother anyway—and had received a letter of reprimand in her file indicating she violated the department's "use of force policy." She got the sense that if her mother hadn't died that day, they might simply have fired her. But in all honesty, her mother's death had nothing to do with her rough treatment of Thick Jay.

"Do you really believe that?" Dr. Ewing asked.

Caroline suddenly felt sleepy. Twenty-one days since her mother's death and still she had trouble sleeping for more than an hour or two at a time, as if she were still trying to reach out, to catch her mom in the act of dying. "I don't know," she said finally. "If it was someone else, I'd assume the two things were related. But all I was thinking about was how that guy hurt that baby. I just wanted to hurt him."

"Any children yourself?"

"No."

"You talked about a boyfriend . . ."

"He's a little younger than me, but I wouldn't call him a child."

Dr. Ewing laughed. "That's not what I meant . . . how much younger is he?"

"I don't see what that has to do with my mental health."

"Five years younger?"

Caroline shrugged and smiled at the floor.

"Ten years younger?"

"Okay," Caroline said. "My boyfriend is six. He's in first grade."

Dr. Ewing checked her watch and looked up genially. "We're five minutes over. We'll talk about your boyfriend next time."

"We're having a next time?"

"You don't want to come back?"

"If they wanna pay me to come in here and girl-talk with you . . . well, fine. But quite honestly, I don't know what the point is. I mean, no offense . . ."

"No. Of course not."

". . . but I don't need it. I had a tough month at work and my mother died. That's it. End of story. You want to know if I resent my father for leaving my mom? You bet. Do I worry that I'm getting older and will never get married and have kids? Every day. Am I burned out busting kids with dime bags of pot? Like you can't believe. But I'd be crazy if I didn't feel those things. Don't you think?"

For a long minute, Dr. Ewing stared with a half smile. "You went after a suspect who was handcuffed and lying on the floor. You hit his head against a brick fireplace. That's not the kind of thing police officers are supposed to do."

"You'd be surprised."

They were quiet again and then Dr. Ewing stood. "Be patient, Caroline," she said. "You know, sometimes it takes two sessions to repair a good brain."

13

Figure 450,000 people in the greater Spokane area—counting from the city of Coeur d'Alene in the Idaho panhandle to the college towns of Cheney to the west and Pullman to the south and the town of Deer Park to the north. If roughly half those people are female, that leaves you with 225,000 males, half of whom would be between sixteen and fifty-five—the potential age range for a serial killer.

Dupree spun the notebook to face Pollard and Spivey. "That leaves 112,500 potentially viable suspects," he said. Pollard looked over Dupree's figures as if they were the work of a lunatic, but Spivey copied down the numbers in his own notebook. Dupree turned it a little more to accommodate him.

"Let me get this straight," Pollard said. "You want to interview a hundred thousand guys?"

"No. I'm just sayin' that in a city this size, it would be feasible."

"Feasible."

"Maybe feasible is the wrong word. But the way we've been doing it isn't much better. Three weeks and we're still chasing phone tips and going over field interview cards. Screw that. Let's make a file on everyone. A hundred thousand suspects."

Pollard looked as if Dupree were speaking French.

"Look," Dupree said, "a serial killer can't operate in a city too much smaller than Spokane. When's the last time you heard of a serial killer in a small town? After the first murder, ol' Andy'd trudge down to the barbershop, grab that weird Floyd the barber, and haul him off to a cell with Otis, and Aunt Bea would bring him sandwiches. In a big city, your suspect pool might be a million. A hundred thousand guys sounds like a lot, but if we get ten detectives doing ten a day? Shoot, in a hundred days we'd solve every crime in the city."

Pollard kept searching for the joke; Spivey seemed to be actually thinking about it. When Dupree failed to land a punch line, Pollard threw his coffee back, squeezed the Styrofoam cup, and stood to leave.

"I'm worried about you, buddy," he said to Dupree. "I gotta go interview the pawnshop guy. Looks like you ain't gonna win that pot after all."

Since Dupree had been assigned to head the serial killer task force, Pollard had been given his caseload, including the two Lenny Ryan murders.

Pollard left the cafeteria and Dupree looked over to Spivey, who was staring intently at the numbers he'd copied onto his notebook. "What about transient populations—a truck driver, or someone else from out of town?"

Dupree considered the kid. He had short, dark hair, a little curly patch in the front hanging over his forehead, and big, semicircle eyebrows that heightened his constant look of confusion. Dupree had complained about him to the lieutenant, who defended the kid by saying he had tested out of the park, the highest aptitude of any detective candidate, and had gotten A's in college. The lieutenant said he was earnest and eager; if Dupree was more patient, he might even learn something from Spivey.

"We're not gonna interview a hundred thousand guys," Dupree said. "I was sort of . . . illustrating how tough it's gonna be to find this guy."

Spivey allowed his mouth to curl in a grin. "Oh, a joke." He winked, as if he'd just help pull one over on poor Pollard.

Dupree stood, peeled off a dollar bill, and draped it over the uneaten half of his Danish. Spivey followed him out of the courthouse and across the small courtyard to the Public Safety Building. Inside, Dupree punched in the short code, the door buzzed, and they were in a hallway connecting the offices of the various detective units.

Behind Major Crimes was another coded door. Dupree entered the number and the door opened into a small conference room that had been turned into a command center for the serial killer investigation. Three sets of desks faced one another, covered with desk calendars, phones, Rolodexes, and in and out boxes. The phones led into a central CID panel, identifying the name and address of anyone who called in tips. There were three computers in the room, and a secretary sat in front taking phone messages: Tips came in at all hours, ever since the city announced a five-thousand-dollar reward for information leading to the capture of the "Southbank Strangler."

The name had been Fleisher's and so he won the twenty-five dollars. Fleisher's entry had everything a good serial killer name required: precision, alliteration, and, as the real estate agents say, location, location, location. Other entries had included the Riverbank Killer, the Peaceful Valley Strangler, and Spokane's Slut Snuffer, which everyone agreed was in poor taste. Dupree had tossed in his five bucks and suggested they name the killer "Brandon"—he'd read that it was the most popular American boy's name now—but more and more his genius seemed to be going unappreciated. So the newspaper and television editors happily sent their graphic artists into fits of creativity coming up with Southbank Strangler logos and maps, shadowed backdrops for headlines. All we need now, Dupree thought, is a theme song.

Pictures of the three victims were tacked on the wall of the task force office, above a map of the riverbank. The first picture was of Rebecca Bennett, killed almost two months earlier, at the beginning of April. That trail was the coldest, with few people even remembering the woman. The second picture showed the most recent victim, a twenty-nine-year-old prostitute named Sharla McMichael, who'd been dumped in the same clearing where Rebecca Bennett was found. But no one could remember seeing Sharla for days before she was killed, and even though it was more recent, that trail was as cold as the first. The third picture was of a thirty-one-year-old prostitute from Portland named Jennifer Skaggs, who had last been seen five weeks earlier.

Dupree didn't think the killer could have found people who would be missed less. He marveled at the lack of discernible effect from the killings: No witnesses. No parents calling police. No friends or family or even pimps to worry about these women. It wasn't much better at the crime scene: No footprints or tire tracks; nothing of the killer left behind except forty bucks in the victims' hands. No fingerprints on the money or the girls, all of whom had fingernails torn off and whose hands had been washed with bleach by the killer, just to make sure. And although the attacks seemed sexual, there was no semen, a detail strange in itself. They weren't even sure how the killer had gotten the bodies there. They were chasing a ghost.

Dupree, Laird, and Spivey were the city detectives assigned to the case. They were joined by a sneaky sheriff's detective, a state patrol trooper, and, as a consultant, the muscular FBI profiler Jeff McDaniel, who'd stayed for two days and then promised to check in from Quantico—although from Dupree's vantage point his main talents seemed to be having lunch with the brass and hitting on secretaries. McDaniel promised to return and do a "full-blown profile" on the Southbank Strangler. Dupree promised to hold his breath.

In the days following the discovery of the second and third bodies prostitution nearly stopped along East Sprague, the strip where generations of hookers had worked. Hundreds of tips flooded the police department; the best ones were funneled to the task force office, where every day Dupree and the other detectives came in, grabbed a handful of telephone message slips, made phone calls, and went out to interview the nonexistent friends and relatives of the victims. Most of the tips were patently ridiculous.

"My boyfriend's weird," the tip sheet might say, or "My neighbor watches porn." But each of them had to be checked out, because nothing was more embarrassing to a police department than the interview four months after the arrest in which a neighbor tells a TV reporter that she called the police about the cannibal with the strange movie rentals. But in the weeks since the killings the world had started to get back to normal; now the hookers were starting to venture out on East Sprague again and the tips were dwindling in number. Dupree found himself reaching for the losers, the tip sheets that contained little chance of adding anything substantive to what he knew.

A stack of twenty or thirty tip sheets filled Dupree's in box. He grabbed two: a man on probation who had given a cabdriver "the creeps" and a guy's brother who had been robbed by hookers and still held a grudge. He decided to try the second tip first, tapped out the number, and introduced himself.

"It says here your brother was robbed by a prostitute?"

The guy on the other end cleared his throat. "Yeah. Or a dancer, I'm not sure."

"How long ago was that?"

"Boy, couple years."

"He ever display any violence toward women?"

"He beat up his girlfriend. That's why he's in jail."

"He's in jail now?"

"Uh-huh."

"You say he's in jail now?"

"Yeah."

"How long's he been in?"

"Couple months."

Dupree slumped. "You know the most recent murder was three weeks ago?"

"Yeah, I thought maybe you could see if he got a furlough or something."

"A furlough."

"Yeah. So, do I have to testify to collect the reward?"

After he hung up, Dupree ran the name of the brother and found out he'd actually been in jail for three years. He printed out the guy's rap sheet, stapled the pink message sheet to it, and dropped it into the out file.

Next, he tried the cabdriver, but got no answer. He reached for another message from the thick stack in the in box, but his hand just rested on the pile. This process felt more random to him than if they *had* just decided to interview every male in the region. This was the coldest trail he'd ever seen. Most murders, the cops knew who had done it within twenty-four hours of finding the body. There was still the problem of proving it, but the suspect was obvious. Woman gets shot, talk to the husband. Tavern owner gets shot, talk to his partner. Gangbanger gets shot, find out who he pissed off. If he did the math, Dupree figured he could graph the results of murder investigations based on the amount of time it took to generate a suspect. Find a suspect within the first twenty-four hours, you had a ninety percent chance of getting a conviction. Seventy-two hours? Probably sixty percent. Then the curve fell quickly. And now, three weeks since the last body? Dupree put their chances at about one in twenty of ever getting a suspect strong enough to stand trial. Especially with prostitutes as the victims. All he had to do was read the teletypes and intelligence reports from other cities to realize how long their odds were of ever solving this. Portland had eight active prostitute murder cases; Vancouver, B.C., had more than thirty. Almost every city seemed to have active prostitute murders. And for some reason, it was worse in the Northwest. Even Spokane had other strings of prostitute murders; they'd seen nearly a dozen over the last decade unrelated to this case, most recently a woman named Shelly Nordling, who had her throat slashed and was then tossed from a car. Then, of course, there was the king of them all: the Green River Killer, outside Seattle. Forty-nine women, almost all with a history of prostitution. That case was never solved.

Dupree's task force was trying other things, of course, looking at paroled sex offenders and men charged with assaulting prostitutes, conducting routine stings of johns and prostitutes, even posting surveillance cameras at a few pickup spots. A handful of women detectives, including Caroline, were out interviewing hookers on the street, compiling lists of rough tricks—johns who scared them. And Special Investigations was setting up a john sting tonight, posting a female officer—probably Caroline—on a corner, then questioning every guy who stopped to talk to her. But such steps were long shots. Hell, maybe one in twenty was too high. One in fifty was more like it, or one in a million. Of course, Dupree knew what would improve the odds. Another body. A new crime scene to sift through. In the meantime, he would just sit here making phone calls so unlikely they might as well be random, and wait for it to happen again.

Dupree took the next tip sheet from the basket. It was from a woman named Amend who lived in the West Central neighborhood, near the river. Her neighbor often left his house at 7 P.M.

and returned at 2 A.M. Twice, he had returned to his house with women she described as "slutty."

"Lucky guy," Dupree said.

Dupree turned the tip sheet over. That was it? He was about to toss it in the out file when the man's name caught his attention. Verloc. The name was familiar. Dupree dialed the woman's number but received no answer. Verloc. He tapped the sheet against his glasses. Next he opened the telephone book and found the listing for "Verloc, Kevin." That name rattled around in his head and he found himself getting excited. He entered the guy's name into the NCIC computer, but came up with no criminal record. Still, the name seemed significant. He knew he should wait until he'd talked to the woman, but after three weeks of dead ends his curiosity was too great. He looked at the deep box of worthless tips and knew he couldn't stomach sitting here all day, inching along. Sometimes, you just had to drop a bomb. He tapped out the number.

A man answered after one ring. "This is Kevin."

"Mr. Verloc? This is Alan Dupree, with the police department. I'm with the task force investigating the murders of three women who worked as prostitutes and we received a call suggesting we talk to you."

"Sure. What can I do for you?"

Sure? Dupree was dumbfounded. He expected denial, defensiveness, even confusion. But friendliness, enthusiasm? He was caught off guard and launched into full bluff mode. "Yeah, we're just looking for anyone who might have some information and, like I said, your name came up."

"Sure. Well, I do have a crew that works down on East Sprague, at Landers' Cove, the boat dealership down there. They see their share of hookers during their shifts—always have to run 'em out of the boats, you know? I can hook you up with 'em or I have their log reports, if that's what you're looking for."

"Log reports. Mmm-hmm."

Kevin Verloc continued. "You know, as far as myself, I work in the dispatch room—kind of half graveyard, half swing shift—so I don't really see anyone."

"The dispatch room?" Dupree began to feel uneasy.

"For my security business. That is why you're calling, right?"

That's when it hit him.

Kevin Verloc was a state patrol trooper who'd been shot in the back, what, eight or nine years earlier during a routine traffic stop. A real inspirational story. He'd gone on to start this security business, providing security guards to patrol neighborhoods where rich and elderly people lived, and also for concerts, schools, and businesses. Dupree felt sick. Kevin Verloc had been a good cop and he'd hired a lot of former badges to be security guards. But that wasn't why he couldn't be the killer.

"Hello?"

"Yeah. Sorry. I just got a note from the receptionist here."

Verloc sounded confused. "So what's this about?"

"I'm terribly sorry . . ." Dupree rubbed his head.

On the other end Kevin Verloc burst into laughter. "Jesus. I'll bet Mrs. Amend called you. She thinks I'm a serial killer? That's hilarious. The woman is insane. I can't even get the newspaper without her running away from me. That is so funny."

"Look, I'm sorry. When I saw your name, it looked familiar, but I didn't put it together." Dupree slowly placed the phone tip into the out box. "I just . . . I'm sorry."

"No, you got me. I should've known I would get caught." Kevin Verloc laughed. "I confess. I run over these women with my wheelchair."

Since being shot, Kevin Verloc was a paraplegic.

Dupree's head fell against his desk as Verloc laughed on the other end.

"My accomplice is an old blind guy. But he just drives. I do the heavy lifting."

Dupree took the ribbing—almost unbearable coming from another cop who'd know how sloppy he had been on this tip. When Verloc finally finished laughing Dupree retreated as gracefully as possible.

He stared at the stack of remaining tips. Was this how things were going to be? Messages about creepy taxicab drivers and guys in prison and ex-cops in wheelchairs? He swung with the back of his hand and the box fell over, spilling pink message slips across the floor. And the beauty part was, none of the other detectives even looked up.

14

She couldn't be twenty, even though that's what she claimed. Thin and pale, with short greasy hair, dull eyes, and a ring in her eyebrow, the girl lost her breath wolfing the soup that Caroline had bought her, and when her sourdough roll was gone she reached over and grabbed Caroline's whole wheat.

"I told you about the guy who likes to bite?"

"Yeah."

"And the guy who burned me with the lighter?"

"You thought his name might be Dave or Mike."

"Sup'm regular like that, yeah." Finished with the soup, the young prostitute tore into a package of crackers. "There's another guy likes to pull hair an' shit. Whole handfuls. You interested in that?"

Caroline said yes and pushed her own soup across the table to the girl. After several deep breaths and some pondering outside, she'd finally come up with the name Jacqueline as if she were trying on a hat. Caroline didn't want to alienate the girl so she let it slide.

"You don't want your soup?" Jacqueline asked.

"I'm not very hungry."

Two spoonfuls disappeared into her mouth before she continued. "Yeah, I been with this guy, I don't know, we've had three, four dates. Always wants a lay and a blow job and then yanks the shit out of your hair while you're doin' it. I'm like, hey, I'm tryin' to work here. I oughta charge him extra for the hair."

"You know his name?"

"It's something regular."

Caroline paused over her notebook. "Mike or Dave?"

"Somethin' like that."

"He have a last name?"

"I'm sure he does." Jacqueline sopped up Caroline's soup with Caroline's roll.

"What's he drive?"

"A truck."

So far, every bad date seemed to be a white guy in a truck named Dave or Mike. "American truck?" Caroline asked.

"Guess so."

"What year?"

She shrugged.

"New? Old?"

"I don't really know."

"What color?"

"It was dark. I didn't really see."

"Can you give me a description? Is he tall?"

"Average, I guess."

"How old would you say he is?"

"Oh, he's old. Thirty or forty or something."

"Thirty or forty? Is he bald? Does he wear glasses? Does he wear a suit? Long hair? One leg? Parrot on his shoulder?"

"No. Nothing like that. He's just . . . you know, regular."

"Mmm-hmm. How about guys who don't wanna pay. You ever have dates try to rape you, force themselves onto you?"

Jacqueline laughed, then stared down at her soup and became serious. "How many pages you got in that notebook?"

Thirty minutes later, when they were finished, Caroline paid the bill and bought a sandwich for Jacqueline to take with her. She tried to get her real name, but Jacqueline insisted that was her name and said she didn't have any ID. Caroline pressed a business card into the girl's hand and told her to be careful, to work with other women and to call if she thought of anything else or was approached by a guy who gave her a bad feeling.

"What do you mean?"

"You know," Caroline said. "If a guy gives you the creeps, makes you feel unsafe or scared in some way."

Jacqueline looked down at Caroline's business card and gave a small laugh. "Ma'am, they all give me the creeps."

In the car, Caroline leafed through notes from the six interviews she'd done with hookers that day. Words leaped from the pages: "bit" and "punched" and "knifed" and "choked" and "bruised," stories of gang rape at knifepoint, of violations with beer bottles and guns, of molestations by uncles and teachers and probation officers. Words stuck in her throat, names and details ran together, descriptions, regular guys all—Mikes and Daves—and Caroline wondered if they weren't going at it the wrong way, looking for the guys with the scary perversions. It might be easier to eliminate the white men in pickup trucks who didn't scare these hookers. *Ma'am, they all give me the creeps.*

Caroline could always recognize a street hooker. The police unit that she was in had grown out of the old Vice Squad, which had been in charge of prostitution, gambling, and drugs—a funny collection of crimes once known as vices. After the proliferation of drugs in the seventies Vice became Special Investigations and began focusing on drug dealing, although they still coordinated an occasional prostitution sting, dragging a woman from patrol to dress up and stand on a street corner looking skanky. Caroline did it herself when they couldn't convince a patrol officer or some girl from the academy to demean herself for an evening. The other cops joked that she was too healthy and good-looking to be a hooker. Hookers in movies looked like Julia Roberts and Jamie Lee Curtis, but most of the ones who worked the street were ugly or fat or sickly or strung out. And even the decent-looking ones who worked mostly hotels and escort services, even those women were usually in need of a shower.

It was her least favorite duty, but when the task force investigating the serial murders had asked the Special Investigations Unit for help, Caroline knew she would volunteer, just like she'd volunteered to interview hookers, which was hard enough since these women did their best every day to avoid cops. The interviews would be followed tonight by a fishing trip—a john sting with Caroline getting all dolled up and walking the strip in front of adult bookstores and topless bars. Whore duty.

All day she'd been dreading the cheap clothes, the lie of it, the wire beneath her shirt, standing under a street lamp, trying to keep the lipstick off her teeth, sticking her ass out so far that the next morning her back always hurt. Maybe that's what she should've asked Jacqueline—how you stand like that without hurting your back.

It was odd now, to be investigating something they usually ignored. Most of the time prostitution was just a given, not even worth mentioning. Many drug dealers had a hand in the business; Burn, for example, pimped a couple of crackheads out of his apartment. But it was nothing more than a fact of their lives, a detail on a rap sheet, like their age or hometown or place of employment. She doubted if most cops even thought of prostitution as a crime anymore, but more as a symptom.

Caroline glanced over the list of bad dates the women had given her. She wasn't surprised that the men who paid cash for straight sex seemed all right to these women. After all, they had some control in that transaction, the lies of power, position, and commerce, the hooker as sales representative, billing agent, and service department rolled into one. And, of course, product.

That's why she wasn't surprised that they had so few names to go on. This was a business set up to give the client anonymity, in which all customers were known by the brand name of saints and Baptists, Waynes and Kennedys, the most Christian, most American of names. Johns. Or "dates," which the women simply called the men, or, if you preferred magic, "tricks." Anyway, through anonymity or deceptive casualness or magical disappearance, the men remained hard to find, and the women . . . well, to Caroline, they were all dead or dying.

She flipped the notebook to the first page of her interview with Jacqueline. After the girl made up her name, Caroline had begun the interview by asking for a date of birth and the girl had just shrugged. Jacqueline said she was from a small town near Spokane ("rather not give the name"), had a baby ("eight months old, foster care"), was a regular drug user ("heroin, meth, pot"), had never been arrested ("says she's too smart"), and might be HIV-positive ("refuses to be tested").

Caroline tossed the notebook on the seat next to her and started the car. She would go back and type up the results of her interviews for the task force and then change into her hooker outfit. Joel had seen her setting the clothes out that morning—the short vinyl skirt and tiny T-shirt—and hadn't said anything. That was the kind of thing that kept her from being able to trust him completely. It wasn't anything he did or said, but what he didn't do, what he didn't say. She sets out trampy clothing and he just goes off to lift weights without raising an eyebrow?

Caroline also hadn't told Joel about tomorrow, that her father was coming to begin going through her mother's belongings. She supposed she didn't talk about it because she didn't want to think about it. It seemed too soon, just three weeks after her mother's death. She'd tried to get her brother to come too, but Peter said he couldn't handle it. Caroline would like to have spoken to Dr. Ewing about the next twenty-four hours, about dressing as a hooker, what to do with the embarrassment and guilt she felt sticking her ass out to trap these guys. And she wished she could talk to Dr. Ewing about her father and Peter. She supposed her father couldn't have been expected to be there to see his ex-wife die, but she was disappointed in Peter, who had come for the funeral but hadn't been back. When she asked him, he dodged the question, saying that his kids had soccer games. But then he cleared his throat and said, "I can't face it, Caroline. I'm just not like you."

And what was she like? Someone who stared into rivers, who held the hands of dying mothers and drug dealers, who bought sandwiches for dying hookers during the day and dressed up like one at night, who could pose as a hooker but couldn't handle posing as a mother in a park, who loses her own mother but obsesses over a drowned drug dealer? She shifted the car and turned back toward downtown, past the tavern where Jacqueline hung out. The young prostitute was leaning against a light pole, already eating the sandwich Caroline had bought for her. From the car Caroline could see a guy in the doorway of a tavern behind Jacqueline, watching her. The guy wore sunglasses and a ball cap. As Caroline passed the tavern the man stepped forward, probably to begin the long, slow dance of negotiation with Jacqueline. That was another movie misconception—the deal itself. The movie john drives up, rolls his car window down, and asks, "How much?" In fact, the deal was more often a sad, empty flirtation, the man maybe trying to convince himself that she really likes him, the woman convincing herself she isn't what she is, the money sometimes an afterthought, other deals made in dope or booze or a ride somewhere or the offer of a roof to sleep under. This barter was another form of denial, the lie that the intimacy of this transaction was no different than the transactions of straight lives, the trading of years for a ring, sex for stability, the factoring into the deal of babies and houses and comfort and meals and entire lives. Caroline felt a kind of mocking dare from these women during these interviews, an accusation from them that a deal was inherent in any relationship, whether the woman charged forty bucks for a blow job or got forty years for a lifetime of them. What is a marriage but a contract, the recording of a deal? Is eliminating loneliness a better motivation than greed?

As she drove, Caroline wondered if Jacqueline saw the world that way, or if she had her own fairy-tale fantasies. Maybe that dark view of male-female relationships was something Caroline was beginning to believe herself. That got her to thinking about the man in the sweats, putting the picture she'd just seen back together in her mind: Jacqueline leaning against that light pole, the man coming from behind her . . .

The man.

Something familiar . . . He'd been shaded by the ball cap and sunglasses and was partially shielded by cars along the curb and the light pole, but something about the way he stood or the tilt of his head reminded her of someone else, and when she realized who, the shock pulled her to the side of the road.

It had to be her mind playing tricks. No way the man she'd seen talking to young Jacqueline was Lenny Ryan. It was an understandable mistake. He hadn't been far from her thoughts since he pushed Burn over the bridge railing. Of course she would imagine the quick glimpse of a man to be him, transposing the flatness and evil of what he'd done onto this guy killing prostitutes, and then transposing some innocent guy talking to Jacqueline into a serial killer.

But the idea was rooted now, and so she turned the car around and sped down Sprague, past weedy car lots and motels with hourly rates, taverns with blackened windows, adult bookstores. She parked in front of the Eight Ball Tavern, Jacqueline's hangout, but saw no sign of the young hooker or the man in the cap. She went into the bar and asked if anyone had seen her talking to the man in sweats, if Jacqueline had gotten into any cars, but the bartender and the four men drinking flat drafts at 4 P.M. shrugged and said they didn't know Jacqueline and hadn't seen her.

"The guy was just standing in the doorway ten seconds ago."

The bartender shrugged.

"Out front," Caroline said, losing patience. "You didn't see a girl out front?"

They didn't say no, didn't shake their heads, just stared at her.

In front of the bar, she put her hand on the light pole and tried to piece the image together again. It seemed less and less likely. The conventional wisdom held that Lenny Ryan was long gone—back to California, most likely. His uncle's car had been found at a truck stop, leading detectives to believe he'd hitched a ride out of state with a trucker.

She hadn't even seen the guy's face. The more she thought about it, the less likely it became that the man she'd seen was Lenny Ryan, and the more embarrassed Caroline became over her recent obsessions. What would Dupree say? That she was taking it all too personally. And Dr. Ewing, what would she say at their next session? That she was suffering anxiety over her mother, over what happened at the falls, that she was still horrified by the choice that Lenny Ryan had given her, that she was still replaying what she'd done, that she couldn't live with her inability to save the young drug dealer. Or even her mother. She didn't know why exactly, but it galled Caroline that Burn's body had never been found. Of course, for that matter, neither had Lenny Ryan.

They were both out there, waiting for her next move, drifting in the undertow, their movements guided by cold, black currents.

15

On his way to the hospital Dupree tapped his cell phone against the steering wheel, the phone number covering the screen. He'd been about to place the call—"Sorry, I'm gonna be late"—when he'd been drawn by something out his right window. It was one of those incongruities he sometimes got while driving, an image he had to convince himself he'd actually seen, that he wasn't filling in details that weren't there.

It was on the corner of a busy four-lane in a residential neighborhood, a few blocks from the Public Safety Building. A guy with a Mohawk haircut stood in a yard leaning against a car, in front of a sign. On the sign were written the words "Beanie Babies for Sale." The car was an AMC Javelin from the early 1970s.

And that was it, but it had the effect of freezing Alan Dupree, so that two blocks later, when the light changed, he just sat there, staring out the passenger window, where the image had been. He composed the image again, disparate details from different times: a 1980s haircut leaning on a 1970s car in front of a sign offering 1990s toys for sale. Was that even it? Was that what unsettled him, or was it some other memory, some dream, some other reference to that car or that haircut or Beanie Babies?

He looked down at the phone in his hand, at the number, and didn't recognize it at first. His thumb rested on the send button and he must have pushed it without realizing, because he was caught off guard when the phone rang on the other end and she picked up quickly, saying "Hello" as if she had been waiting for the call, which of course she had.

He put the phone to his head, said, "Hey," and snapped out of his trance. As he pulled out into the intersection, he was amazed to see the light change to yellow above him. How long had he sat there?

"Alan?"

He tried to remember what he was going to tell his wife. Everything felt so out of place, so *disturbed*. So unreal.

"Did you forget where we live?"

"I'm sorry." He shook his head, clearing this fog. "I'm driving. I got distracted."

"How late are you gonna be?" He could hear the TV in the background and tried to picture them, Debbie on the kitchen phone, the kids sprawled on the floor of the living room, engrossed in whatever was on Nickelodeon.

"Could be a while. At least an hour or two."

"What's going on?"

"I gotta go talk to a pawnshop owner who got shot last month."

"I thought maybe it was the other thing." Debbie had taken a deep interest in the serial killer investigation, more interest than she'd shown in his job in years.

"I'm just chasing my tail on that." In fact he'd spent the morning going through a good-sized stack of worthless tips and the afternoon comparing the three Southbank murders with other unsolved murders in the area, including a couple of murdered hookers, trying to connect a few dots but coming up with nothing.

"Alan?"

He gripped the phone. "Yeah. Sorry. I was waiting for you to say something."

"Yeah," she said. "Me too."

When they had said good-bye and, as an afterthought, "I love you," Dupree pressed the phone against his head, then held it out in front of himself. He tried to remember the last pleasant call he'd made on this thing, this transmitter of anxiety. Of bad news. He turned into the hospital parking lot and parked in one of the spots in the emergency lot reserved for police officers. On the way up he stopped at a nurses' station and bummed a cup of coffee, hoping to wake himself up. He rode the elevator with a nurse and a tiny boy with a shaved head, avoiding their eyes.

Pollard was pacing the hallway in the intensive care unit, his sports coat with the felt elbow patches draped over the back of a chair. "What took you so long?"

"Sorry, honey. I should've called." He handed Pollard the five six-packs he'd requested—thirty mug shots in all, the same photo lineup they'd shown Caroline three weeks earlier.

Pollard jerked his head toward the hospital room and Dupree followed him inside. The light was dim, and something struck Dupree as odd about this hospital room. Then he realized: He'd never seen a hospital room that didn't have flowers or cards in it. The pawnshop owner, Denny Melling, lay on his back, his head propped on a pillow, IV lines snaking over the headboard of his inclined hospital bed. Bandages and a plastic mask covered his face from upper lip to hairline, as if he'd just come from a costume ball.

He breathed in shallow fits and spurts, sputtering a tiny whimper with each exhale. Pollard bent close to his ear and spoke quietly.

"Mr. Melling. It's Detective Pollard again."

"You said I could have . . . more morphine."

"Sure. Sure. As soon as we've asked you a couple of questions. Okay?"

He hummed an answer and Pollard opened his briefcase and removed the first six-pack photo lineup. "Mr. Melling, Detective Dupree here brought some pictures. The guy you mentioned before might be in here. Now I gotta read this, so listen." He turned over the first six-pack and breezed through the boilerplate on the back. "Okay, 'The suspect may or may not be portrayed here. Keep in mind hairstyles, beards, and mustaches can change a person's appearance.' Okay, I'm going to uncover your eyes. The light is going to be kind of severe at first. Are you ready?"

The mask had a flap made of surgical tape that covered Melling's eyes. Pollard pulled it back and Dupree lost his breath. The right eye was fine, although bloodshot, but beyond it was a mess of bone and skin, unrecognizable as a face. The left eye socket was caved in beneath the bandage and his nose was essentially gone, replaced by bumpy red skin held together with the black thread of fresh sutures. Dupree had read the report—"the victim sustained a gunshot wound to the face . . ."—but that description seemed so incomplete now as to be inaccurate. The victim no longer had a face.

Melling's one eye drifted across the faces on the first photo lineup card. "Anything?" Pollard asked.

"No," Melling said. Pollard flipped to the second page and Melling ran his eye across quickly. "Number four," he said and his eyelid drifted shut. "That's him . . . now can you . . . get me some morphine? I need to go to sleep."

Pollard patted his shoulder and let the flap fall back over his eye. He handed the photo lineup to Dupree, who looked at the fourth picture, even though he knew who it was. For weeks he'd been imagining a critical mass of evil, but he never really imagined it could really be one person. But here it was. Their crime spree. Lenny Ryan.

"Can you tell Detective Dupree here what you told me earlier," Pollard said, "what this guy Lenny wanted from you?"

"I told you," Melling blurted, as if he were about to cry.

"I know. Just once more and then I'll have them up your painkiller."

"He came in the day before . . . he shot me and . . . he wanted to know about . . ." Melling took more shallow breaths. ". . . kid who sells dope in the park."

Melling concentrated, trying to come up with the name.

Dupree edged toward the bed. "Burn," he said.

"Burn. Yeah." He took a deep breath.

"Why did he want to find Burn?" Pollard asked.

"I don't know. He wanted to buy some dope. And the kid runs hookers."

Pollard shot a glance at Dupree. "Did this guy ask about hookers?"

"Well, at first, he was all friendly and he wanted to know where they hung out."

"And did he mention any particular hookers?"

"Yeah. That's why he was in my shop. I get a lot of 'em come in. And I guess some hooker he knew pawned a bracelet in my shop a while back."

"Did he have a pawn ticket?"

"Yeah. He got mad that I wouldn't sell it back for the pawn price."

"Do you know how we can find the ticket number?"

"No. I don't keep very good files."

Dupree didn't doubt that. Pawnshop owners kept notoriously bad files to protect the thieves they relied on for merchandise.

"So what happened?"

"He just left. Then . . . he came back mad. He wanted the bracelet."

Dupree stepped in. "Did he tell you her name? The hooker?"

"No. He said she was dead."

Pollard looked up at Dupree again, triumphantly. "Then what happened?"

"When he came back the next day, he was different. He was . . . he had me get on my knees." Melling began to cry, his chest heaving in and out.

Pollard patted his shoulder again and pressed the buzzer to bring the nurse. "Okay, Mr. Melling. You get some rest now and we'll talk later."

In the hallway Dupree stared at the picture of Lenny Ryan and rubbed his jaw, trying to piece this thing together. A few dots connected but didn't exactly finish the picture, just added more questions, making the thing *more* incomplete, like Melling's face. You had to be careful not to imagine too much, to assume that a second eye would follow the first, that these images had to connect, that the Javelin belonged to the guy with the Mohawk who sold Beanie Babies. You had to adjust your vision for the addition of new details, the ignorance of others.

He'd been trying to explain that to Spivey, but now he could see that such subtleties also were lost on Pollard, who stared at him like a dog who's dragged a dead bird back to his master's porch.

Dupree handed back the photo lineup. "Let's think about this."

"Look at the timeline," Pollard said. "Ryan got out of prison two and a half months ago. The first hooker was killed two months ago."

It was tough sometimes, keeping the pieces from falling together too soon, imagining the connections before you even know what it is you're connecting. But Dupree was excited. He began moving down the hallway, Pollard following. He should call Spivey, but the thought of explaining this to the young detective made him ill. So he looked to Pollard. "You got some time to help me out on this, Dan?" Dupree knew he didn't really need to ask. Pollard was on his second divorce. All he had was time. And the task force was a plum assignment.

Pollard nodded. "What do you want me to do?"

They walked out of the hospital together, Dupree thinking about Debbie and about Pollard's divorce two years earlier. The cops of his generation were almost all divorced, their marriages dissolving over time, in streaks: none for a while and then a whole bunch, as if a storm had passed through. The separation was a lightning strike, catching your attention, surprising you. The divorce was thunder, taking away your breath as you calculated how close it had come to *you*. Pollard's divorce had been like that. Close. Dan's wife had been named Natalie, and at one time they were the weekend companions of the young Duprees. Alan remembered one night throwing back drinks at a family-style Italian restaurant and talking about . . . what?

He couldn't remember. He remembered Dan and him laughing, their arms around their wives' chairs, the glasses of wine shuddering with the moment. They were other people then, the tuft of hair on the front of his own head, Pollard not so thick around the middle. But mostly the difference was in the way they were so unafraid. Or unaware. Like Spivey. Dupree could see that night so clearly, the pasta and the wine and the laughter. But for the life of him, he couldn't remember what had been so funny.

16

The headlights would be the first thing, and every time they fell on her Caroline was surprised that they generated no heat, just cold light. Sometimes the driver would hit his brakes or back up. But usually the car would cruise by once, the driver thinking himself smart by driving around the block and checking for police cars. But the car always came back, the driver leaning over the passenger seat and smiling, not so different from the smiles of men in taverns and grocery stores and the hallway of detective offices, a sizing-up, an inventory of her respective parts. Out here, cars coursed like blood cells, drivers cruising for sex or drugs or a combination. There was no incidental traffic on East Sprague. No one just passed through.

Caroline paused in front of a bus bench that advertised a buffet-style restaurant. She wore little makeup, had no fur coat or thigh-high leather boots, none of the trappings of the TV hooker. Instead she wore clothes from a secondhand store, the short, tight vinyl skirt and a small button shirt that left her midriff exposed. It was no more revealing than what other young women would be wearing in the clubs that night, just cheaper and tighter. The rest was body language. Attitude. And movement. The walk. Unattached street hookers didn't lean against light poles, they moved in a flowing display of parts pointy and curvy, the contrast between convex and concave, ankle to knee to thigh to hip to waist to breast to neck. Everything a man wanted was contained in those contrasts and so she told herself what girls like Jacqueline presumably told themselves every day, that it wasn't so much about her but her parts; if a john could separate *her* from *her parts*, then so could she. She sauntered along the section of Sprague Avenue that functioned as a market for street hookers, an odd collection of car lots for people with bad credit, Chinese restaurants, pawnshops, dive taverns, hourly-rate motels, bottom-feeder businesses like karate shops and Swedish massage parlors, and a few legitimate daytime businesses. Most prominent of these was Landers' Cove, a high-end boat and yacht dealership hiding stubbornly behind a high chain-link fence and taking up the entire block on which Caroline now resumed her walking.

Over her shoulder she heard a motor decelerate, and a man in racing leathers pulled up on a newer crotch-rocket motorcycle, his weight thrust forward like someone traveling terribly fast, even though he was pulling to a stop in front of her. She pegged him right away as a guy from Fairchild Air Force Base. They were all over the place and most of them were harmless, but there were always a handful of aggressive little assholes that attracted the attention of police. Nothing serious: statutory rape, simple assault—teenage girls and bar fights. They hired hookers and bought speed, raced around in their little roadsters and plastic motorcycles, which were the only thing of value they would acquire during their years in the service. "What's goin' on?" this guy asked, the intensity of his stare very different from the nonchalance of the words.

"Hangin' out," she answered. "Waitin' for a date." She was careful to straddle the line of entrapment, to not be the one to make the offer.

"Yeah. You been anywhere fun tonight?"

"No. How about you?"

He shrugged. "I was goin' to the state line. Unless you give me a reason not to."

This guy was so obvious, his move like a beginner's serve in tennis. No subtlety or power. Just lob it out there. She smiled. "I suppose I could think of some reasons."

"I bet you can."

And then nothing. He just sat on his bike, his helmet on, staring at her. Caroline worried for a moment that she wasn't attractive enough, or that he wanted a different type. She felt another pair of headlights, saw the car slow down and then move on.

The air force guy stood his ground and she looked at him with growing irritation. "You want somethin'?" she asked finally. "'Cause you're blockin' the street."

This rattled him a little, as if he wasn't sure what to do next. She could see what he was attempting—what they all did, what they were all told to do to keep from being arrested. Get the hooker to initiate the deal. That way, if he was hitting on a cop, his lawyer could convince a judge that it was entrapment.

He looked her up and down. "I don't know. You look like a cop to me."

"Yeah? You look like a prick."

He seemed really hurt. "Hey, there's no reason to get upset."

"Get the fuck outta here. I don't got time for games."

He took his helmet off and she saw his military haircut and thin mustache. Air force, all right. She was proud that she'd nailed this guy.

"I didn't mean nothin' by it. I've just never seen you out here before."

"You ever go to the Derby? Up north?" It was a small tavern in her neighborhood, the kind of place this guy would never find himself.

"No."

"Well, I ain't welcome there anymore. So for the time being I'm here, and I'm tryin' to work, so why don't you move on?"

"Damn! Don't get all upset. I'm just makin' sure you ain't a cop." Now he was off the bike and Caroline could feel her own adrenaline rise. He was being drawn in, forgetting his caution. "You oughta relax. Maybe we could, you know, go somewhere."

She nodded at his motorcycle. "I ain't goin' nowhere on that thing."

He looked down the street. "We could get a room."

"You want a room? Mr. Romance?" This was actually good. The part she hated was climbing in cars, that moment before the other detectives came out from the staging area to cuff the guys, Mirandize them, and begin the process of impounding their cars. If they were using a young patrol officer or a student as the decoy the staging area would be much closer and there would be no climbing in cars, but with Caroline the cavalry could lay back a little farther. And so the car was the most dangerous, the most vulnerable part. And the worst part too, from a cop's point of view, because if the john tried to use the car for the sex act then it could be confiscated, which meant the nuisance of filling out property forms.

Caroline glanced kitty-corner across the street, to the low-slung motel where Gerraghty and Solaita were watching and listening to the wire she was wearing. "I suppose I could come up with a room."

"How much?"

Bingo. Felony. Caroline imagined Sergeant Lane, always so anxious as he listened to wires. He would be relaxing now, nodding even. Caroline stepped toward the air force guy. "Depends what you want."

"I don't know. Half-and-half?"

Blow job and a lay. This guy was more energetic than he looked. "I might have that in stock. Eighty-five and you pay for the room."

"Bullshit. Sixty and you pay for the room. I know those guys give you a deal."

It was true. Hookers usually got a break on hourly rates or could work a trade—a blow job for four hours' credit, something like that. The guy already had implicated himself, but Caroline knew she had to keep negotiating, even though she was losing interest. "I oughta get fifty for standin' out here talkin' to you. How about seventy-five?"

"Too much."

She acted as if she were disappointed. "Seventy-five and I pay for the room."

He smiled. "You ain't a cop, right?"

"Me? I'm chief of police."

He laughed and she checked for traffic and began crossing the street. He followed her, reaching out to run his hand across her ass. It was all she could do to not turn and strangle the little shit. This guy probably grabbed asses his whole life. She hated guys like that, bump into you in the hallway, press against you in crowds, get his kicks by rubbing against strangers, like some junior high kid.

He talked as he followed her, a nervous chatter that made him seem even younger. "My name's Albert," he said. "I'm from Salem. How about you? Where you from? You know, not that it matters, but it's surprising how many people, I say, 'Hey, I'm from Salem,' and they say, 'No shit?' You know, 'My uncle lives there,' or something."

She led him toward the lobby of the motel and through a door into the stairwell. There, sitting in a chair next to the landing, leaning against the ice machine, was Gerraghty. "Howdy, son."

Albert jumped and grabbed his chest. Caroline glared at Gerraghty. *Howdy?* The worst cops, Caroline thought, were the ones who pretended they were in their own little movie, tossing around catch phrases and snappy comebacks that sounded as if they'd been practiced in front of men's room mirrors.

"We're police officers," she said, turning away from Gerraghty and showing her own badge since he seemed in no hurry to show his. "You're under arrest for solicitation of a prostitute."

"No way!" He seemed to be shrinking, getting younger by the second. "I never said I'd pay for sex. I thought this was . . . you know . . ."

But Gerraghty was coming across the landing, his hand on the gun in his waistband. "Put your hands behind your head and turn around."

"Nuh-uh. This is not happening." He was incredulous. Caroline reached for his arms and he allowed her to close a handcuff gently around one of his wrists.

"You have the right to remain silent . . ." Gerraghty began.

In the dim light of the stairwell, Albert burst into tears. Caroline dropped his cuffed hand. "Please, don't!" he cried. "This is my second one. I'm gonna lose my bike and get a dishonorable." He babbled something about getting loans for college and then brought his hands up to his face, the handcuff clattering.

His crying seemed to amuse Gerraghty, who cracked a huge

grin and rolled his eyes. But Caroline felt bad, and when Solaita came out of the first floor observation room to finish Mirandizing the kid, Caroline eased back out the door.

She stood in front of the motel and let a breeze brush her face, the air cool with impatient spring. She could hear the air force guy still crying while Solaita patiently explained to the kid that an attorney could be provided for him. She took a deep breath and walked through the motel parking lot, back across the street, pausing to look at the kid's motorcycle. She supposed they'd come pick it up later, after the sting.

She began walking again, away from the motorcycle. "God, I hate this," she said under her breath, still knowing that all the officers would hear that on the other end of this wire—Gerraghty and Solaita across the street, the sergeant and the other detectives in the warehouse two blocks away. They'd look at each other and raise their eyebrows, just more proof that Mabry wasn't cut out for this, that she was slipping in some way, that she was too soft. She walked on.

The serious johns parked on the dark side streets perpendicular to Sprague, waiting like fishermen in their boats for women to swim past. Or they trolled Sprague or Pacific behind it, and when another set of headlights fell on the sidewalk, Caroline stepped out into the light, giving the driver a chance to window-shop. But the car didn't slow down and Caroline was surprised to find that she felt a low-grade rejection. She walked two blocks down Sprague, then back toward the boat dealership as several more cars passed. After ten quiet minutes, Caroline saw Sergeant Lane pull around the corner in his unmarked car. At the same time, Solaita and Gerraghty emerged from the motel across the street, a subdued Albert handcuffed between them. Sergeant Lane parked his car behind the Japanese motorcycle and climbed out.

"We're done," the sergeant said, handing over her athletic bag. "I sent the patrol units back with five suspects and your friend here"—he gestured at Albert, who sat slumped on the curb—"makes an even half dozen. I'd say that's a good night's work."

Caroline checked her watch. "But it's only ten." The second shift for hookers was only beginning, the time from 10 P.M. to 3 A.M., an hour after the bars closed.

"I told 'em we'd give 'em a couple hours. We gave 'em a couple hours. This isn't our case. Let Major Crimes do their own grunt work." He looked over at Solaita and Gerraghty, who had the slumping air force kid between them. "Who wants to ride this Japanese hunk of shit back?"

Gerraghty shrugged, feigning indifference. "I guess I could."

"You don't think we should give it another hour?" Caroline asked.

"This is just an item on their checklist, Caroline. They want to be able to say they tried everything. I appreciate your commitment, but are we gonna catch anybody who isn't an idiot doing this?" To illustrate, he turned to Albert. "The guy they're lookin' for ain't gonna come riding up to some hooker he's seein' for the first time."

"It's your call." Caroline felt relieved, even as she wondered if Lane didn't trust her out here, or was worried that she'd snap again. Or maybe he did think this was a waste of time. It didn't really matter to her, as long as it meant she was done for the night. Caroline turned her back, reached into her shirt, removed the taped wire from between her breasts, and dropped it in the bag. She pulled a sweatshirt from the bag and pulled it on over her shirt, then slid a pair of sweatpants up to her hips, unzipped the skirt, and dropped it to the pavement. When she looked up they were all watching, the other detectives and the air force kid. The sergeant cleared his throat.

Gerraghty climbed on the bike, turned the key, and it fired up. He gave the other detectives a half smile.

"Front end's a little loose," the air force kid said. He looked at Caroline apologetically and shrugged. "I hit a tree."

Caroline's car was parked a block off Sprague Avenue, behind the cyclone-fenced boat dealership. The sergeant walked her halfway there, praising her for the john sting and for the way she'd come back after her suspension with enthusiasm and professionalism. On Dr. Ewing's advice, Caroline was trying not to be cynical, not to hear condescension in the voices of the other detectives, to take the words literally, as if she were encountering them written on a page. But Caroline couldn't help hearing the subtext of what he was saying. If she were praised for coming back with enthusiasm and professionalism, then those things must have been missing before. If her work now was the exception, then her screw-ups and emotional explosion from last month were the rule. *Thank you for not being so female this time.*

"Well," Lane said, turning to walk back to his own car, "I just wanted to tell you I appreciate it."

"Thanks," she said, and they separated, began walking toward their own cars, but Caroline stopped. From the sidewalk she watched to see if he turned back, if he betrayed what he was really thinking, but he just walked, as she had before, beneath the streetlights on Sprague, until he got to his car. He got in, started the car, and drove away.

She was going crazy, looking for significance in every movement, every utterance, drawing lines between things that weren't connected. And worst of all, she'd begun to expect reasons and patterns beneath the behavior of people. That could be dangerous for a police officer, to start thinking the world was like a children's book, to start believing that good would be rewarded and evil punished.

Caroline tossed her bag inside the car, suddenly aware of the darkness all around her, the contrast between this shadowed side street and the garish lights from the rows of Chinese restaurants and dive bars on East Sprague.

Someone was watching her. She felt it before she heard it—across the alley, a soft footfall, a crunching, a shoe on broken blacktop, someone trying to step carefully. She turned, but the alley was shadowed and dark and Caroline couldn't see inside, even when she shielded her eyes against the lights on Sprague. She reached into the bag, fumbled for her handgun, and tucked it into her waistband. Then she stepped into the road and crossed halfway into the shadows, recalling that day in the park, the way she ran away from Lenny Ryan and toward the doomed Burn. In the center of the street her eyes began to adjust and she could see into the shadows, forty feet away, a man turn and walk with purpose back into the alley.

"Hey," she called, and he began walking faster, past garbage cans, the tongue of a loading dock. She began running and entered the mouth of the alley as he reached the other end, and even though she knew this was wrong, Caroline hurried along the narrow and rough pavement, fully aware that she should return to her car and use her phone to call for help, and aware, too, that the man she was following was not some subconscious reaction to stress, some anxious trick of her eyes. No, she was certain now. It was him. She was chasing Lenny Ryan.

17

By 10 P.M., the picture Dupree had in his mind was larger, if not yet any clearer. Pollard had run Ryan's photo past families and friends of the three victims and had found nothing. Dupree checked to see if any of the victims lived in Northern California but that was another dead end. They checked Burn's case files and Melling's pawnshop records against the names of the dead hookers. Nothing.

As for Ryan himself, the caliber of weapon in the three prostitute deaths didn't match the caliber from Melling's shooting. There were no credit cards or rent payments or anything that established his whereabouts after leaving prison two months ago. His probation report indicated he went to just one meeting and then disappeared. No trail of him in Spokane until he shoved Burn over the bridge. No fingerprints or semen samples on the dead women to compare to Ryan. In essence, there was nothing.

The job was like that. Information trickles in so slowly, you begin to obsess over isolated details at the exclusion of all the rest. Take for instance what had happened two weeks earlier, when the lab prelims came back and Dupree found that two of the victims had similar traces of chicken sandwiches in their stomachs and he started imagining the killer waiting outside a certain restaurant or buying them chicken sandwiches before he killed them. And that detail became primary, sending him spinning in pointless, time-consuming directions, until he found himself casing out restaurants and reading packages of frozen chicken breasts. In the end, the chicken turned out to be just an entree from the menu of a restaurant on East Sprague where hookers routinely met late at night. So from that flurry of singular information and action emerged a detail that was meaningless and capricious, amounting to nothing.

In truth, things didn't always connect, or if they did, the point connecting two separate facts might very well be the least important property of each fact.

Coincidence, in other words. Hardly a thing to contemplate for most people, whose experience with coincidence was usually pleasant. Dream about your old eighth grade teacher and the next day bump into her at the store. What a nice coincidence. But to someone investigating a crime? There are no "nice" coincidences. Coincidence is the devil. Some cops—Spivey was the type—pretend they are immune to coincidence, that every bit of information is equal and that investigating is the same as finding truth. But Dupree knew better.

When you get a break like today, with Melling, the pawnshop owner, pointing to that picture of Lenny Ryan and moaning about hookers, you chased it with a kind of superstitious caution. Because a guy like Lenny Ryan has paid for his share of sex and dope and these worlds will certainly intersect, but you don't know where; you only know separate facts: the fact of Lenny Ryan showing up in town and killing at least two people and trying to kill a third; the fact of Lenny Ryan asking questions about where to find hookers and talking about a dead hooker. Across the ledger was this man killing prostitutes. You look for intersection in the time frame. In the brutish confidence. In dates and blood samples and credit card receipts and twenty-dollar bills.

But these two independent sets of facts may never intersect. Or maybe they bump up against each other but it doesn't mean a thing. Or maybe there are other details connecting them, things you know, but which aren't on the surface anymore, points of true

intersection, shadowed, hidden away. An investigation is like trying to remember something without knowing its nature. It was
the application of analysis to intuition, trying to see a smell. And
that process changed a person, dulled his sense of the present, of
the living, of the fabric of a life, of a marriage, even.

They pay a person to piece together lives and pretty soon he
begins to piece his own, to see the dark motives, sitting up at the
bar, wondering, "What happened to me?"

"What is it?" Pollard asked.

Dupree blinked away the trance. "Hmm?"

"You were staring," Pollard said. "It was kinda creepy."

Dupree checked his watch. "It was . . . I was thinking . . ." He
stretched his arms, and his eyes narrowed as he took in Pollard.
"Remember that Italian place we used to go to a couple years
back? You and me and Debbie and Natalie."

Pollard considered for a moment. Then his face softened and
he smiled. "Yeah. On Hamilton. Geez. I haven't been there in . . .
shoot, years." He checked his watch. "You think they're still
open?"

"I'm not talking about now. I was just trying to remember that
night."

Pollard settled into his chair. "Yeah, that was fun. Debbie's a
hoot."

"Natalie, too."

They smiled at the old habit of complimenting a guy's wife like
she was his car. Gentle, meaningless words, they were not meant to
condescend, but it was impossible not to read into them the short
significance of marriage in their lives.

"I was trying to remember what we were laughing about."

Pollard wrinkled his face again. He stared at the desk, then
looked up. "I don't . . . geez, Alan, I must be getting old. I don't
even remember us laughing."

"How long after that—"

"A year," he said before Dupree could finish the question about
his divorce.

That dinner was a singular fact: They'd had fun. Now add the
singular fact of Pollard's marriage: Within a year it would be over.
It wasn't just coincidences, but also aberrations. How could you

know, when you stood so close to something, if you were looking at a structural flaw or a harmless crack? He hadn't talked to Debbie since six. He was now five hours late for dinner, three hours later than his last estimate of eight o'clock.

Pollard stood. "Let's get a beer. Maybe it'll come back to me."

"Yeah. Okay." Dupree put loose sheets back into file folders, file folders back into boxes, boxes back under his desk. For a moment, he fantasized that if he were more organized at work he might be a better man at home, that his problems with Debbie were organizational and not structural. Maybe he just needed to remember more, to be conscientious. His anniversary was coming up, and he knew she wanted a mother's ring. What were the kids' birthstones? Hell, when were their birthdays?

The thought of birthstones brought him back to jewelry. He looked up at Pollard. "Lenny Ryan came into the pawnshop for some hooker's bracelet."

"That's what the man said."

"And he has the ticket from the dead hooker, yeah?"

"But we checked Melling's records," Pollard said. Indeed, they had gone over all of Melling's receipts and hadn't found the names of any of the three dead prostitutes.

But Dupree was already up and dragging over the boxes of receipts. See, that was another thing that happened. You tried to connect these things by focusing on one set of details and you forgot the other set. They had looked through the receipts for the names of dead hookers. But they hadn't looked for bracelets. Dupree handed one box of receipts to Melling, took the other for himself, and began paging through them.

Pollard took his box reluctantly. "What am I looking for?" he asked.

"Jewelry," Dupree said, without looking up from his work.

"Jewelry."

"That's right."

"At a pawnshop."

"Right."

"Are you nuts? There might be five hundred receipts for jewelry. And twice as many without receipts." Pollard was right. If Melling's shop was anything like the other 125 pawnshops in Spokane, then much of his merchandise was stolen. This was especially true of jewelry, the first thing burglars stole, since it was easy to carry, and the first thing pawned, since it was rarely marked with serial numbers. Pawnshops were required to keep detailed books, so if a pawnshop owner like Melling thought for a minute that a piece was stolen he'd buy it under the table with no receipt, or fill in the receipt with bogus information to protect his client. Melling's receipts were as vague as he could make them, just a number and a word: "jewelry" or "electronics" or "coins." Many of the names were obviously fakes—Smiths and Johnsons and one Dr. Seuss.

They stacked the jewelry receipts on the desk between them, looking over the names one by one and comparing them to the known aliases, addresses, or phone numbers of the victims. Dupree had resigned himself to two more hours at the office when he pulled just his tenth receipt, checked it against the victims' aliases, and then set it down behind him. But he stopped, turned, picked it up again, and stared at the word "bracelet" and a name he never expected to see. Shelly Nordling. Dupree stood.

"What?" Pollard asked.

He walked to a file cabinet, opened it, and found a large folder labeled "Unrelated Cases"—cases of unsolved prostitute murders, assaults, and disappearances from the last ten years in Spokane. He grabbed the last file. "Nordling, Shelly, DOB 9-16-72. Homicide victim, 8 Feb." Dupree had gone over this case a dozen times, like he'd gone over other unsolved murders and disappearances of women in the city. But he'd seen nothing to connect Shelly Nordling to the three more recent prostitute deaths. The details were completely different. The kind of details that serial killers simply didn't change, for instance, the fact of hiding bodies. Such details weren't coincidental, but were basic. Shelly Nordling had been slashed across the throat with her own knife, apparently after an argument with a john or a pimp. The latest three had been strangled and then shot. Shelly Nordling had been dumped in an alley, with almost no thought. The latest three had been prepared, some of their fingernails removed and forty dollars pressed into their hands. The bodies had been planted carefully in shallow graves and covered with branches. So their killers had to be different. Didn't they?

Dupree read the file, sliding each page across to Pollard. Almost four months earlier, in February, a woman's body was found in an alley, her throat cut, no fingerprints or other evidence to lead to her killer. Small, manageable traces of methamphetamine, cocaine, and prescription drugs were found in her system, along with signs of sexual activity, but no signs of rape. No skin was found beneath her fingernails, only some cotton clothing and some carpet fibers. The theory was robbery or an argument with a john. For a long time they had trouble identifying the woman except by her street name, Pills. Pills hadn't been seen by anyone on the street for about a week. She was a leech, a street hooker who stayed with men for long periods of time, weeks sometimes, trading sex for a place to sleep, meals, and drug money. Unlike most hookers, Shelly Nordling had no file in Washington State. No record or fingerprints. No family or friends came forward, and so Jane Doe 22 sat in the morgue for a month until some woman remembered she had been holding a box of Pills's belongings.

That's how investigators found her, by opening the box and finding an old California driver's license for a girl named Shelly Nordling. She turned out to be from Richmond, in the Bay Area, but they found no family there, just the Nordlings, foster parents who hadn't seen Shelly for years.

And that was it. Dupree stared at a photocopy of the driver's license. Again he found himself staring at a partial picture, looking for that point of intersection, knowing full well there might not be one, that perhaps Lenny Ryan had come to Spokane looking for Shelly Nordling only to find she had been killed in a robbery or a squabble over payment and that was that. When Pollard was done reading he looked up, trying to catch up with Dupree, who'd been a page ahead of him but seemed even further now.

For his part, Dupree couldn't stop staring at the photocopy of the driver's license. In the photo, Shelly Nordling had straight dark hair, to her shoulders, and round eyes set far apart. She was what he would call cute. Dupree set the driver's license on the desk and reached for the clipboard where he kept his copy of the photograph of Lenny Ryan and Ryan's dead uncle from San Francisco. He'd forgotten the young girl in the photo, her straight black hair and round eyes, standing between Ryan and his uncle. He turned the picture to show Pollard. It was Shelly Nordling.

Pollard was just now catching up. "Ryan was in prison when she was killed," Pollard said.

"Right," Dupree said.

"She's his girlfriend *before* he goes to prison? While he's inside, she moves to Spokane, someone kills her, and it makes him mad?"

"Maybe."

"And then he starts killing hookers too, because he's so mad?"

"Maybe." Dupree opened another file, the detective's notes from the investigation of Shelly Nordling's death, and ran his finger down a column of phone numbers until he found the one he wanted and tapped in the number. When the man answered, Dupree apologized for calling so late. Mr. Nordling assured him he wasn't sleeping. "I'm a night owl." He made it sound like an affliction.

"There are some other cases that we're investigating that may have some connection to Shelly's death," Dupree said. "I need to ask you a few more questions."

"All we know is what you guys tell us."

"I understand. I was just wondering if you knew whether Shelly had a boyfriend in prison," he said. "A man named Ryan."

"Boy, I just don't know. We really hadn't been in contact with her for . . . I don't know, six years. I'm sorry. She didn't have a whole lot of use for us." Dupree set his pen down and was about to find a way out of the conversation when Mr. Nordling added, "It's just like I told the other guy."

"The other guy?"

"Yeah. The detective up here."

"A detective contacted you about Shelly?"

"Yeah. Couple months ago."

"What did he want?"

"He just said he was working on a case that she'd been involved in. You have to understand, when she was living up here, it was fairly common to have the police looking for her about this or that." Mr. Nordling laughed bitterly. "Speaking of which, you guys should communicate better with the cops up here. He didn't even know she was dead."

"What do you mean?"

"Well, he just seemed surprised. Really surprised, like he was taking it personal. I asked if I'd screwed up his investigation and he said, 'Yeah.' Then he asked if I knew anything else, so I gave him the shoe box of stuff you guys sent . . . her belongings, or what was left of them. He took the box . . . and that was about it."

The shoe box she'd left with a friend. "Do you remember what was in the box?"

"Coupla earrings. A parking ticket. Stuff like that. I remember when it arrived, Theresa just cried and cried. It's hard to believe that's all that's left of a person, you know? Just a box of crap, things you might toss on your dresser or in your glove box—scraps of paper that don't mean a thing, you know, in the end?"

"This is important. When did this detective come by?"

"Mmm. I guess it was March. Early. Maybe middle of March."

Dupree locked eyes with Pollard across the desk. "Do you remember," he asked, "if there was a pawn ticket in the box?"

"Yeah," Nordling said. "That's the kind of stuff. Exactly. I think she'd pawned some jewelry or something like that."

"Anything else you remember from the box?"

"Prescription. A pair of gloves. A couple scraps of paper with numbers on 'em."

"Phone numbers?"

"Yeah, or pager numbers maybe."

"You remember the numbers or names?"

"Nah."

Dupree reached for the photo of Lenny Ryan and Shelly Nordling on the pier in San Francisco. "Mr. Nordling, I'm going to fax a photograph of a man to the police there in Richmond, and tomorrow a detective will contact you, and I wonder if you'd look at some pictures for us and see if you recognize the man who came to see you."

"You mean he wasn't a cop? Then what was he?"

Dupree shifted the phone. "I'm not exactly sure."

18

The alley opened into the parking lot and back entrance of an adult bookstore, a chipped-brick building with a handful of cars parked alongside. Caroline caught a glimpse of a man in a dark jacket going inside and ran to the door behind him, emerging in a narrow hall as dark as the alley outside. She stood between racks of shrink-wrapped magazines and paperbacks with lurid covers. A handful of men stood hunched in the chest-high racks that filled the place, shoulders pulled in on themselves. As Caroline looked around, she heard the bell on the front door and hurried down the narrow aisles, past a wall of sexual devices and porn videos, locking eyes with an older man in a tie and jacket, who chewed so hard on his bottom lip the skin was white beneath his teeth.

Caroline burst through the front door and only then realized she'd been holding her breath the whole time. On Sprague, she saw the dark-jacketed man on the sidewalk rounding another corner, back to the darkness of the side streets.

She ran down the sidewalk after him, pausing just before she reached the corner. This was insane. She was three blocks from her car. What if she did catch Ryan? Then what? She stood still, three feet from the corner, staring at the place where the brick wall stopped and the darkness began. She listened for his footsteps, but it was quiet. A car blew past and Caroline jumped. She thought about Jacqueline. Then it *was* Ryan she'd seen watching Jacqueline earlier. That's what finally made Caroline take the next step and the next, around the corner. She desperately wanted the little girl with the big appetite to be safe, just as she wanted this man to be someone other than Lenny Ryan.

She eased around the dark corner, her eyes adjusting like those of a person walking down a staircase at night. She gasped when she saw him, no longer running but facing her at the end of the short block, his hands in his pockets, waiting for her. His hair was shorter and he'd grown a mustache, but it was him. When he was sure she'd seen him, Ryan turned casually and walked behind the building, into another alley.

Caroline's breath was short, her muscles tense. "Goddamn!" No way she should follow. She looked back at the businesses on Sprague, where there would be telephones, where there would be help. She shuddered once, a chill of anger and frustration. Then she pulled her gun from her waistband and plunged forward, no longer trying to hide her footsteps on the pavement, just marching forward stubbornly and stupidly. "All right," she said quietly. "I'm coming."

The alley led to another side street and another alley, closed at the far end by a cyclone fence that turned it into a kind of narrow courtyard, filled with old building supplies—appliances, windows, doors, and odd scraps of lumber. The light from a street lamp cast half the courtyard in dull glow, and threw the other half into darkness. He must be in the shadows, watching her. She stood for a moment at the edge of the courtyard, reached up and felt where the chain-link gate had been pried open. She pushed on the gate, and it swung open with a rusty sigh.

"Mr. Ryan. You're under arrest." She was surprised by the frailty of her voice. No response. She slipped inside the gate, both hands on her gun. Building supplies were stacked against brick walls and divided into rows and like piles—cracked doors, cabinets and rotted window frames, odd lumber pieces, appliances, and plumbing supplies. She backed into the shadows and allowed her eyes to adjust again. Nothing. Farther into the courtyard, she walked through plumbing supplies—mounds of old sinks and tubs—and at the end of the courtyard an old refrigerator, lying on its back, had been pushed up against the chain-link fence. It looked as though he'd escaped that way, or wanted her to think he had. She approached carefully, her mind racing: Why would he urge her on like that, coax her to follow him, only to escape over a fence? Even in the dark she could see the silhouette of something on top of the refrigerator. A shoe box. Caroline stepped carefully toward it, checking behind each row and stand of appliances before moving forward. A wet, moldering smell crept up on her as she moved toward the box. She crouched, covered her mouth and nose, and used the barrel of her gun to nudge the top off the box. Inside were some papers and a pair of earrings. She lifted one of the earrings from the box and turned it toward the light. It was a pinpoint, a stone so small it had to be real. Caroline had been holding her breath, but now she breathed in and the smell hit her, stronger than before. But there was nothing in the box that could make that smell.

The refrigerator. She set the shoe box on the ground. Three other refrigerators sat beneath a loading dock fifteen feet away. They were chained and padlocked shut. But this one wasn't locked. What am I doing here? Caroline thought. She began to back out of the alley, the gun in front of her, pointed at a forty-five-degree angle to the ground. She could feel him watching, his disappointment. He wanted her to open the refrigerator.

"Jesus, don't do this," she told herself quietly. But she thought about Jacqueline again. She clenched her teeth, stopped herself from backing up, and stood in the center of the fenced-off court-yard, surrounded by stacked lumber and building supplies, half in the glow of the streetlight and half in the shadows, like a magician's assistant cut cleanly in half. Brick walls rose up four stories on either side. She could hear her own heart.

Caroline pulled the neck of her sweatshirt over her nose and mouth, and eased forward until she reached the refrigerator and rested her hand on its door handle—the old kind that latched shut. She lifted. It clicked and opened easily, and Caroline pulled the door up a few degrees, the streetlight revealing a decaying body. Patches of darkened flesh. A tangle of black hair, blue jeans, a flowered blouse. Even with the shirt pulled over her nose, even though she was holding her breath, the smell knocked Caroline back.

The door fell shut and latched itself and Caroline stood facing the other way, breathing into her cupped hand, ordering her stomach to settle, her nerves to cool. Her eyes moved back and forth along the courtyard as she waited for Ryan to come at her any second. But he didn't.

Finally the face in the refrigerator began to rearrange itself in her mind, and with horror Caroline found it familiar. She knew by the smell and the early decay that it was too soon to be Jacqueline, who'd been very much alive earlier in the day. Still, the familiarity was a knot in her chest.

When her pulse evened out, Caroline took a breath and walked back to the refrigerator. She lifted the door and looked down on the decomposing face.

Of course it wasn't Jacqueline. This girl had been dead at least a week, maybe longer, depending on the effect the refrigerator would have on the body's decay. But Caroline *had* seen that face before, and not while this woman was alive. It was the particular drift of the eyes and mouth—all the elements in the right place, but everything slipped and dislocated. Not at all like a sleeping person. On patrol, Caroline sometimes came upon a sleeping transient and nudged him with her foot, worried that he might be dead. She would never again mistake a sleeping person for a dead one. The detachment in a dead person's face was the saddest thing Caroline had ever seen. How many dead people had she seen in twelve years as a police officer? Maybe a dozen a year: car wrecks and suicides and all manner of cruelty. But until her mother died she'd never *seen* dead people, not the way she saw live people, with empathy and understanding.

Caroline lowered the refrigerator door and closed it purposefully, then backed out of the courtyard, keeping her gun pointed at the ground. At the gate she swung around, but no one was there. She backed up to a brick wall and leaned against it, her head back, trying again to slow her breathing. She could hear traffic out on Sprague, the bass thud of car stereos. And she could hear faint footfalls, or imagined she could, careful steps on the other side of the courtyard, as someone walked away.

19

The tires bounded once off the curb and then Dupree stood on the brakes, squealed the car to a stop, and was out. Lights from patrol cars rolled across the brick facades of buildings on East Sprague and along the expectant faces of people who stood shoulder-to-shoulder behind the police tape. The lights and activity had a flow to them, a current that pulled Dupree, or that he followed instinctively, until he arrived at the mouth of the alley where the latest body had been found.

He'd been on his way to a beer with Pollard when Caroline's phone call came. In the scramble to get to the scene Dupree wasn't sure whether he was more angry at Lane for leaving her behind after the sting or at Caroline for traipsing through alleys after Lenny Ryan. The drive from the Public Safety Building to East Sprague had been filled with imaginary lectures for both.

In the alley the first evidence tech was waiting for the rest of the crew so they could begin processing and videotaping and photographing, once the detectives had made their first run through the crime scene. Patrol officers were hanging around too, waiting for instructions on traffic flow and interviews of potential witnesses.

They all looked at Dupree, and something—the late hour or the impotent sameness of the process—left a bitterness in his mouth. They all knew what to do. What did they want from him? He'd been at work eighteen straight hours. There was no telling when he might go home now. Five? Six? Would he make it home before Debbie got up with the kids at seven? Would he go home at all? Hell, why not just work around the clock, cataloguing bodies forever?

A portable electric lantern lit the alley until the light stands arrived with the crime scene van. But even with the lantern the alley was dark, and Dupree fumed at Caroline for venturing down this strip of pavement by herself, with Ryan hiding in the shadows.

He walked to the refrigerator, pulled a handkerchief from his pocket, and carefully opened the latch, touching as little of the surface as he could manage. He propped the refrigerator door with his elbow and used the handkerchief to cover his mouth and nose. When he saw the body, Dupree felt the tug through his chest again, as if a cord connected his toes to his balls to his throat. A flashlight beam lit the body from over his shoulder.

"Victim is female," he heard Spivey say from somewhere behind the flashlight. "GSW. Strangulation. Ligature marks. Apparent homicidal violence."

Dupree lowered the handkerchief from his face. "So you're ruling out accident?"

Spivey ignored Dupree and continued speaking into his microcassette recorder. "Evidence of environmental activity." He was talking about bugs into his tape recorder. Maggots. "Memo to bring in an entomologist to pinpoint microbial and insect activity."

Dupree was too tired to fight with Spivey now, so he put on his gloves and turned back to the body as the young detective continued to narrate. "Entrance wound in left upper quadrant of victim's torso. Body's position is covering possible exit wound. Apparent ligature on the neck. Body is decomposing."

She was curled up on her right side in the refrigerator, so Dupree reached in and eased her back slightly. He shined his flashlight beneath her and saw what he expected to see, two twenties attached by a rubber band stretched around her clutched right hand. "Ah, Jesus," Dupree said quietly.

"Victim displays signature twenty-dollar bills banded to right hand," Spivey continued. "Two fingernails appear to have been removed . . ."

Dupree eased the refrigerator door closed and turned to Spivey. "You wanna get the techs in here? Then talk to the people in the building supply place; find out who's been poking around the alley." When he realized Spivey was recording the instructions, Dupree grabbed the microcassette recorder and spoke into it. "Memo to self: Tell chief he has sweet ass."

Spivey swiped his recorder back and trudged off. Dupree watched him walk to the end of the alley, where Sergeant Lane was talking to the sneaky Special Investigations detective, Gerraghty. Dupree walked over and addressed the sergeant. "So the whole time you're running this sting, Lenny Ryan's watching Caroline? Is that what you got?"

"Yeah," Lane said, not meeting his eyes. "Seems like that, huh?"

On Sprague, Lane pointed out the blocks that Caroline had paced, the motel down the street where Gerraghty and Solaita had been, and the warehouse where he and the other officers had been waiting to arrest the guys and confiscate their cars. Dupree looked across the street and then back, trying to imagine the thing—Caroline cruising back and forth under the harsh streetlights, Ryan somewhere nearby. But where? One of the bars?

"Do me a favor," Dupree said. "Before the bars close, take a picture of Ryan and just ask around, find out if anyone's seen him."

"Actually"—Lane shuffled his feet—"Caroline's doing that."

"She didn't go home?" Dupree was incredulous. "She's out there by herself?"

"I'll send Gerraghty to help her."

Dupree waved him off angrily. "Don't bother. I'll do it."

Lane shifted his weight and made eye contact finally with Dupree. "I don't get this, Alan. This guy Ryan is killing these women? Then why does he lead Caroline into the alley and not . . . Why didn't he . . ."

Gerraghty followed Lane's gaze back toward the alley. "Once he got her in there," Gerraghty said, "why didn't he . . . I mean, it would have been easy to . . ."

Dupree nodded to get him to stop talking. "I don't know." He walked off toward the closest tavern, not wanting to think about what it would have been easy for Ryan to do with Caroline in the fenced-off alley.

Dupree pulled his cell phone and called her. When Caroline didn't answer right away, he hung up and hit redial; this time she picked up but continued what she was doing, interviewing someone above the tinny music of a country jukebox and the scattering of pool balls.

"You've never heard of a girl named Jacqueline?" Dupree heard faintly over his phone. *"Uh-huh. Uh-huh. I see. How about this guy?"* Dupree walked down the block as he listened to her conduct the interview, feeling strangely close to her, this shared intimacy, listening to her use the skills and style he'd taught her a decade earlier. *"And you're sure he wasn't in here tonight?"*

The phone shuffled and she was on the line. "Mabry," she said simply.

"What do you get for a game of headboard Yahtzee these days?"

"Guy was gonna give me seventy-five."

He dropped the casual air. "Jesus, Caroline. You chased this guy into a fuckin' alley? By yourself? What are you doing?"

But she was ready for the lecture. "If I go for backup, I lose him."

"You didn't have your phone?"

"I had my gun. What would you do?"

Dupree sighed. "Where are you?"

"On a beach in the south of France, tanning my stomach." He saw her then, straight down the row of businesses, two blocks away, emerging into a streetlight. She must've stepped out of a bar, but from his angle it was as if she'd materialized out of the wall, from the darkness. She had the tiny phone to her ear; she was wearing sweatpants that seemed to exaggerate her long legs and narrow waist. She looked good. They locked eyes and walked toward each other, continuing their phone conversation.

"What do you think he wanted?" Dupree asked. "Why'd he let you follow him?"

"I don't know . . . he wanted to show off the body?"

They were two blocks apart now, staring at each other as they spoke into their phones. "You think he killed her?" Dupree asked.

"I don't know," Caroline said. "What about you? What do you think?"

"His girlfriend was a hooker who got killed here a couple months ago. While he was in prison. For what it's worth."

"What *is* that worth?"

Dupree crossed at the corner and they were speaking from opposite ends of the same block now, still staring at each other. They slowly lowered their phones as they met in the middle of the block.

"So you're all right?" Dupree asked.

"Tired." She reached down and flipped his tie. "Things have gotten pretty formal around the Dupree estate."

"Actually, I haven't made it home yet. I was putting in a late night."

"You should go home."

He knew that. He was thinking of another theory, how if you paired a young man and a young woman on patrol duty, they would end up sleeping together. Other cops attributed that to adrenaline or the huge amount of trust required for the job, but Dupree had a better explanation: The attraction between two people was directly proportional to their proximity to death. For cops, male and female officers were most susceptible to affairs during times of stress and danger—this case, for instance. Or six years ago, when Caroline shot the drunk during the domestic violence call. She was right; he should definitely go home.

But he didn't answer and they walked slowly back toward the body, Caroline telling him about the girl who'd given her name as Jacqueline and everything that had happened that night, Dupree updating her on what he'd found out about Lenny Ryan from the pawnshop owner and Shelly Nordling's foster father.

"So we think his girlfriend's death made Ryan decide to kill hookers," Dupree said. "Some kind of displaced rage or . . . I don't know."

"So he's your suspect?"

"For now? He's a person of interest, I guess."

"What'd you call it? Displaced rage?"

He shrugged. "I don't know, Caroline. Until we find a better theory. Hell, he's responsible for every other crime in this town."

"Is the psychology good?"

"I don't know," he said. "In the morning, I'll run it past the FeeBIes." The local FBI agent Jerry Castle—Pyle—had become the task force's contact with the Bureau's Behavioral Science Unit in Virginia and would likely contact the muscle-bound Bureau profiler, Jeff McDaniel.

Caroline stopped walking near the adult bookstore where she'd begun her chase of Lenny Ryan. She looked up at the dirty curtained windows, heavy wood door, and yellow neon sign. Suddenly the fatigue seemed to hit her. "He ran through here," she said. "I chased him through here."

Dupree looked up and saw what it was—the peep shows and sex toys, the dirty magazines. He felt strangely embarrassed. "Why don't I have Spivey take care of it?"

"That'll be fine," Caroline said. "I'm gonna hit a couple more bars down the other way, see if I can find this girl. She said her name was Jacqueline," she said quietly, an afterthought, and Dupree saw how Caroline hoped that a name, even an obviously fake name, would somehow give this girl an identity, a place in the world.

"I'll go with you," Dupree said.

She didn't bother objecting and they walked down Sprague together, the flashing lights at their backs, past rubberneckers who stood at the police tape like people waiting in line for tickets. Dupree and Caroline walked next to each other without saying anything until Caroline glanced over.

"Are you gonna tell Debbie that we worked together on this?"

He didn't answer right away. Six years earlier it probably had saved Dupree's marriage, the promise that he would no longer work with young Caroline. They spent only that one night together, hadn't even made love, but Dupree convinced himself that it would be best to tell Debbie straight out. And so he had. That continued to be his only betrayal of his wife, and his deepest temptation, the night Caroline shot the drunk wife beater—after the mess at the crime scene, talking quietly in her apartment, her shaking, Dupree holding and then kissing her, the two of them tossing and rolling and then stopping suddenly, but holding each other tightly so that they couldn't go any further, couldn't undress anymore, until finally they just fell asleep. Afterward, when they had pulled apart and he'd driven around for a couple of hours, Dupree marched into his own house and told Debbie flat out, and the next day announced to Caroline that he was requesting a transfer out of patrol. He told her that he was happy with his wife, that it wasn't his Debbie he didn't like, but his life.

On East Sprague, the neon lent a crass, peripheral glow to his memories. "I don't talk to Debbie much anymore," he said.

"Don't be like that, Alan," Caroline said quietly.

"I'm trying," he said. "But . . . I'm losing something."

"You're fine," Caroline said. "You've always been fine." She kept walking until they reached a dark, smoky bar with a sign that simply said "Drinks." Dupree followed, and it took a minute for his bleary eyes to adjust. A dingy blue carpet ran the length of the floor and a foot up the walls. Four stools leaned against a chipped bar, which was manned by a sickly bartender wearing a back brace. Three round wobbly cocktail tables and a pool table with torn felt—the whole bar was home to just two broken old guys and a drunk woman whose filthy jeans gaped where her zipper was broken.

The bartender recognized them as cops and began hovering around his drunk customers. The bar must've been cited for overserving recently, the way the bartender suddenly nurtured these people who likely hadn't shared a sober day in a year.

"Looks like last call," the bartender said, smiling to Caroline. "Finish 'em up, guys. Bill . . . time to go."

Dupree sat at the bar next to Caroline, who was standing and who reached in her pocket for Lenny Ryan's mug shot. She waited patiently as the bartender moved down the row away from her, toward his paying customers at the other end of the bar. He stood over one of the old guys, who held his beer close to his chest, between his two hands. The bartender was overly polite, smiling back at Caroline and then speaking gently to the old man. "Hurry up, please. It's time." The old man looked up at the bartender. "Bill," the bartender said quietly, and Bill drained his beer and gingerly offered it to the bartender, who took it and moved down the row to the woman and the other man. "May, are you ready? Lou?" He held out his hands for their beer glasses. "Hurry up, please. It's time." He had gotten all three glasses now, but none of the old people budged and the bartender could apparently think of nothing else to do, so he put the glasses in the sink and turned to face Caroline.

"I'm looking for a young white hooker who might go by the name Jacqueline. I don't know her real name."

"What's she look like?"

"Twenty. Mousy brown hair. Short. Eyebrow ring. Buggy eyes. Thin, kind of sickly."

He smiled. "That's half the girls out there." He gestured down the street. "That ain't the girl they found . . ."

"No," Caroline said. She slid the photograph across the bar. "How about this guy? Only with shorter hair. You seen him?"

The bartender shook his head. "Boy, I don't think so."

"Look again," she said. "I want you to be sure."

He lifted the picture and stared hard at it. "No. I've never seen him."

"Is there a pimp or a dealer who runs a lot of girls around here?"

"There are a couple of guys. Kids, mostly. Whoever has the dope."

"What about names?"

"There's a guy named Michael."

"At last!" Caroline turned to Dupree. "The break we've been looking for!"

Even the bartender laughed. "I'm sorry. I don't know his last name. I just seen him in here a couple of times. It's Michael . . . something."

"And where does Michael something live?"

"No idea. I just seen him around, you know? Guys come in, ask about women or dope, and people, they say, 'Talk to Michael.' You know, something like that."

"Who says that?"

"Hmm?"

"You said people say to talk to Michael. So what people?"

"I don't know—guys."

She held up the picture of Ryan again. "This guy?"

The bartender laughed again. "I told you, I don't know that guy."

Caroline smiled back and Dupree marveled at the way she charmed people. "Just testing you."

"I'm not saying that guy never came in here. We get guys all the time coming in, waiting for whores to pass by on the street. I don't pay too much attention."

"I'll make you a deal. You start paying attention and maybe I won't talk to the liquor control board about you serving these people into a coma, okay?"

The bartender nodded.

Dupree looked away from the bartender and his eyes fell on Caroline's waist, which was at eye level at the bar next to him. All of her weight was on one foot, her arms spread on the bar, this perfect picture of balance. It was strangely erotic, watching her interview this bartender—one of the most mundane functions of their job. Dupree reached out with his hand and held it over her waist and her hip, inches away from where her shirt was tucked into the elastic band of her sweatpants. But he didn't touch her. When he looked up the bartender was eyeing him strangely, and Dupree let his hand fall.

Caroline turned to face him then and he felt himself blushing. "Can you think of anything else I should ask this guy, Sergeant Dupree?"

He shook his head no.

"You all right?" she asked.

"Fine."

"Okay," she said. She gave the bartender her business card and gave him one more look at the photograph of Ryan. "If you see this guy around, or if Michael comes in or if you see a young woman like I described, you call me. Deal?"

"Yeah, sure." The bartender shrugged and chewed his thumbnail and looked back at Dupree, as if he knew what the detective had been thinking and sympathized with him.

"Hey, can I get a beer?" Dupree surprised himself by asking.

"Yeah," the bartender said. "You bet." He raised his eyebrows at Caroline, but she shook her head and sat on the bar stool next to Dupree.

"You sure you're all right?" she asked.

"Just thirsty."

She looked outside and then back at Dupree. "You think it's a good idea to drink before you go out there and investigate a homicide?"

"I can't imagine a better time." When the glass arrived he held it up and drained the first half. He tried to sound casual. "So, are you goin' home?"

"I think I'll try to find this girl Jacqueline, at least see if I can figure out her real name. I mean, if I'm not in the way."

He felt a surge of relief and an attraction to her that was something like nostalgia. "No," he said. "You're not in the way." Holding her that night six years earlier, Dupree had told her about his theory that life ought to include mulligans, just like in golf. So that you could make one mistake a round that doesn't cost you, that doesn't hurt anyone. *It's not that I want to leave my wife,* he'd said that night. *I just want a mulligan.*

Dupree finished his beer and they stood. Caroline walked out and Dupree began to follow, but first he turned to the other end of the bar, where the old drunks were waiting for the cops to leave so the bartender could continue overserving them. He wanted to ask them if their lives slipped away or if there was a moment of epiphany, like someone throwing a switch and bang, you realize that the best life has to offer is a bottle of fortified wine. The old people looked nervously at him and Dupree bowed and dropped a ten-dollar bill on the bar.

"This one's on me," he said. And he was happy that he remembered their names. "G'night, Bill. G'night, Lou. G'night, May."

20

The thin, exhausted girl, who had decided to change her name that very morning, walked slowly down Sprague, her eyes on the flashing police lights six blocks ahead. *Jacqueline*. It sounded older. Sophisticated. It didn't sound like someone who would get all caught up in street shit, that's for sure. Jacqueline would be above all that. She walked barefoot down the sidewalk, carrying her shoes by their straps, slowing with each step closer to the police lights. God, not another one. She looked back toward downtown, thinking maybe she should take a cab to meet Michael and Risa at the motel where they were waiting for her, probably fucking right now (he was such an asshole) or else smoking Michael's rock or the weed that Risa had gotten for them. Even by cab, she wasn't gonna make it back in time for the dope.

Now five blocks away, Jacqueline thought about that lady cop who had bought her lunch today, who asked all those bizarre questions about bad dates. Fuckin' freaks, some of these guys. There was one guy who tripped her out only a week ago. He felt her up in the Lamplight, a bar downtown where she worked sometimes. Jacqueline had stared at the guy the whole time, even in the motel room that he rented, and it wasn't until they were done and he was paying her, his hands shaking a little, that she recognized him.

"Hey," she said, "you teach . . . biology, right? At Ridgeview Junior High."

The guy didn't say a thing.

"Rae-Lynn, remember? I had you for eighth grade."

His stare made her feel strange, as if she wasn't even there.

"Yeah, well, I didn't think you'd remember me. I only went there two months." She shrugged—no big deal—even though it was. "So, you still teaching there?"

Still, the guy didn't speak.

"Hey, I ain't gonna tell anyone, if . . ."

He just stared at her, with the weirdest look on his face, like he'd done something bad to her, but shoot, compared to some of these sick fucks . . . It wasn't like with Michael or anything, where she wanted to wake up with him, where she lost herself and felt safe. But it was fifty bucks and it didn't hurt. She'd wanted to say something to make the guy feel better, but what was there to say?

So she just grabbed her things and left.

That lady cop had asked about guys who made her feel funny, well, maybe she should've mentioned the teacher. He didn't scare her, but she had asked which guys gave her the creeps. And that guy certainly did. She reached in the pocket of her jeans and found the card. Detective Caroline Mabry of the Special Investigations Unit. She turned it over, then put it back in her jeans.

Jacqueline leaned against the bus bench. She didn't want to walk toward the police lights. The lady cop might be there and might run her with questions again. And this time they might see that she had warrants out on her under her real name. Fuck that.

Behind her was the high chain-link fence of Landers' Cove, where they sold boats and trailers. For a while, last fall and winter, it had been the place to take dates, in the cabins of the big boats. Back when Burn was pimping her, before she hooked up with Michael, a lot of girls ran dates through the boat place, because it was cheaper than getting a hotel. But the owner of the boat place had gotten tired of hosing it down and finding rubbers everywhere and so they'd put up a better fence and brought in all-night security guards. It was too bad. She liked the big, luxurious boats.

Jacqueline leaned against the fence and watched the old security guard, Paul something. He walked around the lot with his flashlight. He had gray hair and sunken-in shoulders and walked with a limp, but the guy wasn't so bad-looking, for a grandfather. She thought it was cool watching a guy who didn't know she was watching him.

Paul the security guard moved his lips, singing to himself as he walked around aimlessly. He stopped in front of a huge yacht and ran his hand over the hull.

"So you gonna let me in there tonight, Paul?"

Startled, he turned and shined the light on her and smiled. "Hey there, girlie." He called all the hookers "girlie." "You thinkin' of buyin' a boat?"

"That depends. What would you recommend?"

He turned his bony shoulders back to the yacht he'd been touching. "Can't go wrong with a beauty like this. Only has one on-board TV, though."

"Yeah, that sucks. How many I need?"

"That depends," he said. "You planning to have a crew?"

"Nah. No men allowed on my boat."

He looked back at the boat. "I used to have a boat. I ever tell you that?"

He told her that every time they spoke, but she said no.

"Nothing like these Cadillacs." He walked slowly over to the fence. "Just a little fishing boat. Trolling motor and captain's chair. That was the first time I retired."

"What happened?"

"To the boat? Or the retirement?"

"I don't know. Both."

"Sold the boat. Retirement didn't take after my wife died." He smiled to her. "So my son got me into the glamorous world of all-night security. And here I am."

"How old are you, anyways?"

"Sixty-eight. But I have the body of a sixty-seven-year-old." He had reached the fence now and he shined the light on her arms, no doubt looking for tracks. "You doin' okay, girlie? Bein' careful? Stayin' off my boats?"

"Oh, yeah. I'm good." She nodded. "What time is it, Paul?"

"Little after three. You callin' it quits?"

"Yeah. My boyfriend's got a room down the way."

"You want me to call you a cab?"

"Nah," she said. "Thanks, though."

He nodded up the street. "Do you know; did they find another girlie up there?"

Jacqueline nodded.

The old man chewed on his lip. "You oughta quit."

"Two more weeks," she said, her standard answer when anyone advised her to quit. Probation officers, drug counselors, the lady who handed out condoms at the clinic—she was always two weeks from quitting.

"You were gone for a few days there," he said.

She shrugged one shoulder. "A guy hired me to dance at the state line and I got out there and it's just him and some of his buddies and he says they gotta *audition* me, 'cause there's so many girls wanna dance at this new club."

"What'd you tell 'em?"

"Thirty bucks a blow, fifty for the show. Fucker don't get no free date, even if he owns a club." She smiled. "'Course, if a high roller like yourself wanted a freebie . . .'"

Paul shook his head. "I pretty much avoid sex with beautiful young women . . . messes with a man's expectations, you know?"

She blushed when he called her beautiful. She liked flirting with old harmless guys like this. It reminded her of the movies.

"Besides," he said, "you're assuming I'd give *you* a freebie." He shined the flashlight on himself. "You think this kind of seasoning comes cheap?"

"You're funny," she said. She pushed herself off the fence. "Well. I suppose . . ."

Paul reached up and hooked his fingers in the fence. "Be careful."

"Thanks." She smiled again, reached up and brushed his fingers in the chain-link fence with her own, and turned to leave. She walked away from the boat dealership and paused at the street. There was a pickup truck waiting for her at the end of the block, and a man staring out from it, smiling as she approached.

21

They sat in Dupree's car, in front of Caroline's house. It was funny. Caroline spent the beginning of the night trying to convince men that she wanted to have sex with them in their cars, and now here she was at three in the morning, sitting in a car with a man she wanted to have sex with.

"It's a bad idea," she said.

"It is?" They'd been talking about her being added to the serial killer task force, an idea Dupree had floated at the scene because of her rapport with the hookers and her run-ins with Lenny Ryan. But she hadn't given him an answer and so he'd followed her home and they sat in his car outside her house, discussing it. "You don't want to work on the case?" he asked.

She smiled at him. "No. I don't think we should sleep together."

"I didn't . . ." But he didn't finish the thought and she could tell that he felt caught, somehow. "I'm not putting you on the task force because I want to sleep with you."

"But you can't tell me you haven't been thinking about it. I have too. I just think it's a bad idea. It's always been a bad idea."

He looked away from her and rubbed his smooth head,

135

swallowed, and laughed. "Most good things start out as bad ideas," he said quietly.

"It's not that I don't want to." She touched the back of his hand. "Maybe it'd be better if it didn't mean anything. If we were just horny."

"Oh, I can be horny."

"Yeah, but we can't be *just* horny. Not with each other."

He opened his mouth to object, but again, he couldn't. "I feel like I'm being blamed for something I never even brought up."

"I'm not blaming you. Just look at us. I have a relationship with a twelve-year-old who hasn't uttered an intelligible sound in six months. And I like it that way because it means I don't have to talk about the fact that I don't want to live with him anymore."

"You don't want to live with him?"

Caroline looked at Dupree, but only for a second, because eye contact seemed like a particularly bad idea just then. "No," she said firmly, to herself.

"You're sure?"

Caroline nodded, then said, "No."

They each stared out their window. Dupree laughed and then Caroline did too.

"We should've done it six years ago and gotten it out of our systems," she said. "I don't think it's possible now."

"I'm not *that* old." There was a silence in the car; Dupree cleared his throat. "Look, I didn't mean to . . ."

"You didn't do anything," she said. "Fifteen minutes from now I might've asked you to take me to a motel."

"Mind if I wait?"

She reached over and squeezed his arm, opened her car door, and climbed out.

"So I'm going to request that they assign you to the task force."

Caroline looked serious. "Do you think I'm up to it?"

"I do."

She stood there in the cool air, thinking. "Okay," she said.

"Okay," he said.

As he started the car, Caroline raised her eyebrows good-bye and pushed the car door closed. She watched him drive away and then turned back to the house. That night they almost slept together, he made a stupid reference to golf. Nice pillow talk. But it wasn't even the unromantic idea of a mulligan that got to her. It was the whole idea of what would happen afterward that made her feel so sad, so distant from him. She could imagine the feeling, a cheapness, the flat emptiness of being someone else's infidelity, existing most strongly in that person's betrayal to his wife and his better self.

She opened the front door and set her bag down. Someone was breathing in the room. She switched on the light, expecting to see Joel, but found her father asleep on the couch, wearing a suit without the tie, his short gray hair peeking up from a blanket.

"Daddy?"

He started, and it took him a second to recognize her.

"I thought you weren't getting in until tomorrow," Caroline said.

He sat up and rubbed his face, more lined than she remembered, silvery whiskers already jutting from his solid jaw. "I had some business in Seattle, so I came a day early. Joel got me at the airport. He let me curl up here. I hope it's not a problem."

"No," she said. "Of course not. Is he—"

"He went to bed." Her father yawned. "Where have you been, Caroline?"

She sat down next to him and held his big hand, ran her fingers over the veins and the black hairs, squeezed it tight, and leaned against his shoulder. She hadn't realized how tired she was, but now she felt like sleeping and crying, and the thought of working on this case weighed two tons. Faces ran together—the dead girl in the refrigerator, Burn going over the dam, her mother slipping away—and filled Caroline with a deep loneliness, the panic of a child who realizes she's alone in bed. The faces and Joel and Dupree and her father's hand . . . Caroline buried her head in her father's shoulder.

"It's all right," he whispered to her. "Go on and cry, baby. It's okay."

And she was still crying ten minutes later when her cell phone rang.

22

The guy was gnawing on his tongue because he didn't want the hand job to end, and that pissed Jacqueline off. Normally she wouldn't care one way or another, but a guy can't pick you up on your way back to your motel and then try to stretch a hand job into a fucking relationship. Forty bucks was incredible for just a hand job, but still . . . She ought to just quit, but she was alone with him in the front seat of his smelly pickup—she couldn't put her finger on the smell—and Jacqueline figured she'd be better off if he just finished his business.

The guy's arms were thick and muscular; his neck was a tree trunk. He closed his eyes and spat some words in a growl that made Jacqueline shiver: ". . . Nnnn . . . oh yeah . . . suck me . . ." This kind of talk always bothered her, but at least the guy didn't call out names. More than anything, Jacqueline hated guys who called out names. They could fantasize about their old girlfriends or women at their office or even their sisters; what did she care? But it made her feel bad to hear the names because then she had to think about the poor women who knew these assholes.

When the guy began to grumble more, Jacqueline looked out the truck window because she hated their faces during this part. Risa said it was her favorite part, because even the tough ones get so helpless: She said she could kill twenty guys a week while they got off. But Jacqueline never trusted being stronger than these guys, even for a few seconds. It never lasted. Jacqueline looked over at the guy and he was pinching himself again in the soft, white flesh under his round biceps. She stopped for a moment. Her hand was getting tired, and he was likely to cut off one of his balls to keep from finishing.

"Oh, come on, buddy."

Then it all went crazy: his arm shooting around her head, a hand on the back of her neck, squeezing, pulling her head toward his lap. Jesus, he was strong, stronger than he looked. She figured out what his truck smelled like—bleach—as the hand tightened almost all the way around her neck and then the other hand found her throat and—

The fingers twisted into her windpipe and Jacqueline realized something that normally would've scared her off a guy: He was wearing gloves, suede driving gloves. He squeezed even harder, and it dawned on her that he was not trying to choke her; he was trying to break her neck. Risa always said you had to look out for the short, strong ones, because they're pissed off at the world.

Then he growled again, like a dog, and Jacqueline knew she was going to die in this truck and she gave up to something she'd always understood—that they are stronger than she is, that when they are done with her, this is the way it has to turn out. She knew that first when she was six, that look in a man's eyes—excited and repulsed and . . . angry, all shadows and dark rooms. She'd never known a man who wasn't angry and that was the thing girls never talked about, the thing that was so screwed up about hooking. To a lot of these guys, sex was just the other side of a good beating.

The guy was harder now; didn't that figure? Almost without thinking, Jacqueline reached into his lap and twisted—not to save herself, but just because she felt so angry. The man's hands loosened a bit and then she scratched him in the groin, so hard she felt a nail break off in his skin. He tried to turn his lower body away from her, but she was lying across his lap, pinning him.

Frantic, she brought her right hand in, punching him as hard as she could in his Adam's apple, the way Michael had taught her. His hands fell away, and it took a couple of his wheezing breaths before she realized she could go. She opened the truck door and was on her feet, running across the blacktop, arms swimming, and still she heard him moaning behind her, louder even than the slap of her bare feet. She ran along a row of grocery carts padlocked to a rail on the side of the store parking lot and threw herself into a line of shrubs. Over her shoulder, the pickup fired, shifted, and squealed, all at once.

She should peek around the side of the shrub to get the license plate of the truck, but she was frozen, huddled on the ground next to an empty jug that smelled like sour milk. Her neck was so tender, she felt like crying.

The truck made a few more passes as the driver searched the neighborhood for her. Once, she even saw the headlights against the wall behind her. She swallowed a few times, but otherwise was still. The truck drove off and Jacqueline stayed where she was. A few minutes later it rumbled through the parking lot again.

This time, when it seemed to be gone for good, she stood and ran through the lot, along the front of the grocery store—"Huggies Rebate, Ranier 12-Pak $4.99"—then back toward Michael's hotel room. It was probably a mile and she was in bad shape and began coughing immediately. Her throat felt like raw meat. She didn't think of Michael as protection—and hated whores who mistook pimps for boyfriends—but right now he was the safest thing she could imagine. They had been partying earlier, when Risa and Jacqueline had decided to go out and make some money, and shit if he hadn't told them to be careful, calling her by her real name and everything. That blew her fucking mind, Michael telling them to be careful. But no. She climbs in the first car that stops for her. And on a night when they found another dead girl. It was too much. Jacqueline ran along cracked sidewalks and dead lawns, her shadow thrown by the occasional porch light, ducking under trees and around cars, staying off the busy streets and away from bright intersections. She seemed to run forever.

The motel was down a hill, just off Third, in the shadow of East Sprague. A lot of hookers took their dates here, although Jacqueline preferred to work in cars. The sign simply read "Motel." Jacqueline waited until there were no headlights, then ran across the street to the two-story stack of rooms. She relaxed a little, but her neck was really beginning to ache. She passed the motel office and looked up to the second floor room, where Michael and Risa had probably smoked everything themselves. She wondered why she'd even agreed to give that guy a hand job when the dope was on the way. She was halfway up the landing when she saw the maroon truck with its white and maroon canopy, eighty feet across the parking lot, parked alone under a streetlight.

Jacqueline backed up against the stairwell. At first she thought someone was getting out of the truck, but then realized someone was getting in. Risa.

Jacqueline opened her mouth to scream, but no noise came out. Risa climbed inside, the truck door closed, and for a moment the truck didn't move. Jacqueline took a step down the stairs and then another. Then the truck pulled away.

She ran back up the steps and beat on the door to their room, but no one answered. She opened the unlocked door. A couple of empty forties sat on the table. Nothing else. Her purse was spilled out on the bed, and there was no sign of Michael. It freaked her out that the truck would show up back at her motel, almost as if the guy knew where to find her. Poor Risa. Jacqueline needed to get out of there as quickly as possible, to get as far from the man in the red truck as she could get, back home if she had to. She felt a twinge of guilt, but told herself there was nothing she could do to help Risa.

But there *was* one thing. She reached in her pocket and took out the lady cop's business card. There was no phone in the room, so Jacqueline ran down to the pay phone on the corner. Her hand shook as she balanced the cop's business card on the top of the phone. She tapped out the number, her arms twitching. She had to cover her mouth to keep from throwing up.

After three rings, a lady answered, and it sounded like she'd been crying.

"Is this"—she barely recognized her own voice, rushed and breathless—"the lady cop?"

"Who's this?"

Her words streamed together. "I can't tell you this fucker tried to strangle me but I got away and I just saw him leave with Risa Jesus you gotta help her!"

"Slow down," the lady cop said. "Is this Jacqueline?"

It took a moment for the new name to register. "Yeah," she said. "You gotta do something it's red goin' east on Sprague!"

"Slow down. Tell me where you are."

But Jacqueline slammed the phone into the cradle and just stood there, breathing and staring at the phone. Fuck it. She pulled her hands into tight fists in front of her face and began crying. She had to go. Now. She backed out of the phone booth, then stopped, reached back in, and grabbed Caroline Mabry's business card.

PART III

JUNE
The Fire Sermon

23

Special Investigative Summary

Supplemental Report
Confidential
Date: 4 June

Case Number(s): 01-10643, 01-20054; 01-20154-A, 01-20159, 01-20161, 01-20179, 01-22390, 01-24911, 01-25212, 01-26055.
Suspect: Leonard M. Ryan and/or Unknown Persons
Offense: Homicide (multiple)
Officer: Sgt. Alan Dupree
Unit: Serial Murder Task Force

Facts: On 21 May at approximately 1100 hours, SIU Det. Caroline Mabry observed a WM subject she believed to be Leonard Miller Ryan, DOB 7-20-63. At that time, Ryan was a suspect in at least two active homicide investigations and an attempted murder/robbery (see attached case files). On 21 May, Det. Mabry observed Ryan watching and possibly stalking a young prostitute that Mabry had recently interviewed, a white female subject, approx. age 20, who gave her name as "Jacqueline." Acting on this information, Det. Mabry returned to where she had observed "Jacqueline" and the subject she believed to be Ryan but was unable to locate them or to determine conclusively whether the man she had seen was Leonard Ryan.

Later on 21 May, at approximately 2300 hours, following a prostitution sting on East Sprague, Det. Mabry observed a WM subject she conclusively determined to be Ryan. Detective Mabry followed the subject into an alley between Sprague and First Avenues, at Magnolia Street, where she discovered the body of a deceased WF in a refrigerator. Subsequent investigation by myself and the task force determined that the deceased female was Andrea Jean McCrea, DOB 2-13-81. Cause of death was determined to be homicide by strangulation. Victim suffered fractures to the windpipe and larynx. Victim sustained a .38 caliber GSW to the chest, apparently postmortem. Ligature marks were observed around the victim's wrists but there were no signs of sexual assault. As with other victims, a number of the victim's fingernails were broken indicating possible defensive wounds, yet no tissue samples were recovered from the remaining fingernails. The victim's hands had been washed with a bleach solution and two twenty-dollar bills were attached by rubber band to her hand. The victim McCrea had a history of drugs and prostitution and a "high-risk" lifestyle. Autopsy placed the date of death as approx. 14 May, seven days prior to the discovery of the body. Two latent fingerprints were removed from the refrigerator door and/or handle and were matched to Cal. State Corr. Fac. Lompoc prints of Leonard M. Ryan.

Roughly five hours later, at 0450 hours on 22 May, Det. Mabry received a cellular telephone call from a woman she believed to be "Jacqueline," who said that a WM subject in a red vehicle had attempted to strangle her. "Jacqueline" then observed another prostitute, whose street name is "Risa," climbing into the red vehicle. After alerting patrol units, Det. Mabry proceeded to the Uptowner Motel in the 1200 block of East Sprague but was unable to locate "Jacqueline" or "Risa." Subsequent efforts to identify or locate "Jacqueline" or "Risa" or to locate the subject Leonard Ryan have been unsuccessful.

During the ensuing two weeks, the task force focused on the viability of Ryan as a suspect in the unsolved homicides of at least four prostitutes and the possible disappearance of two others. After an article in the local newspaper (see attached article from 28 May, "Streets of Fear: Police

Doing Little to Solve Serial Murders"), I was asked to prepare this status report detailing the task force's work and to explain my apparent delay in securing an FBI profile of our suspect. To that end, I have requested assistance from the FBI's Behavioral Science Unit and have sent Det. Caroline Mabry to interview a retired FBI agent and expert on criminal profiling in New Orleans, LA.

Background: Lenny Ryan is the primary suspect in the homicide of Kevin Hatch, AKA "Burn," 28 April. Hatch and the subject were involved in an apparent narcotics deal when they attempted to flee an SIU surveillance team. During subsequent chase, Ryan was observed pushing Hatch into the Spokane River. Hatch's body was never recovered and he is presumed dead. Ryan escaped. (See attached case file 01-10643.)

Also on 28 April, Det. Pollard and I responded to a homicide in the 900 block of South Stone. Cause of death was determined to be blunt trauma to the head, the weapon being a pipe wrench found at the scene. Victim was Albert Stanhouse, DOB 7-1-37, and subsequent investigation indicated that he was the uncle of Leonard Ryan. Neighbors described a younger man arguing with Stanhouse and later identified a photo of Ryan as the man they saw leave in Stanhouse's car. The car was later recovered at the Chattaroy Farm and Truck Stop on Highway 395. (See case file 01-20159.)

On 29 April, a pawnshop owner, Daniel C. Melling, DOB 9-4-62, sustained a GSW to the face during robbery of his business in the North 900 block of Division. Melling identified a photo of Ryan as the man who shot him and reported that Ryan had a pawn ticket for a bracelet belonging to a deceased prostitute.

Independent investigation by myself and Det. Pollard identified that prostitute as Shelly Nordling (see case file 01-20161) and revealed Leonard Ryan's relationship with Nordling, DOB 9-16-72, a prostitute who was arrested with him in Richmond, Calif., in 1996 for possession of narcotics with intent to deliver. Nordling testified against Ryan in that case. In late 1999, Nordling moved back to Spokane to work as a prostitute and was a homicide victim on 8 February, her body found less than a block from the 21 May crime scene. Ryan is not a suspect in Nordling's death; at the time he was incarcerated at the State Correctional Facility at Lompoc, Calif.

Ryan was released 5 March and immediately violated his probation. His whereabouts since then are unknown. Forensic evidence and witness interviews (see attached documents) place the death of the first victim (Rebecca Bennett) at about 1 or 2 April, within the time frame of Ryan's release.

Sometime between 16 March and 18 March, according to the victim's foster father, David Nordling, a man fitting Ryan's description visited the Nordling house in Richmond, Calif., posing as a police officer. At that time, Mr. Nordling gave him a shoe box containing Shelly Nordling's personal effects, delivered to Mr. Nordling by Spokane police. That box was later discovered near the refrigerator in which Andrea McCrea's body was found on 21 May.

The task force has had difficulty verifying Ryan's whereabouts between 20 March and 4 June, during the period of four prostitute homicides and the disappearance of two others.

Current Status: The investigation remains open. After exhausting thousands of leads, the task force has identified Leonard Ryan as its primary suspect, the potential motive being displaced rage (see accompanying definition in attached source material from the FBI Behavioral Science Unit) over the death of Shelly Nordling and anger toward prostitutes.

Subsequent to criticism in the local media, SPD officials suggested I apologize to Special Agent Jeff McDaniel of the FBI's Investigative Support Unit, for my being "brusque" and seeming "unimpressed" with his unique abilities and charm. In addition, I was told to contact former FBI profiler Curtis Blanton, now a law enforcement consultant working in New Orleans, LA. I was instructed to ask both experts to evaluate the crime scene signatures and methodology and to determine Ryan's plausibility as a suspect. To that end, Det. Mabry, whose recent work for the task force has been exemplary, is flying to New Orleans, LA, this week to review Blanton's assessment and to receive a general critique of the investigation to this point.

Recommendation: On 2 June, I telephoned Special Agent McDaniel in Sacramento, where he is assisting authorities on a multiple homicide case. He accepted my apology and explained it would be at least a month before he had time to provide any more expertise for our case. The same day I telephoned Curtis Blanton and he expressed, in no uncertain terms, his lack of interest in working on this case and his disdain for our efforts so far. That day, I recommended that we honor Mr. McDaniel's prior commitment and Mr. Blanton's request that we leave him alone and that we actually try to "do our own damn work." Since, two days later, my superiors sent the entire case file to Mr. Blanton in New Orleans anyway, without my knowledge, it is apparent that my earlier recommendation was treated like a flaming turd, so pardon me if I don't squat right down and pinch off another loaf of meaningless opinion for you.

Addendum: This morning, 5 June, at 0800 hours, I was informed that the pawnshop owner Daniel Melling had died during the night of complications arising from his wounds. The attempted murder charge against Leonard Ryan has been amended to another charge of murder I.

24

When she was little, Caroline called the sunrise "Mr. Pink Sun."
An early riser, she loved the look on her father's face when he
descended the stairs to find her sitting there in her footed paja-
mas, holding her blankie, curled up in the window seat next to
the banister, watching the horizon for the tiny shifts in light that
marked the dawn. As she got older, Caroline's fascination with
the sunrise became more scientific and she tried to pinpoint the
precise moment that morning began. She would remind herself
to pay better attention, but some small detail would catch her
eye, the shape of a cloud, the pine needles on a tree, dew on the
lawn, and before she knew it a moment had slipped past—and
perhaps that moment wasn't a defining one, but how could she
ever know? The moments seemed stolen and she felt cheated, a
premonition that there was a danger in missing much of her life,
that she could be so distracted by the details of *living* that she
failed to notice *life*. The next weekend she would be at the window seat even earlier, concentrating even harder, trying to see the
coming light without seeing the details—a kind of unfocusing
that she could sometimes sustain for several minutes.

Her father would come down the stairs, tucking in the flannel shirt he wore on weekends, and find her in this trance, letting the images play on her retinas, absorbing the light without processing it. Caroline would blink the trance away and smile at her father, and if it was Saturday they would put on their coats and walk downtown together while her mother and brother slept, the embers of morning still cooling in the east.

"Amazing," he'd sometimes say, "the prettiest part of the day and ninety-five percent of the people miss it."

On these Saturdays, they slowed down when they crossed the Monroe Street bridge, Caroline's hand lost in his, and she would run her other hand along the concrete railing of the bridge, catching strobed glimpses of the waterfall between the rails.

"Water's high," her father might say. Or, "Late runoff." Or, "Spillway must be closed," or a thousand other remarks about the river, never the same one twice. His knowledge of the flow and the seasons and the string of dams downstream amazed her. Across the bridge, she would sometimes look back over the banks, to that point where the Monroe Street Dam began to coax the river over its face. She remembered seeing an eddied pool of trash once—empty bottles and cardboard boxes—moving in a swirl and then disappearing over the lip of the dam.

At the grocery store, he would buy a newspaper, bagels for him and Caroline's mother, and donuts for Caroline and her brother, and they'd walk home along the same route. And even though she couldn't eat her donut until her sleepy-headed brother woke up, Caroline didn't mind, because for another hour, it would just be Caroline and her father and the revelations of growing light.

Joel's hand on her shoulder brought her back. "You all right?"

She stood at the large window at the end of the tarmac, staring out at the horizon, fully engulfed now in the sunrise. Caroline smiled. "I missed it."

Joel turned to the gate, where passengers were just beginning to board the plane. "No you didn't. They're still doing the back of the plane."

She turned to face him. His eyes were downcast, like those of a kid afraid of saying something wrong. She reached up and touched his short hair, running her fingers along the top of it, like a gust through bunch grass. "I was thinking of something else."

He nodded. He never asked what she was thinking. "You have your books?"

She opened her bag and held them up, two black paperbacks with the same photo on the back, a slightly askance, more than slightly overweight Curtis Blanton, the leading expert in the country on serial murder, a former FBI criminal profiler who had made his reputation interviewing and studying psychopaths, chiefly one nicknamed the Pacific Coast Killer, for his habit of littering that highway with dead hookers. Now Blanton was a kind of free-lance profiler, working with local cops when he wasn't consulting on movies and TV shows. He also was the author of two books, *Hunting America's Most Notorious Killers* and *Catching America's Most Notorious Serial Murderers*. Caroline felt a low-grade nausea when she went to find his books on the Internet. Rather than type Blanton's name in the search field, she typed the words "serial" and "killer." The result: eighty-six nonfiction books concerning serial killers currently in print. Their titles screamed: "Amazing," "Evil" killers and "Fantastic," "Bizarre" cases. There was an encyclopedia of serial killers. Trading cards. A self-published how-to booklet. She had set out to investigate a murder and had stumbled across a genre; this thing infecting her city was a thriving industry. Alive, a woman like Jacqueline was worth a couple hundred bucks a day until her looks ran out or she died of AIDS or hepatitis or was shot by an angry john. But if this monster got hold of her, she could be worth a chapter in one of these books, perhaps even a composite character for the miniseries.

Blanton's books had arrived two days ago. Immediately, she was put off by his descriptions of serial sexual murders. She recognized so many of the details from the case they were investigating, it felt almost like prediction on his part. But it was more than that: The books were a strange blend of overheated, graphic detail and psychiatric guesswork, full of phrases that sounded like the random pairing of pop-psychology terms: "psycho-sexual objectification" and "postmortem, postcoital model infatuation."

She put the books back in her bag. "What are you going to do while I'm gone?" Caroline asked.

Joel shrugged. "Hang out. Maybe go rock climbing with Derek and Jay. Wait for you to come home." He'd been so nice to her since her mother died. And even sweeter since her father's short visit. She wondered if her dad had said something to him, suggested that Joel take better care of his little girl.

Joel kissed her so gently, it made her wince a little bit. She turned then and walked toward the jetway, thinking of her father again. The whole family used to accompany him to the airport for his business trips when Caroline was a child. Each time, he would get halfway down the jetway and then look back and wave with his fingers, the way you wave to little kids. After his trip last month, Caroline had driven him to the airport. They were supposed to go over her mother's belongings, but that's when the case picked up, and a day later she was on the task force and the weekend just got away from them. They'd decided to go through her mother's things later in the summer, and Caroline promised to take vacation in August. Still, she felt as if they'd accomplished something, maybe allowing her to forgive him a little bit. At least that's what she was thinking that day when she watched her father walk halfway down the jetway, stop, and turn. She expected him to wave, but he didn't, just smiled sadly as other passengers walked around him. He stared at her for a long moment and then turned and disappeared down the jetway.

"Ma'am?" The ticket agent had her hand out, and for the second time that morning Caroline shook herself from memory's grip. She handed over her ticket, resettled her bag on her shoulder, and walked down the jetway. Halfway there, she turned to wave to Joel. But he was gone.

25

The girl goalie was coming right at Marc Dupree. He had broken out and run alone into the clear with a couple of long dribbles, and was slowing up to shoot when the goalie left the net and began coming at him, the way goalies were taught to do but rarely did in Marc's experience with eleven-year-old goalies. Yet there was no doubt. This goalie was coming, lips pared back to reveal a scowl built of braces and slitted eyes. This goalie was coming for Marc, and she was big.

He heard Coach's voice—"Shoot!"—but he couldn't. His cleats planted in the dark grass, weight on his left foot, right toe point-down, an action figure die cast in a moment of inaction. Something had frozen Marc, something about this big girl goalie, rumbling out of the net like that. He felt as if he were on TV or maybe PlayStation, the controller paused while someone went to the bathroom.

But after a few seconds, fear replaced Marc's indecision. He forced himself to move, a short dribble to his right, into position to shoot, and then he began bringing his right foot forward, into the ball. The goalie arrived at the same time as Marc's foot, and the ball was kicked from both sides at the same time. It thumped like a drum and didn't move at all. Marc did move, his weight pivoting over the stationary ball, flipping him forward over the ball and the goalie's leg, sprawled onto his back in the grass. Soccer sucks, he thought, and wished he would've played baseball like last year.

Then he was just mad, and he got up like a shot, running after the ball, which had gone from the girl goalie to a defenseman to the good kid on the Lancers, the kid who Brian's cousin said had already fingered a girl, and a seventh grade girl at that, and who was just now taking the black-and-white ball up the right side-line. And even though Coach was trying to teach them positions this year instead of just letting them run "nilly-billy" or whatever he called it, Marc clearly had left his position and was following the ball up the field, teeth clenched and cheeks red, breathing in grunts through his nose.

At midfield, he heard Coach's voice zoom past like a race car— "Dupreeee!"—but Marc ignored him and kept running after the good kid, gaining on him so that when the good kid stopped to change direction, Marc was on him from behind, too close and going too fast to slow down. He ran into the good kid full-bore, like a football player, and for the second time in the last thirty seconds Marc Dupree was on the ground. He looked over at the stunned and bloody-lipped Lancers kid and had the briefest urge to ask what, exactly, it meant to finger someone.

But the ref called a penalty kick and gave Marc a yellow card and Marc felt the glare of his coach as he looked sheepishly over at the sideline, past Coach, trying to find his dad. He finally found him, in a pack of parents with camcorders, his back to the field as he gestured with his arm and talked on that stupid cell phone. Coach sent in Andrew to replace him and Marc slumped over to the sidelines.

"What happens when you run around out there, willy-nilly?" Coach said. "You're in fifth grade, Dupree. Start acting like it." Marc sat down on the cooler between the coach and his father, who still had his back to the game.

"Yes, I'm defensive," his father was saying into the phone. "If you were the lead investigator and the chief went over your head to bring in some retired FBI agent to *evaluate* your investigation, you'd be defensive too."

His father listened for a moment. "I know who he is. I got a TV. But Christ, Lieutenant, I asked the guy for help and he made it very clear he had better things to do." He listened and then launched right back in. "The guy treated me like I was a groupie for his rock band. So now I gotta send my best detective to Louisiana so Officer Gump can read our reports, pull a bunch of voodoo psychology out of his fat ass, and tell us that Lenny Ryan is mad at hookers? Fuck that!"

Marc looked around at the other parents. A couple of them had turned when his dad raised his voice. They looked at Marc, then back to the field. Marc looked at the field too. The good kid for the Lancers had cleared the cobwebs and was stepping into his penalty kick, a real wussie kick that went wide right by five feet. Marc looked back at his dad. He'd never heard him use the F-word, although he said "shit" when Marc dropped Hot Wheels into the cold air return. Marc had heard other adults use the F-word before and it always sounded funny, like they were crazy people or criminals or were trying to show off to their kid's friends or something. Marc didn't like to think of his dad as one of those adults who used the F-word.

"I'm not making excuses." His dad rubbed his forehead. "But when I read the chief's letter, sucking up to these FBI pricks . . . maybe I got carried away."

Without the cusswords, whatever his father was talking about sure was boring. Marc guessed it had something to do with the problems between his mother and father and the apartment his father had rented. Not that Marc was entirely opposed to them getting a divorce, if that's what happened. At first it had made him angry, but shoot, his mom didn't seem any sadder, and his dad always took him and Staci for pizza and hamburgers. And some kids whose parents were divorced got more stuff, like his cousin Andrea, who had a phone and a Sega Dreamcast in her room.

"If Ryan was in town, we'd have him by now." His father took a step away from the game. "He's gone now. He's got no reason to stay. And if he is here, how will some retired fat FeeBIe in New Orleans help us catch him? You put way too much stock in these federales."

Boring crap. Marc stood and opened the cooler beneath him,

pulled out a juice box, and drank it. He looked up at Coach to see if he might get back into the game, but Coach didn't even look at Marc.

His father paced back toward the game now, finishing his conversation. When he moved out he told Marc it was temporary, that as soon as he and Mom "worked through some things" he'd come back. But Marc hadn't seen them working at all, just avoiding each other. When he came back from his dad's apartment—which wasn't so awful except it had only basic cable—Marc didn't know whether to say anything about it to his mom. It was like a giant game where they pretended with their mother that their father was dead. His dad sometimes asked about his mom, but like you'd ask about a sick person, like you don't really want an answer. "How's your mom doing?" "Fine." "That's good."

Brian said Marc's dad would start dating a babe; Marc thought that would be okay and maybe he'd see her in her underwear or something, but that hadn't happened yet, and anyway, when he thought about it, his dad didn't seem like the babe type.

"It was a joke, Lieutenant. One joke in a dry report." His father listened, nodding and mmm-hmming as he walked back toward the sideline, right past Marc and between two parents with camcorders. "I can't come down right now," he said. "I'm at my kid's game. First thing in the morning. I'll see you then." He turned the phone off and slid it back into his jacket. From behind, Marc watched him try to look casual as he focused back on the game. Marc was suddenly aware that his father didn't even know he'd come out of the game. It gave him a weird thrill, to know this thing that his father didn't, to watch his dad scan the field and slowly realize that the person he'd come to watch wasn't even there.

It was good, in a way, that he was out. Otherwise, Marc would never have known that his dad drifted off with his phone and didn't even watch the game. Afterward, he would've told Marc to play with more discipline, or pass sooner, or any of that crap he said after games, and Marc would've just taken it as truth. But the truth was, his dad hadn't even watched the stupid game. It was an amazing revelation that made Marc feel both sad and powerful, and when his father began moving his head more frantically, up and down the field, Marc thought about hiding behind the coach, to keep this going as long as possible. But his father spun around and saw him sitting on the cooler and grinned.

"There you are," he said. "What happened?"

Marc just shrugged. Staring at him, his dad got a weird look on his face—not a look that had anything to do with the game, but the kind of look that Marc imagined on his own face, the way you look when everything around you changes and you feel like you don't have a say in anything anymore.

"Are you okay?" his dad asked.

And even though he was fine, Marc didn't answer, just turned back to the game.

26

Burgundy Street stunk. Not like Bourbon, of course, which ran a small stream of vomited hurricanes and daiquiris along its cobblestone curb, but it stunk nonetheless, with the more general stench of the French Quarter, seeping down narrow streets, currents of hot wet stink that flowed around the posts of sagging balconies and tired rowhouses. At Burgundy and Dumaine, a young white guy in sunglasses, maitre d' coat, surf shorts, and flip-flops stood with a garden hose, spraying some unidentifiable soup from the sidewalk in front of his door, with no hope of cleaning it, just moving it down a ways.

"Hey, sweet," said the man, and he winked, as if he were not hosing down vomit, but playing the piano or bench-pressing. "What's ya hurry fo'?"

She moved along without making eye contact, without straying from the thought that had bewitched her all day: The French Quarter was below sea level. No matter how long Caroline contemplated that detail, she couldn't comprehend it, not without forgetting everything she knew about water. The place was so languid she found it impossible to think of it as anything but under water. This afternoon, with an hour to kill, she had taken a passenger ferry across the mud-colored Mississippi and was surprised how forgettable the great river was, how it didn't offer any relief to the world around it. It moved at the same pace and with the same murkiness as the city. The Spokane was a minor river, sure, but it carved a dramatic path through basalt and granite, in contrast to the city around it, provided a speed and severity that said a river was still a formidable thing—not exactly beyond human control, but a thing nonetheless to be feared. The Mississippi, on the other hand, was no more fearsome than this block. Less so, maybe.

From behind she heard the sound of footsteps and sensed the maitre d' following her. "Now, they ain't no call fo' rudeness," he said.

She waited until he was close and then spun on a heel and allowed his momentum to bring them face-to-face. She found that most men shrink away from a direct stare. This guy was no different, stopping suddenly, his body language changing completely as he pulled back into himself. "I don't mean to be rude," she said clearly, careful not to apologize, "but I'm in a hurry." And then she turned and walked away.

She had about six steps on him before he answered. "Well," he called after her, "y'all know where I live."

Caroline turned down St. Philip and found the bar on the corner: Lafitte's Blacksmith Shop, a dark-stained, wooden structure that still resembled the livery stable it had once been. A small sign declared it to be the oldest tavern in America. The building seemed to revel in its chipped-paint shabbiness, its darkness. The front was open to the street, but there were no windows and the interior opened like a shallow cave, as if it had been dug out of this old, stained hunk of dark primordial wood. Candles flickered on each of the tables and Caroline stood in the doorway, waiting for her eyes to adjust before she stepped inside. When she could see in the darkness, she encountered a narrow bar with a blending machine for hurricanes and zombies, a cash register, and a couple of domestic taps. Above the bar, the only obvious electric light was aimed at the cash register, along with a video camera to catch pilfering bartenders. The camera caught Caroline off guard and caused her to take another look around the place. There were more lights than she'd first seen, green neon exit signs along the ground and small lights illuminating the steps that led to the back of the bar. The owner of this business had gone out of his way to hide the lights and the camera, retaining for tourists the old darkness in the face of late-century zoning ordinances and emergency exits.

"Ms. Mabry?" Curtis Blanton was heavier than in his jacket photo, mostly in his neck, which was pinched by his collar, even though his shirt was unbuttoned. His thick right hand swirled a mixed drink—bourbon and something—while he draped his left hand over that massive neck. He had a close-trimmed beard, round eyeglasses, and a blockish face that flushed red at the cheeks. He rose to shake her hand.

"Thank you for meeting with me," she said.

She had expected to see the files they'd sent down spread out, or at least sitting on the chair next to him, but there was nothing on the table except his drink. She sat down across from him, and he raised his arm for the bartender.

"Your first time to New Orleans?" he asked.

"Yes. It's nice."

He stared for a moment. "Not too hot for you?"

"It's fine."

"But it's hotter than Spokane," he said, and she noticed that he pronounced it right, rhyming it with "can" and not "cane," the way most people did.

"You've been to Spokane?" As soon as she asked it, she knew it was a dumb question and, indeed, he smiled with disappointment, like a teacher who realizes his student hasn't done her homework.

"I worked on Green River," he said. "One of our suspects lived in Spokane."

William Stevens. Caroline remembered. Stevens had been cleared by credit card receipts that established an alibi for him during some of the murders. And then he just up and died. Some people still believed he committed some of the murders. In one of his books Blanton wrote that he thought Stevens wasn't the killer, although the methodology of Green River led him to believe that not all forty-nine murders were committed by the same killer. "I should've remembered that," Caroline said. "I did read your books."

He emptied his drink and waved the glass at the bartender. "On the airplane."

For a moment, she considered lying. "Yes. On the plane."

He nodded. "When your lead detective up there . . . Dupree?"

Caroline nodded.

"When your Sergeant Dupree called me to consult on the crimes up there, I told him that I was too busy on this case. But I'd worked a little with your assistant chief on Green River, and he sent the case files anyway. I told him I didn't have time to look over the files and he said no problem, they would send a detective down here with all the details to pick my brain. I said I didn't want my brain picked. They said it would be no trouble. I told them I couldn't guarantee that I'd have time to even look at the case files."

The bartender arrived with another drink for Blanton. He looked at Caroline, but she shook her head at him. "But you read the files?" she asked Blanton.

He stared at her again, then looked down at his drink. "Your guy is white. Between twenty-four and forty-eight. Drives an American sedan. Never been married. Sexually dysfunctional. Comes from a fairly well-off family and seems easygoing, even smooth, but he isn't. There will be trauma involving the mother, maybe something you can find, like a death or a divorce, maybe something you can't, like him witnessing the mother having sex." Blanton smiled. "He smiles at the wrong things. He may have moved a lot as a child or been beaten up or it may have been something as simple as his being a latecomer to puberty. But from the beginning, he is the classic insider/outsider, seeming to have his shit together, when in fact . . ." He tailed off and picked up his drink.

Caroline opened her purse to get out her tape recorder, but Blanton shook his head. "No," he said. "Have a drink. I hate drinking by myself."

"I guess I'll have a Gibson," she said. Blanton waved his hand again and the bartender appeared. Then he drank his cocktail like it was water.

"Bring the lady a Gibson and I'll have another of these." The bartender disappeared again. "I don't work two cases at once, Ms. Mabry. It's one reason I left the FBI. Each case has its own language and context. I couldn't assist on your case from here any more than I could predict your weather. How many women victims have you?"

She noticed the strange form of the question as the bartender arrived with her Gibson. "Four, for sure. Probably others we haven't found."

"How many were whores?"

She flinched at the word but didn't break eye contact, thinking this must be some kind of test, seeing if she would flinch at his crude language. In his books he wrote in a kind of detached yet overheated, clinical voice—"the rage model taking over through the insertion of foreign objects," and on and on.

"All of them," Caroline said. "They're all prostitutes."

"Chronic drug users?"

"All of them."

He stared at her again. "Profiling is fairly simple, Ms. Mabry. You examine the crime scene and build your man from the ground up. But therein . . ."

He reached into his suit jacket and pulled out a photograph. He handed it over to Caroline, the kind of school picture snapped in front of a glittery blue backdrop. The girl in the picture wore braces and looked all of twelve.

He rattled off the numbers: "Nineteen victims in New Orleans over the past three years. Twelve prostitutes, five other women with histories of heroin or cocaine use, one college student, and this"—he tapped the picture—"fifteen-year-old girl who snuck out of her parents' house planning to walk down to a fraternity party at Tulane and who, quite obviously, never made it." He took the photo back from Caroline. "Each of these women got into a car of her own free will, was beat in the head and then driven into the swamp. About half died from the beating, the other half were still alive and quite possibly conscious for what must have been a terrifying drive. Can you see my guy arrive at the swamp, yeah?" Caroline thought she picked up a Cajun affectation at the end of the sentence but Blanton didn't pause, just waved his empty glass at the bartender again. "Sometimes, the women, they're alive. Other times, dead. Can you imagine that?"

"I suppose," Caroline said.

"You think my guy treats the living ones different from the dead ones?"

"I don't know."

"Well, what do you think?"

"He would have to," she said.

"You would think so. But he doesn't. Just think of that one detail. He doesn't even care whether they are alive or dead. Doesn't care. Dead or alive, he drags them from his vehicle, by the hair. Then he has intercourse with them, sodomizes them, and then again with, I don't know, something, a pipe, a tire iron . . ."

Finally, Caroline had to look away.

"And then he sets about beating them again, not with the tire iron either, with a rock, a stick, something at the scene. Now the ones who are still alive, this is when he kills them. And then the rape occurs again, in the same order. And finally, he poses them, spreads their legs or crosses their arms on their chests. So how long does my guy spend with each victim?"

Caroline shook her head, unable to answer.

"Come on," he said. "How much time?"

Again she shook her head.

"Four to six hours. I mean, that's a lot of activity, all that beating and fucking and posing. But four to six hours between the first sexual activity and the second?" The bartender arrived with another drink and Blanton paused to drink it in two long gulps. "A lot to do at the crime scene, but four to six hours? What's he do the rest of his time?"

Caroline felt too sick to answer, but he just stared at her, not letting her off the hook. She blinked. "He drives around, or just sits there. He lets the rage, whatever it is, he lets it build up. He takes pictures. Maybe he feels regret."

"Yeah," Blanton said, nodding as if glad to have some agreement. "Yeah, that's what I think." He looked slightly embarrassed, as if he'd just realized he'd slipped from the "intercourse with the victim" of his books to the "beating and fucking" of this conversation. "Did they tell you what I said when they asked me to consult on your case?"

"Sergeant Dupree said you weren't interested unless our suspect killed someone other than hookers."

"What else?"

"He said you might be interested if we got more bodies."

"Is that exactly what I said?"

She looked down at her drink. "He told me that you were an arrogant prick who said not to even call back until we got to double digits."

He smiled and nodded at the better translation. "That's right. That's what I said. Double digits. Are you a fan of baseball, Ms. Mabry?"

"No."

"It's all statistics, baseball. That's what I like about it. The numbers. You got a handful of bodies, that's single A. I got nineteen down here. Triple A. Thirty-one waiting for me in Vancouver. Only twelve in Detroit, but two are housewives. And Seattle, Green River . . . shit, forty-nine bodies? Come on! That's DiMaggio. A fifty-six-game hit streak. Ain't no one gonna break that record. Not in the U.S."

Caroline looked down at the table, trying to keep her composure.

"Do you see why I'm telling you this, Ms. Mabry? There are active serial murderers in a couple dozen American cities, preying on the kind of women that your guy is hunting. Drug users, hookers, the homeless. These women are fodder, the trash we throw out so these sick bastards won't go around picking up our secretaries and our housewives and our fifteen-year-old daughters.

"It sounds coarse, but you need to know, I don't have time to do all of them. I don't have time to talk nice." He looked perturbed, as if he were having trouble making his point. "Your first prostitute who died up there, tell me again . . ."

Caroline was confused by the way his language went back and forth: hooker to whore to prostitute, from Cajun to something vaguely Midwestern to East Coast clinician. "Rebecca Bennett," she said.

He shook a meaty hand in front of her face. That wasn't what he'd wanted. It was as if names were some sort of violation of his rules. "I didn't ask who. How?"

"Strangled, then shot. Dumped along the river."

He nodded. "And what did you do, what did the police in Spokane do with this horrible crime?" Now he mispronounced the word, Spo-CANE.

"It was before I was involved."

He stared at her, clearly disappointed.

"Not much," she said. "One investigator. Regular crime scene work-up."

"And if it had been a housewife?"

She sighed. "We would've gone door-to-door for a month."

"That's right. And the last one?" He answered for her. "You form a task force, the FBI gets involved—lasers and carpet fibers and computers and the whole Quantico road show. You offer a big reward, beat the bushes for meaningful interviews. What would you say, ten times the effort as the first victim? Twenty times?"

Caroline felt sluggish, as if she'd been boxing with Blanton rather than interviewing him. "I don't . . . sure, twenty times."

"That's right," he said, tilting his glass toward her as if he'd just proven some point. "So the fifth victim is twenty times as important as the first. Now imagine how important the fifteenth victim is, or the nineteenth. And housewives are twenty times as important as hookers, right? Now what about a fifteen-year-old girl? Huh? Do y'all see what I'm saying, Ms. Mabry? Do y'all understand the concept of triage?"

Again, he'd slipped into a Louisiana drawl. "Yes," Caroline said.

"Because if y'all can't even get past the triage, then the surgery itself . . ." He didn't finish. He picked up the candle between them and swirled the melted wax in the glass so that the light flickered and almost went out. Then he set the candle down and again he was the professor. "How do we catch a murderer, Ms. Mabry? A run-of-the-mill killed-my-wife-over-an-argument murderer. Where do we start?"

Caroline thought about it. "Motive."

"Right," he said. "So when we get a serial murder, we assign our best homicide detective—for the sake of argument, let's say your man Dupree—and he launches into it the way he does all his other simple little cases, looking for motive. But that won't work. It's different with these guys. Motive is only the surface.

Sex. Control. Every one of these cases, the motive is sex and control. So you have to go deeper, to inhabit these guys, to find the thing that lives beneath the motive."

"Beneath the motive?"

"The fantasy. With these guys, it all goes back to fantasy. You piece the fantasy together, you start to piece your guy together. Everything—location, weapon, staging, appearance of the victims—fits into the fantasy." He leaned forward across the table, engaging Caroline's eyes. "You go to the crime scene and you imagine what he's thinking—why the bite marks on the shoulder, why the body is facedown. What is the fantasy? By the third or fourth body, you look for the pattern. By the tenth, you look for the aberration. Because in the end, that's where you'll catch him. In the aberration. In the one that's different. That's where he'll reveal himself."

Blanton stared at the table for a long moment, then began speaking without looking up. "We found her forty-eight hours after he finished with her. The others, it was as much as a year later, because they were whores or crack addicts and no one noticed they were gone. We needed forensic dentists to tell us who they were. But this girl was fifteen and when she went missing, people noticed. We broke out da hounds and went out into the swamp and found her. I'd been here three weeks . . .

"He only had sex with this victim once. The rest was the same, the beating, the tire iron, dragging her by the hair, the posing. But only one sexual assault. And only while she was alive. Why? What's different?"

Again, Blanton seemed to lose his concentration. "We tested the contents of her stomach. You know what we found?"

Caroline shook her head no.

"One of them cinnamon rolls from the mall. You got them up in Spokane, them cinnamon roll shops?" He pronounced it Spok-UN this time. She thought he did it without thinking, as if screwing around with people was a habit, like chewing his nails. He waved his empty glass at the bartender again, and when the bartender brought another drink he handed over a credit card. "That's it for me." He raised his eyebrows to Caroline, but she still hadn't finished her Gibson, and she shook her head no.

"So tell me about my guy," he said.

Her throat was hoarse. "Your guy?"

"Yeah. Why did he only have sex with this victim once? What was the difference? The aberration? What went wrong with the fantasy?"

Caroline searched her mind for details from his book, trying to come to the kind of conclusions about the guy's psychology that Blanton seemed to draw so effortlessly from the evidence. But she felt so tired, so overwhelmed all of a sudden, so weary from trying to stand up to it, that she couldn't picture anything from his book, just a cloud of assumption and bad science. All she could think about was movements, patterns, currents of flow, where people had been and where they were going.

"I guess," she began, "I think . . . he bought her a cinnamon roll."

Blanton looked surprised. "Why do you say that?"

"You said he raped her when she was alive. For the cinnamon roll to be in her system still, she must've eaten it just before . . ." She tailed off. "So I'd say it's his mall, not hers."

"Yeah," Blanton said. "That's right. The mall wasn't close to her house and I can't imagine a girl running off to a frat party stopping for a cinnamon roll."

"So I guess," Caroline continued, "the first thing I would do is see if there's a photography shop at that mall."

Blanton cocked his head.

"You said he poses the bodies more than usual. Maybe he takes pictures," Caroline said. "Well, he can't take those to One-Hour Photo, so he must run his own darkroom. And he must buy equipment somewhere. I mean, it's a longshot, but . . ."

Blanton stared blankly.

"Then," she continued, "I'd go to the camera shops around that area and check their credit card receipts to see which customers have a history of sex crimes."

He was quiet for a moment.

"Should we do my guy now?" Caroline asked. "What did you say? Twenty-four to forty-eight. American sedan. Never married. Middle class. Some trauma involving the mother, maybe big, maybe small. Late through puberty. Classic insider/outsider."

Blanton stared at her, emotionless.

Caroline continued. "But then, that describes every one of these guys, doesn't it, Mr. Blanton? That's the standard profile. Boilerplate four out of five times. No, I'll be more curious to see what you think *after* you've read our files."

For the first time, he smiled. "All right, Ms. Mabry. I'll read your files tonight. I have to meet with the medical examiner tomorrow morning. They fished a young woman out of Lake Pontchartrain and I need to make sure it's not related to the killer down here. You-all wanna come?"

He signed the bill and she caught a glimpse of the number he wrote, sixty-eight dollars. A lot of booze.

He noticed her watching him. "I had some friends here, earlier," he said. He stood and stared down at her. "Do you want to know my theory of why women don't like baseball as much as men?"

She found herself smiling at the word "theory" and thinking of Dupree. "Sure."

"Well, of course, women can be baseball fans, but they don't inhabit the game the way men do. They don't worship the numbers. We talked about it before, the importance of the numbers. Five, nineteen, forty-nine, fifty-six. The numbers mean nothing if the fantasy isn't there. If you can't imagine yourself as the baseball player. Men do that. They're trained to do it, and even if they weren't trained, it's . . . natural. They can picture themselves playing the game. Do you understand? Even those of us who never played baseball . . . we understand the fantasy. The fantasy is all that matters. Do you see?"

"Yes."

His eyes drifted from hers to the floor. "I apologize if I made you uneasy, Ms. Mabry. At Quantico, we always had one woman in the Investigative Support Unit, but to be totally frank, I've never met a woman who contributed much to these kinds of cases. Fortunately for them, they don't have the capacity for understanding this type of killer, for understanding the fantasy."

"And you think that's essential."

He thought about it. "Yes. I do. Of course, there is a need for . . . cinnamon rolls. But in the end, you can't catch these guys if you can't conjure them up, if you can't see them in your mind."

He looked up at her with the same expectant stare he'd had when she came in, and she had the feeling that every word was a test, a cruel game. "So, can you conjure him up, Detective Mabry?" His voice dropped to a hoarse whisper. "Can y'all see your man?"

She stood, exhausted, and looked around a bar that strived so hard to remain dark. In the darkness she saw that Lenny Ryan would forever push Burn into the river while she watched helplessly, that he would turn ever so slowly to stare at her, waiting for her to do something. "Yes," she said, "I see him."

27

It wasn't long after the drunk girls joined their table that Joel felt things getting out of hand. The waif—he would have carded her in his own place—had settled onto his knee and was pretending there was nothing strange about using a guy's leg for a chair in a crowded bar. Across the table, the girl angling to be Derek's was telling one of those long, anecdotal jokes, a string of implausible coincidences about a woman whose boyfriend drives them into a muddy ditch and must use her clothes as traction to get the car out of the mud. Derek was laughing like it was the funniest story he'd ever heard, his arm around the booth behind her. Jay, too, was listening to Derek's girl's story, turning every few seconds to laugh with the girl who had been assigned him. As her story built to its improbable climax, Derek's girl slid out of the booth, stood, and removed her shoes. "So she walks up to the farmhouse and knocks on the door, buck naked." The girl held her shoes over her crotch. "'My boyfriend's stuck. Can you help get him out?'"

Joel laughed politely while the girl on his knee laughed harder, shifting her weight, catching his eye and smiling.

"God, Sandy. That is disgusting," said Jay's girl, the only one of the three with dark hair. Jay put his hand on her leg.

"That is so funny," Derek said. "That is really funny."

"Hilarious," Jay said. "Really hilarious."

They were crowded in this booth at the tail end of McCool's, a long, narrow pub with predictable Irish decor—green walls and clovers and Irish flags and maps of the island and Notre Dame banners and the rest.

"Really funny," Derek said again.

"Great," said Jay. *"My boyfriend's stuck."*

The laughter trailed into hums and smiles and then, like a football huddle that breaks to reveal the formation, the three girls turned separately to the guys they were sitting near and engaged in single conversations.

"What do you do?" asked the girl on Joel's knee.

"Bartender."

"Really?"

"No, I just say it to impress people."

"That's cool." She nodded at the leg she sat on. "You're not married?"

"No, but I'm seeing someone."

"Where's she?"

"Out of town." Joel wondered why he'd told her that. Why not *She's at home*, or, *We're meeting her later*? He felt transparent. Why did there have to be this gap between who you are and who you want to be? He finished his drink and moved the girl off his leg so he could stand. "I'm gonna get a drink," he said. "You want something?"

"A Manhattan?"

Of course. These days, everyone drank martinis and martini derivations. Three years ago, Joel's job had consisted of jerking beer taps, but now every college student wanted to drink like a salesman. Booze had come back because things just naturally come back, and so now you had frat boys lecturing you on what kind of gin they wanted and clear-eyed twenty-one-year-old girls ordering Manhattans. It was funny. That had been the thing about Caroline that first caught his attention, when she ordered a Gibson, one of the few booze drinks that hadn't come back.

When Joel mixed her a vodka Gibson, she spoke to him like he was a ten-year-old, instructing him on the proper mix of a Gibson, right down to the number of cocktail onions. So, when she asked for a refill, he brought a pint of gin in a beer pitcher with fifteen cocktail onions strung in a necklace, looped around the rim of the pitcher, like booze-soaked pearls.

At the bar, Joel pulled his money roll from his pocket and peeled off a couple of bills. He watched the bartender, a bald guy with decent concentration, if not the best technique, fill a row of glasses with ice. He could tell from the moment the ice went in that this place short-poured, filled the glasses mostly with ice and mixer and went light on whatever booze they were serving up. He looked up at the better bottles, stacked along the bar like guys in bleacher seats. Usually if a place short-poured, it practiced other kinds of cheapness, too—watering down the booze or mixing the cheap brands with the good bottles, blending the plastic-bottled gin with the Bombay or the cheap whiskey with the Glenfiddich. Hell, some twenty-two-year-old kid ordering eighteen-year-old scotch isn't going to know the difference. Maybe people get what they deserve.

"What can I get you?"

"A Manhattan, a shot of Knob Creek, and a glass of ice on the side." Joel was going to make sure he got his entire shot of whiskey. "That *is* Knob Creek in that bottle, right? Or should I order something else?"

The bartender considered him briefly. "No, that's a good choice."

The drinks ordered, Joel turned his back and surveyed the bar, the same thing every other guy in the world did when he ordered a drink. More disappointment. As he turned to the left he saw a man at a small table staring at him and it took a minute to recognize Caroline's friend Alan Dupree sitting by himself with a drink in front of him. Dupree raised his drink in a short salute.

"Hey." Joel walked over. Dupree likely had seen that girl sitting on his lap and Joel felt a moment of panic. "How's it goin'?"

"Good," Dupree said. "How about you?"

"You know. Buddies are gettin' a little wild."

He looked back at the bar, but the bartender was still fussing with the limes in a couple of G-and-Ts. "I don't know if you saw, you know, that girl, I mean . . ."

"Yeah, I saw her. She's cute."

"I didn't do anything, she just sat on my knee."

Dupree nodded and Joel detected in the movement a kind of disappointment, as if he wished he'd seen Joel hitting on the girl. "Heard anything from Caroline?"

"She's not big on calling." Joel looked over at the table, then back at Dupree. "Hey, do you want to join us?"

Dupree looked over at the girls, and Joel thought he saw the older man sigh. "That's nice. But I have kind of an important meeting in the morning. Thanks anyway. But if you talk to Caroline . . ." He stared at the empty drink in front of him. "Go on back to your friends. I'll talk to her when she gets back."

Joel began to edge away. "Okay," he said. "Well . . . take it easy."

Joel got his drinks and left a buck tip on the bar. On his way back to the table, he snagged a chair, disappointing the waif, who fanned a couple of singles in his direction. He shook her off and sat down on the new chair at the end of the table.

When he looked back down the length of the bar, Joel saw Dupree edging through a crowd of people. The wiry detective reached the door, went outside, and stood beneath the streetlight, staring at the sidewalk. And in that moment, Joel pictured himself on that sidewalk, at forty-five, balding and losing his form. Suddenly the very struggle of Joel's life seemed both predetermined and petty, like a lab mouse in blind pursuit of one of two paths, solitude or settlement. As he watched, Joel couldn't imagine a way out and felt a chill inevitability, the claustrophobia of age.

The door swung closed and Dupree was gone. Joel drank his shot of whiskey and turned back to the table, where Derek's girl was starting another joke: "There was this girl who had fish for tits . . ."

28

Bourbon after midnight was a thin but enthusiastic stream of staggering idiots, listing down the center of the street in puddles of booze and water that bubbled up from overworked sewer grates. The crowd was overwhelmingly male. They took off their shirts, danced outside taverns, and formed lines in front of store-front windows where bartenders sold plastic "To-Geaux" cups containing every imaginable mixture of poisons. The street surged with men, the young and the old marked by their inability to handle alcohol, the rest blurring into one type, something between twenty-five and fifty, shuffling along with the same look of buzzed horniness, joints lubricated, eyes glazed, but their ability to function at least still arguable. One swerved in front of Caroline, bleary-eyed and weaving, his lips glistening with what-ever he'd just drunk from the Big Gulp glass in his hand. "Hey, where we headed tonight?"

Caroline stepped carefully around him and continued down Bourbon. When she'd checked in yesterday, the desk clerk had assured Caroline that June was "slow" in the quarter: no festivals, the college students either gone home for summer or still taking finals. The weather was too hot and muggy for sustained debauchery, the clerk said, and so New Orleans in June offered a kind of bucolic sentience, a sluggish old-South charm.

"Show us your tits!" It came from a group of tall young men facing her from the street—possibly a team of some kind—and at first Caroline paused on the sidewalk, pondering it, the idea of shocking them and herself. Hell, she'd have done it when she was in college. But the fleeting thought was replaced by lingering disgust from her conversation with Blanton, which was replaced by the urge to shoot the young men. It took her a few minutes to realize they weren't even talking to her, that the team was looking above her, to a balcony. Caroline stepped from underneath the balcony and looked up, to where, among twenty or so drunk revelers, a group of young women leaned over the balcony, dancing and holding their hands out for the Mardi Gras beads that served as currency even after the festival season.

One girl, earnest in the face and Thanksgiving plump, hoisted her shirt eagerly, and the team whooped and hollered, pelting her bare chest with two-dollar strings of beads. Another girl made more of a production, swinging her hips and teasingly revealing one breast at a time, then both in a flair of showmanship. She got even more beads.

What am I doing out here? Caroline wondered. After the meeting with Blanton she hadn't been able to sleep, too haunted by his photograph of the fifteen-year-old victim, and so at 2 A.M. she'd gotten out of bed and opened the phone book, looking for cinnamon roll shops at the local malls. She wrote down three of them on hotel stationery and cross-referenced these malls with photography shops.

She'd gone back to bed, but still couldn't sleep. She'd gotten up, put on a pair of sweatpants, and gone outside, planning to walk along the river. But outside her hotel she heard the music and cheers of Bourbon Street two blocks away and had walked down here, merging into the crowd along a stretch of storefronts that promised live sex shows. Was it simply her cop training that drew her to the sound of an out-of-control party or was it something else, something connected to this thing she was chasing, this troubling idea that had begun to form inside her head?

It had started with the fatalism of the prostitute Jacqueline, and now found voice in the unflinching depravity that Curtis Blanton described. Police, like popular culture, liked to imagine serial killers as a nonnegotiable evil. There was a book on these guys, containing the details that Blanton had quoted to her: single, twenty-four to forty-eight, and so on. These things, in combination with other factors, created a monster, a thing *out of the norm*, superhuman, the bogeyman: Jeffrey Dahmer, Ted Bundy, Hannibal Lecter. Ghost stories to keep your fifteen-year-old from going out at night.

But the book itself troubled Caroline. Twenty-four to forty-eight? Single? Problems with relationships, with intimacy? Unresolved issues involving their mothers? Every man that Caroline had ever known had the urge to be single, had problems with intimacy, and wouldn't meet her eyes when talking about his mother.

What had Jacqueline said when Caroline asked which guys gave her the creeps? *"Ma'am, they all give me the creeps."* Caroline recalled the list of bad dates, guys who bit and punched and pulled hair and forced themselves on her. These were just men, not monsters. Bankers and salesmen and ranchers and biology teachers. Cops, presumably, and bartenders.

It was that list of bad dates that haunted Caroline as she thought about Curtis Blanton's conviction that only a man could catch a serial killer. The ramifications of what Blanton was saying were inescapable: A serial killer was not an aberration, but an amplification of male fantasy. Maybe there were no monsters. Maybe every man who looked at a *Penthouse* was essentially embarking on the same path that ended with some guy beating a woman to death and violating her with a lug wrench. No wonder Blanton was dubious of Caroline's role in the investigation. If she couldn't imagine the violent fantasy, what could she imagine? The victim. The fear. And what good were those?

Caroline watched the team of young men stare at the balcony, their mouths open slightly, their bodies taut and expectant. On the balcony a new girl had emerged, or rather had been pushed: young and thin, in jeans and T-shirt, her head lolling to the side, her body limp. Behind her, an older guy—maybe twice her age—propped her up, one arm around her waist, the other lifting her arm to wave at the crowd. The girl opened her eyes and smiled back at the man holding her, but then her head fell back against his chest, her eyes closed. The man lifted her shirt and ran his hand along her small breasts, and the team went crazy. The cheers awoke the girl and she smiled again at the man holding her on the balcony, then looked down at the boys on the street, then allowed her head to fall back into his chest. The boys threw beads and the man reached down and grabbed a handful, draped them over her chest. Then he lifted her shirt and rubbed her breasts again. The girl grinned sleepily, eyes closed, head moving in small circles.

"Show us her pussy!" yelled one of the boys on the team.

Caroline began walking down the street, but stopped and looked back over her shoulder at the group of boys standing in the middle of the street. Finally, she turned and made her way purposefully through the crowd into the bar beneath the balcony. It was packed and it took a couple of minutes to negotiate the pawing hands to the back of the building, where the staircase was blocked by a red velvet rope. Next to the rope, a huge man in a wooden chair waved his fingers up and down like he was fanning her.

"Let's see 'em," he said.

Caroline's hands were pulled tight into fists. "What?"

He raised his eyes to the ceiling. "That's my balcony." He pointed to her chest. "People expect me to put on a good show. So let's see what you got." He had several strands of beads in his lap and he held one up for her.

Caroline just stared at him.

He reached for her shirt. "Come on. If you afraid to show me, then what good you gonna do me up there?"

She pushed his hand aside and spoke clearly and plainly. "There's a girl up there who looks about sixteen years old."

The guy just stared at her.

"And there's a forty-year-old guy undressing and fondling her for the crowd."

Still, he stared.

"I'm an off-duty police officer and I'm hoping to stay off-duty. So what do you say we take care of this and you keep me from making a phone call?"

The guy sighed, got off his chair, and lowered the rope. They climbed the steps and emerged in a dark hallway with ornate wooden doors on each side. At the end of the hallway she could see the silhouettes of swaying dancers and hear the cheering below.

The doorman chattered as they moved down the hall. "I can tell ya, they ain't no underage females in here. We card very aggressive, ma'am, very aggressive."

They emerged on the narrow balcony, crowded with people swaying and swinging mugs of beer and daiquiris, the women lifting their shirts and reaching for strings of beads thrown from the street. Caroline pushed past the doorman and through the tightly packed group of people. She found the plump girl and her friend, but couldn't find the girl who just a minute ago had been on the verge of passing out.

She glanced down at the team, still gathered on the street. Down there, they were so tall, their body language so insistent and demanding. But from this angle, their upturned faces were the simple faces of boys. She turned away.

"Har!" A thin guy in glasses stepped in front of her, revealing the wide smile of the hopelessly drunk. "Har-rar-u?" Caroline squeezed past him.

"I don't see no sixteen-year-olds," the doorman said stupidly.

Caroline looked around the hallway. "What's behind these doors."

"Hotel rooms, ma'am."

"You have a master key?"

He grinned out one side of his mouth. "You wanna go into all them rooms, I 'spect you gonna have to make that phone call."

Caroline left the doorman and returned to the balcony. She found the plump girl, who had adopted the more patient dance of her friend, one breast at a time. Caroline grabbed her arm and she turned nervously, as if she expected to see her mother.

Caroline yelled into her ear above the music. "There was a girl standing next to you! Wearing jeans and a T-shirt! Very drunk, like she was going to pass out!"

The girl turned to face Caroline, her cheap plastic beads jangling. "Is she in trouble or something?"

"I don't know!" Caroline said. "Did you see her leave? With an older guy?"

"They went downstairs for another drink!" The girl smiled. "To loosen her up!"

Caroline left the balcony again and ran past the doorman, who was now bored with the whole thing. "That it, ma'am?"

Caroline spoke to him without slowing down. "If that girl is harmed in any way, I'll have this place shut down."

The doorman hurried to catch up but didn't say anything.

At the top of the stairs, Caroline paused and took in the crowded bar. Thick wooden beams held up the ceiling and made it hard to see the whole room. She finished descending the stairs and pressed through the crowd, from table to table, until she reached a small booth on the wall facing Bourbon Street. Sitting at the booth were two couples, facing each other, including the man and woman that Caroline had seen on the balcony. The woman was older than Caroline had imagined, maybe twenty-five, the man younger, maybe thirty-five. They were both laughing as they related for their friends their brief moment of balcony stardom. The woman was covered in Mardi Gras beads. Her head bobbed drunkenly as she spoke and a white string of spittle connected her lips, but she was very much conscious, very much an adult.

"It made me seasick being up there," she said, slurring the words to something like *thea-thick*. "Fucker hasn't been that interested in my tits since our honeymoon!"

The man defended himself. "Hey, you're the one who wanted to go up there . . ."

"I'm kiddin', babe." The drunk woman fell against her husband's shoulder and he kissed her gently on the top of her head.

The husband noticed Caroline then, standing at their table. He turned toward her. "Hey," he said, "can we get another round?"

Caroline nodded, then walked away from the table and left the bar. Outside, she made her way down the sidewalk until she hit the first cross street, left Bourbon, and walked with her hands in her pockets down an increasingly quiet side street, past pawnshops and bookstores, the noise and grate of Bourbon Street fading behind her. She walked until she'd reached the Cafe du Monde, the all-night coffee shop in the French Market, where she sat and caught her breath and had a cafe au lait, thinking about the unreliability of human perception and memory. She thought of a robbery victim she'd once interviewed: The woman spent ten minutes describing the man who'd broken into her house, and it wasn't until Caroline held up the police artist's sketch that she realized it matched almost perfectly a photograph on the mantel of the woman's dead son. She supposed some people see what they want, others what they dread.

Caroline sat in the wrought-iron chair, watching the waiters in their dirty paper hats. The air was moist and smelled slightly septic. About twenty people were in the cafe—groups of men taking the edge off good drunks, couples in serious conversation, lonely men with newspapers and novels and sketchbooks. Men. Not monsters.

Caroline finished her coffee and left, walking until she reached the levee along the northwest bank of the Mississippi. A light wind moved with the river, seemingly at the same pace, stirring the thick, soupy air. She was relieved to be along a river, even one as broad and languid as this. Maybe she could stay here the rest of the night.

After her father had left the family, Caroline's mother suffered bouts of insomnia that became progressively worse. Caroline remembered the heightened anxiety of her mother's 2 A.M. phone calls. She would begin speaking before Caroline even answered, so that it seemed her mother was starting mid-sentence, some hyperspeed version of herself, apologizing for a long-forgotten remark, obsessing over the menu for an approaching holiday meal at which it would just be she and Caroline, offering names—boy names and girl names—for Caroline's future children. Maxwell and Corinna. Blake and Sandra. Caroline would listen patiently as her mother exhausted two or three topics and then started on television programs or something she'd seen that day in the newspaper. "Go to sleep," Caroline would say.

"Can't," her mother would answer, "too tired to sleep," her voice pained and manic, "too much to do."

Caroline's own insomnia had begun after her mother died, when she awoke one morning at three and imagined the phone was ringing. In her confusion, Caroline imagined it was her mother on the phone, asking whether Caroline thought soup could be served in the pasta bowls she'd brought home from Genoa, or whether Tracy was a better name for a boy baby or a girl baby. But when she got up the phone wasn't ringing, and she couldn't help thinking she'd missed the call somehow.

Since that night, Caroline had stayed awake all night at least once a week. She wouldn't mind so much, but when she got up the phone was never ringing and her mother was never on the other end. So she paced around or wrote notes to herself or went for walks, until she was raw with fatigue, ready to debate the names of children who would never exist or to plan the Labor Day dinner. Or, she supposed, to mistake a married couple on a balcony for a man molesting a girl.

Caroline had mentioned her insomnia to Dr. Ewing, the police psychologist, who told Caroline it was perfectly normal considering the pressure she'd been under: her mother's death, her relationship with Joel, the trouble with Lenny Ryan and Thick Jay, her unresolved guilt over shooting the wife beater six years ago, and, of course, this case.

This case. It had its own irrational and manic voices— Dupree, Jacqueline, and now Blanton—which had replaced the voice of her mother's insomnia. These voices kept Caroline awake tonight, Blanton stressing the elemental importance of the male sexual fantasy, Jacqueline talking about the man who pulled her hair, Dupree's theory of Lenny Ryan spinning out of control like a top. And other voices, ripples on her subconscious.

Her brother: "I'm not like you, Caroline." And her father: "You all right, baby?"

She walked until she reached a park bench overlooking the Mississippi. From here, the river didn't seem so different from the Spokane. All waters are connected, of course. Burn might as well be in this river as in the Spokane, or the Nile or the Indian Ocean for that matter. And her mother too. Eventually, the water rises up and claims us all and we float away. That fact was inescapable in a city like New Orleans, a city built below the sea. In a city like that, you can't bury people in the ground and so you shove the bodies into family crypts, two-hundred-year-old marble and granite casings that might hold the remains of a hundred people. They just open the crypt, slide the old dust and bones to the back, and put in the next body. The oldest cemetery in New Orleans was called the City of the Dead and from a distance, that's what a person saw, a skyline of crypts and statuary that became, up close, a rough assemblage of exposed brick and chipped granite. The cemetery had been full for years and was useful now only as a tourist attraction and a place for muggers to hide in the shadows of the crypts.

Let the criminals have it, Caroline thought. It doesn't matter. Eventually, the water prevails, even in cities of the dead. Eventually, the water comes for us all, washes over the statues and through the crypts, topples the headstones and tumbles the graves. Caroline sat down on the park bench, too tired to sleep. There was so much to do. She curled her legs up and began rocking, turning her face to the breeze.

29

Spokane Police Dept.
Office of the Assistant Chief
Meeting Transcript

Date: 6 June, 0800 hours
Case: Serial Murder Task Force

Present at Meeting: Asst. Chief James Tucker, Major Crimes Lt. Charles
Branch, Major Crimes Sgt. Alan Dupree

[Begin transmission]

TUCKER: Okay. Is this thing on? Okay. For the record, this is Assistant
Chief James Tucker and—do you want to—

BRANCH: No, why don't you go ahead.

TUCKER: —and from Major Crimes, Lieutenant Branch. We're waiting for
Sergeant Dupree to review his status as lead investigator of the serial
killer task force and, specifically, his behavior—

BRANCH: Can we say his performance instead?

TUCKER: Yeah, that's better. Yeah. His performance, okay.

BRANCH: Because I think this is going to be hard enough without getting into, you know—

TUCKER: Personal things. Right. Okay.

BRANCH: Because he's had some personal difficulties lately and I just think—

TUCKER: Yeah, I heard. Left his wife, huh?

BRANCH: —that the more we stay away from that—

TUCKER: I couldn't agree more.

BRANCH: He's going to have enough trouble taking this—

TUCKER: Yeah. I can see that.

BRANCH: Okay.

TUCKER: And you don't think Detective Spivey should be present for this?

BRANCH: Oh, God no. Not unless you want to clean the blood off your desk.

TUCKER: Okay. You want some coffee?

BRANCH: No. Thanks.

TUCKER: Well, I guess we'll just wait for Sergeant Dupree.

[End transmission]

[Begin transmission]

DUPREE: Hi, honey. I'm home.

TUCKER: Please come in, Sergeant.

DUPREE: Probably be easier if I stayed out here and you just shot me from your desk there.

BRANCH: Hi, Alan.

DUPREE: Sit here?

TUCKER: That's fine.

DUPREE: Look, I know my report was the wrong place for that joke. I want to apologize and . . . what's with the microphone?

TUCKER: With your permission, we'd like to tape this meeting because of the nature of the discussion.

DUPREE: What nature is that?

TUCKER: Well, we try to tape personnel meetings having to do with employment status. As a precaution.

DUPREE: What the [expletive deleted] I'm being fired?

BRANCH: No one's firing you, Alan. We're just trying to get a handle on this investigation. Sit down.

TUCKER: At this time, I am providing Sergeant Dupree with—

DUPREE: [Unintelligible]

TUCKER: —a copy of a memo dated 5 June relating to—

DUPREE: Six pages? You have six pages?

BRANCH: Alan. Sit down. Let's just get this finished. Okay?

TUCKER: —relating to his performance as lead investigator of the task force investigating a series of recent homicides. As you can see, Sergeant, under the first heading, we have uncooperative and confrontational behavior toward colleagues and investigators from other agencies. Now below that heading are items one through nine detailing Sergeant Dupree's uneven and occasionally improper conduct in this area. And so on.

DUPREE: What's this one? Confrontational attitude toward other agencies?

TUCKER: I don't think we need to go over each point.

DUPREE: Just tell me about this one.

TUCKER: I think it's pretty clear. On 22 May, you sent the FBI a previously discarded lead that Lenny Ryan was seen caddying at a golf course in north Idaho and said that you couldn't investigate it because to do so would mean crossing state lines.

DUPREE: I thought it was funny. I thought the federales would appreciate it. I didn't think they'd really waste a day looking into it. You're punishing me for their stupidity?

TUCKER: And after that, you ridiculed Agent Jerry Castle for investigating the lead, a lead that you sent to his office.

DUPREE: [Unintelligible]

TUCKER: At a subsequent task force meeting, you continued mocking Agent Castle by throwing a golf ball at his leg.

DUPREE: Actually, I was aiming for Secret Agent Castle's nuts, but the target was too small.

BRANCH: Yeah, that's a good idea, Alan. Just keep joking your way out of this.

DUPREE: Where did this [expletive deleted] come from? What's this one? Failure to properly record interviews?

TUCKER: Our goal is not to go through each of these points, Sergeant Dupree. The entire report will be entered into the record of this meeting. So if we could—

DUPREE: What's this one? Failure to coordinate outside support? This is crazy.

TUCKER: Again, our intent is not to go over this entire memorandum in this meeting, Sergeant Dupree.

DUPREE: Failure to utilize necessary investigative techniques? What is that about?

BRANCH: Damn it, Alan. The fact that you don't even know what we're talking about is half the problem. We applied for a ten-thousand-dollar grant for the FBI software that set up a computer database for analyzing and prioritizing evidence and you haven't used it at all.

DUPREE: I got tips coming in that Lenny Ryan left on a spaceship. You want me to put that in the computer so it can tell me that we should be looking for a little green man? Come on, tell me where this is coming from?

TUCKER: What about the entomologist?

DUPREE: The what?

TUCKER: Another detective claims that you ignored his request to bring in an entomologist to analyze the insects and microorganisms on the victims' bodies to gather a more accurate measure of the decomposition of the bodies.

DUPREE: Spivey. That [expletive deleted]. I should've known. Spivey didn't get his bug doctor and so he came running to you. That little puke.

BRANCH: This is a different kind of investigation, Alan. We're not convinced you appreciate the full spectrum of investigative techniques at your disposal and maybe a detective with more recent investigative training—

DUPREE: I appreciate how to be a cop! I appreciate when someone's trying to clean me like a [expletive deleted] fish!

BRANCH: Alan, even if these other complaints weren't true, you have screwed up every chance to bring in a profiler—

DUPREE: Bunch of voodoo crap.

BRANCH: That's what I'm talking about. Whatever you think of its effectiveness, this kind of case requires behavioral profiling. And your antagonistic attitude toward Agent McDaniel and Curtis Blanton has kept them from consulting on our case—

DUPREE: My antagonistic attitude? Blanton told me to go [expletive deleted] myself until we got to [expletive deleted] double digits! My [expletive deleted] attitude?

TUCKER: The purpose of this meeting is not to debate the merits of these points, Sergeant Dupree, nor is it to hear your quite impressive range of profanities, but to provide you with the rationale used in deciding to replace you as lead investigator.

DUPREE: Replace me? So what do I do now?

BRANCH: That's up to you, Alan. If you want to continue as an investigator on the task force, under a probationary period—

DUPREE: What about this one? Provided the public with false and misleading information at a crime scene? What's that?

TUCKER: On 28 April, while responding to a homicide at the home of Leonard Ryan's uncle, you in fact told a television reporter that the victim had been castrated and that his heart had been extracted from his body.

DUPREE: [Unintelligible]

TUCKER: Sergeant, could you speak into the microphone?

DUPREE: I said [expletive deleted] Spivey that little [expletive deleted].

BRANCH: Come on, Alan. Sit down.

DUPREE: So who's taking over the task force?

BRANCH: Alan, I don't think—

DUPREE: Are you bringing someone in from outside? Or are you going to promote someone? Pollard?

TUCKER: We're promoting Detective Spivey—

DUPREE: He's [unintelligible] ten years old!

BRANCH: He's thirty-one, Alan.

DUPREE: He's an idiot.

BRANCH: Spivey didn't come to us, Alan.

TUCKER: We asked him for an assessment of your performance and McDaniel likes him. McDaniel will work with him.

DUPREE: I thought I was training him.

BRANCH: Frankly, Alan, I had hoped when I paired the two of you that you might benefit as much from his recent training—

DUPREE: What?

BRANCH: —especially his expertise in the areas of evidence recovery and forensics.

DUPREE: I don't . . . This is . . .

TUCKER: Sergeant Dupree, the task force's failure to apprehend Mr. Ryan or, quite frankly, to provide enough evidence to prosecute him if he is arrested would be enough to replace you at this point. Those things coupled with your failure to—

DUPREE: You don't understand. This guy Ryan, he's like a black hole, like this concentrated darkness, like a top—

TUCKER: Time will be provided at the end of this meeting for you to defend your behavior—

BRANCH: —performance.

TUCKER: Right, your performance.

DUPREE: I don't know what to . . . I've never been fired before.

BRANCH: I told you, no one is being fired.

DUPREE: You give all you have to a job and you wake up one morning and everything [unintelligible]—

TUCKER: Detective Spivey has made it clear you can continue with the task force if you like.

DUPREE: This is hilarious.

BRANCH: Or you can return to the Major Crimes Unit and your previous assignment.

DUPREE: No. No. If you don't want me on this thing, then put me back in a car.

BRANCH: Alan, let's not make this worse than it is.

DUPREE: I've apparently made it as bad as it can be. No, you want me off this case, I'll just ride out the rest of my time on patrol.

TUCKER: Sergeant Dupree. Sit down. I promise, you will have time for rebuttal.

DUPREE: Put me back on the street. You guys win. Motion passed. Vote is unanimous. Let's move on to new business.

TUCKER: Put the microphone down, Sergeant.

DUPREE: Point of parliamentary procedure. Motion for consent decree. Meeting is adjourned.

BRANCH: Alan, come on—

DUPREE: Where does this thing lead?

TUCKER: Sergeant Dupree, put the microphone cord down.

DUPREE: Ah, there it is—

[Transmission ceased]

30

"Okay, now apply the models of pre- and post-offense behavior to your guy."

Caroline was lost. "I'm sorry."

"The models." Blanton gritted his teeth and turned away from the steering wheel briefly. "The models. What were we just talking about?"

"Organized and disorganized crime scenes."

"That's right."

Caroline concentrated, tapping her pencil against the yellow legal pad as Blanton cornered in his rental car and McDonald's wrappers flew from one side of the car to the other. Curtis Blanton seemed more energetic today, and also more patient, although patience on him came across as somewhat forced and manipulative, pushing her to the things she needed to know. His speech today was flat and gave no hint of Cajun inflection or dialect. He also seemed absent-minded, a trait that didn't exactly complement his tendency to drive like someone on speed. The combination was like taking a college class from a stoned professor while trying to elude the police.

"Remember this when you go back to Spokane," he said, his

pronunciation of the city perfect once again. "Disorganization is different from impulse. Your guy could be impulsive and still be organized. The tools, for instance, can be in his car at all times, showing a planning stage, while the predatory behavior itself— the choosing of the victim; in other words, the hunting—can still be spur-of-the-moment."

The light changed to yellow and Blanton stepped on the gas until it became clear the car ahead of him was planning to stop. He stabbed at the brakes, and soda cans and McDonald's trash flew forward as the car squealed to a stop.

Caroline ignored his driving. "I'd say he is both organized and impulsive."

"How is he organized?"

"There seems to be a preparation stage. He stores the bodies, washing the hands with bleach, breaking off the fingernails. And then, of course, he puts money in the girls' hands. And he covers them with branches and debris."

"Good. What about impulsive behavior?"

"Well, when we find a body, he seems to need to replace it with another."

"Right." Blanton looked over at her. "Good. That is the key behavior. The replacement of bodies. I saw that with my guy in the Pacific Coast Highway case. Killing and then storing and then moving the bodies when he needs them. These bodies are his tools, his chess pieces. That's what the fingernails and the money is about. Your guy feels a need to communicate through these bodies."

She winced every time Blanton called the killer "your guy." She supposed that was partly because of the fact that she felt a very real responsibility for Lenny Ryan, for blowing the drug bust in the park and allowing him to escape.

The light changed and Blanton was quickly around the cautious driver and had the car flying again. "So why does your guy leave forty bucks on these women?"

"So the world knows these are hookers he's killing."

"And why does he replace the bodies?"

"He wants people to see what he's done?"

"People?" Blanton ran the car up over the curb and into a small parking lot. "What people?"

"I don't know. Everyone."

The funeral home was a two-story, white building with huge pillars in front and two hearses parked bumper-to-bumper along the side. Blanton parked next to the hearses and they climbed out. He looked over the car at her. "Think about which people he wants to notice."

Caroline followed Blanton past the hearses to a narrow side staircase that led to a basement door. He beat on the door with his open hand. A droopy-eyed white man in his fifties, wearing a long, shiny gray apron and matching shiny gloves, pushed open the heavy door. They followed him into the dark basement hallway.

"Hey, Curty," said the man. "How you been?"

"Hey, Russell." Blanton dropped right back into his wet delta drawl. "This here's Agent Mabry. Specialist from Washington."

Caroline looked curiously over at Blanton, wondering why he would imply she was an FBI agent, but he didn't meet her eyes.

Russell gave her a slight bow. "It is my pleasure to meet you and let me say you a pretty lady for a gub'ment man."

"Russell's that rare gen-a-man who can be embalmin' one minute and flirtin' the very next," Blanton said.

"Ren'ssance man," said Russell.

"The ME here yet?"

"No, sir," Russell said. "He called and say he be 'bout an hour yet. It's just you and me. And the lady, of course."

They followed Russell through a metal door into an ice-cold embalming room, with two deep, stainless-steel gurneys wheeled up against the wall. What looked like an old reclining barber chair leaned against the opposite wall, and Caroline had turned to nod at the old man sitting in it when she realized the man reclining in the chair was dead. He was naked, covered with a thin blanket, everything about him pinched and wrinkled and pale. The fingers on his left hand were clenched in a rigor fist, but the right hand was reaching out, like he'd died shaking hands. The fingers had apparently stiffened in perfect position to hold a Coca-Cola.

Blanton followed her eyes. "Russell, you-all . . . uh . . . your friend, there."

"Oh geez. M' cupholder. I'm sorry." Russell walked over and took the Coke from the dead man's hand.

All three of them stared at the dead man still, and Russell clucked with his tongue and took a drink of his Coke. "Eighty-one years old. Died in his sleep night 'fore last. We should all be so lucky, eh Curty?" Russell pushed the dead man's hand down but it popped right back up. Russell ran his hand over the man's rooster hair. "I gotta help these nice people, here, Mr. Beauchamp. I'll be with you in jus' a minute."

Caroline tried to make eye contact with Blanton but he was looking at Mr. Beauchamp with a cocked head, staring into the dead man's empty eyes. He noticed Caroline watching him and shuffled his feet. "I can't remember the last time I saw someone who died of old age," Blanton whispered.

Russell left Mr. Beauchamp and shuffled over to another door. "You wanna wait for that ME then?"

"Naw," Blanton said. "Ain't gonna hurt nothin' if we just take a little look," He turned to Caroline. "If you wanna wait out here . . ."

"I'm fine," Caroline said.

Russell offered them each some VapoRub and they spread it on their upper lips, beneath their noses, to combat the smell. They went through another metal door to a smaller room, with a large stainless-steel tub in the center of the room and rust-colored streaks leading to a drain in the floor. The body was in the tub, covered with a plastic sheet. Even with the Vicks on her lip the smell choked Caroline, reminded her of the formaldehyde and decay of her college biology lab.

"I don't guess this is going to do much for my insomnia," Caroline said quietly.

Blanton turned and gave her a strange, understanding smile, and she wondered what *his* dreams must look like.

"Girl was in the water at least two days," Russell said. "Didn't bloat so much, which is the su'prisin' thing with the heat and all, but then she jus' float along, right beneath the surface and soak up half the damn lake. Weigh t'other side of two hundred pound when they finally fished her out."

Blanton pulled on a pair of rubber gloves and offered another pair to Caroline but she shook her head no. Russell and Blanton stepped toward the body, but Caroline stayed back a step. The plastic sheet was pulled away and Caroline watched Blanton for a reaction, but saw none. She looked past Blanton to the girl's feet—one of which was still contained in a tennis shoe. A Reebok. An old one. Like the kind Caroline used to wear to her aerobics class.

"Excuse me," Caroline said. She turned and left the room and walked to the embalming room. She sat down in a chair with her back to Mr. Beauchamp, pulled out her notebook, and continued making notes of her conversation with Blanton.

Blanton and Russell were in with the girl for about ten minutes. When they returned, Blanton peeling off his rubber gloves, Russell finishing his Coke, they both seemed embarrassed. Caroline could tell they'd been talking about her, and she felt as if she'd flunked some test by leaving the room, as if she were no longer the specialist from Washington, D.C., but just some squeamish girl from Washington State.

"I apologize for my insensitivity earlier, Miss Mabry," Russell said. "I forget myself down here, sometimes."

"No apology necessary," Caroline said. She turned to Blanton and tried to speak the way he would. "Not your guy."

"No," Blanton said, the drawl put away again. "No signs of sexual assault or violence. There was enough water in her lungs to wash a car. She just drowned. The family doesn't want an autopsy, 'cause they don't want to know what drugs she was on."

"So there won't be an autopsy?"

"That's up to the medical examiner."

Russell walked them to the door and bowed good-bye to Caroline. Blanton was quiet while they walked to the car.

She sat down and picked up her yellow legal pad where she'd left it on the floor of the car. Blanton turned the key to start the car, but then turned to face her. "Ms. Mabry, have you considered getting off that case in your city?"

"I'm sorry?"

"No one will blame you. And they'll find your guy without you. But there's a very good reason I don't see very many women investigators on cases like this. It's not natural, standing over the bodies of women who have been raped and murdered and even drowned. But if you can't face up to it . . ."

Caroline interrupted him. "Did you read about the kid I tried to save?"

"I'm not implying that you can't do the job . . ."

"That's exactly what you were implying." Caroline felt some need to explain herself. "The kid I tried to save, the kid who was selling drugs to Lenny Ryan, did you read about that in the report?"

Blanton sighed, turned forward, and shifted the car. He began driving away from the funeral home. "Yes, of course. On the dam."

"Right. His hand hit mine and for just a second, I thought I had him, but actually he was pulling *me*." She felt a chill just describing it. "And I . . . I tried to hold him. But maybe I let go. Maybe I was too scared by the river."

"Is that what you think?"

"I don't know. I thought I did everything I could. But your mind won't let it go, plays it in all these different ways. You start to wonder. I mean, they never recovered the body. I think of that kid in the water all this time, and I feel terrible. And I think of what would've happened if he'd pulled me with him."

Caroline jerked her head toward the funeral home. "Back there, when he pulled the sheet off, I could see by her shoe that she wasn't killed by your guy."

"Her shoe?"

"You said he poses the bodies. He's a perfectionist. He's not going to leave one shoe on. And I guess the truth . . ." She sighed. "The truth is that I just didn't need to see another body, Mr. Blanton, especially a drowning victim. My dreams are specific enough." She turned to look out the window. "Now if you think that makes me weak . . ."

They drove in silence, Caroline staring out her window as they passed grand homes with dark vines climbing the gated walls and wrought-iron porches.

"Did he watch you?"

She turned back. "Hmm?"

"Your killer. Mr. Ryan. Did he watch you try to save the young drug dealer?"

"I don't know. I guess I never thought about it."

"Well, if he did, what do you think he felt, watching you do that?"

Caroline tried to imagine what he was proposing, but her thoughts were like a dense fog. "I guess I don't follow—"

"You said he gave you a choice. Arrest him or save the boy. Okay, after that, you don't think he watched you try to save that dealer? And if he did watch that, you don't think he felt something?"

Caroline tried to picture herself from Ryan's vantage point on the other side of the footbridge, looking down, seeing her hanging by the catwalk, swinging by her legs while Burn's body slipped over the foaming edge of the dam.

"Your guy is very distinctive. I have to tell you, when I read the report, I was somewhat confused, Ms. Mabry. The combination of behaviors he exhibits is unlike any serial murderer I've encountered, or rather, like many of them. The fingernails and the money, the preparation of the bodies, the movement of them, the tokenism, the changing fantasy, sometimes posing, sometimes acting out; the only thing that doesn't change is the rage. He nearly breaks their necks with his hands *and then* he shoots them. That sort of overkill, Ms. Mabry, is a sign of great anger, a tremendous urge for retaliation."

After not sleeping all night, Caroline felt sleepy, at least two steps behind.

"Crimes like this are committed along a psychological continuum," Blanton said, running his hand along the dashboard. "At one end is excitation. Sex. At the other end is pure anger, retaliation against a symbolic victim. So where does your guy fall?"

When Caroline didn't answer, he continued.

"In none of his murders has he left any semen. That, in itself, is notable. Whatever excitation is present early on quickly becomes retaliation. Rage. Your Mr. Ryan was in love with a prostitute. So he longs for prostitutes. But when he went to prison, she returned to being a whore, to sleeping with other men, and he hates her for that. He hates whores and he longs for whores. He couldn't save his girlfriend and now these other whores can't be saved either. And at some point when he's with them, he knows they will go off to sleep with other men. And he can't take that.

"Let's say that when he picks up the first one, he intends to have sex with her. He can't do it. He can't orgasm. He has slid along that continuum from sex to rage and so he breaks her neck and finds his . . . release in that. Afterward, he doesn't even want the money from the transaction. He hides the body along the river, and the next opportunity he has to pick up one of these women, he repeats the cycle. So you have bodies number one and two. My guess is that there are more like this you haven't even found yet. So far, it's unremarkable. The fantasy is moving along a standard continuum." He turned to face her. "But what did I say, where do we catch these guys?"

She thought back. "In the aberration."

"That's right. So where is the aberration? What is different? What changes?"

"I don't . . . after we find the first body, he changes. He replaced the body we found along the river with a new one."

"That's right. That's right. The entire fantasy changed. Something caused him to change, something happened that makes him want to show the bodies off, to use the bodies to communicate with the outside world, to replace the ones that the police find with new bodies. To begin killing other people—his uncle, the pawnshop owner. So what is that trigger? What happened to Lenny Ryan that changed him? Who is he trying to communicate with, Ms. Mabry?"

Caroline covered her mouth. "Oh, my God."

Blanton drove slowly, maybe ten miles per hour, along the shoulder of the road. The slower he drove the faster he spoke.

"He watched you try to save that boy and he was moved. He changed for you. He plants bodies for you to find. He led you down an alley to show you a body and after you found it he went to get another whore. And which one did he go after? Jacqueline, a girl you'd recently talked to. Don't you see? He's acting out your initial meeting, giving you the opportunity to save these people."

Caroline's breathing felt shallow and rushed.

"You said he replaces the bodies because he wants people to see. That's right. Now keep going. Who does he want to see? Who does he think can save these hookers? Who does he wish could go back and save his girlfriend?"

Her voice was rusty and weak. "Me?"

"Yeah," Blanton said. "You."

31

Lenny Ryan's beard was coming in nicely. He turned from side to side, dragging his fingers through the thick, dark whiskers. He finished running the razor over his bald head, and when it was shaved clean, wiped off the rest of the shaving cream with a towel. He put his glasses back on and considered his face in the mirror—like a reverse portrait of himself, no hair on top, lots of hair on his chin, the weakest prescription of glasses he could find. When he was done, he held up the driver's license and turned side to side, checking it against the picture of Angela's ex-husband, David Nickell, a bald man with glasses and a beard.

He heard Angela outside the bathroom. "Gene? You 'bout done in there?"

He came out and she was standing there in her bathrobe, smiling at him. She rubbed his bald head. "You take longer in the bathroom than a damn woman."

He watched her walk into the bathroom. He didn't like heavy-set women but there was something about Angela that made him feel good, made him feel safe and unhurried. He walked into the kitchen and pulled on a pair of boots. That was the best thing about meeting Angela at the truck stop that night. Her husband had run off in such a hurry, he'd left not only his driver's license but his car and most of his clothes too, and damn if they didn't mostly fit, except the pants, which were a little loose in the waist and a little too short. But these boots were great; whatever eventually happened with Angela, he was going to keep these boots.

He went out. He liked stepping outside and not hearing any cars, just the hum of the single power line and the clicks and whispers of the woods around Angela's cinder-block cabin. The house was an hour north of the city, in a narrow valley where the farmhouses and trailers were spaced almost a mile apart along the highway; the minute he saw it, Lenny remembered how much he liked the country.

It was warm already, the sun baking down between the pine and fir trees. He trudged across the dirt driveway toward the chicken house, reached over, and unlatched the hook. Inside the pen, alfalfa and straw crackled beneath his feet. He reached beneath the roost into the first nest and found an egg, causing a hen to protest by pecking at his leg. Without thinking, Lenny swung his foot toward the chicken—much harder than he'd planned, like a punter—raising a great cloud of straw and dirt and at its center, one howling chicken. He found himself shocked again by his stored-up anger and he stared at his wake, at the dirt settling into the beam of sunlight, at the agitated bird racing from the henhouse.

After a moment, he went back to looking for eggs. He found eight. Holding out the bottom of his white T-shirt, Lenny made a little pouch to carry them back to the house, taking small, careful steps. He opened the back door without looking away from the nest of his shirt, the bell jangling as the door swung closed behind him. He eased the eggs from his shirt to the table. He could hear Angela showering in the bathroom down the hall as he cracked the eggs and plopped them into a metal mixing bowl. He added a little milk and a sprinkle of cinnamon, the way his momma had always made eggs. He supposed she added the milk to stretch out the few eggs they had, but he'd learned to like the taste of eggs done that way. He whipped the egg mixture and set it aside, then grated some onion and cheese, chopped up a green pepper and the little bit of ham they had left over from dinner last night.

The gas flame sputtered and sparked and glowed blue. Lenny dropped a chunk of butter into the pan and held it just above the flame, until the butter was completely melted and just beginning to brown. Then he poured the eggs in and set the lid on the pan.

"Boy. Smells good." She trudged past him and started upstairs to get dressed. But she paused on the bottom step. "So what are you doing today, Gene?"

He lifted the edges of the omelet and let the uncooked egg run beneath it. Then he put the lid back on the pan. "Going into town."

"Spokane?"

"Mmm-hmm."

"I gotta work tonight, but if you want to come back by two, I could go with you."

He didn't look up. "I'm gonna be later than that."

"That's okay, I guess. I got plenty I can do around here." She went upstairs.

He dropped two slices of bread in the toaster and poured two glasses of orange juice. He folded the cheese, ham, and vegetables into the omelet and put the lid back on. And then he sat reading last Sunday's paper, which Angela had brought home from the restaurant. He flipped to the real estate section and ran his finger along the commercial section. Nothing. This was crazy, thinking he would ever figure anything out. He leaned over the newspaper and stared out the window.

She came back down in her waitress dress and shoes, something on her mind. He cut the omelet into two halves and put one half on a plate for her with a slice of toast.

"So what do you do when you go to Spokane, anyways?"

"I told you. Get my mail. See a couple people. Do some things."

"What kind of things?"

He looked up and finished chewing, but didn't answer.

She picked at her own eggs. "You gonna be late, then?"

"Don't know yet."

She stared at her fork. "It's just, you haven't been to Spokane in quite a while."

"A few weeks."

"Seems like things are going pretty good around here, yeah?"

He chewed a mouthful of eggs and watched her. She took a drink of her orange juice. This wasn't like her to ask a lot of questions, even though Lenny knew she had good reason. She had to know he was hiding. After all, he'd moved in the night they met; the next day he'd shaved his head and started growing this beard. But if she found it strange that he looked more and more like her ex-husband, Angela never mentioned it. She seemed like the kind of person who had decided long ago there were things she didn't want to know. So she rarely asked about his business unless Lenny brought it up first—which he realized he had to do now if he wanted to enjoy the rest of his breakfast.

"What is it?" he asked finally.

"It's just . . . you'd tell me if there was somebody special in Spokane, right?"

"There's nobody special."

"But you had a woman like that, for a while?"

"Yeah."

"She's not around anymore?"

"No."

Angela nibbled around the edge of her toast. "I'm sorry. I probably sound like a jealous old biddy."

He looked up. "You sound fine."

She rolled her eyes at herself, laughed, and took a bite of omelet. "Boy, them's good eggs, Gene. You're gonna make somebody a good wife some day."

Lenny ate his eggs.

32

Caroline shifted and squirmed from New Orleans to Salt Lake City, falling asleep and waking up seconds later, staring at her watch, unable to comprehend that virtually no time was passing. They hit storms across the Midwest and had to climb, and before sliding the cover down on her window, Caroline could see flashes of lightning beneath the plane. The engines groaned and the plane rattled as it climbed, adding sound to Caroline's brief dreams—glimpses of women drowning in refrigerators, the embalmer Russell having coffee with her mother, the Mississippi River curling over a great falls.

Next to her, a woman hushed a baby already asleep—"Shh, shh, shh"—and that sound, too, scraped at Caroline's nerves, until she had to get up and go to the rest room at the back of the jet. She walked down the narrow aisle, faces turning up toward hers, as if these people wanted something from her too. She felt beads of perspiration on her face.

At the back of the plane a man was crouching in the aisle, talking to an attractive girl. Caroline waited patiently until the man stood, without looking at her, without breaking his conversation, and pressed himself against the seat back for Caroline to pass.

In the rest room, she washed her face and stared at herself in the mirror.

The flight was delayed an hour out of Salt Lake, so she sat in a coffee shop and wrote out a rough report of her meeting with Blanton in longhand on the yellow legal pad. He'd jotted down a brief profile of an unknown subject—UNSUB—that matched Ryan perfectly (". . . UNSUB acts out retaliation fantasies pertaining to deep trauma through the creation of a surrogate for the subject of the original trauma . . ."). Thankfully, the section of his report pertaining to Caroline (". . . possible involvement of Det. Mabry as a rival or symbolic figure in his evolving fantasy . . .") was short and understated.

Salt Lake City to Spokane was an easier flight, and Caroline settled into a window seat without anyone next to her. She closed her eyes, eager to sleep, but the pilot's voice interrupted her. "We're beginning our final approach into Spokane—"

Caroline checked her watch and couldn't believe it. She'd slept the entire flight, and if she'd dreamed, she didn't remember.

She felt drugged as she walked down the jetway, behind the woman and baby she'd sat near on the first leg of her flight. "There he is!" the mother kept repeating. "There he is! There he is!"

The baby's father, a tall man with long hair, wearing a knee brace, stepped from a crowd and swallowed them both in an embrace. They pulled off to the side of the flow of passengers, and Caroline's head turned as she passed them, and she saw the man kiss his baby on the top of her head.

Even at midnight the airport seemed strangely crowded. Joel was sitting away from the people, two gates away, and he stood when Caroline approached, reached out and took her travel bag. She didn't offer any resistance. He bent down and kissed her.

"Hey," he said. "You look tired."

She let him carry her bags to his Jeep. They climbed in and fastened their seat belts, but he didn't start the car.

"What's the matter?" Caroline asked.

He turned. "I have to tell you something. I was going to wait until we got home, but I have to tell you now."

Caroline felt sluggish, doped. "Okay."

"Last night, I was out with Derek and Jay . . . it was the last thing I thought would happen, but . . . I met this girl and . . . I'm sorry . . . I went home with her."

Caroline nodded, said "Okay," leaned back in her seat, and closed her eyes.

PART IV

JULY

Death by Water

33

As always, the first sign was the disappearance of the rapids near stateline, where the river dropped to reveal rocks as white and shiny as cleaned bone—rounded boulders and fingered slabs picked up ten thousand years earlier by glacier and deposited dumbly along the gravel and dirt riverbed. A few miles downstream, the receding water brought three old men with metal detectors to a calm stretch of midriver, where there were rumors of a sunken ferry boat and lost mining treasure. The old men combed the newly exposed banks, each listening to his own progress through headphones, each playing in his mind some version of the story of old coins and silver nuggets, each willing to settle for a narrative of old plows and car parts—for anything containing mystery, really, since that's what their lives lacked. Like all people, they realized too late that mystery was the key to staying interested in the whole business, to distracting themselves from the surety of what came next; that a man strives and settles and strives and settles and this pattern eventually kills him. But the old men didn't acknowledge the affliction, not to one another. Instead, they passed on the glistening riverbed with nods and raised eyebrows, sweeping their metal detectors before them like blind men with canes, oblivious to the deep water at their backs, where life goes on—swimmers and fishers and boats carving the river into sheets and beads that explode in tiny prisms and rain back on the river.

All along the Spokane, for twenty miles, for a hundred years, people came down to the tame July river, shadowing it from Lake Coeur d'Alene in the rich Idaho woods to the channeled scablands to the west, where the river paused to note the end of the forest and the return of the great, hard western desert. Smack between rock and forest was the city's center, where a low river felt more like desperation than recreation. Here the rocks weren't white and shiny, mere ripples in the flow, but black and hard: volcanic basalt columns flaked and knapped by the current into giant arrowheads, into massive Clovis points. Here the rock battled the water, bending it through tight channels and around craggy islands, beating it onto each ledge of the falls. And if there was another surety in the water's eventual victory, each summer these hard black stones promised it wouldn't be any time soon. But with the falls dried up to a deferential trickle, the spectators stayed away. After all, who takes pictures of rocks?

So maybe that's why they just didn't notice the drought. Whatever the reason, it snuck up on the city, this lack of rain. Fifty-four days, by the time the newspaper recorded it with a color photograph of a second-generation wheat farmer rubbing dry dirt between forefinger and thumb, as if that meant anything. The people saw the photograph and read the story about the drought as if they were watching a program on television—something detached and theoretical, marking time between dinner and bed. Did they actually believe that water came from the sky anyway, that farms still existed? Taps still ran. Cans of food were replaced on grocery shelves. What did a drought matter when every morning the sprinkler system greened the lawn?

These things were the true measure of water, not some exhausted river limping through the falls, shuffling out of downtown and lying down to die in the flatland between Peaceful Valley and Nine Mile. With the dams closed, the water beyond downtown pooled and became mostly still, a series of lakes safe enough for drunk rafters and whining Jet Skis and dogs chasing tennis balls. What was left of the river was allowed to squeeze through the turbines and past the wastewater treatment facility, where round ponds of sludge were separated from water, past housing developments, horse and cattle ranches, until it was just a stream, curling past the Spokane and Colville Indian reservations until finally it fed the Columbia, which had long since stopped being America's great river and had itself become just a series of dams and lakes.

In the mythic river of the west there is balance and peace, a fly fisherman harmonizing with the water. But the streams had all been toileted by cattle or muddied by roads. The rivers had all been broken. What rocks failed to do, dams accomplished with disappointing ease, turning the big rivers into pools of beaten and still water.

It was in one of these dam-formed lakes, just twelve miles from downtown Spokane as it turned out, that the water pulled far enough back to reveal the skeleton of an old horse-drawn swather, which had been abandoned by a farmer and overtaken by water eighty years ago and which emerged from the river during periods of drought, every ten years or so, to be discovered by someone poking around the riverbed. The swather was discovered this time by two boys making their way upstream with sticks, stirring the mud flats for frogs. Long metal railings like ribs stuck out from the swather just above the water level, along with a cab seat that looked to the boys like an exaggerated bicycle seat.

They picked their way out to the rusted tractor; the boys would tell TV reporters that there was a funny rotting smell. Then they both saw what appeared to be a man constructed of balloons tangled in the metal ribs of the swather, his body bloated and unrecognizable, his clothes long since torn away, his flesh washed clean of features and bleached the color of the mud flats. Anyone who had known him when he was alive would have had trouble believing that all the head-busting and pussy-chasing and law-breaking would amount to this, that a young man who had been so feared and desired had become nothing but a dilution of his own parts, a watered-down soup of the complex recipe of chemicals and compounds that make a man. It was the river's oldest trick and now it was done. Three months after taking Burn, the river had finally given him back.

34

To her surprise, Caroline found that she rather liked working for Spivey's newly organized task force. He was professional and thorough, and his nerdy, detail-oriented personality—which had seemed simply officious before—was perfect for a job that was essentially that of investigative accountant, criminal bean counter. In six weeks, he had transformed the small conference room that had been Dupree's cluttered clubhouse for the cynical and anxious into something that actually looked like headquarters for a multiagency task force—maps and charts and photos lining every wall, reports on soil samples and carpet fibers and bacteria slides filed neatly on a sort of lazy Susan filing cabinet available to investigators at any time. Dupree had done some of this, of course, and so the main differences were in organization and atmosphere. Gone was the feel of an old police squad room, cops drinking coffee, their feet up on their desks, talking endlessly on the phone. Where before, investigators had gone home every day having failed to catch a killer, now they went home having completed a review of prostitution case files, or an "environmental activity report" of the insects found on the corpses, or some other some small, managed task. The computer evidence database was up and running, organizing reams of information: tips, interviews, intelligence, forensics, reports, follow-ups, field interview cards, and similar data from other cases around the country. The detectives gathered this raw data as if the weight of the information might solve this crime, as if Lenny Ryan might be hiding in the paper itself. Each detective had a terminal on his desk, and each contact he made was entered into the computer, filed and cross-referenced and available in the database at the stroke of a Function-2 key. A technician worked full-time simply adjusting software to the task force's needs and keeping the frustrated and computer-illiterate Detective Laird from firing his handgun into his terminal when it didn't do what he thought he'd asked it to do. The six detectives had divided up different areas to concentrate their investigative work—backgrounding victims and interviewing other prostitutes (this was Caroline's area), crime scene assessment and forensics, and the tracking of Lenny Ryan. They met every day to report their progress and to brainstorm.

Of course, many things about Spivey still grated on Caroline's nerves, such as his habit of pushing up the sleeves on his suit coat like a banker about to reach into a toilet, or his insistence on providing coffee and baked goods to the investigators. During daily meetings he seemed less a task force commander than a condescending waiter.

"You look like you're eyeing that last scone, Caroline."

"Nope. All yours, Chris."

"More coffee then?"

"No. I'll just have the check."

"Jeff? That scone has your name on it."

McDaniel raised an eyebrow at Caroline. "I don't eat processed sugar. Bad for the metabolism." That was the other major change, of course, the full-time involvement of the profiler Jeffrey McDaniel. Spivey's first order of business had been to secure McDaniel's help by convincing the FBI's Investigative Support Unit that Spokane would be a great public relations opportunity to have its experts go beyond consultation and theorizing and actually help local police catch a serial murderer.

His first day in the office, McDaniel made a beeline to Caroline's desk and pretended to be interested in her dealings with Lenny Ryan. He leaned on her desk, an obsessively fit, overly muscled man with graying hair furiously parted to the side, a guy who, at forty-seven, still described himself as "in my late thirties," and who, if Caroline saw him on the street, she would bet a month's salary on his being a cop. McDaniel had been in the office only an hour before he hit on her, leaning on the corner of her desk and crossing his arms, roping the muscles beneath his tight dress shirt.

"I'm hoping for someone to work out with while I'm here," he said, looking her up and down. "Seems like you keep in pretty good shape."

"It's amazing what they can do with prosthetics," she'd said.

"Come on. You must go to the gym."

"I don't think I'd be a very good spotter for you."

"I don't need spotting," he'd said. "Just a workout partner. I like working out with women better. They're more trustworthy. I need someone I can trust."

"Well," Caroline said, "good luck with that."

When he wasn't hitting on Caroline or the receptionist, McDaniel's role in the investigation was less defined. He dominated entire meetings theorizing about Lenny Ryan's "down time" or explaining why his signature changed: "Rubber bands hold money in the victims' hands as well as show his increased need for power and organization." Dupree called FBI profilers the "hindsight experts," and that struck Caroline as an apt description. Every time the detectives unearthed some new information about Ryan (his father was arrested for beating his mother), McDaniel would nod and say, "That fits," or "Textbook," and then add the detail to his ever-expanding profile.

The rest of the time he was Spivey's private mentor, following the eager young detective around and telling war stories. He sauntered around the office and the only time he seemed uncomfortable was when Curtis Blanton's name came up or when they discussed the report he'd given Caroline in New Orleans. McDaniel's lips would go white and thin and he'd stare at his shoes until the subject changed. He was outwardly dismissive of only one of Blanton's conclusions, the idea that Lenny Ryan was obsessed in some way with Caroline. "Ridiculous, melodramatic tripe," McDaniel spat.

"He's clearly communicating with the entire outside world, with all of us."

She heard McDaniel acknowledge Blanton only once, one morning when Caroline took a phone message from a woman who claimed to be McDaniel's agent. "Tell Jeff he didn't get the Court TV thing," the agent said. "I explained to the producer that he's retiring next month and would be available, but they wouldn't budge. They're going with that fat bastard again."

When Caroline gave him the message, McDaniel shook his head bitterly and muttered to himself, "If I'd retired first, I'd be a millionaire." Then he looked up at Caroline. "Have you ever seen him on TV? He stammers. Repeats himself. Guy's as telegenic as a warthog." He looked around the office, then leaned over and spoke quietly. "He didn't actually retire, you know. He was forced out. Just between you and me. He's . . . unbalanced. You know?" He stood at Caroline's desk, nodding his head and rocking on his heels and reading the message over and over. After more than a minute of this, he balled up the paper, threw it in the garbage, and walked out of the office.

But if Blanton was McDaniel's sworn enemy, their profiles of the Southbank Strangler were nearly identical. Both profilers attributed the crime scene evidence to an extreme example of "excitation/retaliation serial homicide"—Ryan being both attracted to and repulsed by prostitutes, the victims being symbolic of the girlfriend who betrayed him by sleeping with other men for money. The lack of semen on the victims and the obsessive cleaning of their hands after the killings showed his intense disgust for these women; he wouldn't even allow himself to orgasm with them. And while he wanted the police to know that he was the killer (why else lead Caroline to a body?), he didn't want these women to have any trace of him on their bodies or under their nails. The money he left in their hands was his way of letting police know that the victim was "only a hooker," and both profilers believed it was possible Ryan felt a kinship with police; he was doing them a favor by ridding the streets of unclean women. But the money also was a final, bitter gesture to one particular hooker. Ultimately, both profilers wrote, Ryan blamed his girlfriend for her own death and for his killing spree. *She made him do it.*

If McDaniel expanded Blanton's profile, it was within his particular area of expertise, which also was his doctoral thesis: childhood commonalities among serial sex criminals. McDaniel offered a template for the kind of kid who might grow up to murder women and taunt the police. As they checked Lenny Ryan's past against McDaniel's profile (". . . as an adolescent, offender likely experienced run-ins with authority and has a history of juvenile crime . . . offender's early experiences with intimacy occurred with prostitutes . . ."), the two lined up perfectly.

When Caroline first saw McDaniel's report, she experienced the disorientation she'd felt in New Orleans, the sense that it might be better to *not understand* someone who would kill so easily and so effectively. McDaniel's report had seven headings. The first was: "Perception among offenders of parental neglect or sibling rivalry during preteen years." She didn't know a single person who couldn't claim that. The headings got progressively more specific, including one that jogged an old memory: "In a display of the early use of surrogates for his anger, the young offender exhibits cruelty toward animals." She thought for a moment about the awful realization she'd had in New Orleans, that these "profiles" were so horrible because they were so common. She remembered the first time she'd heard at the grade school bus stop that a boy in her neighborhood amused himself by putting cats into garbage cans and shooting them with his pellet gun. She tried to remember his name, Pete something. Was this Pete something now a serial killer? Pete . . . Pete . . . What the hell was his last name? It would come to her sometime today, and when it did maybe she would enter his name into the computer, just to see what happened; the thought made her smile because she knew how Dupree would appreciate such a gesture. At first she wished he'd stayed on the task force, or at least stayed in Major Crimes. But after a month with Spivey at the helm Caroline realized that Dupree couldn't have existed on a task force run by profilers and accountants so contrary to the things that twenty-six years as a cop had taught him.

He would especially hate the daily reviews—Spivey's signature morning meeting. Once they dispensed with Spivey's muffins and coffee, the procedural improvements, McDaniel's latest insight into the boyhood habits of Lenny Ryan, and the irrelevant information they gathered the day before, there was nothing to review. No sign of Ryan. No new bodies. No sign of Jacqueline or Risa, the missing prostitutes. Details drifted in, but led nowhere—the odd blood spatter, a bit of curious carpet fiber.

At this morning's meeting, McDaniel sat champing gum with his mouth open, patiently waiting for his turn to lecture while Spivey progressed beyond the ever-improving computer system to the actual work they were accomplishing. At the chalkboard, Spivey wrote the word "Victims" and turned to Caroline.

"Caroline, we'll start with you," he said. "Anything new on the prostitute front?"

They'd been over her report before, of course. Spivey checked with each of his detectives throughout the day, but she knew his reasons for wanting to share the information with the group, in a formal setting, to make sure that nothing slipped through the cracks, that information culled by the suspect investigators was available to the victims' investigators and so on.

Caroline handed out six copies of the transcript of her interview with Lynn Haight, an exotic dancer and occasional prostitute who had left a suburban club approximately three weeks earlier and was approached by a white man in his late thirties or early forties in a red sedan. The man claimed to be a police officer investigating the serial killings. He seemed friendly and asked some questions about prostitution: Had she seen anything suspicious? Did she ever work along East Sprague? During the questioning he offered to give her a ride, but the woman became suspicious and asked to see a badge. When the man stalled she got scared and ran back into the club. The dancer hadn't reported the incident because of an outstanding warrant for failing to show up for court on a drug possession charge.

"Textbook," McDaniel said. "Ryan's posing as a cop again, just like he did in California. He actually thinks he's one of *us*."

Caroline cut him off before he had a chance to take over the whole meeting. "Still, the biggest problem we're having is getting prostitutes to cooperate," she said, thinking again of Jacqueline. "That lack of trust."

She explained that the man who tried to get Lynn Haight into his car had been wearing a baseball cap and had a full beard, and so she had been unable to pick him from a photo lineup that included Ryan. But one of Spivey's new toys was a computer program that allowed police to manipulate photographs, and so beards were added to all of the men in the same six-pack of mug shots and placed in front of Lynn Haight. She immediately pointed to Lenny Ryan.

"The prosecutor doesn't think we'd ever get a manipulated photo ID accepted by the courts," Caroline said, "but I guess we'll worry about that if we ever get to trial."

"Outstanding work," Spivey said. "And what about the prostitute registry? Where are we with that?"

This had been one of Spivey's better ideas. Starting with police reports, Caroline had gotten together with social workers, outreach ministers, and others who came in contact with street hustlers, dancers, and call girls, and had set out to compile a kind of hooker catalogue, as complete a list as they could make of every woman who'd turned a trick in Spokane in the last five years. She had come up with more than three hundred names or street names of women, two-thirds of whom she could locate, half of those in jail, on probation, or already dead. The hope was that this registry would allow detectives to figure out if other hookers might be missing and to keep track of the rest, but the result was merely to drive home just how daunting their task would be. There were more than a hundred hookers on the list who could not be accounted for, most of them women like Jacqueline, for whom they didn't even have a real name.

Prostitutes were a transient population, most of them chronic drug users; a woman might run off to Seattle when her dealer got arrested, or move to Portland to look up an old pimp. "We've sent names to shelters across the Northwest, and we're getting other police agencies to do sweeps. That's all we can do, I guess."

"Outstanding," Spivey said. "More coffee?"

Most of the other detectives were engaged in hunting for Lenny Ryan. A motel owner in Spokane had called in after the photograph of Lenny Ryan ran in the newspaper and said that a man matching that description had stayed at his motel from April 22 to April 27 under the name "Gene Lyons." They'd found no matching fingerprints from Ryan at the motel, but a handwriting analyst had matched the rigid signature on the guest registry to a signature from his file at Lompoc.

Spivey beamed and nodded appreciatively to the group. "Great work, people," he said. "Top drawer. We have an alias. We have Mr. Ryan posing as a cop and trying to get hookers into his car. We have him in Spokane at least five days before the drug bust in Riverfront Park. And, best of all, we can add some more information to our timeline."

The timeline was Spivey's pet, a huge grid that took up half of one wall. The names of Ryan and his victims ran down on the far left column. Dates ran across the top of the chart. Whenever a detective found information to add to the timeline—like when Caroline had found out that the first victim, Rebecca Bennett, visited a friend in the hospital on March 14—Spivey said, "Outstanding!" and made a production of printing out the new information, clipping it with scissors, and gluing it to the timeline, like a salesman recording a big week on the thermometer marking quarterly totals.

Despite Spivey's enthusiasm, it struck Caroline that the investigation was in most ways no better off than it had been under Dupree. No new bodies had been found, and except for a couple of unreliable witnesses, there was no sign of Ryan or Jacqueline or Risa. Their last official contact with him, their last positive identification, had been two months earlier, in the alley where he led Caroline to the body of the fourth victim. The media had been flashing Ryan's picture every day ("Serial killer suspect still at large"), and still all they had were two sightings, two women who claimed that a man who looked like Ryan, wearing a ball cap and a beard, stopped to talk to them. That was it. The timeline, the prostitute registry, the pet torture—none of it meant anything if Lenny Ryan had packed up and moved on.

"Great work, people," Spivey said.

There was a light knock at the door, and a senior volunteer in wire-rim glasses came into the conference room, looking confused, as if he had been trying to find the rest room. He looked around the table and then saw Caroline, walked over, and handed her a message. "Is this you?" he asked.

She looked down. It was a phone message with her name on top

217

and one short sentence below: "Body of Kevin Hatch located near Nine Mile." She stared at the note and held her breath. For so long it had been the natural order of things, to have him floating out there. The note fell to her lap as if it weighed fifty pounds.

"Yes," she said weakly to the senior volunteer. "This is me."

35

Dupree bent down, shined his flashlight beneath the tree limbs, and caught a glimpse of braces, a white bra, and a boy pulling up his pants. He thought for a moment about walking away and just letting the young couple reach whatever base they were nearing—third, by the look of their clothes and his memory of teenage sexual progression—but it was too late. They'd seen him. They'd been caught, and religious kids like these had high expectations of punishment once they were caught. They emerged from the bushes straightening their clothes, the girl staring at the ground, trying to avoid Dupree's eyes, the boy having trouble fastening his belt.

"There are better places for that kind of thing," Dupree said.

"We were looking for something," the boy said.

"I know what you were looking for." Dupree shined the light into the boy's eyes. He looked about fourteen. The girl too. "Go on back to the concert."

Thankfully, the concert was winding down in the grassy meadow beneath the old railroad clock tower in Riverfront Park. It featured a band called Loaf and Fish, which the promoter explained to the disbelieving Dupree was a "fundamentalist Christian rap-punk band with ska influences."

Dupree followed the ashamed boy and girl back to the edge of the meadow, where they disappeared into a crowd of three hundred people shaking their fists or holding their palms up toward the flatbed trailer that functioned as a stage. Dupree pulled out his earplugs and concentrated on the words coming from the white singer with blond dreadlocks. It took a while to catch up to the lyrics, but he heard: *Jew and Gentile . . . Abel's brother Cain . . . Fire from heaven, cursed writhe in pain!* Dupree replaced his earplugs. But the radio strapped to his shoulder crackled and he had to remove one earplug, turning his head away from the music to hear the call on the radio. "David-four to David-one," the voice on the other end repeated. "You there, Sergeant Dupree?"

David-four was a roundish black kid with glasses named Kelvin Teague, and from what Dupree had seen after a month back on patrol, the brightest officer on Dupree's shift. Dupree pressed the button for the microphone and covered his earpiece with his hand so that he could hear. "What's up, Teague? The Christians giving you trouble?"

"No, sir. I was just wondering if it would be reasonable force if I was to put this band out of its misery."

"I think we could justify that."

"This is unbearable. It's like the opposite of music. Think they'd stop if I just started firing blindly toward the stage? I'll try not to hit anyone."

Dupree checked his watch. "Ten minutes. You can make it ten more minutes. Then we'll sweep through the park once and call it a night."

"Okay, but if these guys scream one more song about God, I'm gonna become an atheist and you're gonna have to explain it to my mom."

Dupree put his flashlight back on his belt. He had gotten right back into the feel of being in uniform, especially the weight and security of the belt, the holster buckled over the handle of his gun. The belt gave him an odd sense of moral authority, an unambiguous idea of right and wrong that he had lacked as a detective in street clothes. *Of course I'm a good guy. I'm wearing the belt.* He sat down on a park bench.

Teague continued talking into his ear. "What church encourages this shit, Sarge?"

"No idea."

"Well, I wish they'd just pass out the poison Kool-Aid and get it over with."

"What do you say we keep the radio clear, Teague?"

"It's just . . . when the Bible says to 'sing unto Him and talk of His wondrous works,' you don't think . . . ?"

"I honestly don't know."

"I mean, this ain't a race thing, is it? Like am I maybe missing something? This ain't, like . . . gospel for white people?"

"No. I don't think so."

"I'd just hate to think of these guys in the same section of heaven as Al Green."

Dupree leaned back on the park bench. "Keep the radio clear, Teague."

The concert ended with a punk version of "Amazing Grace" and then the singer asked anyone who wanted to be saved to come toward the stage. The crowd parted and about twenty people came forward, palms in the air, and what had been a punk concert was now a revival, the sweating lead singer taking off his leather coat, getting down on the knees of his leather pants, and placing his hands on the foreheads of the people, mumbling as each of them came up. At the edges of the crowd those who had come for the music drifted away, but most of the people stayed, joining hands as the lead singer led them in prayer—"*. . . and finally, Lord, we ask that the spirit moving this band may live inside each of these people . . .*"

Teague was coming toward him across the meadow. "This is gonna stick with me for a long time," he said.

As the band packed up its gear and the crowd dispersed, Dupree and Teague walked once more through the park, every few minutes Teague returning to the topic of the concert. "I can't comprehend what I just saw. It's like I saw a chicken driving a car. I'm God and I hear that shit, some bald kid with a nose ring singing about me like that? *Fireballs*, man. Grasshoppers. Plagues and shit."

At the west end of the park they dropped down a hill to the river and Dupree found himself at the base of the narrow footbridge where Caroline had chased Burn and Lenny Ryan three months earlier. This is where she stood, staring at Lenny on the bridge, at Burn in the water, trying to decide. He'd imagined it dozens of times; when he was on the task force he would go over it in his mind as if there was something in the short drama that he'd been missing, some key to the whole thing. But nothing ever materialized. Just the choice, three points on a triangle, the points in motion. Caroline here. Lenny Ryan there. Burn in the river. And that's it. Dupree walked to the edge and looked over, but it was impossible to picture her desperation now, with the river just a trickle, the exposed black rocks of the waterfalls like something out of a horror film, the water behind the dam a shallow, still pool.

Teague stood next to him. "So I guess they finally found that dealer that went over the dam. You hear that?"

Dupree turned to him. "Yeah. That's what I heard."

"Some kids found him this morning, up in Long Lake?"

"Mmm-hmm."

"And the guy who pushed him into the river, the guy killing all the hookers, you think he's still in town?"

There were no secrets in a police department, and Teague was constantly hitting Dupree up for some juice about his last assignment, something grisly perhaps, some bit of autopsy gossip he could trade over coffee with other patrol officers. Ever since coming back to patrol, Dupree had been fending Teague off. "You should ask Detective Spivey about that."

"Yeah, well, if he is still in town, that's fucked. Guy's like a killing machine, something out of the movies, huh?" Dupree didn't respond, and Teague finally just shook his head and followed Dupree's eyes to the dry riverbed beneath the bridge. They stared for a long time, at the water pooled up in the holes in the rock, at the small stream flowing at the center of a rock bed that, a few months earlier, had barely contained its rushing torrent, a river so loud and impressive, it ended conversations.

"I hate floaters," Teague said finally.

"Yeah."

When they reached their cars at the turnout in front of the

park, Teague asked Dupree if he wanted to kill the last ten minutes of their shift getting a latte at a new coffee house—the name of which Dupree didn't recognize.

"Right over by the cop shop. That old brick building on Monroe across from the bail bondsmen. The body-piercing clove-smokers hang out there. It's fun to go in and watch 'em all check the stashes in their pockets."

Dupree said, "Why don't you go ahead."

Teague climbed in his patrol car and drove off and then Dupree started his own car. He waited for Teague to clear himself to the radio dispatcher and then did the same.

He drove slowly through downtown, the cast from the streetlights rolling across his patrol car, cruising slowly past the downtown bars that would cause trouble at closing time, four and a half hours from now, when they would release toxic clouds of wife beaters and drunk drivers and date rapists and vandals and worse. For now these men were loading up on booze, getting ready. Swing shift ended at nine-thirty, so Dupree would be off work when the drunks hit the street, home in his small apartment, watching *Sports Center* and waiting for the microwave timer to ding on his frozen burrito.

At a traffic light some laughing kids looked over and saw him and became sober and still, staring straight ahead. Dupree followed their Ford Escort for a couple of blocks, but then lost interest and turned down Sprague.

His car passed beneath a railway underpass, and Sprague Avenue around him turned from legitimate businesses to seedy storefronts, adult bookstores, and taverns—the center of prostitution in the city for as long as he could remember. But to his surprise the strip was all but deserted tonight: just a few cars parked in front of the same old taverns, no sign of the women who usually cruised Sprague or perched on the backs of bus benches, all but wearing "Open" signs on their tiny shirts. He had seen this before, of course, the fear driving hookers off the strip. He remembered, twelve or thirteen years ago, when Los Angeles gangs first made an appearance in Spokane and began a turf war that extended to the prostitutes run by the gangbangers. What Dupree thought of as the professional hookers had moved indoors then, or to the taverns and low-rent motels or to West Central on the other end of downtown, where a lower class of prostitute worked: teenage runaways, young male hookers, street people, mental patients.

But this empty street felt different. That summer everyone seemed to sense that it was temporary, that the young men with guns would shoot each other and shoot each other's whores until the thing was settled and then the women would return to their perches on the bus benches, to their walking routes. But there was something about the way Lenny Ryan had eluded capture that made this different. Since returning to patrol he'd noticed how people talked about Ryan, like a ghost, something other-worldly. It reminded Dupree of his first opinion of Ryan, as a natural phenomenon, a concentration of all the shit and darkness and everything.

By the time it crossed Napa Street, Sprague was returning to legitimate shops and businesses that reflected the city—a city that in its heart was more used car than computer, more mobile home than condo. Spokane was what some people used to mean when they said "old-fashioned," which was what some people said when they meant "unsophisticated," which was what some people said when they meant "lower middle class," which was what some people said when they meant "white trash."

Dupree listened to the radio traffic. Nothing much going on. He turned the car up Freya and began climbing the steep South Hill. The South Hill complicated the popular notion of Spokane as the trailer park of the Pacific Northwest; there were vast old money and culture in Spokane and pools of new money, and whatever vintage it was, the money in Spokane lived for the most part on the South Hill, between the streets of Twelfth and Fifty-seventh. As the lower middle class crept higher each year, the wealth had begun to slop over the backside of the South Hill, or to the far north, to new neighborhoods with a slot in the garage for the motor home and street names made up by the developers to sound English, exclusive, and rich: Lancaster Circle and Nottingham Place. Still, the numbered streets were home to some of the oldest and best neighborhoods in the city, and it had been important to Debbie to live up here, to send their children to South Hill schools on his salary as a cop and hers as a part-time speech therapist. So they'd followed that essential rule of real estate and bought the worst house in a good neighborhood, a little too far east, but as far south as they could afford, a nice, low-twenties block of the South Hill.

Where the South Hill neighborhoods to the west were made up of Craftsman or Victorian, the houses on this street were newer, ranch-style or California splits, whites and browns, the basketball hoops and bicycles reflecting the ages of the kids in the neighborhood. It had seemed perfect six years earlier, for Debbie and Alan to move in with their children when everyone else on the block had children, as if they had found some perfect demographic center, someplace where they would always fit in.

Her house—Dupree's house too, he supposed, at least until the paperwork went through—sat in the middle of the block, white stucco, pitched roof, one story with an attic and basement, slightly smaller than the other houses. One-car garage. Every other house on this street had a two-car garage. Dupree slowed and stopped in front of the house. The lights were off. No strange cars in the driveway. No toys or bikes left out in the yard. Dupree shifted into park, turned the key back, and listened as his patrol car shut down. The neighborhood was quiet. He checked his watch. It was after ten. His shift was officially over. He thought about his apartment northwest of here and couldn't imagine going there right now. He stared at his old house and imagined Marc inside, all twisted in his covers, facing sideways or backward, his feet hanging off the edge of the bed, and Staci, so still while she slept that sometimes he succumbed to the urge to put his hand in front of her nose and feel for warm breath.

Dupree turned the radio off and sat quietly in the dark of his patrol car, watching the house. Wednesday night. He wondered if Debbie had gone to her book group meeting. What were they reading now? The last book he remembered on her nightstand was something like *Yo-Yo Sisters*. That had been right about the time he'd moved out. Surely, the book group had already discussed that book and moved on, but Dupree felt the sudden urge to find out what the *Yo-Yo Sisters* had been about—probably some female rapper's self-help thing, or else just some excuse for women to talk about sex. That was the thing he'd realized about her book group: One of its chief reasons for being was that women need a context to talk about sex. It's why all the magazines had those quizzes about sex ("Rate your lover!"). For all their reputation as noncommunicative, men could talk to buddies about sex anytime, during a football game, standing at the urinal, at a funeral. Women needed someone else to bring it up. Still, it kind of turned him on, thinking about the book group, imagining his wife in a roomful of equally fit and proper mothers and wives, talking about sex under the pretense of talking about a book about sex. And the funny thing was, the reading part is what made it seem so exciting to him. He didn't care much for reading himself—no patience for it—but for some strange reason he had always been attracted to women who read, and if there was one thing about Debbie, she did love to read. And not just to waste time, or to appear smart; it was really important to her—the reading, of course, but also the fact that he liked that side of her. She once told him that he treated her as if she were the only person in the world capable of reading a book, and even though she was making fun of him when she said it, they both recognized the truth of that statement, a thing important to the core of their relationship, a thing that operated like a pilot light as the years slid by, maybe burning low, but ready to flame up when the partnership of raising kids and running a house gave way to the horny college freshmen they had once been. He didn't know exactly where her reading and his appreciation of it fit into their lovemaking, but it did, somewhere between undressing with the lights off and squeezing their eyes closed, biting their lips, and falling off each other with great sighs.

But over the years they dented and chipped away at too many things that would turn out to be important. That included Dupree's appreciation of a well-read wife, and so they rarely talked about the books that Debbie read anymore. It seemed to him now that it had begun to get away from them at the Christmas party eight years ago—before Caroline had shot the wife beater, before they'd spent the night together, before he'd transferred off patrol—when Debbie insisted on having his entire shift over for a holiday drink. But you can't have one drink with a cop, and so late in the evening Caroline and Debbie had found themselves standing next to each other in one of those awkward conversational circles, the two of them standing across from Dupree and Caroline's date, some dope she'd known in high school. The dope brought up the full bookshelves all over the house, Debbie's bookshelves, and Caroline—slopping beer on the carpet—drunkenly admitted to studying poetry in college. "Poetry . . . and criminal justice! Can you beat that? It's like studying taxidermy and veterinary medicine." She'd laughed. "My adviser just looked at me like I was nuts." And Debbie had caught him staring at this young woman, and maybe that was the first time she had been jealous of Caroline, or at least his first awareness of it. Poetry and criminal justice. When Dupree had looked away from the young and vibrant and drunk and well-read Caroline, his wife was staring at him with eyes that showed both accusation and admission. And Dupree had just looked down at the wet carpet.

It was funny. For twelve years Dupree had fantasized about being single and being with Caroline. And now that he'd finally left his wife, he hadn't said a thing to Caroline. In his mind he felt like he was waiting for something, but what? Maybe it was Joel. Maybe seeing him at the bar that night had gotten to him, watching Joel struggle the way Dupree struggled to be a good person, to be a faithful, stand-up guy. Maybe he wanted to give Joel every chance to succeed where he failed. Or maybe he didn't feel worthy of her, since he'd been removed from the task force and Caroline remained on it. Or maybe it was just simple guilt over hurting his kids and Debbie. Or maybe or maybe or maybe . . .

He stared at the big picture window in the living room and noticed that the curtains were open. That was strange. Debbie always closed those curtains at night. Well, almost always. Dupree could think of only a handful of occasions when he'd come home late and found those curtains still open, Debbie having fallen asleep with a book or with the TV on. So maybe she'd just fallen asleep again. He looked around the neighborhood. This was a quiet, safe place, no halfway houses nearby, no homes ornate enough to draw burglars of any repute, no taverns down the street spitting out drunks. He couldn't think of a neighborhood in the city in which he would feel better having his children live.

Still, those open curtains bothered him. There had been a petty burglar he'd arrested once, a guy named Turner, who would case houses by looking for open curtains. The thought of Turner or some other degenerate standing in front of his family's ground-level window, checking out his family's TV and stereo, just about made him sick. He unbuckled his belt and leaned back in the seat and fantasized sitting there all night in his patrol car, every night, guarding the house, protecting the people inside without having to deal with them. He imagined sitting in his car forever, the kids passing by every morning, avoiding his eyes as he started the car and drove slowly behind them, maybe running the lights without the siren, just to make sure they got to the bus safely. After a while they'd get used to it, and their friends, too, having a police car tail them every time they went for a ride on their bikes. He tried to remember the last time Marc had met his eyes. He felt irrelevant to the boy, as if he'd stopped existing once he'd moved out of the house. He thought again just how nice it would be to live in his car outside the house, to be able to see his children grow up without having to face how he'd hurt them.

36

Caroline was flipping through the channels when she saw footage of a swamp on CNN. Three or four channels later, she realized what she'd seen and flipped back. A perky news anchor was saying that a suspect had been arrested in the murders of as many as nineteen women in New Orleans, in the deadliest serial murder case in the last three years. The suspect was the custodian at a high school in the Lakeshore neighborhood. He had been caught on a security camera stealing photography supplies from a high school yearbook class. The high school principal sat the custodian down to question him about the darkroom supplies and the man had shocked the principal by suddenly confessing to being a serial murderer. Just like that.

Curled up on the couch, Caroline marveled at the ironic sense it made. For all Blanton's efforts and expertise, a high school principal accidentally catches the guy. She opened her briefcase and found Blanton's office number, grabbed the phone and punched in the number. Her call went straight to his voice mail. She considered paging him. She checked her watch. It was almost eleven; it'd be closing on one in the morning there. While she amused herself thinking about what Blanton might make of a 1 A.M. page, the recorded message ended and his voice mail beeped.

"Oh," she said, "hey, Mr. Blanton. This is Caroline Mabry with the Spokane Police Department. I just wanted to"—she started to say "congratulate," but thought better of it—"I just called to say I was just glad you caught your guy. I guess that's all."

She set the phone down and a minute later, it rang.

"Am I crazy or did you just call to congratulate me?" Blanton sounded deadened or drunk, like the first night they'd spoken. Caroline was sorry she'd called.

"I didn't know what else to say. Are you in the office?"

"Yeah."

"What are you doing there?"

"Sitting."

"At one in the morning?"

"Is it? Well, I guess that explains why the office is so empty."

"Why didn't you answer my call if you're just sitting there by yourself?"

"I didn't feel like talking."

"But you called me back?"

"I wanted to know what I was being congratulated for."

"I thought you might be happy that he got caught."

"I had some drinks with some of the detectives earlier. They certainly seem happy. Perhaps you'd like to talk to one of them?"

Caroline noticed there was no more trace of New Orleans twang, as if now that the crime had been solved, he could put that tool away for next time. His voice was flat and hollow and its bitterness made her feel cold, like the first time they'd met.

After a short silence, he sighed. "So, aren't you going to ask how my profile stacked up against the real thing?"

"How did your profile stack up against the real thing?"

"Fair in most respects. But I overestimated intelligence again. I had this guy as a college graduate. He's an imbecile, a fuckin' janitor. It's a wonder he didn't kill himself."

She didn't know what to say, and again there was silence on her end.

"So, aren't you going to ask me if I'm troubled by that fact?" he asked.

"Are you troubled by that fact?"

"Good question. Yes, I am. It troubles me that this guy could be so much more interesting in the abstract than in reality. Makes me wonder what I'm looking for. I seem to need these guys to be formidable and, I don't know . . . evil. This one's just broken."

"You interviewed him?"

"Yeah."

"What's he like?" Caroline was surprised at how quiet her voice was.

Blanton answered as quietly. "Like every one of these sick fucks. Unremarkable. Just over forty. White. Short, dark hair. Just . . . forgettable, you know? Forgettable." He sighed, and she heard him take a drink. "What about you, Ms. Mabry? Do we need to send this high school administrator to *Spow-kaine* to solve your crime?"

"It couldn't hurt," Caroline said. "Although we did get a profiler finally."

"Who'd you get?"

"McDaniel."

"You didn't."

"*I* didn't. The lead investigator brought him in."

"McDaniel?" Blanton sounded engaged, the way he'd been the afternoon they saw the drowning victim and Blanton had clued her in about how Lenny Ryan's fantasy involved her. "Christ, Jeff McDaniel couldn't profile himself!"

"What is it with you two?"

Blanton was quiet for a moment. "What do you mean?"

"He practically leaves the room when your name comes up."

For the first time Caroline could remember, Blanton seemed unsure of what to say. "I retired first and got all the good TV gigs." He paused and seemed suddenly concerned. "Why? What has he told you?"

"Nothing. I'm just wondering if he is going to be any help to us."

"McDaniel? Nah. He's completely Freudian. Guy will spend the next six months figuring out that your guy had a fucked-up childhood."

Caroline smiled to herself. "He does talk a lot about the offender's parents moving and being an outsider in school. Torturing pets, stuff like that."

"I always thought McDaniel would be a great help if the killer was nine."

They were both quiet for a moment.

"I asked my guy here about the fifteen-year-old girl," Blanton said finally.

Caroline didn't say anything.

"Says he doesn't remember picking the girl up."

"Is he just screwing with you?"

"I don't know. He volunteered to take a lie detector test on it. And he confessed to everything else. But not her. Not the girl."

"Copycat?"

"No. It's him. Same DNA, prints. Same everything. I think he can justify the others in his simple mind, the crack whores and speed freaks. But I don't know, maybe even he can't imagine what kind of person would do that to a fifteen-year-old girl."

And then, quietly, Blanton added, "So how come I can imagine it?"

Caroline didn't answer and he filled the quiet with a deep breath.

"We weren't quite right about the mall, by the way," Blanton said. "The mall with the cinnamon roll shop wasn't near his house. It was near the school. The girl went to the school where he worked. That's probably why she got in his car."

"You were right about the girl being different," Caroline said. "You said the way to catch him was in the aberration."

"Yeah?" Blanton sighed. "I say a lot of things."

"You should get some sleep," Caroline said.

After a moment, he said, "You too, Ms. Mabry."

The phone went dead and Caroline stared at it. She checked her watch. It was a little after eleven. She switched the TV over to a local news channel, which was doing a story about Burn's body being found. The reporter stood on the roadside above Long Lake, gesturing down the hill. Caroline turned up the volume.

". . . a body that investigators believe is that of convicted drug dealer Kevin Hatch, who was pushed to his death in April by Leonard Ryan, a man police now want to question about the deaths of . . ."

So how come I can imagine it? Blanton's words barged into her mind. At the moment he'd said it she'd thought about Burn resurfacing, and about that day in the park. Why didn't she tell Blanton that Burn's body had been found? If anyone might understand her ambivalence, her difficulty comprehending Burn's return and the sequence of events on the bridge that day, it was Blanton. He would appreciate her effort to find some meaningful distinction between—what had Blanton called it, *broken and evil*—some distinction between the Kevin Hatches and the Lenny Ryans of the world. Some elemental difference between them and her.

So how come I can imagine it?

Caroline closed her eyes and saw Lenny Ryan on the bridge again, reaching over, pushing Burn. Then what? The look. Ryan had looked at her with . . . what? The look haunted her. She'd always figured Ryan pushed Burn over the bridge as a way to escape, to force her into choosing to save one or arrest the other. But was that the look? There were easier ways for Ryan to get away. And if he was trying to create a diversion, why didn't Ryan run after pushing Burn? Why just stand there? Looking at her?

There was another choice she could have made, of course. She could have shot Lenny Ryan. Certainly, part of her had wanted to do that. And maybe that was the look in his eyes: some combination of anger and challenge and resignation.

In her mind, Lenny Ryan's eyes became the eyes of the drunk wife beater six years earlier, the man she killed. In that instant on the bridge, the idea of shooting Ryan had passed through her head, just as it had with the wife beater. Sometimes, as she played it in her head, Caroline allowed hindsight to create enough time to shoot Ryan just as he reached for Burn, before he pushed him over the edge. But that wasn't what happened. Ryan pushed Burn and she decided to go after Burn rather than face Ryan. Did she really choose to save Burn? She was filled with so much self-doubt lately, she'd even begun to wonder if she went after Burn as a way of ignoring Lenny Ryan, her fear, the fact that she might have to shoot a man to death again. Or be killed by him.

She stood, walked to the kitchen, and got a glass of tap water. She stared out the dark window into her backyard, seeing the day in the park and all the things that seemed wrong with it, a string of impossible coincidences and well-meaning slapstick, a string of overreactions.

There was a notebook on the kitchen table. Caroline opened it and drew a small map of the center of the park, where they had set up the surveillance of Burn. She drew X's to mark herself and the other detectives and the letters B for Burn and R for Ryan. She stared at the page as if she could imagine the letters into action.

From the moment Ryan approached (she could see him even now, loose khaki pants and black T-shirt, bushy hair) they had figured him for a drug customer. He had the look. But no drugs changed hands. She wrote on the page: "Why didn't Burn hand over any drugs? Maybe there was no drug deal."

Burn and Ryan had run away and hidden. Together. That made no sense. It was easier to be caught that way. She remembered Ryan holding Burn's arm as they ran, dragging him along. She wrote in her notebook: "Why not split up? Why run away together? Why would Ryan need to keep Burn close by?"

Then the bridge. She flipped back to her simple drawings, the X's, the B and R. Now she drew another map, of the bridge, herself, Burn, and Ryan. And then Burn went over the edge. She remembered the look in Ryan's eyes after he pushed Burn. Stubbornness. Resignation. He was not going to be arrested. She would have to shoot him. But she couldn't. She thought about Jacqueline, as she often did now. No sign of her since the night her friend Risa disappeared. Were they both dead? Were they dead because Caroline hadn't been able to deal with Ryan, either by arresting him or by shooting him? She wrote on the page: "What the hell's the matter with me?"

She threw the notebook across the room and it hit the wall and slid down to the small table where she kept her telephone, teetered on the edge, and fell.

So, how come I can imagine it?

She tried to think like Blanton, by applying the test of aberration, looking for the pattern that was revealed in the breaking of the pattern. The New Orleans janitor might've gone around forever picking up and killing prostitutes and drug addicts that he didn't know. But the fifteen-year-old girl? He worked at her school.

Caroline imagined Lenny Ryan's patterns: He kills hookers

because he blames his girlfriend for betraying him, for being a hooker and getting herself killed. He killed his uncle and the pawnshop owner during robberies. So why kill Burn? They'd always assumed he killed Burn to create a distraction. Could there be some other reason?

This whole time she'd been focusing on Ryan. They all had. But what about the young drug dealer? It shocked her, how little she knew about Burn. She'd read his file and had never found any connection to Lenny Ryan, other than the one they heard from the pawnshop owner, that he occasionally pimped some girls. They had gone over his files and talked to his friends and associates, but none of the dead prostitutes' names had come up. She tried to compose Burn's file from memory, but she couldn't, and realized she wouldn't sleep until she went down to the office and read the whole stupid file. She went to her bedroom, slipped into a pair of sweatpants, socks, and tennis shoes. She pulled her hair back in a short ponytail. In the living room, she turned off a light and caught a sliver of headlight through the drawn curtains of her window as a car pulled up to the curb across the street.

Dupree. She had been expecting him for weeks. Wanting him to come some nights. Dreading it other nights. Tonight, she didn't know how she felt. She turned the deadbolt, opened the door, and stepped out onto the porch. And then she froze. It wasn't Dupree idling across the street from Caroline's house. It was a man in a small, red sedan, and from her porch she could see his baseball cap and beard.

37

Dupree lurched awake in his car, in front of his old house. He checked his watch. Eleven-thirty. He must have fallen asleep. He wiped his mouth on his sleeve, stretched, and looked up at the house. The curtains were closed now. He imagined Debbie waking up on the couch and seeing the patrol car parked in front of the house, staring for a while and then pulling the blinds. This must have seemed to her perfectly in character for a husband who, for so many years, came home without ever really coming home.

He started the car and drove off, blinking away his fatigue. At the end of the block he turned on his headlights. His shift had ended two hours ago. He didn't know that he could work any harder to get himself fired. At the end of his shift he was supposed to turn in his patrol car, or at least call in and say he was going to be late. The dispatcher would be going crazy trying to locate him. Understandably, the brass took it pretty seriously when a cop fell asleep in his car, especially at the end of shift, because for all the dispatchers knew he could be lying dead somewhere. Dupree switched his radio back on, prepared to be excoriated on the air. But the radio exploded with the frenzy of a call. "Charley-ten, en route . . . Charley-two, en route." Patrol units headed for something. "Be advised, the caller says male subject has a knife." The dispatcher was apparently on the phone with a witness who described a man and a woman fighting. "Baker-six. You need assistance there?" Cars from other sectors offered help.

Groggy, Dupree turned on his siren and lights and stepped heavily on the gas, the idea forming inside his sleep-dulled mind that perhaps his two-hour disappearance would be lost in the confusion of a big call.

He should tell the dispatcher he was en route, but that might just further confuse the situation. He listened, picking up bits and pieces. A domestic? A woman being beaten. He picked up the address, the East 800 block of Sprague, and understood the frenzy. It was right in the middle of the strip where Lenny Ryan was trolling for victims.

He sped down the rest of the Freya Hill, the trunk of his car slapping against the road as the car leveled off each flat side street and then bounded down the steep hill again. He ran traffic lights, slowing enough to give himself time to dodge drunk drivers, and within a couple of minutes he'd pulled up to Landers' Cove, the boat dealership surrounded by the high cyclone fence. Two other patrol units were there already, the officers yelling at a couple on the sidewalk across the street, a tall Hispanic woman in a miniskirt and a drunk white guy in dirty jeans. They were locked at the shoulders like Sumo wrestlers, screaming and swinging from close range at each other's heads.

"Let go of her!" yelled a cop Dupree recognized as being named Vasquez. Dupree moved to the other side, so that he, Vasquez, and the other officer were coming from different angles, each with his hands out, trying to calm the situation.

"She's tryin' to kill me!" the man yelled. As if to show that he was telling the truth, the woman brought her other hand up and cut the man across his side with a stubby little knife. The guy yelped and hit her in the face and she cried out as they lurched away from Dupree, squawking and swinging at each other.

They danced this way over to the other cop, a younger guy that Dupree didn't know, who tried to grab the woman's arm. She jerked her head up—blood spraying out from her nose and mouth—and swung the knife at the officer, who leaped back. The woman's movement caused the couple to lose their balance and they tumbled to the pavement. The woman landed on the hand holding the knife and it squirted free, but before Vasquez or Dupree or the other cop could do anything the man reached over, grabbed the knife, and tried to slash the woman across her already bleeding face. She got one of her hands up in time and the knife opened her palm and more blood spurted.

Vasquez threw himself into the man and knocked him off the bleeding, crying woman. The knife flew out of his hand and they rolled off the sidewalk onto the street, and suddenly the man was on top, grabbing Vasquez by his hair and slamming the back of his head into the curb. The other officer was there in a flash, swinging his side handle baton across the drunk man's shoulder. From Dupree's vantage point, it looked as if the man had actually been lifted in the air, the blow from the baton raising him off Vasquez and depositing him a few feet away, on his side in the street. Dupree pounced on the man, cranked his left arm up, and pushed his own baton into the man's neck.

"Don't move!" he yelled, and then over his shoulder: "You all right, Vasquez?"

"I'm gonna kill that fucking bitch!" the man beneath him screamed.

"I'm okay," Vasquez said. He started to say something else, but stopped. Dupree could hear a rustle of activity behind him. "Watch out!" Vasquez yelled.

The next thing Dupree felt was a sharp pain in his shoulder.

"Let him go!" the woman yelled. "Donnie! Donnie!"

Dupree brought his side handle baton up and hit the woman and she fell back, leaving the blade in his shoulder. The other officer grabbed the woman and wrestled her to the ground.

"You okay, baby?" screamed the man on the ground and he squirmed beneath Dupree. Not knowing what else to do and wanting to tend to the knife in his shoulder, Dupree cranked a little harder on the man's arm. "Aaah!" yelled the man, but he finally went limp and allowed Dupree to handcuff him.

Other police cars were arriving, as well as paramedics. Dupree reached back over his own shoulder and felt for the knife handle. He pulled it out. It was a small kitchen paring knife. It had gone straight in and not too deep, maybe a couple of inches. Still, Dupree knew what this meant. The Big Worry. There were plenty of small worries on patrol. Break up a street fight and it's like you're wading into a giant petri dish of unknown germs and bacteria and viruses. Drag some old transient to detox and you automatically start scratching, whether you've picked up his head lice or not. But the Big Worry was something else entirely, something that dried out your mouth every time you noticed a scratch on your arm, every time you found someone else's blood on your skin.

He didn't know a cop who hadn't been strapped with the Big Worry at least once. In the everyday buzzes of adrenaline on the street, you don't notice the bite marks or the dried blood until later, when you're alone with your thoughts. Of course, the odds were astronomical, but that didn't matter at three in the morning, after your shift, lying next to your wife, wondering whose blood cells were mingling with yours. Dupree had never known a cop or paramedic to get it that way, but that didn't stop the Big Worry. This little paring knife had slashed both of these drunks and then had been calmly deposited in Dupree's shoulder, joining their blood as plainly as a transfusion.

A paramedic arrived and Dupree took his uniform shirt off and then his T-shirt. The blood made a circle on the back of his T-shirt the size of a baseball

"I love you, Donnie!" the drunk woman was yelling as the paramedics finished bandaging her wounds and the cops eased her into a patrol car.

"I love you too, baby!" Donnie yelled back.

"That's touching," Dupree said quietly, under his breath. The paramedic applied some cream to his shoulder. It burned worse than the stabbing.

"You need stitches," the paramedic said.

Dupree rolled his eyes. "Can you do it? I don't want to go to the hospital."

"Sorry. I'll bandage it for now, but you're gonna have to go in and get stitched." The paramedic reached for his kit. "When was your last tetanus shot?"

"I had one for lunch today," Dupree said.

The patrol corporal came by with his camera and snapped a picture of Dupree's wound, and then Dale Henderson, the zombie-eyed graveyard sergeant for Charley Sector, came over to look. He was a few years younger and Dupree was taken aback by the condescension in his voice, even as he tried to make a joke. "I guess this is what happens when you respond to a call off your shift."

"I guess," Dupree said.

"You had us a little worried," Henderson said. "Why'd you turn off your radio?"

"I don't know. My shift ended . . . and I guess I wasn't thinking."

Without looking up from Dupree's shoulder, Henderson asked, "Where were you drinking tonight, Alan?"

"I wasn't drinking!" Dupree didn't like the snap in his own voice. It was a natural question for Henderson to ask. "I wasn't drinking," he repeated more quietly.

Henderson checked his watch. "Okay, but you understand my asking. Two hours after your shift ends, you just happen to be driving past a call in another sector?"

"I wasn't drinking, Dale." He blew a mouthful of air toward the other sergeant.

Henderson shrugged as he wrote something in his notebook. "It's no big deal. You're clearly not drunk. I was just curious."

But Dupree couldn't shake the desire to explain himself. "Debbie and I split up almost two months ago," he said. He told Henderson everything that had happened, from the Christian concert to his decision to drive by his wife's house when his shift ended. Henderson quietly took notes. "I was sitting outside her house and it was so quiet," Dupree said. "I guess that's why I turned off my radio, because of that quiet." He told Henderson about the fight and the knife in his shoulder, and when he was done Dupree laughed ironically. "Just put down that I was drinking. That's a lot less pitiful."

Dupree remembered Henderson's own messy divorce, six, seven years earlier, in that same cluster of breakups as Pollard's. Henderson had been dating a woman in the prosecutor's office, a clerk he later married. Dupree's story seemed to have softened him. "Well," he said, "you were a big help with the homecoming king and queen over there."

"Yeah, I should've stayed asleep."

"You should've called in and told someone you were off work," Henderson said, a scolding tone in his voice. "You're gonna have to write this up yourself, you know, explain how you got stabbed outside your sector, two hours after your shift ended."

"Yeah," Dupree said. "I figured as much."

Henderson flopped his notebook closed and considered Dupree carefully. "You takin' care of yourself, Alan?"

Dupree just nodded and watched Henderson walk away. The paramedic finished taping the bandage on his shoulder and handed Dupree a handful of antiseptic creams in small packages connected at the ends like sausages. "After they stitch you up, you're gonna need to keep an eye out for infection," the paramedic said.

"Thanks," Dupree said. He put his uniform shirt on, and gave the T-shirt to a patrol officer to take to the evidence room. When he stood up to button his shirt, Dupree noticed an old man across the street, pressed against the chain-link fence of the boat dealership, watching him, a guy in a security uniform. Dupree walked over.

"I don't envy you guys," the old man said. "I don't know where you get your restraint, how you don't just shoot idiots like that."

"Did you witness our little party here?"

"I'm the one who called the police. They were just walking along, both of 'em as drunk as the day, just laughing, and I'm watching 'em, thinking how nice it is that even drunks get to fall in love. And then she wanted to go one way and he wanted to go the other and next thing you know . . . Battling Bickersons."

Dupree looked through the fence, past the old man to the rows of yachts and smaller boats in the sales yard of Landers' Cove. In the center of the huge lot was a glass-and-steel showroom that was in the process of being remodeled. Construction crews had set up a trailer and a small crane, and the one-story, glass storefront had been stripped to its metal frame, which apparently was being expanded.

"What's going on here?" Dupree asked.

The security guard noted the construction and turned back.

"They're expanding, adding Jet Skis and snowmobiles. What do you call 'em? Snowboards. I guess they're gonna call the new part Landers' Mountain."

Landers' Cove had been here at least forty years, and during that time the wealthy South Hill people had been forced to come down to this ever-worsening neighborhood to buy their boats. The owner had continued to pour money into the place, hoping to wait out the neighborhood. Of course, Dupree had seen neighborhoods gentrified. But he never would've seen it coming in this neighborhood. Across the street, a three-story brick building also was being remodeled. It had housed a dive bar and two levels of lowlife apartments for as long as Dupree could remember. Now the facade was being scrubbed and a demolition crew had set up a chute leading to a dump truck and was gutting the building of its lathe and plaster.

"What's going in across the street?" Dupree asked.

"Electronics store," the old man said. "'Course, if they keep cleaning up the neighborhood, I'm gonna be out of a job."

Dupree remembered when he'd been on the task force, mistaking Kevin Verloc for a potential suspect, only to be reminded that Verloc ran the biggest security company in the city. "You must work for Verloc," Dupree said.

"That's right," said the old security guard.

"How long have you worked here?"

"At the boat shop? Six, eight months."

"And how long have you worked for Kevin?"

The old guy smiled wryly. "Ever since the doctor slapped his butt."

"You're his father?"

"Paul Verloc," the man said and gestured toward the fence, as if to show he would shake hands if they weren't separated by the chain link.

"It's good to meet you," Dupree said. "I'm Alan Dupree."

Verloc's father nodded. It seemed like years ago that Dupree had been fishing for tips and had mistakenly called Kevin Verloc.

"You ever talk to anyone about these murders?" Dupree asked.

"Couple weeks ago," Paul Verloc said. "A woman came by and asked if I'd seen anything out of the ordinary." The old guy laughed. "It's amazing what you start to think of as ordinary. I've walked around corners and seen kids, fifteen, sixteen years old with a needle stuck in their arm, givin' some old drunk a smoothie. And a cop asks if I've seen anything out of the ordinary and I can't come up with a thing."

Dupree nodded. "I know what you mean."

"I do miss the girlies, though," the old man admitted. "Some of 'em were rude and you couldn't trust 'em, but most of 'em you felt kinda sorry for." Absentmindedly, Paul touched his middle finger to an age spot where his hairline had once been, running the finger across the lines of his brow beneath his silver, receding hair. "You figure they moved to another neighborhood?"

"For the time being," Dupree said. He finished buttoning his shirt and checked his watch. Going on three now. "Well," he said, "it was good talking to you."

Paul Verloc touched his radio to his temple and tipped it toward Dupree.

In the car, Dupree sat for a moment staring at the blood-streaked sidewalk. He'd been punched or kicked or scraped weekly as a patrol officer, usually breaking up a fight like this one, but this stabbing was the most serious injury he'd ever sustained as a cop. As a young man he'd imagined police work as a series of Walter Mitty daydreams, in which he was stabbed or grazed by a gunshot while protecting some beautiful young woman, solving some master crime. But this was the truth of the job—a paring knife in your shoulder from a drunk woman you were trying to help.

Dupree pulled a small notebook from his pocket and jotted down a few notes to make sure he included them in his incident report. He wrote down exactly what he'd heard the woman yell, the name of the side street, the closest businesses and the distance between the chain-link fence and the sidewalk. He started the car and had begun driving toward the hospital when it occurred to him that he should probably write his report tonight, before he got his stitches. He turned the car and headed for the cop shop.

He drove over the Monroe Street Bridge and pulled his car into a space in front of the Public Safety Building, saving his explanation at the garage for later. He used his ID card to go in through a back door, emerging in the dark hallway outside the detectives' offices, and was on his way to the front desk when he realized he was standing in front of the door to the task force office. Dupree stood outside it for a moment, listening. It was quiet inside. He pulled out his ID badge, with the dark magnetic strip down the side. By now they should have changed the lock or taken his ID off the list of those that would open the door. But when he swiped his card through the runner, the lock clicked open.

It was dark inside, the entire room lit by two desk lamps left on by detectives. Dupree walked straight to Spivey's desk, his old desk. The thing that galled him wasn't that a shit like Spivey was valued more than he was by the police department. He'd been around long enough to know that police brass were as impressed as anyone by the power of youth, the lure of a person who seems to know new things. This was especially true of cops, who fell all over themselves before a cop who could turn on a computer. But even that didn't really bother Dupree. To be honest, he had been slow to make adjustments. He should have gotten a profiler on the case. He should have gotten the computer database up and running and done a better job with follow-ups. What bothered Dupree was that he hadn't seen it coming. From a purely political standpoint he'd underestimated Spivey completely, allowed his dislike for the kid to translate into dismissiveness. He could have used the kid's expertise and it would have helped them both, but instead he shunted Spivey to the side. And for what?

Two spots over, her chair was pushed deep into the well of her desk, a sweater draped over the chairback. Spivey had gotten the job in Major Crimes that Caroline deserved. That's why he gave the kid such a hard time, why he did so many things.

He walked to Caroline's desk, picked up the photograph of her mother, then set it down. Absentmindedly he pulled one of the drawers in her desk, but it was locked. He stepped away from her desk and took in the whole room, the room he'd once commanded—without Spivey's knowledge of science and profiling and computers, surely, but with a certain integrity. Mostly life is an ascension, it seemed to him, and he wondered what happened when you stopped climbing, when your progress began to be measured in the other direction and the best a person had to look forward to is retirement, the loss of responsibility and opportunity, the loss of function and friends.

He put his hands palms-down on her desk. For twelve years this was the only relationship he could have with Caroline, that of sergeant and officer, of mentor and student, and so he approached it with the heat and passion of an affair. He taught and inspired and cajoled her. He worked behind the scenes on her behalf, praising her in reports, whispering her name for promotions and big cases, coaxing her career with an honest zeal. He did more than that, of course, more than he should have, and more than she knew. It was ironic: To this woman, he had been faithful. And now that she was finally on the inside—everyone he cared about was inside now, it seemed, the curtains drawn on every house he drove past—Dupree was stuck on the outside. He ran his hand along the sweater on her chair, ashamed of the tactile thrill of her clothing, and his life suddenly seemed to him like a ship that had gone off course somewhere—although that wasn't quite right, because he knew exactly where and when. He wondered how many times he'd replayed that night in his head, how many times he heard her frightened voice on the radio, still two blocks away. Yelling at her to wait, he was almost there, her saying there wasn't time and then the terrible clap of a gunshot. Stumbling out of his car and down the driveway, finding her in the backyard beneath the sizzling bug lamp, pointing the gun at the drunk wife beater, who lay still at her feet. The mess at the crime scene and the interviews, the crush and bustle, then back at her apartment, the night stretching until dawn and seeming heavier than the collective weight of every night since, so that Dupree found himself believing that if they had just made love, it wouldn't be such a vivid and haunting possibility, would be just a memory: simple, sweet, and gone.

38

Shaking, Caroline backed into her house, grabbed her cell phone off the dining room table, and unholstered her gun from the shoulder strap hanging over a chair. She punched 911 on the phone, but already her mind was telling her that maybe she hadn't really seen Lenny Ryan, so she didn't hit the send button right away. She pressed herself against the wall to keep from being silhouetted by the lights in the house. She edged across the room to the wall, turned off the lights, and then crouched in front of the front window. The red car was gone, and immediately she wondered if it had ever been there. She grabbed her car keys from the entryway desk, dropped to her stomach, and crawled to the open front door. Nothing. She looked both ways, then came outside slowly and stood in a crouch, keeping the gun pointed to the ground as she came down the porch steps and climbed into her car. Her tires chirped as she backed out of the driveway.

She lived only a few blocks from Division, the main north-south street in the city, so she went that way, her head swinging from side to side as she looked down residential streets for some sign of the red car. She tried to be calm, to second-guess herself the way she would question an unreliable witness. She had just interviewed the exotic dancer who was approached by Ryan in a red car. So maybe she had just seen a red car slow down in front of her house (it happened all the time; she lived at the corner of an uncontrolled intersection) and imagined the man inside to be Ryan in a beard and baseball cap. Had the car even been red? It had happened too quickly for her to get a license plate number or a make and model, and colors at night were tough to see. But it was a small sedan, she knew that. Four doors. Maybe a GM product but more likely Japanese, a Nissan or a Mazda, she thought. Yes, Nissan. A Sentra, maybe. And yes, she was sure it was red.

If patrol got out now, they might have a chance of finding him—again, her mind cautioning, if it was him. And if it wasn't? Who knew what Spivey would make of this. She turned on her radio, but the dispatcher was on something else right now, two drunks fighting on East Sprague and some patrol officers who apparently had gotten into it with the drunks. Then, as she was fiddling with the radio, six blocks ahead Caroline saw what looked like a red car pass under a streetlight and turn right onto a side street. She stepped on the gas and flicked the switch to turn on her grille lights, veering past the cars until she reached the side street.

Her fingers clenched the wheel. The gun was a dead weight in her lap—a dumb place to carry a gun when you're speeding around like this. She carefully put it on the floor of the passenger side. When she reached the side street that the red car had turned down, Caroline cornered hard and saw it only three blocks ahead now, its driver as calm and even as someone on his way to work.

Within two blocks she caught him and he pulled over slowly, then seemed to reconsider, veering out toward the street, then settling back on the shoulder, in front of a clapboard house. The driver turned to the side and she could see the silhouette of a baseball cap; he turned forward again and sat still.

She should call for backup. She should have called for backup the minute she saw the car, but this second-guessing, this inability to trust herself, made her decisions slow and muddy. Without looking away from the figure in the driver's seat, Caroline reached with her right hand, patting the floor in front of the passenger seat until she found the butt of her handgun. She climbed out of the car carefully, using her door as a shield. She pointed the gun toward the red car and edged out from the car door to her left, sliding, staying low. The driver's side window on the red car came down slowly.

"Both hands out the window!" Caroline yelled. She steadied the gun.

He did and right away she knew by the skinny, shaking arms that this wasn't Lenny Ryan. Caroline edged closer until she could see that it was a boy in this car, maybe eighteen, nervously waiting for a ticket. She allowed the gun to slip to her side as she approached the red Nissan Sentra. A boy in a baseball cap looked up at her.

"Did you just drive past Corbin Park?" Caroline asked breathlessly.

"No, I swear," said the boy too quickly and more than a little defensively, as if driving by Corbin Park was illegal.

Caroline stood next to his car, breathing heavily. She looked in every direction, then back at the car and the nervous boy. She could see a bottle peeking out from just beneath his car seat. He moved his foot to cover it. "Hand me that," she said.

He reached down and handed her a bottle of Mickey's Wide Mouth beer.

"Is this any good?" she asked.

He shrugged. "Uh, it's not mine."

She laughed, releasing tension, then dumped the beer on the ground near her feet and tossed the empty bottle in the backseat.

"Recycle that," Caroline said. "And"—she tried to think of something—"signal when you turn, okay?"

Caroline walked back to her car and climbed in. She opened the glove box and put her gun inside, then closed it. Her cell phone flashed at her from the passenger seat—the numbers 9, 1, and 1 still on its face. She picked up the phone and turned it off.

When had she lost confidence in her senses? In New Orleans, when she'd been so certain she'd seen a girl being molested on a balcony? Or earlier, when she'd failed to stop Ryan from pushing Burn over the bridge? Or had the erosion begun six years ago?

Caroline started her car and drove back through her neighborhood, cutting up a side street along Corbin Park, a slim crust of pleasant homes around the park, fading quickly to apartment buildings and run-down houses with backyard sheds and cars on the lawns, to her neighborhood of small brick homes and remodeled bungalows.

She was surprised to find her house completely dark, then remembered turning off all the lights when she hid—apparently from some kid in a red Nissan with his first beer.

She hated going into a dark house, and anyway, this felt like one of those nights when it wouldn't be worth the effort of trying to sleep, when her mother's insomnia would get the best of her. She drove south on Monroe, a street of fifty-year-old, three-story brownstones mixed in with newer burger joints and appliance shops and convenience stores. Every third car she passed seemed to be red.

She parked at a meter in front of the Public Safety Building. At the turnout in front of the building Dale Henderson, the graveyard patrol sergeant, was climbing out of his car. He'd been Caroline's sergeant for a while, after Dupree had transferred out of patrol. Henderson waited for her and they walked toward the building together.

"What are you doing here so late?" he asked.

She smiled. "The fellas like it when I come in early and make coffee. What about you? Sounds like you guys fell into the shit tonight."

"How'd you hear about that?"

"Radio."

Henderson nodded and held the front door for her. "Can I ask you something?"

"Sure," Caroline said.

"Well. You're still close with Dupree, right?"

"Ye-e-e-ah," she said cautiously, wondering at the way he said "close," at the meaning of "still." "Why, what happened?"

"Well, for one, he showed up two hours after his shift was over, without calling in. And he jumped into a street fight and got stabbed in the shoulder for his effort."

Caroline felt her neck muscles tighten. "Is he all right?"

"He's fine. Couple of stitches. But when I asked him why he

didn't call in, he got all bent out of shape and finally said he was asleep in his car in front of his wife's house."

They stopped and faced each other in the large open foyer of the Public Safety Building. Directly ahead was the police sergeant's desk and behind that, the door to the detectives' offices.

Caroline had a bad feeling. "Why are you telling me this?" she asked.

Henderson glanced at his shoes. "Well, maybe this isn't my place, but having gone through a divorce myself, well, some-times"—he struggled to find the words—"the other party doesn't understand how much is at stake for the one leaving his family."

Other party? Caroline's hands balled up into fists. "I don't know what you think, Dale, but—"

He interrupted her. "A single person like yourself just goes . . . with the flow, so to speak. But for a guy like Alan . . . well, his decisions have an impact on other people."

Caroline turned and walked away.

He followed her. "I know it isn't my business—"

She said over her shoulder, "There is no *business*, Dale."

"I'm not being judgmental—"

She stopped and spun back to face him. "No, that's exactly what you're being. And you're full of shit." She stalked off, and this time he let her go. She punched in the code on the door to the detectives' offices and found herself in the long, bright hallway in front of the Special Investigations Unit, her anger bleeding away into worry about Dupree. She shouldn't be surprised by Henderson. There were no bigger gossips in the world than cops; you can't ask people who traffic in the flow of information in the community to turn it off when they return to the office.

Caroline swept her card and entered the SIU office and was immediately struck by the differences between her old office and her new digs. In the task force office, there were pictures on the walls of dead women, maps of where their bodies had been found or where they had disappeared, and, of course, Spivey's ubiquitous timeline.

The SIU office seemed almost quaint by comparison, pictures of busted drug houses here and there, photographs of cocaine and methamphetamine in its most common forms, charts of ecstasy and other designer stuff. It could be a high school science lab. Caroline went to her old desk and opened it, pulled out the thick file on Burn, with copies from all his court cases, adult and juvenile, and newspaper clippings after his death. The headline on the biggest story, a month after Burn washed away: "Family Still Waiting for Drowned Drug Dealer." That story was accompanied by a photograph of a young-looking black woman, Burn's mother, holding a picture of him in his sixth grade football uniform, his helmet proudly in the crook of his armpit.

Caroline picked up the thick file and backed out of the SIU office into the hallway, made sure the door lock clicked, and started for the task force office. She thought about Henderson, the way he implied that she was to blame for Dupree's situation, and although it made her mad, she felt the tug of guilt nonetheless.

She slid her ID card, entered the room, and there was Dupree, as if he'd just popped out of her thoughts. His back was to her, and he was standing at her desk holding her sweater. When the door closed, he jumped, dropped the sweater back on her chair, and turned.

There were only two lights on in the room, dim desk lamps turned downward. Seeing him there in his uniform reminded her of their time on patrol together, and she realized, maybe for the first time, just how long they had been wrapped up in each other like this and how much it had taken out of both of them.

"You scared me," Dupree said.

"Sorry."

"It's okay," he said. He looked around, realizing that she must wonder why he was in the task force office. He waved his ID card. "I didn't think my key still worked but it does. They probably ought to get that fixed."

"What are you doing here?" Caroline asked.

"I was on my way to write a report about how I went to a concert, fell asleep in my car, and got stabbed by a couple of drunks. How about you?"

There was a time—when she used to see him in that uniform regularly—when Caroline would've called Dupree the minute she saw that red car in front of her house, but everything felt different now, and she couldn't get Henderson out of her mind. *The other party*. "Catching up on some work."

He noted the dismissiveness in her voice, and he felt suddenly like a swing-shift patrol sergeant snooping around in the office of a top-priority task force.

She moved around to the worktable in the middle of the room, so that the table and her desk were now between her and Dupree. "Where'd you get stabbed?" she asked, as if she were asking where he'd gone for the weekend.

"Shoulder," he said.

"Oh." She put her files down on the table and began leafing through them, avoiding Dupree's eyes. "Did you get stitches?"

"I'm on my way." He was baffled by her matter-of-fact, condescending tone. "What's the matter?"

"Nothing."

"You can't talk about it? What, I'm a security breach now?"

"No. It's nothing like that. I just needed to look something up. You know how that is, one of those details that you can't shake."

"Yeah," Dupree said, "I know about things you can't shake." Her cold reserve ran across him like sandpaper, and it struck him as ironic that the woman he thought about most had pulled the furthest away. "Well," Dupree said, "I should go file my report. I don't want to hold up my firing."

Caroline smiled sadly as Dupree backed out of the office and let the door close.

He stood in the hallway, trying to comprehend what had just happened. He could handle it if Caroline didn't want to be with him; lately, he didn't want to be with himself. But that pitying tone was unbearable, and he thought again about Debbie drawing the curtains, about being outside, and suddenly he had the urge to just lay it out there for Caroline, his feelings and the blame and everything. Everything he had done was for her, to be with her, to take care of her. She could ignore him, but she couldn't ignore that.

This time he slammed his key card into the runner. It flashed green and he pushed the door and found Caroline staring at the floor in front of him, as if he hadn't just walked out of the room, but melted into the carpet. She looked up at Dupree and he wondered if he could swallow the words that were rising in his throat or if there was some reason to say them—*I have loved you for so long*—because as soon as he thought the words he knew they would sound trite and empty and beside the point. She knew that he loved her. And that wasn't the point, anyway. Love is easy; the drunks on the street tonight loved each other. What he had given her was what he couldn't even give his wife: six years of loyalty, fidelity, and sacrifice. He stood before her now, playing the years in a split second and believing right then that the job and the marriage and every assorted unhappiness was just a symptom of her, and he felt the need to explain himself, to show that he had fallen because of her. His shoulder ached, and even that seemed to be her fault, as he racked his memory for words more powerful and revealing than "I love you," something that would show all he had done for her.

"When I got to the house that night six years ago," Dupree said quietly, evenly, "you were standing by the guy you'd shot. And the knife—" He closed his eyes and tried to stop, knowing this would only break her in two. But part of him knew this had been the point all along, hurting her the way he hurt now, making her need him again.

"What?" she asked, but she could imagine what he was going to say and it made her sick. "The knife was what?"

"On the floor in the kitchen," he said, "near the woman. The guy didn't have the knife when he came at you. I picked it up and dropped it next to him."

39

Lenny Ryan found himself thinking about the dog he'd had growing up in Vallejo. His old man got the stupid animal—Lab mix of some kind—as a watchdog, but it just whimpered by the door all night, Lenny's dad throwing shoes from his bedroom and yelling at it to shut the fuck up. Then each morning his dad took the dog outside and leashed it to the front porch, and the minute he let go of its collar the dog tore through the yard, its leash uncoiling until he got twenty yards away, where it snapped like a whip and jerked the dog back by its neck.

The dog would get up then, take a piss, and run in the other direction until the leash snapped at exactly the same point on the other side of the yard, Lenny's dad yelling and laughing and getting the dog more agitated, until it raced off in another direction and . . . *snap.* Every morning began this way. His dad thought it was great, but Lenny found it sad that the dog seemed to forget every day what it learned the day before. Each morning it bolted as quick as ever, and even when it approached the ring of dead grass marking the end of its leash the stupid dog picked up speed, as if everything it had learned about the world was untrue, as if this time it might finally break free and just keep running.

Lenny was surprised to have that dog pop into his head while he lay flat against the ground, watching the street from beneath a van in a used car lot on Division. He'd been forced to hide just a mile from the lady cop's house—way too close. The streets should be full of police any minute now, and then he'd be on his way back to Lompoc or whatever version of state hole they had in Washington, where he'd live out his days walking the yard with the bangers and addicts, the stupid and mean and sick, all talking about the action they'd have when they got out, this piece of ass or that job or that bit of revenge, how when the doors opened *this time,* they'd break free and just keep running.

Lenny lifted himself onto his elbows so that he could see the dark street from the shadows beneath the van. Nothing. Was it possible the lady cop hadn't seen him? No way. She walked out of her house and stared right into the eyes. She must have seen him. Maybe they had set up a perimeter and were closing in. He pressed himself flat against the ground again.

Then again, they might not go for prison. What did they use in this state? Gas, electricity? He thought this was one of the states that gave you a choice. Hanging might even be one of the choices. Jesus, what would that be like? *Snap.*

Shelly had a dog. It was always yapping and so Lenny hadn't paid any attention that morning when it went all crazy and the cops came, searched the house, and found Shelly's stash—enough meth for an intent-to-deliver charge. Since it was his house, he was the one who got popped, but he figured he could do a year easier than Shelly, anyhow. He hadn't counted on catching five from the bitch prosecutor—some pinched old broad who stood at the podium in a short, gray suit flexing her calves. She talked the jury into a nickel upstate because it was Lenny's *third strike,* making that sound like the first two were slicing the heads off babies instead of theft of a car stereo and assault.

He spat and thought that he had some legitimate strikes now for the lady with the twitchy calves.

He rolled out from under the van and crawled under one parked closer to the street. He peered down Division but still didn't see lights. A few cars trolled easily down the street. Obviously they hadn't cordoned off traffic. The only explanation was the one that made no sense: She didn't call for backup.

Nothing this woman did made sense, from the first time she drew down on him and the pimp. After Lenny pushed the pimp into the river he tensed up, expecting to be plugged by her but she didn't shoot him. She ran downstream after the pimp and Lenny wouldn't have given her one in a thousand, but goddamn if she didn't just about do it. Leaning over the bridge watching her, Lenny caught himself rooting for her.

Then, when he saw the lady cop again on the street, posing as a hooker, something clicked. He couldn't stop staring at her. She wore her hair the same length and color as Shelly used to. He hadn't noticed that before. While she walked along Sprague that night, he broke into her car and went through her glove box until he found an envelope with her address on it. He'd just left her car when she came walking down the street. He showed her the girl in the refrigerator because suddenly it seemed important that someone know what he was doing. He supposed that was why he left her the box with Shelly's stuff. And why he drove past her house sometimes. Like today.

He hadn't even planned to come to Spokane today. He spent the morning working around Angela's cabin in the woods north of town—stringing new barbed wire, repairing a pump house that collapsed under the snow. Sometimes, when he was working, Lenny imagined that he was like the other men he saw on the ranches around Springdale, and his old life seemed like someone else's. In that life, he and Shelly were always longing for better shit—better sex and better highs and a better life. Maybe Angela had been knocked down enough that she understood what a waste of time better could be. Better is the dog running against his leash. Maybe life could be a string of small, bearable moments—work in the sun, come in for a sandwich, watch TV.

Today at noon, Lenny had come inside for a sandwich, switched on the TV, and caught the beginning of the news. The pimp's body had finally surfaced. Lenny stood in front of the TV in his work clothes for a long time, holding his sandwich at his side. He wrote a note for Angela and took her car into Spokane.

He parked outside city hall, checked his shaved head and beard in the mirror, took a breath, and went inside. All this time, he'd been worried that someone would recognize him, but that turned out to be the easiest part. Most of the people didn't even look up from their windows, and the one person who asked for his identification didn't even compare the picture of Angela's ex-husband to him. The other part turned out to be more difficult than he'd imagined, though, and he bounced from department to department collecting building permits and zoning applications, wondering if this would be easier if he'd gone to college.

For the deeds he had to go to the county courthouse, right in front of the police station and the jail. He even passed a cop in uniform, nodding and saying hello as he walked through the metal detectors and into the old courthouse. An hour later, he had everything—deeds and transfers and the paperwork from the city. He'd even requested some court documents on a civil suit and slipped a guy twenty dollars to mail them to him. But none of it added up to anything. What had he expected? A mention of Shelly? He had a few drinks, drove around, and found himself outside the lady cop's house, and that's when the shit exploded.

He checked his watch again. Forty minutes and still nothing. They weren't coming. That was the only explanation. He thought back to the alley, how she had followed him and didn't even call for backup until after she'd found the body. The lady was just plain nuts.

Lenny rolled out from under the van and made his way back to Angela's car. He started it and left Division on residential streets, turning whenever he saw a pair of headlights in front of him. He had made it a couple of miles north and east—thinking about how much work this had all turned out to be—when he stopped the car, beat his thumbs against the steering wheel for a minute, then turned to go back to her house again.

He made his way west on side streets past her neighborhood, then cut down Maple until he was at the bottom of the North Hill. He cut back east on more residential streets and alleys, crossed Monroe and found himself across from Corbin Park. He cruised through the lady cop's neighborhood, and tried to be nonchalant as he drove past her house. It didn't matter, anyway.

Her car was gone. The house was dark. And Lenny was suddenly tired, like he'd been straining against something for a long time.

With the dog, after they finally got fed up with its whimpering and took to leaving it outside on its leash all night, an angry neighbor cut the leash and the dog ran three blocks, right down the middle of the street, and got hit by the first car it saw. His dad said that was okay, the dog was "out of its misery." No animal that Lenny's family owned ever just died. They all got put out of one misery or another, and if that made Lenny feel better about the animals, it didn't do much for his opinion of life.

He drove around the block again and parked across from her house, right where he'd been when she came out before. He idled in front of her house and thought about switching the car off, leaning back in his seat and closing his eyes. If he did that, it would be all over. The lady cop would come home, find him asleep, and have him arrested. That might be okay. The truth was, he'd never minded being locked up at night. It was quiet and at least he was never tired inside, not the way he was out here. He knew most guys saw it the opposite way and couldn't hack it at night, the dead-heavy loneliness, but it was the endless days that got to Lenny, the grind of time in the dayroom, the sad shuffle of guys waiting for the pay phone, the collective weight of threats on the yard.

He couldn't do any more days and he certainly couldn't handle hanging. So the idea of waiting for her to arrest him faded away and he shifted into gear and started back for Angela's house. But even as he left, Lenny knew that he would show up here again, confront her with what he'd been doing and force *something* to happen, even if that meant that one of them killed the other.

When he imagined that, it was in a kind of daydream, the way kids daydream about war—as valiant and painless. His vision was even more specific: him slipping easily over the dam, the lady cop reaching out and taking his hands, the two of them drawn over the edge together and drifting away, out of their misery and into sleep.

40

Her first thought was to turn herself in, call Internal Affairs in the morning, admit what had happened, and hope there wouldn't be much fanfare when they fired her. She even felt a kind of relief about it. Forget Lenny Ryan. Forget Spivey and McDaniel and Curtis Blanton. But there was still one person she couldn't forget. Caroline slumped into a chair. "Alan," she said, and then nothing else. He stood in front of her, still.

"I'm sorry," he said. "I shouldn't have told you."

If she turned herself in it would end his career. Simple as that. Once the investigation was over, she might survive in a less vital job, on the DARE team or teaching at the academy or working on some community program. After all, knife or no knife, the wife beater had been within the kill zone of twenty-four feet, that area police officers were taught is close enough that your life is in danger, even from an unarmed subject. Any threat within that area created a judgment call about whether to respond with deadly violence. The shooting would take some explaining, but it would hold up. But Dupree had tampered with evidence. He would go to jail for trying to help her.

He leaned across the desk and tried to make eye contact. "I'm really sorry, Caroline. I don't know why I told you that."

But she figured they both knew. Henderson knew, Dupree's wife knew, and more than likely the whole department knew. That's because what happened in bed between two people was less significant than what the world saw, the sum of all the smiles and stares, the eye contacts that last a bit too long.

The promise of a thing was in many ways worse than the thing itself. She could pretend to everyone else that Dupree's leaving his wife had nothing to do with her. She could tell herself that they hadn't slept together. She could wait a respectable amount of time before they got together, but had there ever been any doubt, either in her mind or in Dupree's—or in Henderson's, for that matter— that they would end up with each other? A bitterness rose in her throat, and she thought that self-deception was a thousand flavors that all tasted the same.

"I didn't expect anything from you," she said. "I didn't ask . . ." She didn't finish the thought, that she hadn't asked him to leave his wife.

"I know," he said and looked at his shoes.

It was true; she hadn't asked him to leave his wife. But in some ways what she had done was worse. By *not asking* him, she had strapped them both to the potential of this thing. If they'd just gone ahead and had sex that night, any night, if they began to make demands of each other, they could have begun the long process of letting each other down, of disappointing and betraying each other; instead they allowed this to become the worst thing an attraction could be: pure. They trapped the moment of first infatuation and had selfishly kept it pristine.

No wife or husband or twenty-four-year-old bartender could live up to the person you were trying *not* to sleep with. Daydreams never have bad breath or forget important dates. Add up Dupree's sacrifices for her, the small ones she'd known and the big one she'd discovered, and it made a thin lie of every stare and smile, of every hard swallow during six years of working together and avoiding each other and imagining each other. But now, Caroline felt as guilty as if they'd been caught in bed together.

"I wanted to help you," he said.

"Should I thank you?" she asked coldly.

"No. Of course not."

"You had no right to make that decision for me, Alan. If I screwed up, then—"

"You didn't screw up," he said. "You did the right thing. You didn't know that he didn't have the knife anymore. What if he'd grabbed your gun?"

"Jesus, he was stone drunk!"

"No! It was a good shoot, Caroline."

She had been on the way to forgiving him, to understanding him, but his condescension boiled her blood. "Listen to yourself, Alan? Who the hell plants a knife on a *good* shoot?"

He raised his hands. "You were upset. I was trying to make it easier for you."

"But now you *want* me to be upset. Now you *want* it to be hard."

Dupree rubbed his temples. "No. The reason I told you now . . ."

"You should leave," Caroline interrupted.

"The reason I told you was so you'd see how much I—"

She leaped up and interrupted again, shaking in front of him. "How much! How much!" She took a breath. "Goddamn it, Alan! You think I don't know how much? I've been here the last six years too. And most of that time I've spent alone!" Her voice quavered and she set her jaw. "I want you to leave, *now*." She stood and opened the Burn files, pretending to work, even though she couldn't read the type through her bleary eyes.

When she looked up, he was holding his hands out to the side, either a sign of surrender or a plea for understanding, but she was accepting neither right now, and so his arms fell and he nodded. "Okay," he said.

He took a few steps toward the door, then turned back, but decided not to say whatever it was that had stopped him. He left the room and the door hissed closed behind him. Caroline held her breath until the lock clicked into place. She waited for another minute, then walked to her desk and dropped the Burn file on it. Then she picked up her phone and threw it halfheartedly across the room. It clanged harmlessly against the side of a desk and to the floor.

That night six years ago, Dupree held her, stroked her hair, and told her she'd done the right thing, all the time knowing what she knew, that she had panicked. Later, her mother had done her best to console Caroline with her expertise in the field of television police. "So you shot someone. Isn't that why they gave you a gun?" Caroline knew only one other cop who had killed someone, and yet her mother was right in a way. In the way she was always right. They *had* given her a gun for just such occasions. And that was the thing she had allowed herself to forget. It wasn't the shooting that had shaken her. It was pretending she hadn't screwed up the shooting. She hadn't known about Dupree planting the knife, but she engaged in her own deception by ignoring the voice that told her the shoot was bad. Instead, she'd said nothing and allowed an official lie to replace her own intuition.

That night, she'd had another second or two before she needed to fire and maybe she didn't need to fire at all. And yet the other cops had always been supportive. She had shot a man from twenty feet away, a drunk, enraged man closing fast, a man coming at her after nearly killing his wife. After her senses returned, after Dupree apparently worked over the scene, Caroline had been relieved to see the knife lying next to the wife beater's body; but in truth, that was the first time she remembered seeing it. That was the disconcerting part, feeling like a fraud, hearing her colleagues say she'd done the right thing, even that she was courageous—*courageous!*—all the while knowing she had only been afraid.

Glenn Ritter. That was his name. She hardly ever thought of him by name, just as "the wife beater" or "the guy." After the funeral, Caroline had stepped up and introduced herself to Ritter's wife, a bruised and bandaged woman leaning between two crutches. Mrs. Ritter said that when they were first married, her husband's drinking seemed random and the violence merely a threat, but soon the threat was replaced by casts and purple bruises and the sounds of his boots in the hallway. Over the years he began to get drunk every weekend, and some weeknights too, and the violence developed a pattern, with some connection between the frequency and the severity. With all seriousness Mrs. Ritter told Caroline that if she had paid better attention she might even have charted it, like the tides.

But then Mrs. Ritter got quiet, matter-of-factly thanked Caroline for saving her life, and turned away. What Caroline had gone there expecting, of course, was some kind of forgiveness, a release from her guilt, but that was probably too much to ask from a woman who had endured tidal beatings from a man she loved.

While Caroline imagined that her colleagues doubted her ability, all along the doubt had come from herself. She'd shot an unarmed man. This wasn't about the procedural validity of the shooting or whether the man deserved it or even whether Caroline might have been in danger. These things were as arguable as they were beside the point. What was inarguable was whether Caroline *believed* she had exhausted every other way out of the situation. She hadn't. Six years hiding behind the idea of a police kill zone dulled her intuition and her faith in herself. She could live with her own fallibility more easily than she could live beneath so many layers of deceit.

For all those years, to buy into the necessity of Glenn Ritter's shooting was to buy into the simplicity of good guys and bad guys, to believe some people didn't have consciences, which was the defense she saw other cops use, but had refused to allow in herself. It was why she had been so intent on the double major, not just criminal justice, but also poetry, not just investigation, but humanity as well. It wasn't an issue of compassion as much as it was honesty and effectiveness. You get nowhere investigating bad guys. But if you search for truth, she really believed, it reveals itself as tiny breaks and fissures—cracks through which we can glimpse our own darker natures.

Again, she heard Blanton: *This one's just broken.* That was the easiest thing for cops, to imagine *them* as broken, and us as whole. But what if our own cracks and fissures differ from theirs only in degree, and if we engage in the same brand of self-deceit? Most cops didn't like to think of crime in such terms. They saw absolutes like the baby in the back room of Thick Jay's drug house. And she wasn't thinking that her shooting of Glenn Ritter was the same as Lenny Ryan pushing Burn into the river.

But there wasn't as much distance as she'd like to believe, and if she knew anything about herself, it was the shudder of fear and self-loathing that accompanied those things she regretted. She had to imagine that Lenny Ryan felt the same shudder, that he felt *something* she would recognize. She'd never met a criminal who thought he was evil. There was always someone worse; even child murderers and rapists could describe those people whose acts had less justification and more brutality. In the end, Caroline believed, we all expect *our* sins to be forgiven. That was the thing she had forgotten, the thing Dupree had unwittingly returned: The lies we tell the world are nothing compared to those we tell ourselves.

She looked down at the files in front of her, ran her fingers across the name on the tab. "Hatch, Kevin C. DOB 11-9-81."

Blanton said you catch these guys in the aberration—the difference—but that wasn't quite right. At the slightest provocation from his principal, the custodian confessed to being a serial murderer. Yet he wouldn't admit killing the fifteen-year-old girl. Somewhere deep beneath the cracks and fissures the custodian clung desperately to the lie that he hadn't done it. So maybe you find these guys in the same place you find yourself. In the lie.

Whatever the actual reason Lenny Ryan pushed Burn over the bridge, there was another reason that he clung to, and even if it was bullshit that was the reason Caroline needed to find. Guys like Blanton pretended to want to understand these killers, but they wanted only to exclude them, to separate themselves and their own dark fantasies from these monsters. That was Spivey's lie and McDaniel's and Dupree's too, she supposed. And, of course, Blanton's. *This one's just broken.*

Caroline felt herself dissolve into the pages of Kevin Hatch's criminal files. The first entry was from 1986, an order from family court to have custody of the boy granted to the grandmother while the boy's mother was in a drug rehabilitation program. In 1988 the mother got out of rehab, and Kevin Hatch went back with her. In 1989 the boy's father died in Seattle and probate court listed the sum of Kevin's inheritance: "a 1983 Ford Escort, a wristwatch, and assorted personal belongings." Kevin's first contact with juvenile court was in 1991, at the age of nine, for theft. The arrests came regularly after that: possession at thirteen, assault at fourteen, auto theft at fifteen. Intelligence reports from SIU and the prosecutor's office had Burn heavily involved in a gang, running drugs and hookers from an apartment off East Sprague. By the time he was seventeen Burn had been arrested nine times, convicted five. She quickly did the math; from fourteen to seventeen, he had spent more time in juvenile detention than on the street. In the last couple of years of his life Burn was arrested three more times, but convicted just once, of a minor possession charge. She recognized the pattern, not of a young man who was no longer breaking the law, but one who was learning how not to get caught.

Caroline had read all of this before, of course, but this time she tried to look beyond the words, for something she might have missed. She was frustrated by how limited police reports were, by their narrow focus, their lack of context and background. Reports like this were written to prove one small point, that "Kevin Hatch was in possession of methamphetamine when he was questioned on 9-11-98" or that "a black male subject identified as Kevin Hatch was observed leaving the scene on 1-4-96."

She reached down into her desk and grabbed a pen and notebook, drew a line down the middle of a notebook page and on one side listed every address, every business, and every date in the files. On the other side, she listed every name from the files: "Hatch was observed selling narcotics to Carl M. Higuera . . ." and on and on. She filled four pages of the notebook with dates, addresses, and incidents, as well as a list of thirty-four names of relatives, associates, lawyers, and witnesses to his crimes, and when she looked up at the clock she was stunned to see that it was almost three in the morning.

Finally, she turned on the computer. When the database was up and running, Caroline typed in the names from her notebook, one at a time, checking them against other names that came up during the investigation, during interviews with hookers and victim profiles. Another hour passed, the first fifteen names revealing nothing, and then she came to the name "Rae-Lynn Pierce." She looked back at the file the name had come from, Burn's 1998 arrest for possession of narcotics—a charge that was later dropped because of some sloppy evidence room procedures. A young woman with no identification, who listed her name as Rae-Lynn Pierce, had been in the car with Burn when he was arrested.

She spun in her chair and typed the name into the first field of the database. A hit came from Caroline's prostitute registry.

Pierce, Rae-Lynn, DOB 4-9-81
Conviction, Solic. Prost. 1996.
Conviction, Poss. Narc. 1999.
Warrants: FTA, 10-13-00
Last Contact with police: 1999.
Last Known Address: 2144 W. First Ave., Spokane 7-1-00

She stared at the date of birth. Eighty-one. That would make Rae-Lynn Pierce twenty years old. Twenty. Caroline jumped up and her chair spilled over. She bumped into desks crossing the room, pulled the reverse address directory from the bookshelf near Spivey's desk and leafed through it. Rae-Lynn Pierce's last known address was a drug halfway house.

Caroline returned to the computer, righted her chair, and searched another field for Rae-Lynn Pierce. The computer returned one more match, meaning she was mentioned in one other file that had been entered into the computer—the homicide file of Shelly Nordling, Lenny Ryan's old girlfriend. Again, Caroline knocked her chair over when she stood up. Across the room, in the cabinet beneath Spivey's timeline, Caroline opened a drawer and found the Shelly Nordling case file, which was filed under "Unrelated Cases," since she had been killed by a john or a pimp before Lenny Ryan began his string of murders.

Caroline tore through each page of the report, her eyes running down every disappointing detail of Shelly Nordling's life until she reached what was apparently the only mention of Rae-Lynn Pierce anywhere in this case, at least under that name.

Identification was made possible after a female acquaintance, Rae-Lynn Pierce, came forward with a shoe box of material left in her care by a prostitute Pierce knew as "Pills." Through that material, detectives were able to determine that the body was indeed that of Shelly Nordling.

So the girl who turned over the shoe box belonging to Lenny Ryan's girlfriend also knew Burn. Caroline felt the fog of coincidence lifting. Lenny Ryan had history with Burn. If nothing else, this girl, Rae-Lynn Pierce, knew both Burn and Ryan's girlfriend. With every revelation came a measure of disappointment and self-doubt. In this case it was the knowledge that Rae-Lynn Pierce had been there all along, on the fringe of the case, waiting to be discovered, and that Caroline hadn't seen it, hadn't put it together. She stared at the name and the date of birth. Rae-Lynn was twenty. There was one outstanding warrant against her: FTA, failure to appear in court, which gave her reason to lie about her name.

Caroline walked across the room to the computer reserved for NCIC and WASIC searches, a local and national database of people with criminal records. She typed in "Pierce, Rae-Lynn" and the date of birth, and even before the mug shot appeared Caroline recalled the nervous, skinny girl who had paused so long to invent a name, the girl for whom every man seemed threatening. Caroline had been looking for her for so long that her very existence had become wrapped up in the cords of Caroline's self-doubt. Two months of flipping through mug shots, asking every tavern owner and social worker, visiting hospitals and shelters, and yet until now Caroline had no clue who the girl might be. Now here on this computer screen, she emerged a little fuller of cheek, but definitely her, and if she was somehow still alive, this runt of a girl might connect Lenny Ryan to Burn, might throw light into rooms full of shadow. When the picture had downloaded she sat back, her arms at her side, suddenly exhausted. She ran her eyes over the inscrutable face of Rae-Lynn Pierce, who had worked over a sandwich like it could save her life, and who had called herself Jacqueline.

41

The recipe called for golden mushroom soup, but all she had was regular. Rae-Lynn stared at the can, wondering what made mushroom soup golden. She thought about calling the store. If they could tell her that, say, it was brown sugar or butter or just more mushrooms that made the soup golden, she could try to add it to the recipe. Or she could just go with the regular mushroom soup and hope for the best.

That's what she did, in the end, layering the Tater Tots, hamburger, and regular mushroom soup into a deep casserole dish, setting the oven at 425, sliding it in and noting the time. It was six-thirty in the morning, half an hour before Kelly was due home from his graveyard shift at the hospital. She liked saying that to herself, that he was due home from the hospital, even if he was just an orderly. Sometimes he told people that he was a physician's assistant or that he was an intern, but he usually winked at her later and explained that the person had been acting all superior and had deserved it. Anyway, that kind of stuff didn't bother her.

He loved having a meal when he got off work and it had become

Rae-Lynn's favorite time of day too, getting up before the sun rose, showering, putting on something nice, and having dinner ready for him when he came home at seven. They'd eat and he'd tell her stories about patients he'd saved from the laziness of doctors or from the stupidity of nurses. Even if most of it sounded like bullshit, it was still really interesting and she felt proud that he could even think of stories like that. Then they'd smoke a bowl, have sex, and he'd go to bed. When he was asleep, Rae-Lynn would head off to her job making lattes in a little drive-through espresso stand just off the freeway.

When the hamburger–Tater Tot casserole was done cooking, she turned off the oven and figured she'd just leave it inside to keep warm. At seven-thirty, she turned the oven back on, called the hospital, and found out Kelly had left at six-thirty, like always.

At eight, she pulled the casserole out of the oven and was officially worried. She stared out the window of the duplex and chewed on her fingernail. A little before nine, the door finally opened and Kelly came in with a guy she recognized as one of his friends from the hospital, a short, older guy named Scott. They spoke quietly about something as they came in the door, Scott saying something like, "Good light," Kelly whispering to Scott that he should be quiet, that Kelly would take care of it.

I'm not mad, she wanted to say. *You don't have to be quiet. Don't worry.* But when she looked up at Kelly, she could see it was something else.

"Hey, baby," he said and kissed her cheek.

"Where you been?"

"Remember Scott?"

"Sure," Rae-Lynn said, and she nodded to him. He was half a foot shorter than Kelly, with glasses and thinning hair. He smiled without showing his teeth, and his heavy-lidded eyes were aimed right at her tits.

"It sure smells good in here," Kelly said.

She didn't like how small her voice sounded. "Geez, what took you so long, Kelly?"

"Oh, Scott and me just had a beer and talked about some stuff. Remember, I told you, he's into computers and all that."

"I didn't make a very big casserole," she said.

"Don't worry about it," Kelly said. "Let me talk to you for a minute, baby." He led her toward the kitchen.

"I'm gonna go out and get the stuff," Scott said.

"What stuff?" Rae-Lynn asked.

But Kelly was pulling her into the kitchen. He set his car keys on the hook next to the refrigerator, dipped his finger into the top of the casserole, and tasted it. Then he winked and shook his head. "Boy, that's good, Rae. That's really tasty."

"It got cold."

"No, it's good."

"I had to use regular mushroom soup," she said.

"It's great, baby."

"I didn't have the golden mushroom."

"Oh, I like it better this way," Kelly said.

"Have you had it the other way?"

"Oh, yeah. This is way better."

"You promise?"

He pulled her to him and she disappeared into his chest, smelled cigarette smoke and beer on him. He kissed her on the forehead, patted her butt, and pushed away from her, back to the table. He picked up a fork from one of the two tidy place settings and took a bigger bite. "Oh, yeah. It's really good," he said through a full mouth.

Rae-Lynn heard the door close in the living room. "So what stuff is he getting?"

"Hmm?"

"Your friend. He said he was gonna get some stuff."

Kelly rolled his eyes as if it were nothing, but continued chewing when his mouth was empty. Finally, he said, "I told you about Scott before. Remember, from work?"

She held her hands out. "I don't . . . What do you mean?"

"You know, the computers and stuff. I know I told you." He kept eating the casserole, ignoring the two plates she had out on the small kitchen table. "He does those Web sites and makes a shitload of money. He's gonna be like Bill Gates one of these days. Own his own computer company. That's why I'm trying to get in on the ground floor with him now. It's a good time to get in."

All she could think to do was nod.

"I told you, I don't plan to be at the hospital forever."

"What does he do?" she asked.

"You mean with the computers and stuff?"

"Yeah."

"Well, I know I told you this, but he's got these two Web sites, like I said." Kelly turned to the sink so his back was to her and poured himself a glass of water. He stared at the glass as it filled with water. "One is mostly topless stuff, some beaver shots. The other is really tasteful too, you know, but definitely more hard-core."

He returned to the casserole and took another forkful from the middle, leaving the browned edges. He chewed without looking up at her. "Like I was saying, Scott's a genius when it comes to the computers."

"Kelly, I don't—"

"What kind of soup did you say you used here?" He waved a forkful toward her.

"Regular mushroom."

"It is really good." He chewed the bite of casserole and then set the fork down on the table and took her limp hand. "I think you oughta write them people and tell 'em your way is just as good as the other."

"Kelly, I don't—"

But he interrupted her. "See, Rae, this is real important for me. I know I talked to you about this. It's not fair for you to change your mind now that he's here and all."

Rae-Lynn could hear something being unpacked in the other room.

Kelly smiled. "It's no big deal. It's just like it's you and me except Scott's gonna film it. What's the difference between this and what you and me do every morning?"

Rae-Lynn couldn't look up. "What about him?"

Kelly shrugged and looked at the floor. "You know, when we're done, if you wanted to do some stuff with him . . ."

"Kelly . . ."

"No," he said, "it doesn't have to be that. You could just, you know, blow him or something."

"Kelly, I don't *want* to be with another guy."

"Hey, I don't mind, Rae," he said. "I mean it. I'm not jealous like that. I'm fine with it. I mean, if it's all right with me, then I don't see what the big deal is . . ."

She looked down at the casserole, which had a hole carved in it from where Kelly had been eating. She leaned against the table.

"Don't worry, we'll smoke a bowl first. You know, loosen us all up."

Rae-Lynn put her hand against the table.

"Is it that much different from what you used to do?" Kelly asked. "I mean . . . you can do that for me, right? Just this once."

She didn't say anything, just stared at the casserole.

He kissed her and grabbed her butt again. "I knew you'd be all right with this. It's gonna be cool, Rae."

Kelly was eight years older than she was, but they had taken the bus together when she was a kid. She knew his younger brother, Ted. After the guy nearly killed her and then took off with Risa, Rae-Lynn had decided to return home to Moses Lake. She'd been in town only a couple of days when she recognized Kelly at the grocery store. That had been six weeks ago. She hadn't used anything but pot in those six weeks. No treatment or methadone. She had just decided she wasn't a junkie anymore. And it had really felt like something, like a time she would look back on as normal and good. But now that it was over, she wondered what difference it made— six weeks or six months? Or six hours for that matter? Once it's over, the fact that it was a good time meant nothing, no different from having a picture of your birthday party. Real flat, like that, like a picture of someone you thought you loved.

She knew everything had to end. She wasn't a kid anymore. But as she watched Kelly scoop casserole onto a plate for Scott, she wondered if this thing she was about to do would erase all the memories of the first few weeks. See, it wasn't the thing Kelly wanted her to do. She would live through that. She had lived through worse. And it wasn't the leaving. She always left. But this time, it would've meant so much to Rae-Lynn if she could've saved something of what this had been, and all she could wish right then was that she had left just one day earlier.

42

The drug counselor's thick face spread into a smile. "I'm not surprised you had trouble figuring out who she was," he said. "I worked with Rae-Lynn for three months, and in that time, she never used the same name for more than a week." The counselor's corn-rowed hair made him look like Stevie Wonder. He stared fondly at the picture. "One day she'd have a hippie name like Moonlight or, what was it . . . Zenshine. Next time she'd go sexy—Monique or Sasha. You know, the kind of names a little girl would come up with to make herself sound grown-up."

"Jacqueline," Caroline said quietly. She sat across from him at a long table in the dining room of the group home where Rae-Lynn Pierce had gotten treatment.

"Yeah, like Jacqueline," the counselor said. "I liked working with her. A lot of these women come in and start playing you." He nervously pulled at his lip. "When you meet someone like Rae-Lynn . . . I've always liked the kind of people who work hard to remain optimistic in the face of everything. You understand, Detective Mabry?"

Caroline handed the counselor a photograph of Burn and he stared hard at it.

"Yeah. This kid had a street name. I can't quite remember it."

"Burn?"

"Yeah. Burn. We do our best to keep anyone on the outside from finding the women in here." He put the photo of Burn back on the table. "But the women get lonely and call these guys sometimes."

"You think he came in to see Rae-Lynn like that?" Caroline rested her finger above Burn's forehead.

"I just can't remember. I'm sorry. It blurs. I've been doing this a long time."

"But you do think this guy came here to see Rae-Lynn?"

He just shrugged, then his eyebrows raised and he clapped his hands together. "You know, there is one person. Chloe. She was here then." He looked over his shoulder. "She might know more. Sometimes the women keep a better eye on each other than the staff does. I'll see if she can talk to you."

He stood to leave, but Caroline stopped him. She slid another photo forward, the picture of Shelly Nordling.

"How about this one?"

"Shelly." He sighed. "That was really too bad about her. Shelly was here the same time as Rae-Lynn. I think they were even fairly close. Well, as close as people get in here, if you know what I mean."

When Caroline didn't answer, he went on.

"You have to remember," the drug counselor said, "everyone in here has stolen from their parents or their girlfriend or sold their kid's toys to get drugs. I mean, by the time they get here, they aren't the most trusting people." He stood to go check his files. "I'll see if Chloe feels like talking."

Caroline nodded and wrote on the notebook in front of her. "I'll need as much information on both women as you have. Contacts, files, forwarding addresses, insurance information. Anything you have."

"I can look." He stood and walked through the kitchen toward the offices.

Caroline stood and walked around the dining room, two long tables with benches on either side, like a school cafeteria. The treatment facility was in a grand old house in Browne's Addition, a neighborhood of nineteenth-century mansions that had mostly been carved into apartments or group homes. Breakfast for the twelve women in the house had been between seven and nine, and now at ten they were back in their rooms or off at jobs or in school, desperately trying to achieve the kind of lives—a service job and enough money to afford food—that most people would consider hard and unfair. Caroline paced around the long tables. On the walls were posters showing sunrises and kittens and waves at the ocean, each poster with some empty inspiration. But there was one that was more cryptic, and it caught Caroline's attention: a poster of an old wooden bucket filled to the brim with water. The poster read, "Chop wood; carry water." Caroline stared at it.

When she turned, a thin black woman in a wheelchair was in the doorway.

"Kind of makes you think, don't it? What that might mean?"

Caroline turned to the poster and then back to the girl in the wheelchair. "You must be Chloe. I'm Caroline Mabry."

"Chris said you wanted to talk to me?"

"Yes," Caroline said. She gestured toward the table, where the small photographs of Burn, Rae-Lynn, and Shelly sat like a row from a high school yearbook. Chloe hesitated, then wheeled herself over to the table. She lifted herself out of the seat of her wheelchair, and Caroline saw cords of lean muscle in her tiny arms. She looked at the pictures on the table for what seemed a half second at most, sighed, and dropped back into the seat of the wheelchair.

"You came down here to show me dead people?"

"Are they all dead?"

Chloe tapped the pictures of Shelly and Burn. "She's been dead five months and this one got pushed into the river by a cop."

Caroline smiled at her interpretation of what had happened on the bridge, but she didn't correct her. "What about her?" She pointed to the picture of Rae-Lynn, but Chloe didn't even look down at it.

"If she ain't dead, she's gonna be."

"You have reason to think she's dead?"

Chloe smiled. "I have reason to think we're all dead." She lost interest in her own humor though and craned her neck to look into the kitchen. "I wonder if the coffee's on."

"This will only take a minute." Caroline pushed the pictures closer to the woman in the wheelchair so that they hung slightly over the edge of the table.

Chloe looked down at the pictures. "You in some hurry?" she asked.

"Little bit."

"Oh yeah? You gotta get home, take care of your kids?"

"I don't have any kids," Caroline said. "I'm going to a funeral."

Chloe looked rather interested at this. "Whose?"

Caroline nudged the picture of Burn so that it teetered on the edge of the table. "His. They found his body in the river. The family's having a service this afternoon."

"That's too bad."

"Then you liked him."

"No, it's too bad they found his body. Fish could've eaten the fucker, all I care."

"Did he do something to you?"

She shrugged. "Nothin' out of the ordinary."

"He wasn't the one who . . ." And Caroline pointed to the wheelchair.

Chloe looked down at the big spoked wheel and figured out what Caroline was asking. "No," she said, but didn't volunteer anything else.

Caroline smiled. "You want to go?"

"To the funeral?" Chloe smiled. "That'd be pretty funny, huh?"

Caroline pressed the record button on the tape player and slid it into the middle of the table, right between them. "So?"

Chloe looked from the tape recorder to the pictures and then back again.

"Well," she began. "Okay. For a guy his age, Burn did pretty good with the girls. Always had four or five. Rae there was only with him a couple weeks, but old Shelly, she ran with him a while."

Caroline imagined Lenny Ryan arriving five months ago, asking the same questions she was asking now, finding out the same things she was finding out now. "Was Burn your pimp too?"

Chloe rolled her eyes. "It ain't like little girls in thigh-high boots riding with some nigger in a Cadillac. Ain't like that. Guy like Burn, he's someone to party with, you know? Had a place over off Pacific. Nice. Me and Shelly were mostly doing car dates, or taking 'em into alleys or into the big boats on that lot on Sprague, before them security guards got all bent out of shape about it. About that time Burn said we could use his place. Four or five dates a night, you might get a couple hundred, give half to Burn and he'd hook you up with smack or whatever and make sure you get a burger and some fries before you spent all your money and crashed on his couch. You party with his friends and that makes him the Mac and if anyone doesn't pay or tries to fuck you without paying, well, if you're running with Burn, that ain't gonna happen much."

Caroline was concentrating, trying to keep up. "So can you tell me exactly when Rae-Lynn and Shelly were with him?"

Chloe waved off the question, as if measuring time would have been impossible, or at least irrelevant. "Shelly, everyone call her Pills." Chloe looked around the group home self-consciously. "Had a real addictive-type personality. Needs someone to make her think she ain't alone. She was always trying to hook up with some guy. Like she's falling in love, just disappear off the street for a while. Then she come back, all sad, *'He threw me out!'* It was like that with Burn, called him her boyfriend for a while. But a girl like Rae, I think she's smarter, she knows a thing or two."

"Was Shelly working for Burn when she was killed?"

"You asking me, did Burn do her?" Chloe raised her eyebrows.

"Yeah, I guess I am asking that."

"I honestly don't know."

Caroline stared at the girl. "Did people assume it was Burn?"

"People? What people? Somebody do a poll?" Chloe stared at the foot pegs of her wheelchair. "He didn't go around telling people it *wasn't* him, that's for sure. I mean, girl's hawking stuff at pawnshops and sucking a little extra dick on the side and then tells Burn she doesn't need his help anymore . . . shit." She just let it hang there.

"Burn knew she was hawking things?"

"Oh yeah. He come off all sweet, but he keep track of your money for you."

Caroline looked back at her notes. "You said she was turning tricks on the side. Why would she do that?"

"Save some money. Get out of town."

"Burn didn't want her saving money to leave town?"

Chloe nodded. "If you ain't buying drugs from him no more, then you must be buying from someone else. You know?"

"That's what happened? You think Burn got mad at her for going on her own and assumed she was buying drugs elsewhere?"

Chloe shrugged. "Told you, I don't know what happened. But even if he didn't do it, you see why it would be in his interest to let people assume he did?"

"So that was the theory—" Caroline hated to say it, like she was mimicking an old *Starsky and Hutch* episode, but there was no choice—"on the street?"

Chloe just laughed.

"Let me ask it this way. If someone was to ask around about what happened to Shelly"—she reached in her bag and brought out a photo of Lenny Ryan—"let's say this guy. You think he'd get the same . . . hypothetical answer that you just gave me?"

Chloe took the photo of Lenny Ryan. "That's the guy from the paper, huh? The guy doin' all those women." She stared at the picture. "Well, if he's smart, he wouldn't need to ask, but yeah, that's what he'd hear. Girl cut. Still wearin' her clothes. Whoever did it wasn't interested in no freaky stuff. Not like this sicko." She held up the photo. "A girl gets whacked on time like that? It's either the guy paying for pussy or the guy she's paying afterward. See? Ain't a whole lot of other suspects to choose from. Ain't the fuckin' butler, you know?"

Caroline stared at the girl. She couldn't weigh ninety pounds without her wheelchair and here she was explaining the world to Caroline.

"I mean, come on." Chloe tapped her finger on the long dining table, as if she were diagramming a football play. "It don't take a damn rocket scientist."

On her notebook Caroline had written "Burn killed Shelly." She underlined it twice. She had the sensation of watching a road emerge from the fog. She nodded to the picture of Lenny. "You ever see him before?"

Chloe looked down at the picture in her hand. "No. But I haven't been on the street since . . ." She fumbled with the brake on her wheelchair. "I've been in here or in the hospital most of the last year."

"Did Shelly ever mention having a boyfriend?"

"Shelly? Any guy with a wallet was Shelly's boyfriend. Old guys, mostly. I know she moved here with some old guy."

"Did she ever talk about a boyfriend from California?"

Chloe thought for a minute, then smiled. "Yeah. I remember something . . . some guy she was all hung up on. But hell, I couldn't tell you anything. Every whore in here talks about the guy who treated her good. Gets pretty old. We're all just waiting until we save enough money to go back to him. Or until he gets out of jail. Or leaves his wife."

Caroline thought of herself and Dupree and flinched. The counselor came back into the room and handed Caroline two slim files, one with the name "Rae-Lynn Pierce" across the top, the other with Shelly Nordling's name. He kept another envelope close to his chest.

Caroline dug into Shelly Nordling's file. There wasn't much in it, just an admittance sheet, a discharge sheet, and a couple of other reports. Caroline paused right away on the first page, at the address that Shelly listed when she was checked into this treatment center. The address was familiar. Just off the freeway in East Central. She thought about something Chloe had just said, that she failed to follow up on. "You said Shelly moved here with an old guy. Do you remember his name?"

"Shit," she said and stared at the ceiling. "I can see the guy. Booted her out for using dope and stealing stuff. What was his name?"

"Albert," said the counselor quietly.

"Yeah," Chloe said. "I think that's right. She used to call him Uncle Albert. Yeah. Right. I thought that was funny, you know, like the song?"

Albert Stanhouse. Shelly lived with Lenny Ryan's uncle, and that's why Lenny killed him. Suddenly Dupree's random murders—his spinning top—seemed a lot less random. Caroline could imagine Lenny putting it together: Uncle Albert drags Shelly to

Spokane, then tosses her out on the street where Burn pimps her. When she wants to leave she goes to the pawnbroker to get enough money to go back to California, but he shortchanges her on a bracelet. Lenny comes to town and kills all of them. So here was Caroline trying to punish a guy for murdering hookers who was punishing people for murdering a hooker. It shocked her, looking at all that Lenny Ryan had discovered by scratching around beneath the surface and how little they had discovered by working above it.

But something had been nagging at the back of her mind. If Lenny Ryan had reasons to kill his uncle and Burn and the pawnshop owner, then was he the same psychopath they'd been imagining, that Blanton and McDaniel had been dissecting? She had the urge to laugh just then, and she thought about Dupree and his contention that the best response in irrational situations was irrationality. She had another urge too—to find Dupree and tell him what she'd found.

She was startled when her phone rang; still thinking about Dupree, she didn't even check the number. Instead, she held a finger up to the drug counselor and Chloe, turned her back, and took the call.

"Hey," she said, fully expecting to hear Dupree's voice on the other end.

"Ms. Mabry," said Curtis Blanton. "My ticket insists this big Quonset hut is the Spo-Caine *International* Airport."

"Because of Canada," she said.

"Oh. Of course. I guess that makes sense."

She felt two steps behind. "Wait a minute. You're in Spokane?"

"Aren't you going to ask what I'm doing here?"

"What are you doing here?"

"Good question. After we got off the phone I looked over your case again, and I thought of you with that sick twist McDaniel milking this thing for his next stupid book, and I knew you needed my help. So I caught the first flight out."

Caroline rubbed her head. "You know, I'm in an interview right now. Can you rent a car? Or take a cab?"

"No need. I'll wait here for you. But don't tell McDaniel I'm in town. Okay? I want to surprise the big, neckless bastard. He's gonna shit paper when he sees me."

Caroline didn't know how to answer, so she just turned her phone off. Everything was moving too quickly. When she turned back the counselor was bent down, showing Chloe the letter he'd taken from the envelope.

"What is that?" she asked.

The counselor straightened up and patted his corn-rowed hair in the back. "We operate on the same model as AA or NA here," the counselor said. "Even the counselors here, most of us have been . . . are you familiar with the twelve steps, Detective?"

"Somewhat."

The counselor handed her the short letter and the envelope. "One of the most important steps is the acknowledgment of the people we've hurt through our addiction. That's one thing we do here. We have the women write letters to the people they hurt. Some apologize. Some just make excuses. Some aren't even ready for that and they just hit their family up for more money or blame their parents for their problems.

"I worried about that with Shelly because she only wrote one letter. And when I tried to get her to mail it, she begged me not to because she didn't want the man to know where she was. So I put it in her file and never mailed it. Normally, I wouldn't think of violating a patient's privacy like this. But . . ."

Caroline looked away from him then, down at the letter in her hands, which began, "Dear Lenny."

43

An undated letter from the treatment file of Shelly Nordling at the Bright Shining Day Group Home:

Dear Lenny,

Well here I am at another treatment place. I hope you had a good x–mas and not too lonely. Today we're supposed to write letters to people we let down. I was sitting here thinking of a hundred people I stole from, lied to, borrowed money from and did a hundred bad things to.

But you're the only person I ever really LET DOWN. I don't think you can let people down who don't expect anything from you. I think you were the only person who ever thought I could be more than I am.

I'm sorry about Uncle Albert and all of it. I don't know how much you know, but you know me and you know how weak I am and how hard it is for me when I'm alone. Not that it's an excuse. It's what I am.

I wish I could pretend that I didn't know what would happen when I came up here with him. But we've been around too long to be stupid anymore, Lenny. No more time for that.

You know, the day I left with him, I almost came to see you.
But I couldn't look you in the eye. I started hooking again
down there, for a little crank. And up here a lot more. A couple
months ago I sold your uncle's dishes and we got into it and he
beat me up a little and kicked me out. I'm glad you can't see me
now, Lenny.

I wish I hadn't let you go down alone for my stash. I was
just scared. I've been scared so long I don't remember what it's
like to not be.

When I get out of here next month, I'm going to get some
money together and come down and see you, even though I
have no right. I got a few things to pay off but I plan on being
there when you are released. I don't expect you to want to talk
to me or anything, or for us to be like it was before. I don't
expect anything, Lenny, except that it's going to be hard to see
you. I'm even scared of that.

I'm afraid I'll look in your eyes and see how much I let you
down and then I know I'll have to get high. You will want to
know what happened to me and I will have to tell you. And
you will see how weak and ugly I am now. I wish I would
have taken better care.

But what scares me the most is already inside me. It's been
there a long time. It's knowing I didn't deserve you. That I'm
bad for the only person who ever made me feel good. I love you.
I wish that meant more than it does, Lenny.
        Shelly

A note stuck with a magnetic apple to Kelly Baldwin's refrigerator at his home in Moses Lake, Washington:

Kelly,
You fuck! I thought we was going on great! In case you
wonder where your wallet is, I took it, you fuck! That's because
I usually get eighty bucks for that shit you made me do today!
After you fell asleep I got Scott to drive me to the bus station!
How about that! Fuck you! By the time you read this, I will be
long gone and don't try to find me because I'm going back to

my boyfriend in Spokane and he's black and he knows Tie Quan Doe! And will kick your ass!

I don't know why you had to be like that Kelly! We could have been better. You go fuck Scott and his computer and you shouldn't tell people you're a doctor! OK.

luv–u–4–ever (NOT)
Shayla (Rae-Lynn)

A letter typed on Spokane Police Department stationery, folded in half and slid into the mail slot of Assistant Chief of Police James Tucker:

July 26, 2001
Asst. Chief James Tucker
Office of the Assistant Chief
Spokane Police Dept.

Dear Chief Tucker,
This letter is my official request to be considered for early retirement, effective immediately and per our discussion. This decision is based on personal reasons and not on recent decisions showing a lack of confidence in my abilities as a detective.

I ask that you act on this request as expeditiously as possible, although I will continue to perform my duties as patrol sergeant for the David Sector until a reasonable conclusion can be reached in reference to this issue.

I have served the city of Spokane the last 26 years with my deepest energy and commitment. Any errors I made were with the sincere belief that my actions were taken in the best interest of the city, in the department, and in my colleagues, for whom I will continue to have the greatest respect.
Sincerely,
Alan J. Dupree

cc: Lt. Charles Branch, Major Crimes
City of Spokane, Human Relations
Police Guild
Chris Spivey, prick

PART V

AUGUST

What the Thunder Said

44

A jogger found the fifth body in a blind of wild grass on the steep riverbank, a mile from where the first victims had been dumped. From the condition of the remains it was clear this one had been dead for weeks, and only recently had been moved to this spot. Caroline held back, letting the crime scene people do their work, but the moment she edged forward and saw the dried patches of flesh, the sun-bleached teeth, she felt with dread certainty that this pile of orderly bones was Rae-Lynn Pierce.

As Blanton had promised, the pressure increased exponentially with the discovery of another body, and in those first days of August, the office thrummed with activity. Calls came in from psychics, along with tips from prisoners in Texas and Florida, and requests for interviews from CNN and *Newsweek*. The work itself felt natural; with the two profilers and the growing expertise of the task force, the kind of details that had stumped them three months ago were quickly fitted to Lenny Ryan's ever-changing methodology. This time, the twenty-dollar bills were stuffed in the victim's mouth, a detail that sent the profilers into frenzies of supposition that devolved into an argument in the middle of the task force office in which they yelled over each other without making eye contact, like two professors who'd been assigned the same lecture hall.

"He's getting angrier," McDaniel said to Spivey. "He put money in her mouth as a sign of his anguish over oral sex—"

"He ran out of fucking rubber bands!" Blanton interrupted without looking up from a report he was writing. This was a ten-year argument they'd apparently dragged into this investigation and from the two or three times Caroline already had heard it, she surmised that the debate boiled down to whether or not a killer's signature—his unique crime scene behavior—constituted only his obsessive, subconscious activity or also encompassed the more standard MO, the things he did to commit and cover up a crime. Like the others, this victim's fingernails had been torn away with pliers and the fingers scrubbed. Both profilers acknowledged this was part fetish, part reasoned attempt to destroy evidence. Their argument seemed to be over the fine point of whether it was a ritual that also concealed what he'd done, or an act of concealment that became ritualized.

"Pedestrian, small-minded hick," McDaniel muttered as the argument faded.

"Bed-wetting thumb-sucking Freudian," Blanton said.

It seemed to Caroline a ridiculous argument because they agreed on the larger point: that this preparation stage was Ryan's signature. Immediately after each murder he hid the bodies and continued to visit each corpse, baby-sitting it, fulfilling his emotional need for control while also preparing it for discovery by the police. In this stage, he scrubbed the bodies and planted forty dollars and most likely masturbated. Both men said this preparation of bodies was what kept them interested in the case even after it turned from a profiling job to a manhunt. Blanton talked about how Ryan incorporated aspects of five or six killers that he'd tracked over the years (the fingernails, for instance, were right out of a case he'd handled in Texas), while McDaniel talked about the rare chance to catch a monster who was evolving before their eyes.

But after watching them, Caroline believed that each man stayed to get under the skin of the other, to keep an eye on the competition and fight over publicity, to look for material for their next books. They circled each other like vultures and contributed little to the practical aspects of the investigation—the stakeouts and interviews—spending all their time on their insular, peculiar science. At one meeting, Caroline read over Blanton's shoulder: "Due to a lack of early microbial activity and the postmortem displacement of the right clavicle, the remains were moved two weeks prior to their discovery." Caroline was stumped by his mathematical surety.

A week after the fifth victim was found, dental records were compared to those of Rae-Lynn Pierce and determined not to be hers, but likely those of the missing Jane Doe they called "Risa," who still existed only as a street name. While it bothered Caroline that they couldn't even assign Risa a real name, Spivey and the profilers seemed far more comfortable with a body that had no connection to a living person.

With the frenzy of this new corpse, the focus shifted away from Caroline's recent discovery of Lenny Ryan's motive for killing Burn, and she felt herself pushed to the side by this humming and grinding machine, which the remains of poor Risa fed like fossil fuel. In the office, Caroline tended to her own small tasks, trying to forget the idea that had begun choking her thoughts the last few weeks, stopping her cold in traffic or walking to the copy machine:

What if Lenny Ryan wasn't killing these women?

It wasn't some sudden piece of exculpatory evidence that sparked doubt in Caroline; in fact, she found few answers of any kind in the evidence. If anything, the evidence reinforced the idea that they were going after the right man—the great wall of Spivey's timeline surrounding a city of cold forensics, witness interview cards, and credit card receipts that covered every desk in the task force office.

Still, this doubt crept up, catching her off guard like a boom in the distance. If only there were a conclusive semen sample or eyewitness. Instead, the evidence served only to *not eliminate* Ryan. It was like building a house with all windows but no doors.

Of course, she knew thousands of suspects convicted on less evidence. By its nature, such an investigation involved lining up coincidences until you eliminated all other explanations and arrived at a premise. Spivey's timeline provided the premise: the murders, which began about two weeks after Lenny Ryan left prison; his skulking around asking about hookers; the murders of Burn, Uncle Albert, and the pawnbroker; Caroline chasing Ryan into the alley where the fourth body was found; his fingerprints on the refrigerator there; his following Rae-Lynn the day she and Risa disappeared. Even the gloomy county prosecutor had begun talking about this as a death penalty case.

No, she knew her doubts were irrational. Dupree had even invented a name for what she felt—Yearbook Syndrome. Whenever they interviewed the relative of a suspect, invariably that person dragged out a yearbook, pointed to the picture of a shy, pimple-covered kid, and said emphatically, "See. He didn't do it."

That's what I have, Caroline thought, a kind of Yearbook Syndrome by proxy. She had deluded herself into believing that she knew Lenny Ryan. She had stood face-to-face with him and she'd felt the distance between them close. So there it was. The inglorious return of her intuition, six years after Dupree made off with it, telling her that if Ryan had a solid motive for killing Burn, wouldn't there be a motive for killing the hookers too, beyond the psychological backflips described by Blanton and McDaniel?

She never mentioned her doubts to Spivey or to the profilers, of course, who were more convinced than ever that Ryan was the killer. The fact that Ryan blamed Burn for Shelly Nordling's death didn't eliminate the idea that Ryan was acting out his twisted resentment against all prostitutes. If anything, the letter from Shelly's old group home just reinforced their basic theory: Lenny Ryan was acting from a deep-seated obsession over what he felt was Shelly Nordling's betrayal of him.

Whenever she spoke to one of the profilers, Caroline found herself convinced by their surety. Blanton persuaded her that she could never understand Ryan or his violent sexual fantasies. McDaniel convinced her that a monster wasn't something you saw, but the sum of the things you didn't see, the childhood failings and disappointments, the insecurities and rejections.

But when she was alone, at home or in traffic, Caroline remembered Lenny Ryan's eyes. She had been surprised to find not a monster in those eyes, but herself, her fear, her temper, her frustrated attempts to find explanations, to make the world fit into a child's box. And when she felt like this, the evidence and the ever-expanding work of the profilers seemed just a few degrees off, even purposefully misleading, like the illusion of an urn made up of two men's profiles. While the rest of the task force worked to describe the urn, Caroline couldn't stop seeing the two faces.

She looked up at Blanton and McDaniel, physical opposites angled across from each other at the big conference table: Blanton short, squat, and pale, like he'd come out of a can; McDaniel tall, tanned, and buff. Across the table sat Spivey and a slight woman who'd been introduced to Caroline as an assistant producer from *Dateline*. It was McDaniel's idea that some national publicity might bring a tip on Ryan's whereabouts or maybe even draw him out. Key to their plan was creating what McDaniel called the "super-antagonist model," directing Ryan's attention to one police officer, an "alpha cop" that Ryan would imagine as a worthy foe and would find himself irresistibly compelled to contact. Caroline had been that foe early on, both profilers agreed, but for whatever reason, Ryan was no longer engaged by her. So they needed *Dateline* to create a new opponent—actually, two, since neither Blanton nor McDaniel was willing to step aside.

"From the Bureau's standpoint, this is a groundbreaking case," McDaniel told the assistant producer, who was there to do legwork before the rest of the crew arrived that afternoon. She was a slender, attractive woman in black pants, black shirt, and black shoes. A size zero, Caroline guessed. She worked the profilers, shaking her head and saying "Wow!" as they described their harrowing work. McDaniel especially ate it up.

"The role of the FBI Investigative Support Unit has always been just that: to *support* local law enforcement," he said. "But in this case, we're going a step further, using profiling to anticipate Ryan's next move, to actually catch him. And for me?" McDaniel stuck out that ledge of a jaw, and leaned forward until his face was just inches from the assistant producer's. "I need to catch this guy. For me, it's personal."

"Wow!" The producer jotted some notes, "make sure you say that to the reporter when we're on air tonight. Just like that."

McDaniel tried to be nonchalant. "Who will the reporter be?"

The assistant producer tossed off a name.

"Ah," said McDaniel. "Mmm-hmm. It's just . . . people have

said I look like Stone Phillips. I thought it'd be interesting to see the two of us side-by-side."

No one said anything, but Blanton turned and made eye contact with Caroline.

"Yeah, well, Stone doesn't leave the studio much," the assistant producer said.

"There's the resemblance," said Blanton. "Neither does he."

From her desk across the room, Caroline watched McDaniel glare at Blanton. With serial killers fading in popularity, with Spokane in the middle of nowhere, and with only eight victims—five of them hookers—getting the attention of anyone beyond *America's Most Wanted* was going to be tough, and so McDaniel had convinced Spivey to play up the role of the profilers, the idea that the top experts in the country were working together for the first time in a decade to catch a killer. Just as McDaniel had predicted, the angle elevated the story to network newsmagazine fodder. Tonight they were taking Blanton and McDaniel to the dump site along the river, where they would film the two super-sleuths digging in dirt and staring wistfully out at the river, spouting horseshit to draw Lenny Ryan out: *For me, it's personal.*

"What about you, Mr. Blanton?" the assistant producer asked. "How has this case affected you personally?"

"Well, I'm no longer working as a prostitute. So that's good."

McDaniel cleared his throat and stepped in. "It's impossible to *not* take this case personally. Even before we identified Ryan, when we were dealing with an UNSUB—"

The assistant producer interrupted. "Unsub?"

"Sorry," McDaniel said, reaching for her arm. "Bureau talk. Even when we were dealing with an unknown subject, it was apparent his communication with the police, his taunting, was a key part of his fantasy. The killer's focus started with these women, but now it sits squarely on the shoulders of Mr. Blanton and me."

Again, Blanton looked uncomfortable and sought out Caroline's eyes. But she spun away in her chair and picked up the phone to make her weekly calls to Rae-Lynn's family and friends. That list of phone contacts had reached twenty, but no one had heard from her. Blanton and McDaniel said she was likely dead and that her disappearance and the death of Risa marked a new period for Lenny Ryan in which he took longer with the bodies, perhaps out of disappointment over Caroline's reaction to what they called "his gift"—the dead woman in the refrigerator. When no one answered the phone call, Caroline hung up the phone and glanced up at the conference table.

"What about the danger that Ryan poses?" the producer was asking. "If he has moved out of the area, are women elsewhere in danger? The woman leaving the gym? The mother going to the store? Me? Am I in danger?"

Blanton looked over at McDaniel. "Oh, you're definitely in danger."

Again, McDaniel jumped in. "Is there a danger? I would say yes." He nodded, raised his eyebrows to the producer, and spoke more quietly. "Yes."

Caroline couldn't help wondering what Dupree would make of this, of this film crew dragging the profilers down to the riverbank. She hadn't seen Dupree in three weeks, since the night he dropped his bombshell about Glenn Ritter, but she heard he'd requested early retirement. She called him once, but hung up when she got his voice mail and couldn't imagine what to say. And then the new body surfaced and time just got away from her.

McDaniel was holding his index finger to his lip as he thought about a question the assistant producer had asked. He nodded slightly, as if he were about to admit wetting his bed. "For me? This job makes it hard to meet someone. Every relationship goes back to trust for me. A case like this makes it hard to . . . to trust."

There was an awkward silence at the conference table in the center of the room, and then Spivey cleared his throat. All morning he'd been practicing the line McDaniel had given him and he offered it stiffly. "From my standpoint, it's been a real education. If anyone can catch this killer, it's these guys."

There was another awkwardness, and Caroline was saved by the ring of her phone. She grabbed it as if it were a life preserver. "Mabry."

"Where have you been? I've been leaving messages at your house."

It was Joel. "I got them," she said. "I've been really busy."

"I need to see you."

"Can't," she said, "I'm invisible." She smiled because it was so stupid, something Dupree would throw off. In front of her, they were standing at the conference table now, the producer making plans to meet Spivey and the two profilers later at the dump site. The phone at her ear, Caroline watched McDaniel work the skinny, young producer, his pelvis thrust forward, hands on his hips.

"I understand why you're mad," Joel said.

"I'm not mad," she answered, and that seemed true enough.

"Disappointed, then. I understand. I've been disappointed with myself."

"Joel, this really isn't the time . . ."

"I was immature. I made a mistake. I was afraid." The words tumbled from the phone. "Can't I see you?"

"I'm very busy, Joel."

"There's someone else, isn't there?"

"No," she said, "there's no one else." And saying that made her think about Lenny Ryan again, that if he wasn't the killer, there had to be someone else, someone strong, someone obsessed with women, someone still out there.

"Meet me somewhere," Joel said. "I have something for you."

The producer walked to the door and McDaniel walked with her, his hand resting in the small of her back as he leaned down to tell her something.

Caroline caught Blanton's eye and he made a little drinking motion with his right hand. She shook her head and Blanton rolled his eyes. They'd gone for drinks a few times after work and Caroline had begun to worry that she enjoyed his company. Last night, he'd confessed that even though he hated McDaniel's *Dateline* idea, his agent would kill him if he passed up a network appearance. As long as there were serial murders, Blanton could consult on TV shows and movies and write the occasional book and make a living while stabbing away at his own dark psychology.

There's no one else. The killer would be familiar with Spokane, would know how to prepare a body, and, according to Blanton, reflected the unique behaviors of several other serial killers.

"Caroline?" Joel continued. "One drink? Okay?"

She looked across the room at Spivey, his tie knotted so firmly that his shirt collar bunched up beneath it. The killer would be someone physically strong, knowledgeable of prostitutes and police. Taxi driver. Cop. Bartender. "Okay," she said. "One drink."

"Great." Joel sounded relieved.

At the door, McDaniel had pulled his hands out of his pockets and was patting the producer on the shoulder, his hand lingering for a quick squeeze. The producer walked out the door and McDaniel turned to glare at Blanton.

"I'll come get you," Joel said. "Say six?"

"That's fine," she said.

"Caroline, are you sure there's nobody else?"

Spivey and the two profilers drifted back to work. It was chilling to imagine, starting over, as Blanton said, building this guy from the ground up.

"No. There's no one else," she said.

45

The calf had fallen into what Angela called a coulee, what Lenny's dad had called a draw. Those were the kinds of differences he found between Washington and California, little gaps within the names of things that shook Lenny's confidence that he would ever completely fit here. Either way—coulee or draw—Lenny stood at the edge of it, panting from hard work in the late-morning sun. He looked down into a steep gully perhaps twenty feet long and as wide as it was deep, maybe six feet, its sides caved inward like parentheses. It was a sinkhole or small pond in the spring, opening like a sigh in the soft ground, but now its banks were dry and dusty and had apparently flaked off beneath the poor calf's hooves as it tried to escape. Lying on its side in a bed of loose dirt, the dead calf was buzzed by flies that lit on its nose and its mouth and its open eyes.

Lenny dropped his wire cutters, took off his gloves, and crouched at the side of the gully, trying to determine where this calf had come from. A few feet away the cattle trail ran from the creek through this field, and Lenny could see no hoofprints where the calf might have veered off the trail. It was one of the things he'd noticed about cattle the last couple of months; their trails were as thin as bicycle trails, and no matter how many were in the herd or how widely they spread to graze, when they were on the move to the creek or to the salt blocks it was in a single-file line with not a whit of variation. If the lead animal walked in a loop, each animal that followed made the exact same loop.

But for some reason this calf had ventured away from the cattle trail—no more than four feet, but far enough. It didn't make sense. Lenny could see where the lip of the ditch had given way and the calf had gone tumbling in.

He walked back to the cattle trail, trying to figure out what made this calf walk away from the herd. He'd seen these cattle, Angela's neighbor's—maybe thirty head—moving through the field beyond Angela's house, on the other side of the fence he was fixing. In the afternoon they made their way in a tight single file down the trail toward the creek and drinking water. The cattle spread out along the creek like a stain on the earth, and in the evening Lenny would stand on Angela's porch with a glass of sun tea and watch them gather again without any apparent signal and begin making their way single-file back to the fields, where they would graze all morning. More than likely the accident happened at night when the calf couldn't see well, but that still didn't explain it. Maybe something scared the calf away from the herd. A dog. Or a coyote. Lenny looked for prints near the cattle trail, but dogs and coyotes were so light, and he was so inexperienced at tracking, that he couldn't make out anything. It frustrated him, to be able to see so clearly *what* happened—a calf fell in a ditch—without knowing *how* or *why*.

He'd always believed that the *why* of things didn't matter; the outcome was the only thing worth knowing. It was another kind of torture trying to figure out *why*, as pointless and cruel as a calf trying to scramble up the soft walls of a ditch. He stood over the coulee, put his gloves back on, and jumped into the ditch, landing next to the dead calf. The flies buzzed around him, then settled back on the calf's head. The walls of the coulee were almost as tall as he was, and he could barely see out. Lenny grabbed the calf by its ankles, two in each of his gloved hands, and swung it up and over the side of the draw. It landed above him with a sigh of dust.

As he crawled out, the dirt gave way beneath his boots and he experienced for a moment the animal's panic. Outside the coulee, he knocked the dirt from his gloves, picked the calf up by its legs again, swung it in the air, and draped it over his shoulders. He began walking to the neighbor's house, dry grass crunching beneath the boots. He walked through the field, along the creek, and up the dirt driveway between Angela's cabin and the neighbor's tin-roofed house. The house was built around a single-wide trailer and stood among a light stand of birch trees. By the time Lenny reached the driveway he was nearly sick from the heat and the smell of the calf. The neighbor was standing next to the house as if he'd been expecting someone. Pushing seventy, he had a shock of gray hair that rose from his head like a cold flame.

"Whatcha got?" he called when Lenny was close enough.

"He must've fallen into the . . . into the coulee." Lenny came up the driveway and swung the calf down into the gravel between the tire tracks, a few feet from the old rancher's shoes. Lenny coughed and spit into the dirt next to the driveway.

The old farmer's cheeks were dusted with wiry gray whiskers that he scratched as he looked down at his dead calf. A spaniel dog sniffed around the animal's head; the man kicked at the dog and it scampered away sideways.

"Shit," the neighbor said finally. "That's too bad."

Lenny removed a glove and stuck his hand out for the neighbor to shake and he did. "I'm Gene," Lenny said. "I'm . . . uh . . . staying up there with Angela."

But the old rancher didn't introduce himself, just looked down at the calf, and so Lenny did too. Lying on its side like that the calf seemed so slender, almost two-dimensional, like a painting.

"Angela got pigs up there?" the neighbor asked.

"What's that?"

"Pigs." Finally the old man looked up. "I ain't got any pigs to feed it to. I gave up my pigs, shoot, goin' on a couple a years now."

"No," Lenny said. "She doesn't have any pigs."

"That is a shame," the old guy said, then he kicked at the dead animal. "Hate to see it go to waste."

Lenny put his gloves back on. "So what do you suppose happened?"

"Hmm?"

"To the calf. What do you think happened?"

"Fell in a ditch."

"Yeah, I mean . . . well, does that happen a lot?"

He shrugged. "Some."

"Do you know what causes it?"

"The herd runs and a few go in the wrong direction."

"What makes 'em run?"

"Thunder, mostly."

Lenny looked down at the calf and remembered the electrical storm two nights earlier, a couple of quiet flashes and then a flash and a boom right after. "And do they usually die like this?"

"If they don't get out or if I don't hear 'em and pull 'em out."

"You ever seen one fall in?"

The neighbor thought about this. "No. Guess I haven't."

They were quiet for a moment and then Lenny banged his gloves together where his thumbs met his forefingers. He wiggled his fingers in his gloves. "Well, I just couldn't figure out how it happened. That's all."

The old man squinted at Lenny. "You know, they ain't particularly smart animals. 'Specially the little ones."

"No," Lenny said, "I guess not." He nodded to the old rancher and began walking back along the driveway. Maybe he'd be like the old rancher someday, accepting of all the troubles in the world, the basic principle that small ones don't stand much of a chance and that a clap of thunder can panic even the most sedate animal.

Little plumes of dust erupted in front of his feet as Lenny moved along the dirt road toward Angela's cabin. At the top of the hill, the pickup truck that delivered the mail was parked at the bank of mailboxes where the dirt road met the highway and so Lenny headed up that way, thrusting his hands in the pockets of his one pair of jeans. It was a small bearable moment, this one—these boots and these jeans and the neighbor and the dirt plumes of the driveway. He'd shaved his beard and his hair was growing back and Angela dyed it white blond so that it covered his head like first snow.

The big mailbox held a power bill and a Pottery Barn catalogue and an envelope from Spokane County Superior Court. It took a moment for Lenny to recognize Angela's husband's name—David Nickell—on the envelope. Another moment to remember that he had used that name to request documents.

He tore into the envelope. On top was a receipt for the copies and a note from the clerk saying this particular civil suit had just been settled. Lenny flipped through thirty pages of court files, beginning with the complaint, which said the building and alley where the body was found had been owned by SMRC, a real estate company in Seattle and had been purchased for $95,000 cash in January of this year by John Landers, the owner of the boat dealership across the street. When Landers began renovating the building and announced that an electronics company would move in, the real estate people from Seattle sued, saying that Landers had arranged to lease the building while it was still under the Seattle company's ownership and that by not telling them about the electronics company's interest, Landers withheld information that would have made the property more valuable before the sale.

Next came the defendant's statement, a short summary from John Landers in which he admitted having preliminary talks with the electronics company about relocating to the building on East Sprague if he purchased it, but that the deal was

> contingent upon marked improvements being made not only to that property, but to the surrounding neighborhood. Such improvements were by no means guaranteed, and indeed were engendered by Landers' Cove alone in the form of after-hours security, capital renovations, and property purchases at great cost to its business and its cash reserves.

Lenny let the pages fall to his side and he stared down the road to Angela's cabin. It had sounded so crazy that day in the park, like conspiracy talk, like the pimp was just making something up to keep from getting killed. He said that he hadn't killed Shelly—of course, Lenny didn't believe him—and had no idea who did. He said that a few days after Shelly disappeared, some old guy stopped him in an alley, and had warned him that he needed to move his girls out of the neighborhood or it would be on his head. Lenny had thought the whole story was bullshit, but when he began snooping around the boat dealership and the businesses around it, he found the body in the refrigerator.

He wished he was smarter, that he could put things together in his mind. He'd talked to hookers, read through classified ads, looked at deeds of trust, and tried to figure out who would want to get rid of the hookers. But none of it made sense. A person acquires a certain understanding of the world—knows, for instance, that water flows downhill—and anything different is incomprehensible. Maybe he knew no more about people like John Landers than he did about thunder and cattle.

Lenny started back for the house, which sat on a small rise above the creek, in the shade of a stand of tamarack trees. It would have been good to stay here. He liked how Angela sometimes waited for him on the porch in her apron, supper on the table.

At the house, Lenny changed out of his workshirt and dirty jeans and into his khaki pants and black T-shirt, the clothes he'd arrived in. He tried to picture what he would do when he came face-to-face with Mr. John Landers. Would he shoot the man like he'd done at the pawnshop? Would the clap of gunshot surprise him a little and give him pause again? Or was he a different man now?

He grabbed a sheet of paper and a pen. He wrote her name, "Angela," and then stopped and stared at the page. Finally, he wrote, "Had to go to Spokane. Don't wait up." It would have been cool to get some cattle of his own. That would have been something.

He started to write the name "Gene," but crossed it out and wrote "Lenny" on the bottom of the note. Then he lifted the pen to his mouth, chewed on the cap, put it back to the paper, and just above his name wrote "Love."

46

At 6 P.M., halfway into his second-to-last shift as a Spokane
police officer, Alan Dupree sat in his car by the river, using a
radar gun to gauge the speed of seagulls. They were hard to
measure individually, but a few times he managed to get a good
reading. One swooping gull cruised along at eighteen miles per
hour. Another beat its wings and coasted into a headwind to slow
down for a landing, and Dupree watched the red digital readout
decrease to two, the gull hovering in the air for a moment and
then settling onto the surface of the river. Flying at two miles per
hour! Amazing. People made some easy things so hard.

He nodded politely to people walking by his car and they
made faces that seemed like appropriate reactions to a uniformed
police officer measuring the speed of flying birds. This was the
best day he could remember in some time; he wasn't defined by
the fact that he was a police officer or the fact that his marriage
was dying. Today he was just Alan, and Alan was curious about
the speed of seagulls. He'd never thought of the job as the problem between him and Debbie, not really, and he hated guys who

blamed their careers or their friends or anything else for being a shitty husband. But now, when he could so easily imagine *not being* a police officer, the job seemed all-consuming and he was surprised that he and Debbie had made it as long as they had.

Life in the park was winding down; bored with flying, the gulls settled one by one on the concrete steps above the river, waiting for someone to begin tossing bread so they could resume their life's work, stealing from the park's ducks. Dupree looked around for other things to gauge. A duck swam by at two miles per hour, a kid on Rollerblades went by at seven, and finally Dupree started his car.

The dispatcher asked if he could swing by a prowler call on the lower South Hill. They were having trouble getting officers there because of two traffic accidents. Dupree drove along the freeway and got off at the Altamont exit, where he would drive through one of the worst neighborhoods in the city to get to one of the best.

The tired houses and dead lawns at the base of the South Hill reminded him of an old theory. The theory of yard relativity. He believed you could tell a criminal by the amount of yardwork he did. He'd first come up with the theory in neighborhoods like this one, responding to a thousand fights and drug deals and domestics, and after a time it dawned on him that he was almost never called to houses with well-kept yards. This wasn't an economic or racial thing. It was a pure yardwork thing, the basic theory being that criminals don't have the patience for yardwork. That's what crime is, he believed—a lack of patience. Want to get rich quick? Get laid without all the work? Want to get rid of your business partner without the trouble of suing him or paying him off? That's the difference between criminals and real people. Patience.

And in better neighborhoods? Dupree's car moved up Altamont, climbing the South Hill to South Altamont Boulevard, the change in income even more drastic than the elevation. The theory applied here too. There were probably white-collar criminals up here, and Dupree would have bet they hired lawn services rather than trim the roses on the porch themselves. Like those guys responsible for the failure of banks: They probably all had gardeners. Yardwork is a time for reflection, for engaging the subconscious, a time when guilty people can't escape themselves.

Like all good theories, this one might even lead to practical application, assuming he could find some causal relationship between lawn care and crime. Maybe they should force drug dealers to mow their lawns. Turn prisons into groundskeeping companies.

Dupree drove along South Altamont Boulevard, the big, old houses tracing the bluff that overlooked the city. The dispatcher informed him that another car was clearing an accident and would be en route to the prowler call shortly. Dupree parked and climbed out of his car. The house was three stories, a century old, white with pillars. It would cost four times as much as the house he and Debbie had scrimped and saved to afford. Fifteen blocks away and here he was in a different universe.

An old woman with gardening shears was standing in the driveway next door, pointing to the open front door of the white house.

"I saw some lights being switched on in there, and then I saw the door was open," the woman said. "John and Edith are at the lake. That's why I called."

Dupree looked at her manicured rose bushes. "You did the right thing."

Of course he should wait for backup before going into a house where a prowler had been reported, but Dupree didn't think anyone was inside, and these last two days on the job, he was damned if he wasn't going to trust his judgment. He turned off his radio, stuck his head in the door, and yelled into the open foyer: "Any criminals here?"

When no one answered, Dupree went straight to the small security panel; the burglar had snipped the line and taken the battery out of the wall monitor. Dupree went into the bathroom and saw the window the burglar had used, the small window above the shower. This guy was a pro.

It made him nostalgic to think there were still professional burglars out there. In his mind they'd busted all the pros years earlier and all that was left was kids looking to get high, without the patience and intelligence it took to become a real burglar, who went around stealing bikes from garages and rifling through cars. But this guy knew what he was doing, and for the first time Dupree felt a tug of regret over retiring.

Not that he had anything to stay around for. He was forty-eight. He had his twenty in, and six more for good measure—or self-punishment. Most of the guys he'd broken in with had retired or were retiring or were on disability, and now they were playing golf or working as security guards or private detectives, which meant running errands for the sleazy defense attorneys they'd complained about all those years.

Dupree hoped that retiring would keep him from bitching about the continued erosion of the world he'd known. He didn't want to finish up like some old, crotchety fart who couldn't pull his own weight. He remembered when he'd started, how the old-timers still groused about having to read Miranda rights, about women in patrol cars, about waiting for a photographer to arrive at the crime scene before they started fucking with things. He was surprised by his own reluctance to change, his inability to recognize that Spivey might know a more advanced approach to homicide investigation. Most of all, he was surprised to realize how quickly he'd gotten so old.

But the idea that an old-fashioned burglar was out there made him feel vital again. Needed. He thought about some of the old crooks, guys you'd pull over with complete burglary kits in their cars, guys who would get out of jail and single-handedly spike the burglary statistics, guys the detectives spoke about with some measure of respect, the way a pitcher admires a great hitter. The great burglars came from a few families, and there was a time you could just say the name "Gillick" or "Falco" and any cop would nod in grudging admiration.

But as Dupree moved from room to room, his flashlight beam fell on an undisturbed landscape—no drawers thrown open or cords yanked from walls, none of the signs of a first-rate burglary, or even a pothead break-in for that matter. At the end of the house he came to a room with tucked walls and theater seats and a big-screen TV. The thief hadn't even taken the TV. Or the stereo. The VCR was still there. It was strange. He made his way upstairs and found a bedroom, and on the dresser, a picture of the dignified, silver-haired couple who lived there, along with pictures of their three grown children wearing skicoats and posing on a mountain some-where.

Dupree held up the picture. Money. People who had it were happier and better-looking. He didn't care what anyone said. He hardly ever responded to rapes or murders or child molestations in neighborhoods like this. The root of all evil? My ass. From what he'd seen, methamphetamine was the root of all evil. That and booze.

Next to the photograph on the dresser was an unlocked jewelry box. Dupree opened it and could see right away that it hadn't been disturbed, and that's when he knew for certain this wasn't a burglary. Jewelry is the first thing you steal—easy to carry, hard to trace, quick to fence. The neighbor had said the couple was away on vacation. Had she mentioned their names? John and something. He couldn't remember. Dupree looked around for something with their names on it, but didn't see anything.

Someone was banging around downstairs, and a minute later, he heard Teague's voice. "Sarge? You up there?"

Dupree walked out of the bedroom and paused at the top of the curved staircase. Teague stood in the entryway, his hands on his sizable hips. Dupree was glad to see Teague. After thinking about the cranky old-timers he'd broken in with, this doughy black kid with his Elvis Costello glasses might be the only cop down there who measured up to those old guys.

"Hey, Teague. How's it going?"

"I've been calling you on the radio, Sarge. Why'd you go all dark on me?"

Dupree looked down at the small microphone on his shoulder. "Yeah, the radio is too noisy. I can't concentrate when it's on."

Teague smiled. "You'd have busted me to Boy Scout for walking alone into a house with my radio off. On a prowler call? Shit."

"Yeah," Dupree said, "it's not a good idea."

Teague just stared at him. "If you're building a case to get emotional disability payments, you can stop now. I'll testify."

Dupree smiled. "That'd be open and shut, huh?"

Teague looked around the house. "Nice digs. What've we got?"

"A burglar with attention deficit disorder? He breaks in like a pro, then leaves without stealing anything. Woman's got a couple of diamond earrings up there bigger than my nuts."

"That's amazing," Teague said. "You must have some tiny little nuts."

"Yeah, but I got six of 'em."

Dupree came down the stairs and grabbed some mail from a table in the foyer. He flipped through the letters. They were addressed to John and Edith Landers. One was addressed to Landers' Cove. Dupree stared at the letter, his mind scrambling to cover the distance between what should have been two unrelated points, but which seemed to have some fine connection, a filament that you would never even see until it began to burn.

"What is it?"

Dupree looked up at Teague, who had the same look of concern that was on his face when he first arrived at the house. "Nothing. I'm just . . ." He looked down at the letter in his hand. Landers' Cove. "Did you bring your phone?"

"In the car."

"I need you to call Chris Spivey at the task force. Tell him to get up here. Don't fuck with the dispatcher either, just call him."

Teague looked excited. "Why, what is it?"

"I'm not sure," Dupree said. "But tell him it's urgent."

When he didn't elaborate further, Teague trudged out to his car to make the phone call. Dupree set the mail back on the table and walked through the living room, one of those pristine living rooms in which no actual *living* appears to have taken place, filled with hard-backed furniture and no TV. It was surprising there was no red velvet rope across the doorway. Beyond that room was an oak door, left standing open, that he hadn't noticed before. Dupree walked into the doorway of a small office, the walls covered with books and file cabinets, and in the center an oak desk that matched the door. This room had been turned upside down, and Dupree felt the same way he had when he'd come across the murdered hooker—that he should back away and wait for the evidence techs to tell him what he'd found. But the desk drew him in.

On top of it was an architect's model of Landers' Cove and the faux ski mountain they were building. Dupree crouched so that his eyes were at the same level as the Styrofoam model. He looked down at the tiny reproduction of Sprague Avenue and reached out with his forefinger to touch a miniature snowmobile in the lot of

Landers' Mountain. The model covered the entire surface of the desk and represented a six-block section of the East Sprague neighborhood. Dupree couldn't believe the businesses that were represented on this model. Where the hourly-rate motel now stood on the real Sprague Avenue, this model had an upscale grocery store. The new electronics store across the street from Landers' Cove was flanked on either side by an Old Navy store and a restaurant whose sign read, "BIG RESTAURANT, tba." According to the architect, the Happy Stork, Dupree's favorite dive bar, was slated to become a parking garage.

"Huh," he said, and straightened up, rubbing the back of his head. He moved away from the model to consider the desk. The locks on the drawers had all been broken and files were strewn across the floor. Dupree bent over and began reading the files without touching them. There were deeds and legal papers and contracts and contractors' estimates, and the idea that some of this might mean something filled Dupree with the unmistakable adrenaline of the job, the naive belief that the world could be known.

He stepped back and made a mental note of which files appeared to have interested the burglar. Most were just tossed aside but a couple of folders were open on a short cabinet. In one folder, labeled "Security Expenses," Dupree found a pile of receipts from Kevin Verloc's All-Safe Security Company. Dupree pulled out the most recent receipts: two thousand dollars for new fencing in February; a four-thousand-dollar video surveillance system in March; and just last month a bill marked "Miscellaneous" in the amount of two hundred and forty dollars.

The other open file contained a contract of some kind. Dupree pulled his gloves on and flipped the contract to its first page. The contract was between Landers' Cove Inc. and the All-Safe Security Company. He flipped back to the page left open by the burglar.

8. Neighborhood Improvement Bonus

The agreed-upon fee schedule shall include quarterly bonus payments of $2,000 for each of the following ancillary results or circumstances due to the increase in security over the two-year period of the contract, upon meeting such requirements as described and recorded in Appendix A:

(1) A 20% increase in per-square-foot property values in the 1300 block of East Sprague, those values to be determined by an independent property appraiser.

(2) Elimination of prostitution and other criminal activity from Landers' Cove and surrounding properties. (See definitions in Appendix A.)

Dupree flipped to the back of the contract. Appendix A had further definitions and explanations of words like "property values" and "elimination."

"Jesus," Teague said from the doorway. "I leave you alone for a minute and you go all Waco on the poor guy's office."

Dupree set the contract back in the file marked "Security." "Any luck?" he asked.

"No. The task force office was empty so I called Spivey's cell. They're down at the river with a TV crew. I told him you thought this burglary might relate to their case and he said to tell you to go to hell."

"Guy really holds a grudge."

"I told him it was urgent. He said to lock the place up and get hold of the owners and he'd send someone over when they were done. Or else tomorrow morning."

"Got your phone?"

Teague handed it over and Dupree hit redial. Spivey answered on the first ring.

"This is Spivey." There were voices in the background.

"Hey, it's Dupree. I really think—"

"I heard. We'll clear here in an hour and I'll send someone." And then the phone went dead. Dupree tried the number again and this time it went straight to Spivey's voice mail. Fuck him. Dupree wasn't going to do the guy's job for him. He tossed the phone back to Teague, who caught it with two hands.

"Told you," Teague said.

Tomorrow. He'd just be Alan Dupree, private citizen and eligible bachelor. It was funny. He'd dreamed so long of being an easygoing bachelor again, letting go of his twenty-five-year sulk, and the only person he could imagine being impressed by the new, old Dupree was Debbie, who had fallen in love with the easygoing bachelor. He wished she could see who he wanted to be, how carefree he planned to become, how the edges would be smooth again and his jokes would only be funny.

"So," Teague asked, "what do we do now?"

"Now?" Dupree shrugged and looked back at the open files. "Now I go down to the office and file a report. You put some tape up around the house and then you sit here until someone comes by to dust it."

Teague nodded. "Okay. Then what?"

"Then? Then we get a pizza."

Teague just stared at him.

"Hey, Spivey says it isn't urgent. I guess it isn't urgent."

47

"Please, get up," Caroline said, looking down the long hall outside the task force office and the other detectives' offices, hoping that no one was seeing this.

From his knee, Joel looked up at her, pleading. "It doesn't mean anything," he said, "that I love you?"

"It doesn't mean what you think it means," Caroline said. "Does it strike you at all strange that you didn't realize you loved me until after you slept with someone else?"

"I told you, that was a mistake."

"You thought it was me?"

On his knee before her, Joel bowed his head forward, as if he were waiting to be knighted. "I know. I was an asshole. But I'm willing to do whatever I can to keep you."

"Please. Get up." After a moment, he stood. She took his hand. "You can't keep me, Joel. You never had me. Both of us, we were just . . . there."

"How can you say that?" he said. "Is that all it meant to you?"

"I don't really know what it meant to me," she said quietly. "But I know what it meant the night you went home with someone else."

He rubbed his jaw. "Caroline, this might sound idiotic, but before that night I didn't touch another woman the whole time we were together."

"You know that doesn't matter," she said. "We were just holding a place for each other, like bookmarks. And the truth?" She looked over his shoulder and, thankfully, the long hallway was still empty. "I've been waiting for someone else, anyway." Caroline felt as if she were confessing to herself.

"I mean, it's nice that you didn't sleep with anyone while we were together," she said. "But you've wanted to. And you should."

"No, I don't want to—" he started.

"Sure you do," she interrupted. "I know you're trying to be a good guy, Joel. But you're really not. Not yet."

"What if I look back five years from now and realize what a big mistake I made letting you go?" he asked.

She just smiled. "In five years, I'll be seventy-six."

They were still holding hands, her left in his right. With the other hand, Caroline handed him the small engagement ring, nestled in its box.

She heard footsteps over her shoulder. "Caroline! There you are!" She turned to see Dupree at the other end of the long hall; as he realized who she was talking to, his eyes went from Caroline to Joel and then back. Caroline dropped Joel's hand.

"Oh," Dupree said, "I'm sorry."

"It's okay, Alan," she said over her shoulder. "Just give me a second."

"No, it can wait," Dupree said. "I'll . . . uh . . . I'll call you later." He stood for moment as if unsure which way to go, then turned and walked toward the front entrance of the cop shop.

When she turned back Joel had pulled away and was slumped against the wall, staring at the engagement ring in his hand. "I suppose this is the part where you tell me I'm going to make some woman very happy someday."

She smiled. "Maybe when you can afford a bigger ring." She grabbed his hand and pulled him away from the wall.

"I think I did love you," he said.

She hugged him. "I hope so."

312

He squeezed tight in the middle of her back and she felt her eyes clench as she fought the familiar comfort of his arms.

"You know," he whispered in her ear, "maybe for old times' sake, we could . . ."

"That's my old Joel," she said and pulled away from him. She kissed him. "Take care." As she walked down the hall, Caroline had to fight the urge to turn back, because she knew he would be leaning against the wall watching her, the white T-shirt stretched across the ridge of his chest, hands in the pockets of his faded jeans, looking as good as a guy could, perfect in his way, but in no way real or permanent—like a vacation in Mexico, like the test-drive of a car you can't afford.

The task force office was empty, all the detectives home for the night except Spivey and the profilers, who were on the south bank of the river with the *Dateline* crew. She checked her watch. Seven-thirty. She plopped down at her desk and hit the button for her voice mail. Four messages. The first was from Blanton, calling on his cell phone from the river. Caroline put the message on speaker-phone as she looked through an old stack of interview cards.

"Ms. Mabry," Blanton said, "are you familiar with the megalithic statues of Easter Island? Their most striking feature, other than their size, is the fact that the statues have no eyes. Just two cruel, open sockets. It's such a chilling sight—particularly on an island of cannibals—that the first European sailors to encounter the massive heads saw them as figures of great dread, the blind, implacable cruelty of the sea. The statues seem to be crying out that to seek to understand the sea—which, to the Oceanic people, was God—was the same as gouging out one's own eyes. The entire mythology of the statues' meaning and origin focused on that one fact: *The Easter Island statues have no eyes.*"

The voice mail ran out and Blanton was forced to resume his story on the next message.

"I'm telling you about the statues of Easter Island, Ms. Mabry, as I sit alongside your beautiful river, watching McDaniel explain the peculiar psychosis of your man Lenny Ryan to this walking mound of hair spray that the crew of this television program mockingly refers to as *the talent*. Mr. McDaniel has just informed *the talent*, as well as the people out there in TV land, that Lenny Ryan must have surely moved out of the area; otherwise, we would have heard from him by now. We would have found another body. Listening to Mr. McDaniel, who I have begun to think of as *our* talent, I'm disheartened. I'm also reminded that, as with the mysteries of Easter Island, sometimes the most obvious detail is the most obvious because it is wrong."

The voice mail cut Blanton off again and Caroline hit a button to hear him on the third message.

"After a hard century in which the natives of Easter Island were all but wiped out by disease and oppression, a sailor finally asked a holy man why his people built the statues without eyes. There being no past tense in Polynesian dialects, the old islander answered yes, the statues have no eyes. Finally though, he understood and patiently explained that an earlier people had built the statues, and that many grandfathers past, his people arrived by dugout canoe and destroyed the statue people. Then, to the sailor's astonishment, the old holy man reached into a basket and produced a beautifully polished, round piece of dark obsidian with a tiny white shell at its center, a stunning artifact, a single Easter Island eye. The old toothless man smiled. '*We* took the eyes,' he said. The sailor remembered that these islanders were ritualistic cannibals and asked if they took the eyes as a final defeat of the earlier people of Easter Island."

Again, the voice mail cut Blanton off. Caroline listened to the fourth message.

"The tribesman laughed. 'No,' he said. 'We took the eyes out because we were afraid you would steal them.'"

Caroline sat at her desk, staring at Spivey's timeline, which curled around half the office. Finally she smiled and tapped out Blanton's number.

When he picked up she asked, "Was that story true?"

"No idea," he said. "I get drunk and watch *Nova* and the next day I never know."

"How's it going there?" she asked.

"They put makeup on me. It's like putting cologne on a hog. Please come down here and shoot me between the eyes."

"I'm on my way."

"Anyways," he said, and she started a bit at his acquired Spokane colloquialism, "this would almost be bearable if you were here. I have no one to roll my eyes to when McDaniel speaks. The cameraman thinks I'm epileptic."

Caroline rubbed her brow. "Will you tell Spivey I'm on my way down there?"

"If I can extricate him from *the talent's* sculpted ass." She could hear Blanton talking to someone and then he got back on the phone. "He wants to talk to you."

Spivey got on the phone. "Caroline. Where have you been? You're part of this investigation too."

"I got tied up," she said. "But I'm about to come down there."

"Great," he said. "One thing. Do you think you could swing by a grocery store and get some snacks? It looks like this could take a while still."

After a moment, Caroline heard herself say, "Sure."

"Some chips and something baked—maybe a Danish or two, if they're fresh."

"If they're fresh," Caroline repeated. Then she hung up.

The phone rang almost as soon as she'd turned it off. She slapped at the speaker button again and spoke with her head still in her hands. "You want bagels too?"

"What?" Dupree asked from the other end of the phone.

"Huh?" Caroline asked.

"What did you say?"

Caroline picked up the receiver. "Alan? Is that you?"

"Yeah. Hey, Caroline."

"Hey," she said.

"What did you ask me?" he asked after a moment.

Caroline stammered. "I guess . . . I asked if you wanted a bagel."

"Oh," he said. "Not really."

She felt numb having Dupree on the other end of this phone call. It hadn't been as easy as it should have been to tell Joel that she wouldn't marry him. There was some kind of every-girl fantasy in marrying the best-looking guy you knew, a line of thinking that went something like this: *He would look great in a tux.* But for any temptation that his idiotic proposal might have presented, Caroline had known from the beginning exactly what she *should* tell Joel. She knew the right answer. But she felt incapable of speaking to Dupree right now, and if he asked her to be with him tonight she had no idea what her answer should be. For the first time, the only thing keeping them apart was them.

"I'm sorry about earlier," he said. "I don't have great timing. Did you and Joel get everything"—he paused—"resolved?"

"Yeah," she said. "I think so."

"That's nice. That's good." He cleared his throat. "Well, this is probably nothing, but I just wanted to ask if you were going to see Spivey any time soon."

"I was just about to go see him," Caroline said.

"Well, the little dickhead keeps blowing me off. There was a break-in on the South Hill today. A guy named John Landers."

"The boat guy," Caroline said.

"Yeah, right," Dupree said. "Well, it's probably unrelated, but the burglar was clearly looking for something."

"What do you mean?"

"I don't know. There were a bunch of files thrown open and there was a model of the neighborhood down there, and it got me to thinking about Lenny Ryan and the pawnshop guy and his uncle and . . . let me ask you something. Did you ever happen to run into the old security guard at that boat place?"

"Security guard?" Caroline was having trouble following.

Dupree laughed at himself. "You know what?" he said. "It's nothing."

"No," she said, "keep going."

"I'm not even clear about what I'm saying." He laughed again. "Could you just mention to Spivey that someone really needs to dust this house before the owners get home? Just in case."

"Sure," Caroline said. "I'll tell him."

"Thanks." He laughed at himself. "Jesus."

They said at the same time, "How have you been?"

Dupree laughed. "I want to apologize again for what I did the other day. I really had no right to drop it in your lap like that . . . to expect anything from you."

"Alan . . ."

"I could forgive myself for a lot of things, but if I made you think you were a bad cop . . . well, I couldn't live with that."

She squeezed her eyes shut, willing herself not to say anything else, anything that might open her up for a question she wasn't prepared to answer.

"Well," Dupree said, "I've got to meet this guy for pizza. You'll tell Spivey?"

"Yeah."

They were both quiet for a moment and Caroline pictured him six years ago, clinging to her on the couch, her legs wrapped around his, their hands gripping each other's backs, knowing that if they let go they would make love and everything would change. A week before that, she had turned thirty. How could six years go by like that?

"I'll call you after I talk to Spivey," Caroline said.

"If you want," Dupree said.

She replaced the receiver and put her head back in her hands. When she was a little girl, maybe eight or nine, before the divorce, her mother would put her head in her hands like this for seemingly no reason, and Caroline would grow sick with worry. Once, when she was playing with dolls, her mother had come into her room, tears streaking down her face. "Caroline," her mother said, "whatever you do, don't let someone else decide what *you* want." In her eight-year-old mind, the phrase *what you want* took on a kind of sanctity, as if happiness could be guaranteed by gathering around herself some items from a checklist—like a doll's accessories: townhouse, convertible, handsome boyfriend. Her life the past five years seemed like a catalogue of plastic objects, and when she thought about what she really wanted, all she saw was Alan Dupree.

She was reaching for the phone to call him back when she caught a glimpse of a map on her desk. She spun it so that she could see it better. She thought about what Dupree had said. John Landers's house had been broken into by someone looking for files. She tried to picture what that meant. She saw the boat dealership, smack in the middle of what McDaniel called "Lenny Ryan's hunting ground."

She stared off into the distance again, then got up to look for the hard copies of the forensics reports. She found them on the conference table in the middle of the room. She leafed through them until she reached the report on fibers and particles from the first victim,

Rebecca Bennett. She ran her finger down the column listing trace particles, and came to a carpet fiber that had baffled them for a while—a fiber they finally realized had come from a waterproof boat carpet. They knew that prostitutes sometimes took their dates into the boats in the Landers' Cove lot. Caroline went through the other forensics reports, but none of the other bodies carried that particular fiber. Laird was in charge of forensics, and she doubted he would've missed something so obvious as a carpet fiber on more than one of the bodies. Caroline started for her phone, but again she stopped.

This time she went to the file cabinet and removed another forensics file from a case they considered only tangentially related to the others. Shelly Nordling's file. She ran her finger down the fibers and trace particles taken from Shelly Nordling's body and clothing and there it was. The same boat fiber.

Again she pictured Lenny Ryan asking questions and finding out that Shelly and the other prostitutes used to have sex in the boats at Landers' Cove. Now she imagined Lenny Ryan breaking into Landers's house, looking for . . . what? Dupree said he'd taken files. Files?

She felt stupid and sluggish as she tried to piece this together. She rubbed her temples. Files? Where would you go if you were looking for files on someone? She checked the clock. Almost eight. The county offices would all be closed for the weekend. Caroline went to Spivey's desk and found the city/county emergency phone list. She called the county clerk's cell phone. He answered on the first ring, and Caroline could hear the bustle and noise of a restaurant behind him. She introduced herself and apologized for calling him so late.

"I have kind of a strange request that really can't wait until Monday," she said. "Do you keep the names of people coming in to request documents?" She explained that she needed to find out if someone had come into his office looking for court documents pertaining to John Landers.

"The boat guy," the clerk said.

"Right," Caroline said.

"I'll call you back," the clerk said.

The call came two minutes later.

"David Nickell."

Caroline scrambled for a pen. "I'm sorry?"

"Yeah. I just finished chewing out a clerk for mailing a copy of a court file to this guy. Lives up in Springdale. It's against policy. People have to come in to get documents. No exceptions. I don't care how sad your sob story is, how far out in the sticks you live, we don't mail court documents to people."

"When did the file go out?"

"According to my deep-in-shit assistant, he mailed the envelope this week. I think this David Nickell slipped my guy a twenty for the favor. I oughta fire the shit."

"Do you know, did he have ID?"

"He couldn't get documents without ID."

Caroline had to catch her breath. "Do you know what he looked like?"

"Clerk said he was bald and had a beard."

Caroline pushed her luck. "Get me an address?"

"How's Monday?"

"It's no good," Caroline said. "Any chance you could get your assistant down here tonight?"

"I'll see what I can do," he said and hung up.

David Nickell. She started with the Springdale telephone book. She found it: David and Angela Nickell. The address was just a route number; apparently David Nickell lived in the sticks. She called the phone number, but there was no answer, no machine. Next she went to the computer database and entered "Nickell, David," checking it against all the tips they'd received, every witness or suspect or victim. Nothing.

She tried another computer, checking his name against local, state, and national criminal records. Several David Nickells came up, so she narrowed the field by adding the word "Springdale" and soon had a social security number. This David M. Nickell, forty-two, of Springdale, had been arrested for domestic violence against an Angela Nickell, and three separate counts of driving under the influence. Two months ago he had been cited for another DUI on the west side of the state, as well as auto theft and evading a police officer. He was in jail in Tacoma, awaiting trial. His mug shot came up after a moment and showed a balding man with a beard and glasses. She remembered the recent descriptions of Lenny Ryan with a full beard and a cap.

If David Nickell was in Tacoma, then someone else was coming into Spokane asking about John Landers. And if David Nickell was arrested in a stolen car, then the person with Nickell's ID might just have his car too.

Caroline had convinced herself that it wasn't Lenny Ryan parked in front of her house that night, that it was just the kid with the beer. But she wasn't exactly surprised when she ran David Nickell's name and social security number with the state department of licensing, and the description of his car came up—a red 1992 Nissan Sentra.

She fell back against her desk and stared at the ceiling. Like everyone else, she supposed, she believed she could stay separated from the events of her own life, stay dry in the middle of all the rush and tumble, and so it came as a surprise to find herself being tugged by the same current she'd been fighting all along.

48

There was a pinch, and then Rae-Lynn felt a warmth and a tightness in her arm. She wiggled her fingers and leaned back in the stall and felt the warmth move into her shoulder and all over her body, and her calves tingled, and she licked her gums. Tim untied the bandanna around her arm and she fell back against the toilet seat and hummed. A few seconds later her eyes snapped open, and she saw Tim standing at the sink, taking the needle off the syringe. He washed the needle in peroxide and put it back in his kit. She loved Tim for being so clean and safe. She watched him from the stall, where she sat on the toilet, legs spread, the back of her head against the wall.

"That's really nice, Timmy. Thank you."

"My pleasure." His back was to her as he worked at the sink, washing his hands and putting his kit away.

"I'm so glad I ran into you," Rae-Lynn said. "This is gonna be a great night."

"I meant what I said before, you know," he said. "If you got your boobs done, you really could be a dancer."

"Aw, you're just sayin' that," Rae-Lynn said.

"No, I mean it. You'd have to eat better, put a little meat back on your ass and thighs." He turned to look at her, sprawled out in the stall of the men's room at Denny's. "You know, at the better clubs, they don't like it if the girls look sick."

"Do I look sick?"

Tim had the round, soft face of a kid, and blond hair that he parted on the side. His hair made him look sort of stiff, and sorry about things. "A little," he said. "You look like you haven't been taking care of yourself."

Back out in the restaurant Rae-Lynn melted into a corner booth and rubbed her face. It felt elastic. She touched the bruise under her eye where Michael had hit her yesterday as punishment for running away. That could have been worse, certainly. She pressed her small breasts together and stared down at her cleavage. "Would you help me get a boob job, Timmy?"

"Me?"

"If you help me pay for it, they'd be like, half yours."

"So I keep one and you get the other one?"

"No, but you could touch 'em whenever you wanted."

He reached over. "Can't I touch 'em now?"

"You could ask your dad for the money." Tim's dad was a lawyer or something.

Tim opened his menu to the breakfast page. "Hey, Dad. Can I have a couple grand to help this girl get her boobs done?"

"Yeah!" Rae-Lynn laughed without making any noise. She fell over in the booth, then looked up at him. "Hey, can we have pancakes, Timmy?"

"Whatever you want."

She sat back up. "On your birthday, they give you a steak."

"I think that's a different place."

She watched Tim read the menu and wanted to tell him that she liked him, but she couldn't remember if she'd just thought that or if she'd already told him. "After pancakes, we can go back to your place?"

"That depends," he said.

"On what?"

"On how much you plan to charge me."

"How much is a boob job?"

"Couple thousand," he said.

"That's how much I'll charge you."

"How about a cigarette, instead?" Tim asked.

She laughed. "Deal." This was fun.

Tim pulled his wallet out and grabbed some singles, then stood and walked over to the cigarette machine across the restaurant. Rae-Lynn stared at his wallet, still lying where he'd left it, in the crease of the booth.

She was at the door with Tim's wallet before she could remember deciding to do it. She walked around back and hid behind the Dumpster and remembered that night the freak in the truck had tried to strangle her. She wondered what it would have felt like to die that night. Or what if she was dead and didn't know it? Like in that movie. The thought freaked her out a little. Crouching in the shadows, Rae-Lynn opened Tim's wallet. He only had a ten and two singles. She pulled out the cards. A driver's license in which Tim looked fat and pitiful. A bogus gold credit card, the kind they gave anyone, well, anyone but her. She reached in the other side of Tim's wallet. A couple of espresso stand punch cards. At one of the stands, a drive-through a few blocks away, he needed only one more punch for his free latte. A video rental card and a picture of a little girl, only a little bit bigger than Rae-Lynn's baby. She didn't know Tim had a baby. Finally she pulled out a library card and, for some reason, that was the thing that made Rae-Lynn feel bad.

She stood up and walked around the corner to a window on the side of the restaurant. Tim was just sitting at the booth again, turning the pack of cigarettes over in his hands like he was waiting for her to come back, even though he must've known. Outside a woman was walking toward the door, and Rae-Lynn grabbed her by the arm. "Can you do me a favor?"

Rae-Lynn opened Tim's wallet, took the ten and the punch card for the free latte, then handed the wallet to the woman. She pointed to Tim. "Can you take this to that guy at the booth and tell him I'm sorry?"

"Sure," the woman said and started walking toward the front door.

"And don't steal it!" Rae-Lynn said. "I'm watching you."

She watched through the window as the woman delivered the

wallet. Tim thanked her and put it in his pocket without checking for his money. Rae-Lynn thought he would know exactly what she had taken. He was smart like that.

She watched him for a few more seconds, but he didn't look up at the window. He invited the woman to sit down and she did. He opened the pack of cigarettes, gave the woman one, put one in his mouth, and reached in his pocket for his lighter. He took a long drag and the end chirped into flame. The woman said something and Tim laughed and blew the smoke straight up into the air.

Rae-Lynn turned away. With Timmy's ten in her jeans pocket, she started down Division toward downtown. She hoped Michael would be over his anger, because she really wanted to party tonight. She found a cabdriver filling up his car at a convenience store and promised him a blow job for a ride down to East Sprague.

The cabdriver had thin hair and a terrible goatee but he wasn't ugly. Rae-Lynn liked the way he raced his cab, the way it swerved in and out of traffic. Sitting next to him in the front seat, she closed her eyes and spread her arms out like wings. He told her that he owned this cab himself, that he didn't work for anyone else, and that was all he'd ever dreamed of doing, working for himself like this.

The driver turned down Sprague. "To me," he said, "life is a movie. You gotta be the star of your own movie."

Rae-Lynn opened her eyes and stared at the cabdriver. "Wow. That's beautiful."

"Thanks. That's, like, my philosophy."

"I was in a movie once. A couple weeks ago. In Moses Lake."

"Cool," the driver said.

"You want to contribute to my titty fund?" She pressed her breasts together. "I'm raising money for implants. I'm gonna be a dancer."

"Did you see, Pamela Anderson took hers out."

"After you get famous you don't need 'em anymore."

"I ain't gonna contribute if you're just gonna take 'em out after you get famous."

Rae-Lynn jumped over to the passenger window. "Stop the car!"

The cab pulled over in front of the Happy Stork and Rae-Lynn hopped out. "Look, I'll be right back. I just gotta run inside and see if my friend's in here and then I'll come right back."

The cabdriver seemed suspicious but she smiled. "I swear, I'll be right back."

Rae-Lynn giggled at the slap of her bare feet on the sidewalk and tried to remember where she'd taken off her shoes. She needed both hands to pull open the door of the Happy Stork, and as soon as she did, she was hit by smoke and swamp-cooled air. A couple of old guys were at the table near the window and two younger guys were at the bar. They all checked her out. Rae-Lynn felt beautiful.

"Hey." The bartender recognized her. "Where you been?"

"Movies," she said. "And some dancing."

"Cool."

Rae-Lynn fished in her pocket and pulled out the ten. She leaned against the bar to catch her balance. She felt like she was still in the cab, still flying. "I'll buy my first drink, but then I expect somebody to step up."

"Oh, I'll step up," said one of the guys at the bar.

Rae-Lynn considered the forest of bottles behind the bartender. "Tequila."

"Ta-kill-ya," said the guy at the bar.

The bartender grabbed a dirty plastic bottle and filled a shot glass to the rim, then gave her eight bucks change. Rae-Lynn emptied the glass and squeezed her eyes shut.

Rae-Lynn stepped luxuriously away from the bar. She stretched her hands over her head like a dancer and then let them fall to her sides, looking demurely at the men. "You guys wanna see me dance?"

The men all smiled.

"Okay," she said, "I'll be right back." She went toward the bathroom in the back, but kept walking out the back door, into the alley. She was beautiful.

She emerged from the alley onto the dark side street and was surprised to find the cabdriver parked there, waiting.

"Hey!" she said. "I know you!" She doubled over in laughter.

"What the fuck," he said. "You runnin' away from your fare?"

"No," Rae-Lynn said. "I was coming back around front. Those guys in there were all coming on to me and I had to get away. I was coming back."

But the cabbie was angry. Rae-Lynn could see it. Why did guys have to get so angry all the time?

"You owe me fourteen bucks," the cabbie said.

"For two miles?"

"I had the meter running while you were inside." He took a step toward her.

"I don't got fourteen bucks. I told you, we could mess around."

He grabbed her wrist and she swung at him with her other hand, but it grazed off his shoulder. He punched her in the face, right in the eye where Michael had backhanded her. She fell down, and the guy went through her pockets until he found Timmy's eight bucks. He threw two cards back on her, the punch card for the free latte and the business card she'd gotten months ago from the lady cop. Rae-Lynn put the cards back in her pocket. She thought, I am beautiful. I am. Her eyes were bleary and she felt like she was going to throw up. "Timmy," she whimpered

"Fuckin' whore," the cabdriver said. He drove off.

Rae-Lynn stood up, dusted herself off, nearly lost her balance, and then walked back down the side street toward Sprague.

Her arms hung at her sides and she didn't feel like she was flying anymore. Timmy used to have such good smack. But either she was that much tougher to junk up or Timmy had some weak shit, because she could already feel the hunger, the itch at the center of herself. And she didn't even have her eight bucks anymore.

She felt the headlights from a car and turned to show the driver her good side, but the car didn't even slow down. Rae-Lynn continued down the sidewalk, weaving.

She crossed the street, stopped, and leaned her face against the chain-link fence of the boat dealership. When her swollen cheek touched the fence, she jumped back at the tenderness. "Hey!" she yelled. "Are you in there?"

The old security guard came out of the showroom, a look of disbelief on his face. He looked right at Rae-Lynn, then up and down the street, to her right and her left. "Jesus, girlie," he said. "Where have you been?"

And Rae-Lynn started crying then, remembering when she and Shelly and Chloe had used the boats as their own personal apartments, how untouchable they'd felt in the boat yard, sitting on top of the big yachts talking about everything they wanted to be. Back then Rae-Lynn thought her boobs were nice and she would have rolled her eyes at anyone who suggested she needed implants. It wasn't fair that your boobs shrank when you lost weight, that even good things could be undone like that.

The old security guard fumbled with his keys, looked both ways, up and down the street. Then he unlocked the gate, swung it open, and Rae-Lynn stepped inside.

She paused at the construction project on the other side of the showroom, steel girders rising up four stories, exposed on one side like bones, the other side partly covered with gray stucco at the bottom and white at the top, as if it were half ringed with snow. A floodlight shone on the whole thing, throwing its huge shadow across the parking lot and exposing the girder. "What's that?" she asked.

"It's a mountain," the old security guard said, and Rae-Lynn felt better, imagining that when it was complete, she and Shelly and Risa could climb it with a bottle of wine and look out over the city; they would be above everything, then, afraid of nothing. And even though she knew it was impossible, Rae-Lynn found that she couldn't stop picturing it.

"I've never climbed a mountain before," she said quietly.

"It's not real," the security guard said. "It's a building that looks like a mountain." He brushed her hair away from her bruised eye. "What happened to you?"

"Do you think I need a boob job?"

He put his arm around her shoulder. "No. Of course not."

"Can I sleep here? I'm real tired."

"Tell you what," he said. "I'm gonna take you someplace where you can sleep as long as you want. Okay, girlie?"

She nodded. "That would be nice."

He grabbed his jacket and put it over her narrow shoulders. She felt inside the breast pocket for a wallet but there wasn't one. "Thank you," she said.

They walked out the front gate and he turned and padlocked it from the outside.

"You're so nice," Rae-Lynn said, but he didn't answer. He had a

327

Ford Taurus and she climbed in on the passenger side. He reached over and buckled her seat belt and she rubbed his cheek, his gray whiskers.

A few minutes later her eyes snapped open, and she said, "A mountain is a mountain. It doesn't matter why you build it, if it looks like a mountain . . ."

She looked around. The security guard was parking the car in a driveway in a part of town she didn't recognize, or maybe even out of town. It was getting dark. The house was carved into a down-slope, and there were only a couple of other houses built on this hillside. He unbuckled her seat belt and she climbed out. There was an ache between her eyes and neck and Rae-Lynn knew it would get worse, and she would get sick if she didn't get hooked up at some point tonight. "Whose house?" she asked.

"My son's," the old security guard said. It was dark and newer, a one-story ranch with a daylight basement. There wasn't even any grass, just dirt in the front yard along with a wheelbarrow and a couple of shovels.

She followed the old man around the side until they came to the back of the house, perched on a steep bank overlooking the river, a mile downstream from the falls. The backyard had been terraced into the riverbank; beyond that was a five-foot ledge and at the bottom of that, the ground began sloping at a forty-degree angle to the water.

"It's beautiful," Rae-Lynn said. With the sun fading, the river beneath them was like some dark crease in the world, a river of darkness. Across the river were the restored miners' shacks and brownstones of the Peaceful Valley neighborhood, where Rae-Lynn had been to a party once. Downstream were vacant fields of wild grass and scrub trees, and the river made a sharp turn, and the city ended. Beyond that was Moses Lake and Kelly. Rae-Lynn felt sad thinking about him and how he'd fucked up her last chance.

She looked back at the house. There were only a handful of houses on this bank of the river, probably because it was so steep and because it was cut off by a railroad trestle behind the house. "I didn't even know there were any houses down here," she said.

"Ain't many," said the old security guard. "Just us and Mrs.

Amend down the way." He smiled at her and fished in his pocket for the back door key.

Rae-Lynn followed the river upstream, toward the falls and the line of bridges that crossed the river into downtown. Beyond the bridges, the city's skyline rested against the darkening sky. She'd never really seen a whole city before, not like this, where you could see the edges of it, where you could put your hands out and contain all of it.

"You coming?" asked the old security guard.

Rae-Lynn felt a shudder and knew she wasn't strong enough to withstand the shakes and the sickness tonight. Maybe earlier, with Kelly, but now she was tiny and weak and she wasn't beautiful the way people said. She was tired, but sleep only made the itch stronger. For a moment she thought about giving him back his coat and telling him that he shouldn't leave her alone in this house, that she would steal from it. She could see inside the picture window that overlooked the river. From outside, it looked like a huge TV screen. The old man stood on that screen, in front of a big shelf of books, holding a telephone. He seemed so frail, this old man, but she knew that even the frail ones were strong, stronger than she was. They were all so fucking strong.

She could hear her own breathing as she watched the old man speak into the telephone in the huge picture window of the house etched into the bank of the river. At one time such a sight would have sent Rae-Lynn daydreaming about dinner parties and babies and waking up in her husband's shirt, but now she just took a deep breath, pulled the old man's jacket tight around her shoulders, and walked into the house.

49

Kevin Verloc's shoulders were carved and sculpted, and he had the big-veined, round arms of a serious body builder. His neck seemed an extension of his shoulders, and the entire effect was to make it seem as if his weight had all been shifted into his upper body, as if someone had taken him by the legs and squeezed. His hair was short and dark, combed perfectly straight onto his forehead, and he wore small, rectangular-shaped glasses that he removed and slid into his shirt pocket as he came outside. But the thing that surprised Dupree the most was that Kevin Verloc walked.

He leaned on a tripod cane and had to swing his hips heavily to start each leg in motion, but there was no other way to describe it: Kevin Verloc walked. He moved with great concentration as he emerged from the All-Safe Security building—which Dupree recognized by the stucco walls and Spanish style as a former Taco Time. Verloc turned and locked the glass door, and it was only when he was a few steps from the building that he looked up and saw the police car in his parking lot. If he was surprised to see the patrol car he didn't reveal it, walking over with that double hitch, like someone limping on both legs. Dupree stepped out of the car then and stuck out his hand. Verloc stopped, leaned on his cane, and shook Dupree's hand. They were about the same height, but Verloc had a way of tilting his head back, exposing his tree trunk of a neck, so that he seemed to look down on Dupree.

"Something I can help you with, Officer?" Verloc asked.

"Actually, we spoke on the phone a couple of months ago. I'm Alan Dupree. I talked to you a little about the prostitute murders?"

"Sure," Verloc said and his expression didn't change at all. "Dupree."

Dupree laughed. "Yeah. I got that crazy tip from your neighbor and I called you. Remember?"

"Mmm-hmm, it's coming back to me," Verloc said. "You ever catch that guy in the paper? From California? Right? Guy sounded like a real piece of work."

"Lenny Ryan," Dupree said. "No. I guess he's still out there somewhere."

"I'll bet he's back in California again." Dupree didn't answer and Verloc glanced down at Dupree's uniform. "I understand you have two FBI profilers working on the case. That must be fascinating, working with them so closely."

"Actually, I'm not on the case anymore." Dupree ran his hand along the seam of his uniform pants. "I'm . . . uh . . . taking early retirement, finishing up on patrol. That's why I came to see you."

"Oh?" Verloc asked.

"Did I catch you at a bad time? You look like you're racing off somewhere."

Verloc shrugged. "Me? No, I was just going to get a bite to eat. Little dinner break." Then he smiled. "What can I do for you?"

"Well," Dupree began, "yeah, like I was saying, I'm taking early retirement and I'll get a decent pension, but you know what it's like when you get out. I just think I'm gonna need another source of income, not to mention I'd go nuts without something to occupy my time. And I heard that you hire old badges sometimes."

"Sure," Verloc said, "I hire ex-cops. They're the best."

"Yeah, I know some guys who work as private detectives, but I don't think I could stomach that shit."

"Working for sleaze-bucket lawyers." Verloc shook his head. "Hundred-and-eighty-degree turn, man. I couldn't do it."

"Right," Dupree said.

"Come on," Verloc said. "Let's get you an application." He shifted his weight onto the cane and turned back toward the office.

"Are you sure I'm not keeping you from something?"

"No," Verloc said. "It's pretty slow around here right now."

"Because you could just mail it to me if you like."

"No need," Verloc said, "as long as you're here."

Dupree was surprised at how quickly he could move, scuttling across the parking lot. As he walked behind Verloc, Dupree's shoulder radio squawked and he could hear Teague on the other end. "Dupree? Where are you?"

After talking to Caroline, he had planned to go back to John Landers's house, but he'd gotten to thinking about the empty files marked "Security" and his mistaken phone call to Kevin Verloc three months ago. It was probably nothing, but Teague would have to wait at the house while he indulged the nagging little voice in his head one last time. Dupree reached up and switched his radio off. Verloc turned and smiled at him.

He unlocked the door, and Dupree followed him into a small lobby, where a love seat and matching chair sat across from an unmanned desk. Behind the desk was a narrow door that Verloc opened and entered, turning sideways to fit his wide shoulders through the doorway.

Dupree didn't have to turn to follow him into this interior office, which was set up like a small police command center, with a map of the city on one wall and a telephone dispatch panel right in front of the map. Small flags were tacked to the map, apparently marking clients. The desk in front of the map appeared rigidly organized, a can of pencils sharpened to razor points, files stacked so that their edges lined up perfectly with the edge of the desk. "So, mostly you're looking for security guards?"

"That's certainly what we try to do," Verloc said. "That's why I started the business. But a lot of people don't want to bother with guards with all the computerized systems out there—video cameras and fancy lasers and stuff."

"Just like the police department," Dupree said. "Thank God there are still jobs that we can do better than computers, huh?"

Verloc was looking through a cabinet. He turned and smiled weakly at Dupree, then resumed his search in the cabinet. "Anyway, it's awful slow right now, so I can't promise anything. We do a lot of concerts, special event stuff earlier in the summer, and we have a contract with a couple of school districts, so we do some of their events. We had a mall for a few years, but I got underbid last year."

"That's tough. Must be great to have an account like that boat place. Good, steady client, huh? You do any other security work for Landers?"

Verloc straightened up from the cabinet. "Where the hell did she put that stuff? New receptionist. I like things a certain way." He rolled his eyes and stuck his cane out. "I'll check my office."

He disappeared behind an unmarked door at the end of the dispatch room. Dupree picked up a log book and leafed through it. He walked toward the open door and he could see Verloc's cane in the middle of the room, but not Verloc himself. "I know it's here somewhere," he heard Verloc say.

Dupree reached to his belt and unsnapped his holster.

"Ah, here we go." Verloc emerged with a single sheet of paper, his face red. He leaned heavily on the cane and handed the application to Dupree. Then he took the log book from Dupree and set it down, carefully lining it up with the edge of the desk.

"That's great," Dupree said as he looked over the application. "Hey, I met your father the other day. Did he tell you about that?"

For the first time Verloc seemed to flinch, but only slightly. "I don't . . . think so."

"I saw him down there at Landers' Cove. How many guards you got down there?"

"Just my father. How did you . . . come to meet him?"

Dupree reached up and rubbed his own shoulder. "The big wrestling match with the drunks down there, couple weeks ago. I was the cop who got stabbed."

"It wasn't serious, I hope." Verloc looked behind himself for a chair and then eased himself into it, sighing as soon as he was seated.

"It was nothing. Couple of stitches. It changes you a little, though. Most of the time, the bastards are just out there and they can beat each other up and steal from each other and you see it, but it doesn't really touch you, doesn't get to you. But when it's you they're coming after, it's different. It changes you, makes you feel harder, less forgiving . . . But I guess I don't need to tell you that."

"No," Verloc said simply.

"Yeah, I remember when you got shot. Jesus. It affected every cop in the state . . . you know. It's great that you're walking now."

Verloc just stared at him, no expression on his face.

"It must've been hard," Dupree said. "You've made quite a recovery."

"Eight years of physical therapy," Verloc said quietly.

"You still use a chair, then?" Dupree asked. "'Cause when I called you that day, you made this great joke about a wheelchair."

"Sometimes I use a chair. I get tired."

"Yeah," Dupree said. "That's something. So you're pretty well recovered. I mean, as much as they expect?"

Verloc eased himself up out of his chair. "I really should get my dinner."

Dupree stepped aside. "Oh, of course. Sure."

Verloc nodded to the application. "Why don't you fill out that form and bring it in on Monday, and I'll see what my staffing looks like for the fall."

"Yeah, that'd be great."

As they walked toward the glass front door, Dupree walked ahead of Verloc and watched his reflection in the glass. In the window, he could see Verloc staring at his back. Outside, Verloc locked the door again and made his way to a dark red pickup parked in the corner of the lot. Dupree made a note of the license plate, then nodded to Verloc.

"Thanks a bunch. I really look forward to working with you," Dupree said.

Verloc just smiled.

"I'll come by on Monday, then."

"Yeah," Verloc said. "Monday."

He used his upper body to climb up into the truck, fired it, and backed out of his parking spot. He turned on his blinker well before he reached the end of the parking lot, and then pulled out slowly.

In the car, Dupree picked up his cell phone and used his thumb to hit the numbers.

"This is Teague."

"Hey, it's Dupree."

"What the hell's the matter with you? You're acting all crazy. I was about five minutes from calling dispatch and telling 'em you were missing again."

"I'm sorry," Dupree said.

"I gotta tell you, Sarge, this thing is pretty weird."

"What's that?"

"Well, I'm here at the house and the neighbors had a number for Mr. and Mrs. Landers at Lake Coeur d'Alene, so I called. A sheriff's deputy answered and said Mr. Landers was on his way to Kootenai Medical Center."

"What happened?"

"Don't know, for sure. The wife came back from the store and saw some guy driving away from their cabin in a red car. When she went inside, someone had done a number on her husband. Broke his collarbone and his leg, knocked out a couple of teeth, and drained him of a little blood."

Dupree stared back at the office of All-Safe Security. "Are you in the house?"

"On the porch."

"Go inside," Dupree said, "into that office next to the living room, where everything was messed up."

Dupree could hear Teague's footsteps on the hardwood floor. "Okay. I'm here."

"There are a couple of files open there on the safe. They say 'Security' on them."

"Got 'em," Teague said.

"Open the one that says 'Expenses.'"

"Yeah, right here."

As he shifted the car into drive, Dupree looked up at the security business once more. "The most recent receipt, it says 'Miscellaneous.' How much is that?"

"Let's see." He could hear Teague flipping through pages. "Two-forty."

He quickly did the math. Six. Maybe there was one they didn't know about. "Don't move. I'm coming up there." Dupree stomped on the gas and his car bounded over the curb and onto the street just as a red Nissan Sentra was pulling into the parking lot behind him.

50

So fucking cold. She whispered, "Kelly, you took all the blankets," and it was hearing his name that woke her up. She reached out, but he wasn't there. He would come home from the hospital soon; she began wondering what she might cook and whether there were potatoes in the house. It was dark, and then Rae-Lynn realized she wasn't in Moses Lake and that the chills were coming from inside. She sat up on a leather couch and looked around, wondering if she could return to the dream in which Kelly came home. She had no idea where she was or how she'd gotten there. She wasn't wearing shoes. Where the hell were her shoes?

She stretched and yawned and sat up on the couch, reached over and switched on a tall reading lamp. Her hands felt clammy and cold, and the ache in her head was the only thing that seemed at all familiar. She felt a tightness in her left arm, like a bruise, and remembered shooting up. Her eye hurt where Michael and then the cabdriver had punched her; she thought for a minute, reconstructing the day through aches and bruises. And Timmy's wallet. He was so nice. Why had she done that? Maybe when people are shitty to you it makes you want to be shitty to someone else, like kids in school.

She looked around the room, a long, narrow living room or study, a wall of books behind her, the leather couch facing that huge picture window that overlooked the dark river. It was coming back to her now: the nice old security guard taking her to the house overlooking the river. He'd given her something to drink and she must have fallen asleep. She looked for a clock and found a small travel alarm clock open on the bookshelves behind her. Nine-thirty. It was dark. Must be night. The same night or the next night? She still felt stoned. Same night. Then she'd only slept a little while. That was good. She wondered if the security guard had gone back to work.

The leather couch squeaked as she stood up. She yawned again and looked around the floor for her shoes. She looked at the bookshelves behind the leather couch. The shelves were full of row after row of black paperback books, their titles in emphatic capital letters: *CATCHING AMERICA'S MOST NOTORIOUS SERIAL MURDERERS* and *THE TRUE BLOOD MURDERS* and *MINDTRAP: THE LIFE OF AN FBI PROFILER*. There was something strange about the way all the books were perfectly lined up, their spines forming a flat, black wall with these emphatic block letters. It reminded her of the way Kelly constantly reorganized the tools in his garage. Whoever owned these paperback books had even gone to the trouble of alphabetizing them.

Something about the books made her uncomfortable, and Rae-Lynn stepped away to look for her shoes again. There was a carpeted staircase next to the bookshelf and she crept up it carefully, until she was at the landing by the front door. The living room was a few steps up, separated from the landing by a small railing. Rae-Lynn looked through the slats of the railing and saw the old security guard, chewing his thumbnail and watching the driveway intently through the house's front window. A pair of headlights flashed across his body and he seemed to relax. A car was pulling into the driveway. Rae-Lynn peered out the window above the door and saw a maroon pickup.

She felt her body go stiff and then she brought a shaking hand to her face. The truck door opened and out stepped the man who had tried to kill her, thick arms and tree-trunk neck; it was him.

She slid down the stairs and saw a phone next to the bookshelf. She picked it up, thought about calling 911, but remembered the business card she carried everywhere—for luck, she supposed. She pulled it out of her jeans, dropped it, and picked it up. Caroline Mabry. Special Investigations Unit. She found the cell phone number and began punching in her number. The front door opened.

"What took you so long?" the old security guard said.

"I got held up," said the other man. "Where is she?"

"Downstairs. Sleeping."

The lady cop's phone rang once but the men were already on the stairs. Rae-Lynn dropped the phone and ran to the slider, fumbled with the latch, finally got it open, and began running.

She heard them behind her—"Hey!"—and turned to see the old man hanging up the phone as the young man pushed through the doorway. She plunged through the backyard, over the bank, and into the darkness, toward the sound of the river tearing at its banks.

51

Spivey stood a few feet away, chewing on a poppy-seed muffin, watching over the shoulder of a TV cameraman who wheeled his camera along a pair of slender, silver railroad tracks toward a bright bank of lights, to where Blanton crouched, pretending to sift through a handful of dirt, just a few feet from where Rebecca Bennett's body was found. Blanton's suit coat scrunched up over his belt and Caroline could see the waistband of his boxer shorts. McDaniel stood behind him more comfortably, arms crossed, in a cowboy shirt and bolo tie, squinting off into the distance.

"That looks cool," Spivey whispered to the producer.

Caroline paced nervously and took another run at Spivey, speaking under her breath. "I really think we ought to get on this. Now."

The assistant producer held up her hand for Spivey and Caroline to be quiet and Caroline stepped away again, kicking at the ground anxiously.

Her cell phone rang and the assistant producer glared at her. But when she turned on the phone to pick up the call, whoever it was had hung up.

"Does this look to anyone else like I'm sitting on the crapper?" Blanton asked.

"Please, Mr. Blanton," said the assistant producer. "Let's get this shot and then you can leave. All right?"

"I just don't see why he gets to stand and I've gotta look like I'm taking a dump."

They moved the camera to get a different angle, and Caroline took advantage of the break to take another run at Spivey. "Look, I think Lenny Ryan is in Springdale."

Spivey watched the crew set up the camera. "Tell me again," he said.

"A guy has been poking around, requesting documents about Landers' Cove."

"This guy Nickell," Spivey said. "And he lives in Springdale."

She had to admit, it was impressive, how well he could soak up raw information—names and dates—although he had more trouble with concepts. "That's right," she said. "But Nickell is in jail in Tacoma. And tonight someone broke into Landers's house."

"And this somehow puts Lenny Ryan in a red Nissan?"

Caroline stepped in front of him and stared into his eyes. "There is a man with a beard and Nickell's ID requesting court documents on Landers; a man in a beard and a red car is asking about hookers; the car registered to David Nickell is a red Nissan but David Nickell is in jail." She pressed the pages she'd brought into his hands. "And I saw a red Nissan parked outside my house one night."

Spivey glanced at the pages, then handed them back and cocked his head. "I don't remember you saying anything about a car outside your house."

"No," she said. "I convinced myself it wasn't Ryan. But it was. I know it was."

Spivey stared at the ground for a long moment. "You say someone broke into the house of the guy who owns the boat dealership?"

"Right."

"And there were carpet fibers on one of the bodies from this boat place?"

"Two, if you count Shelly Nordling." She looked again at her watch. "I know it sounds complicated, but—"

"It sounds crazy is what it sounds." Spivey wrinkled his brow in thought. "Tell you what. You head back to the office and get a warrant for the house in Springdale." He checked his watch. "In ten minutes, I'll grab these guys and we'll see what we've got."

"And you'll get someone over to Landers's house to dust for prints?"

Spivey's cell phone rang. He picked it up, looked at the number, and turned it off. "Jesus, Dupree," he muttered. "Give it a rest."

"We were talking about dusting Landers's house," Caroline said.

"As soon as we finish here," Spivey said, and he turned back to the shoot.

Caroline threw her hands in the air and stepped away. She circled around the crew and waved at Blanton. He came over, self-consciously picking at the makeup on his face. "This is a good look for me, huh?"

"I know where Ryan is," she said.

"Where?"

"In Springdale. An hour north of here. Will you come with me?"

"Yeah, as soon as we're done."

"I'm going now."

"Just a few more minutes." He looked back over his shoulder at McDaniel, who was talking with the producer about the next shot. He came closer, confiding, "I don't trust him alone with them. I need to listen to what he tells them."

It was too much for Caroline, who spun away and began walking toward her car.

"Ms. Mabry!" He ran to catch up with her, away from the camera and lights.

"Who cares what he tells them!" she said. "So you got fired from the Bureau. Big fucking deal!"

Blanton stiffened. "What did he tell you?"

"Nothing."

"Tell me what McDaniel told you."

Caroline turned to walk away again.

"Ms. Mabry." He walked beside her, speaking quickly as she walked away. "If he told you that I took trophies, that isn't completely true and I'd like a chance to—"

She stopped and faced him again. "What do you mean, trophies?"

"Trophies. You know . . . souvenirs from crime scenes. It wasn't true. I was cleared. But I did have . . . a few things. Some shell casings. Ransom notes. A pair of handcuffs." He stared at the sky. "Some teeth."

Caroline edged away, and Blanton seemed to notice.

"Come on," he said. "It was for research. Bite marks and such. I was working on my first book. It was not . . . I'm not . . ." He looked over his shoulder at McDaniel again and he spit the next words bitterly. "The bastard was jealous that I was writing a book so he told them that I collected goddamn teeth!"

Caroline put her hands up, turned, and began walking again. This time, he didn't follow. She had tromped back across the field and up the bank forty yards before turning back. Blanton stood right where she'd left him, watching her.

Beyond him were the flood lamps of the news crew, and just over the bank was the river, a band of darkness and light, bits of moon reflecting off the black ripples. She felt sick and alone. She looked the other way, upstream, half a mile to the falls, then back at the scrub-grass field where the first bodies had been found, where Blanton was still staring at her.

She thought about the perpetual argument between Blanton and McDaniel over conscious and subconscious activity and realized they were also talking about themselves, their attraction to and repulsion of this twisted psychology. She turned away from Blanton and climbed in her car, sitting for a second and listening to her own breathing as she tried to imagine who would keep a dead woman's teeth. She was alone in this, had always been alone. Those men were investigating one crime and she was investigating another.

The thought made her lonely and she pulled her cell phone from her pocket to call Dupree. She remembered that someone had just called her and hung up. Maybe it was him. She checked the number on her phone, but it wasn't Dupree's. In fact, she didn't recognize it. A 328 prefix. North of the river.

Caroline started her car and drove through the Peaceful Valley neighborhood, along the south bank of the river. Dupree said he was going to a restaurant. She called the 328 number. After two rings, a machine picked up. "This is Kevin. I can't come to the phone. Leave a message and I'll get back to you."

Kevin? She turned the phone off without leaving a message and drove up the hill out of Peaceful Valley and into Browne's Addition. Kevin. She called Crime Check and asked an operator to check the number in the reverse phone directory. After a moment, the operator came back on.

"Owner is listed as a Kevin Verloc."

The name didn't mean anything to Caroline. "Where is it?" she asked.

"Falls Avenue," the operator said, "that little road overlooking the river, just over on the north bank. You know, where it's real steep. There are only a couple of houses."

Caroline was just driving onto the Maple Street Bridge, and she glanced across the river to the steep and dark north bank. "How far west?" she asked.

"Well, like I said, it's kind of tucked down in there so there's no cross street. But I'd say thirty-five, thirty-six blocks."

"Thanks," Caroline said and hung up the phone. She couldn't see anything over the edge of the bridge, but she could make out the faint light on the other side of the river, where the *Dateline* crew was still filming. She looked again across the river toward where the phone call had come from. From the north bank of the river you could theoretically see anything on the south bank.

Caroline turned left and began making her way toward Falls Avenue.

52

The backyard extended forty feet behind Kevin Verloc's house before coming to an abrupt, five-foot ledge onto the steep river-bank, which plunged another sixty yards to the river. The bank was covered with weeds and bushes and scrub trees and a natural dugout about forty yards down the hill, where, pressed against a prickly bush, Rae-Lynn Pierce held her breath and waited to be killed. Thorns poked her skin, and her legs ached from crouch-ing. Behind her, the water chirped and splashed like a running bath. Rae-Lynn knew that her only chance was to break for the river; even if she drowned, it would be better than letting the man in the maroon truck have her again.

From above, a flashlight beam drifted across the bush. Rae-Lynn covered her mouth. She could hear him on the trail above her, grunting as he struggled down the bank. His voice was eerily flat, as if there was nothing unusual about the situation they were in. "Hey, I know you're down here," he said. "Do you remember me?"

He wanted her to start crying, or to try to run away. But Rae-Lynn concentrated on remaining completely still. She watched the flashlight beam move farther down the bank, to the river, and then back across the bush she was hiding in.

"Girlie?" It was the old guy. Their voices seemed to be right on top of her, and Rae-Lynn felt tears roll down her cheeks. "Come on out now. He ain't gonna hurt you."

The guy from the truck laughed. "That ain't gonna work this time, Dad. She knows better." He raised his voice. "You know better. Don't you?"

The old man spoke quietly. "Maybe you could let this one go, Kevin."

"Why don't you go on up to the house, Dad? I'll be up in a minute."

Rae-Lynn's legs twitched from the pain of crouching inside the bush. She leaned forward, thinking she could break for the water now. But once again, the flashlight beam rolled across the bush. "I'll bet you got bruises on your throat from my hands. Is that right? Can you still feel my fingers around your neck?" His breathing was labored. "I didn't get what I paid for, you know. You owe me." He grunted, and it sounded as if he fell. The flashlight beam veered off into the sky and Rae-Lynn heard a clunk.

The old man yelled. "Kevin!"

Rae-Lynn tried to run but her legs felt frozen in place. She opened her eyes and saw the backs of his legs through the bush. He was right in front of her. It had been a trick. He bent over and picked up the flashlight. In the other hand, he held a gun.

"I'm okay, Dad," he said. "Hey, Rae-Lynn. That's your name, isn't it? Do you know how I know your name? Your friend told me. Risa. You remember Risa; I picked her up after you left. Do you want to know what I did to Risa? I'll show you."

Rae-Lynn had to cover her mouth to keep from crying out. She squeezed her eyes shut and imagined herself and Risa and Shelly sharing that bottle of wine on the make-believe mountain by the boat place, above the world instead of always being below it.

"Kevin?" The old man sounded worried. "I think there's someone here."

"Shit. You wait here, Rae-Lynn. I'll be right back." She heard Kevin puff back up the trail toward the house. Rae-Lynn shifted her weight and hugged her knees into her chest and looked up the hillside. Kevin was holding the flashlight with one hand and using the other to slide his handgun into the waistband in the back of his pants.

Forty yards above, on the bank at the edge of the yard, Rae-Lynn could hear a woman's voice. She remembered phoning the policewoman. But was she alone? "Hey there," the woman called down the hill. "Looking for something?"

"Yeah," said Kevin as he pulled himself up the trail. "My dog got out of the house. My . . . my dad let him out."

"Yes, I did," said the old security guard. They all spoke too loudly, maybe because of the sound of the river behind them, but from Rae-Lynn's hiding place on the riverbank, they were like mediocre actors on a stage above her. She peeked around the bush. Covered with weeds and scrub trees, the bank ran up toward the house and was crisscrossed by a couple of trails. She couldn't see the house, only the glow of its lights, which lit up the ridge like a fire. Rae-Lynn crawled out from the bush and saw the lady cop's silhouette and could just make out Kevin, still hobbling with his cane up the trail toward her. The old security guard stood right between them, looking perplexed.

The lady cop held up a badge and shined her own flashlight on it. "I'm a police officer. Just wanted to see what the noise and flashlights were about."

"Oh, sure," said Kevin.

"So what's her name?" the lady cop asked.

Kevin and the security guard didn't say anything.

"The dog?" the lady cop asked.

"Oh, *his* name," Kevin said. "His name is Dutch. Dutch."

The old security guard took a few careful steps down the trail and put his hand out to help his son, who ignored the hand and walked right past him, toward the lady cop. When he got to the steep ledge marking the end of the yard, Kevin Verloc put his cane up above him, then used his powerful arms to pull himself cleanly onto the ledge, which was almost as tall as he was. Leaning on the cane, Kevin got to his feet. He and the lady cop stood on either end of the ledge, twenty feet apart, staring at each other.

"Is there something else I can help you with, Officer?"

"Maybe," the woman said. "Someone placed a call from here to my cell phone."

"Oh?" Rae-Lynn could hear the edge in Kevin's voice, and hoped the lady cop could too. She crept a few steps closer. "Who was it?" Kevin asked.

"Don't know. They hung up before I could answer."

Kevin scratched his head, then began nodding. "You know what? I'll bet I know what happened. What's your number?"

The lady cop gave a number, but it didn't sound to Rae-Lynn like the same number she'd called earlier.

Kevin laughed. "Oh, that's funny. That's only two numbers off my girlfriend's." Rae-Lynn crept up the hill even farther and hid behind a tree, so that she could see them both, standing on the lip of the ridge, silhouetted by the lights from the house. "Yeah," Kevin said. "I started to call her and then I hung up. I must've called you by accident."

"That *is* funny," the lady cop said. "Why'd you hang up?"

Rae-Lynn heard Kevin laugh again, a little more strained this time. "Well, see . . . Dutch is really her dog. I was gonna tell her that he was lost, but then I changed my mind. I got scared."

"Whoa, she must have been mad at you," said the lady cop.

"Yeah, she was pissed all right."

"Oh," said the lady cop, "then you did reach her?"

"Who?" Kevin asked. "Susan?"

"Susan," the old security guard repeated flatly.

"Susan," said the lady cop.

"Yeah," Kevin said. "She ended up calling me and I told her. She was pissed."

"Well, sure," the lady cop said. "You lost Dutch."

"Well," Kevin said. "My dad did."

They both laughed uncomfortably.

"Yeah, I figured it was something like that," the lady cop said.

She shined her flashlight on Kevin and he flinched at the light. From below the ledge, Rae-Lynn saw the shape of the gun sticking out the back of his pants; Kevin's body blocked the lady cop from seeing it.

Then the lady cop shined the light on the old man. "You're a security guard," she said as if something had just dawned on her.

"Yes," he said.

"Where?"

He looked at Kevin before answering. "All-Safe Security, ma'am."

"My company," said the son.

"You work in a mall?"

"Yeah," Kevin said. "He works at a mall."

"I see," said Caroline. "Well, good luck finding your dog."

No one said anything else and the lady cop began walking away. Kevin turned his head halfway toward the bank below him. Twenty yards away, Rae-Lynn slumped behind her bush and put her head in her hands, willing herself to scream for help. But the lady cop just kept walking away and no sound came.

53

The doubts ran through her mind faster than she could name them. It was too dark. She was too far away. Her hand was too sweaty to hold a gun. Caroline concentrated on the side of the house. Maybe ten more steps and she would be in the shadows, away from this man and his father. If she got to the car, she could call for backup on her radio or her cell phone and then hurry back. But she didn't want to let him out of her sight. She wiped her right hand on her pant leg. Nine more steps. So what—call 911 first? Dupree? Spivey? Blanton? Eight more steps. Goddamn it! Was time slowing down, or her thoughts rushing ahead? She urged herself to not look scared, but the side of the house seemed to be a mile away. Seven steps.

Why the hell hadn't she checked in with the dispatcher before walking around the side of the house? Or at least brought her phone? But it wasn't until she stood on that ridge that she remembered giving Jaqueline her cell phone number all those weeks ago, and it wasn't until she saw the security guard that the truth hit her like a slap. Six steps. As soon as she saw the guy with the cane, she should have gone back to the car. She could feel his eyes on her back right now and wondered if he had a gun. Five steps. She swung her head back and to the right, just enough to see Verloc on the lip of the ridge, his arm coming up and the fear exploded in her head, and at first she thought the woman's voice might be her own.

"Oh God! Help!" The voice was faint, coming from down the hillside but it distracted Verloc just enough. Caroline dropped her flashlight, dove, and rolled into the shadows at the corner of the house, coming up on one knee, squared back toward Kevin Verloc. There was a pop and her flashlight jumped in the air and spun around backward. It took Caroline a second to put together what had just happened; no one had ever fired at her before. From the ridge, Verloc swung the gun from right to left, squinting into the bright lights coming from the picture window. He didn't seem to know whether he'd hit her, and he strained to see into the shadows.

"Please don't go!" yelled the woman again.

Verloc spun his head to look down the hill and pointed the gun down toward the woman's voice. "Shut up!" he hissed.

"Put the gun on the grass!" Caroline yelled. Supporting her own gun with her left hand, she put the barrel's sight right in the middle of Kevin Verloc's broad chest and leaned her shoulder against the wall to steady herself. "Put the gun down!" He had fired. She could shoot him at any time.

"Kevin? It's over." The old man moved toward his son. "Put it down."

Kevin Verloc looked back at the house. She could see that he was trying to follow the sound of her voice. His eyes traced the clean line of the shadow from left to right and settled on the corner where Caroline crouched with the gun. Without knowing it, he was staring directly at her.

"Put the gun down," she said again, her voice steady. I can do this, she thought. I've done this before. She closed her left eye.

As he stood in the glare of the lights, the gun at his side, Verloc's right arm twitched once, as if the muscles had been alerted of his intentions. Caroline took a deep breath, then blew it out, ready. The gun's sight sat squarely in the middle of his shirt; she felt dialed in, concentrating so hard, she anticipated his movement before it began. *You can do this.* He began to lean forward, his arm tensing, when the girl yelled again.

"Please. Help me!"

He yelled over his shoulder through clenched teeth. "God-damn it! Shut up!"

"Please," the girl cried again from the riverbank.

Kevin spun toward the river and waved his gun down the bank. "Shut! Up!" Caroline had begun to squeeze the trigger when she saw that Kevin had planted his cane too far forward. The dirt on the embankment gave way beneath the cane and Kevin looked down, then up quickly at his father, his eyes pleading. His knees were locked and he was powerless to stop falling. He let go of the gun and the flashlight and his arms went out to his sides and it looked for the briefest moment as if he might try to fly. His head moved from side to side, and Caroline could see on his face a look of wonder as he pitched forward, over the embankment, like a diver. There was a snap, like a tree branch breaking and a soft thud and then a scream, a little boy's scream: "Da-a-a-ad!"

Caroline ran toward the edge of the lawn, pointing her gun at the security guard. "Get down!" she yelled, but the old man was running to the edge of the bank too.

"Kevin! Kevin?"

He was lying on his stomach on the ground five feet below. One leg was twisted behind him like it belonged to an empty pair of pants. And he was crying. "Dad. Why did you let this happen to me?"

The old man slid down the ledge and reached his son. "Kevin."

Caroline picked up the flashlight and shined it over the ledge. Where he had landed two trees grew out of the same trunk and Caroline could see what had happened. Kevin's leg had become wedged between the two thick trees and had snapped as he fell. It was broken at the calf; the bone had torn through his skin and his pants. "Can you lift him up here?" Caroline asked the security guard. The old man nodded.

He lifted the younger man by his armpits. Kevin just whimpered. When he had Kevin leaning against the embankment his father pushed from below. He flopped on his back onto the lawn. Then his father lifted himself up.

"Drag him up here." Caroline gestured with the gun, and the exhausted old man dragged Kevin by his arms a few feet. Then he fell to his knees.

"I'm sorry," he said to Caroline. Then he looked toward the bank. "I'm so sorry."

Caroline moved closer. "Put your hands out to the sides." Both men did.

Caroline moved to the edge and shined the flashlight down the hill. "You okay?"

"Yes," came a tiny voice.

"Are you Jacqueline?" She corrected herself. "Are you Rae-Lynn?"

There was a pause. "Yes."

"That was brave, what you did. Why don't you come up now?"

"Shoot him first."

"I can't shoot him, Rae-Lynn. Now walk up here. Come on. I'll help you."

She emerged from a scraggly tree halfway down the bank and wiped at her eyes. She was even smaller than Caroline remembered. She wore torn jeans and a yellow T-shirt with a big sun on it. She had no shoes on. She moved slowly up the trail in the hillside until she got to that last, steep ledge—rimmed with tall grass—that marked the end of Verloc's yard. The ledge was as high as she was. She paused, too tired to use her arms to pull herself up. Caroline turned back to see Verloc and his father still lying on their faces, their arms out to the sides. She put the gun in her left hand, set the flashlight down, and got on her knees. She reached down and extended her right hand, and this seemed so familiar to her, the river babbling sixty yards below them, that she was convinced if she just waited long enough her entire life would circle back around and she would be walking with her father across the Monroe Street Bridge to get bagels.

Behind her, she heard Kevin, no longer crying. "I want to talk to Curtis Blanton," he said, with a calm that chilled her. "I'll only talk to Blanton."

His voice stopped Rae-Lynn cold and she stared at Caroline's extended hand. She seemed even too tired for this, but finally she reached out and Caroline lifted her the way you'd lift a child, standing and pulling her over the ledge and into the yard. Once there Rae-Lynn burst into tears, and tried to pull away from Caroline toward Verloc. Caroline held her back easily. She couldn't weigh ninety pounds.

"It's okay," she said.

Rae-Lynn nodded and wiped at her eyes. "I can't find my shoes."

Caroline slipped out of her tennis shoes and slid them over to her. "Here."

"Thanks." She stepped into them. "They're big."

"I need you to do me a favor," Caroline said. "Okay? Are you up to that?"

Rae-Lynn nodded again.

"I don't want to leave these guys alone," she said. "So here's what I want you to do. My car is in the driveway. There's a pocket on the back of the passenger seat. Do you understand so far?"

Rae-Lynn nodded again.

"Inside that pocket are some handcuffs." She looked over at Kevin and his father. "One metal pair of handcuffs and a bunch of plastic ones, like garbage ties. I need you to bring me the metal handcuffs and some plastic ones too. Can you do that?"

"Yeah," Rae-Lynn said. Caroline stood on the ridge, staring at the two men on the ground, listening to her own breathing. She looked over her shoulder, across the river and downstream. She could see a tiny bank of lights where the *Dateline* crew was apparently still filming. Christ! Had they even heard the gunshot? She was still staring across the river when Rae-Lynn returned and handed over the cuffs.

Caroline tossed the metal handcuffs to the old man. "Put these on him," she said.

Paul Verloc got to his knees and grabbed his son's arm. "I'm awful sorry, Kevin," he said. He closed the cuffs around Kevin's right wrist, then his left. When he was done Paul slumped back down on his stomach, turned his face away from his son's, and put his own hands behind his back. Caroline kept the gun on Kevin's head as she came over. She put her knee in Kevin's back and tightened the handcuffs until he winced.

"Where is Curtis Blanton?" Kevin asked again, becoming frantic. "I know he's in town. Is he coming here? Does he know about me?"

She looked down at him lying on his stomach, his big back and arms seeming doughy and restricting. When she saw the bone sticking out of his leg, snapped like a twig, it nearly made Caroline sick.

Then she put the plastic cuffs on Kevin's father and pulled them tight.

"It's my fault," the old man said.

When they were both cuffed Caroline slumped, her heart pounding against her chest. She put her gun in her shoulder holster under her jacket and stood for a moment, listening to the water. "Okay, Rae-Lynn. I need you to call 911 now. Rae-Lynn?"

But Rae-Lynn was edging away from her, staring up at the house. Caroline followed her eyes. A tall, square-shouldered man was emerging from the shadows on the side of the house, and even before he was in the light Caroline knew it was Lenny Ryan.

She felt in her jacket for her gun without looking away from him, but her hand became tangled in the holster, and she had to look down before ripping the gun out and she didn't quite have it when he swung and hit her in the face, lifting her off the ground and dumping her along the edge of the hillside.

She sat up immediately, dazed, and had no idea where her gun had gone. In the light she could see Lenny Ryan, clean-shaven again and leaner than before, wearing his khaki pants and black shirt again, his hair stubble-short and dyed blond. He stood over Kevin Verloc, his fists clenched. "Rae-Lynn!" Caroline screamed. "Go!"

Rae-Lynn ran right out of Caroline's shoes toward the house and Lenny Ryan watched her go, then brought his eyes down again. "Kevin Verloc?" he asked.

"Get down on the grass!" Caroline said as she pulled herself up. She felt woozy and her mouth was full of blood. "You're under arrest."

"This has nothing to do with you," Ryan said, without looking back at her.

Caroline felt through the grass for her gun but it wasn't there. Her hand fell across the old man's flashlight. "I'm a police officer. You are under arrest!" she yelled again.

Lenny Ryan put his foot on the bone sticking out of Verloc's pant leg, parallel to the ground. Ryan pushed it into the grass. Verloc cried out in pain and Caroline was sure he would pass out. But Ryan lifted his foot and looked over at the old man.

"I asked you a question," Ryan said. "Which one of you killed my girlfriend?"

Caroline took two steps and swung the flashlight as hard as she could. Her shoulder vibrated as the flashlight cracked and the batteries flew out and only the shell was left in her hands. Ryan lost his balance and pitched forward several steps, but didn't fall. He turned back and seemed shocked that she had hit him. For a moment they were quiet, and again the only noise was Verloc's whimpering and the river at her back. They stood in a triangle, Verloc squirming on the ground, Caroline and Lenny equidistant from him and from each other. They were both gasping for breath. Caroline wondered if Lenny would agree with her that our lives have a way of eddying back on themselves, offering us the same view over and over, daring us to get it right just once.

"I don't want to hurt you," Ryan said finally.

"Good," Caroline said, her voice seeming to come from somewhere else.

Then Ryan winced, as if the pain from the blow to his head had just reached him. He patted the side of his head and brought his hand forward. The blood glistened in the lights from the house. He started for her. Caroline took a step back, then swung the flashlight again. Just a metal shell now, it whistled as it cut the air. The black tube hit his hand with a slap and he caught it, pulled it away, and threw it to the ground. Then he shoved her with one hand and she fell onto her back again, next to the old man.

Ryan turned toward the younger Verloc, who'd managed to roll over onto his back so that he was facing up, his arms behind him, wiggling with his cuffed hands a few inches at a time. Ryan took a step toward Verloc, who screamed, and Caroline was up and rushing the big man. She hit Lenny in the waist with her shoulder and they both toppled onto the ledge and over it, into the darkness above the river. They rolled through the weeds, and Caroline felt his weight on her chest and lost her breath and then Ryan caught himself on the bank, Caroline still holding on to his legs. He hit her twice with the back of his hand and she fell away. Her head felt as if it had been split open, something dark and warm muddying her eyes. She looked up the hill, and through the blood and dizziness, she could see Ryan pulling himself up the bank again. Caroline took one more breath, got to her feet, and followed him.

Amazingly, Verloc had managed to wiggle on his back about two feet with a broken leg; Caroline wondered at the strength of those shoulders and hands, and thought about the poor women with their broken necks. Staring at the figure of Lenny Ryan in front of him, Verloc began to cry and to mumble. Caroline found the flashlight shell again, then stood and took two heavy steps toward Lenny Ryan. She swung the tube weakly and it hit him in the shoulder without moving him at all. He turned, as if unable to believe she was still trying to fight him. Then his face grew cold and blank and she recognized the look from that day on the bridge, so long ago now. He ripped the black flashlight tube from her hand and lifted it to hit her, but stopped. Dizzy, Caroline lurched forward anyway, onto her knees, and then fell down, her body racked with pain. She threw up in the grass. There was a sound in her ears, a ringing or a siren in the distance. Caroline crawled away, toward a reflection in the tall grass at the edge of the hillside.

Lenny heard the sirens too. He considered the figure of Verloc in front of him, curled up on his side and crying, and Caroline crawling away behind him, toward the edge of the embankment. He felt stumped by something that he couldn't quite get his arms around, as if he were processing this information in a foreign language. Had he come to Spokane simply looking for revenge? Or was it really for an explanation—why he'd lost the only person he'd ever loved, the only thing that made him happy? If that was it, then here he was at the end of it, and all he knew were empty patterns and sad outcomes—the dog on the leash, the calf in the draw. With the sirens in the distance, Lenny felt the urge to talk to someone before he stomped Kevin Verloc to death, to explain what he had wanted. He turned to Caroline, and the empty flashlight fell to his side. But all he managed to say was, "I'm tired."

"Me too," she said. She rolled onto her side, her face streaked with blood, her right arm in the thick weeds. It appeared she was trying to get up.

"You have the right to remain silent," she rasped.

Lenny found himself smiling. Even now, lying on her side, bleeding and beaten, she was trying to pull herself up, trying to arrest him. He'd never seen a woman as strong as this one. Did he know anyone this strong? He thought at one time that she looked like Shelly. But she didn't. Not really. The hair was close, but that was it. He had thought about her so much, had replayed that day on the bridge and the day he led her through the alley to the body he'd found. He had driven by her house all those times and had seen her come outside that one evening. All that time, the distance had allowed Lenny Ryan to begin imagining her as Shelly. But standing over her, he could see this wasn't her. This woman was someone else entirely. Shelly was gone.

She managed to sit up, propping herself on her left arm. Her face was streaked with blood. She brought her right arm forward out of the tall grass, and that's when Lenny saw that she had found her gun. Leaning on her left arm, with her legs out, she pulled the gun into her lap and pointed it at his chest. She was about twenty feet away. If he rushed her, would she do it this time? Would she shoot him? He looked down at her face and knew she would.

He should never have left Angela. He could have stayed on her porch forever. He liked that creek. He liked nights like this, the heat slipping from the air, the hushed cackle of water over rocks and the dry flashes of summer lightning.

Lenny crouched down in front of her, on the balls of his feet. He shrugged and smiled and was almost relieved that it was finally over. "What happened to your shoes?"

A flashlight beam zipped from the house across the yard frantically and then fell on Lenny Ryan, who snapped upright and turned back to look over his shoulder. Caroline could see what it would look like from the house. She and Ryan were at the edge of the lawn, just a few feet apart. He was standing above her with the broken black tube from the flashlight. She was aware then of how gravity speeds everything up, how it even causes events to roll and crash and froth up around us.

A man's voice, Dupree's voice, came from the shadows at the edge of the house. "Drop the gun!"

Confused for a moment, Caroline looked down at the gun in her own hand. She peered into the lights from the house and knew what the flashlight casing must look like. Lenny looked down at it too. Caroline began to speak, "It's okay, Alan."

Lenny's eyes had just turned to hers—locked in pinpoint awareness of each other—when a crack split the air like an ax hitting wood, and another and another, and Caroline screamed, "No!" as Lenny Ryan pitched forward in the grass next to her.

From the corner of the house Dupree's voice was frantic. "Caroline!"

"What did you do?" she whispered as she crawled through the grass and took Lenny Ryan's hand. His eyelids fluttered and he made noises like a child with hiccups. Then his eyes opened and he seemed to focus on her face, but the lids drifted closed and Caroline heard the gurgle of blood in his chest, his breath bubbling out from his lungs back into the air.

She felt Dupree at her shoulder, trying to pull her away, but she wouldn't let go, not yet, and she curled her whole body over Lenny Ryan's hand. There were sirens everywhere now and the sounds of car doors closing and radio traffic, and Caroline found herself whispering, "Shh, shh, shh," trying to hear the river below them.

He heard it too, as he receded into darkness, into himself. And even when there was nothing else to see or remember and no more pain, he felt her grip on his hand and it was a small, bearable thing, the last good thing before Lenny Ryan slipped away.

Caroline held on even after he was gone, remembering how six years earlier she'd been afraid to touch the body of Glenn Ritter as he lay dead in front of her. That night, she hadn't wanted to move at all, as if within that twenty-four feet lay salvation, as if everything she believed could be contained by a kill zone—an arbitrary distance at which a person poses an immediate threat, not just for protection, but for justification too. She had imagined that distance as a great channel, a gulf that keeps us not only safe but apart, that allows us to believe that there are things we are incapable of doing.

But as she sat over the body of Lenny Ryan, Caroline was

struck by just how close twenty-four feet really is, how little space really exists between us. Of course they were different, Lenny Ryan's shooting of the pawnbroker, her own shooting of the wife beater. But that meant there was a difference between what Lenny Ryan did and what Kevin Verloc did, that in the end we are separated not by distance, but degree. And in that truth was another; none of us knows, in the tumble of events, what she is capable of doing.

"Caroline? Did I . . . didn't he . . ."

Caroline looked up at the fear in Dupree's eyes, at the uncertainty, and reached out for the living.

"I'm all right, Alan," she said, and finally allowed Dupree to pull her away from the body. She let go of Lenny Ryan's hand and it fell back into the grass, the fingers now closed around the handle of Caroline's gun.

54

Paul Verloc
Tape Three

Date: 15 August, 1000 hours

SPIVEY: Want some more coffee?

PAUL VERLOC: Sure. Creamer? Thanks.

SPIVEY: Okay, we got the tape changed . . . We all ready? Okay, go ahead.

PAUL VERLOC: Well, like I was saying, at first I was just chasing girlies off the boats. Especially when it was cold outside, they used the boats. It really bugged Kevin that we couldn't keep the girlies away. He was afraid of losing the contract with Landers. Before that I used to bring girlies home to him sometimes. I know that sounds terrible, but because of the shooting, sometimes he had, what do you call it, dysfunction? You know, when you can't . . .

MCDANIEL: . . . achieve orgasm?

PAUL VERLOC: Right. Well, around February, he came back from a meeting and said there was a bonus structure set up now.

MCDANIEL: Bonuses for driving the prostitutes away?

PAUL VERLOC: Yeah. He told me to call him the next time I found someone, you know, having sex in the boats. So I found this one girl and chased off her john. I called Kevin and he came out and took her for a drive.

MCDANIEL: This was Shelly Nordling.

PAUL VERLOC: I guess. I found the next one sleeping in one of the boats. He took her for a drive too. But this time he came back after thirty minutes and said he needed my help. He brought me to the truck and . . . he said she'd tried to attack him and he choked her. But I knew he was lying. See, he's got this problem with dysfunction.

SPIVEY: Yeah, you said.

PAUL VERLOC: Not that it's any excuse but I know he gets . . . frustrated. So we drove her body to the house and Kevin started showing me in all of these books, how if we did certain things, people would assume it was someone else, like in the books.

MCDANIEL: Curtis Blanton's books.

PAUL VERLOC: Oh, he had all kinds of books. He said you guys would make all these assumptions if we did it right and that if they thought there was a serial killer, it might frighten the girlies away. And he was right. So that's why we did a lot of the weird stuff, like shooting them in the head afterwards. He said them books called it . . . oh, what's it called. When you do too much of something?

MCDANIEL: Overkill.

PAUL VERLOC: Yeah. Right. And that you guys would think it was a real psycho who hated women. And he did other stuff, like tearing off their fingernails and moving the bodies. You'll have to ask him, I didn't understand it all.

MCDANIEL: How did you get the bodies down to the river?

PAUL VERLOC: We had a plastic sled and it just pulled over the grass and dirt without leaving a mark. Then he worked on the shallow graves, you know, putting the sticks a certain way. After the second one, he promised he wouldn't do it no more, so I thought it was over.

But he watched you guys find that body by the river with his binoculars, and he kind of liked that and he thought it would really be something if we put another body down there, and it just got so . . .

SPIVEY: But you never tried to stop him?

PAUL VERLOC: Even before they found the bodies, the girlies stopped coming around and we got our bonus . . . I guess I thought he would quit once we got the money. And maybe I knew how much trouble I was in. Since my wife died, Kevin is all I have and after the shooting, he had a hard time. You're probably thinking the apple don't fall far from the tree, huh?

MCDANIEL: You're saying he did all of this . . . for a few thousand bucks?

PAUL VERLOC: At first, I think so. But just between you and me? After a while, I think Kevin kind of got a taste for it.

Spokane Police Dept.
Serial Crime Task Force
Interview Transcript

John Landers
Tape Two

Date: 16 August, 900 hours

LAIRD: We're going in circles here. No one is suggesting that you told Verloc to kill anyone. All we want to know is the general context of your conversations with him.

DARREN MOORE: I told you, my client feels it is not in his best interest at this time to discuss the nature of his discussions with Mr. Verloc, other than to state emphatically that he had no knowledge of any of the crimes Mr. Verloc is alleged to have committed.

LAIRD: So it didn't strike you as strange that when you started paying this guy to clean up the neighborhood, hookers started getting killed?

DARREN MOORE: Look, my client has been through a terrible ordeal. Now he has agreed to cooperate, but I'm not about to let him incriminate himself in some sort of witch hunt!

MCDANIEL: Okay, let's back up, then. The first time you mentioned the bonus situation to him, do you recall what his reaction might have been?

DARREN MOORE: No. I'm not going to let him answer that. I am not about to let my client say anything that might be misconstrued in some misguided attempt to prosecute him until I have a piece of paper from the district attorney that gives my client unlimited immunity from any prosecution in this matter or subsequent prosecution.

SPIVEY: Here you go. Here's your coffee.

Spokane Police Dept.
Serial Crime Task Force
Interview Transcript

Kevin Verloc
Tape Thirteen

Date: 17 August, 1900 hours

KEVIN VERLOC: Yeah. The fingernails were textbook, too obvious, probably. I was conscious of you realizing the killer was a cop because of that, but I just couldn't think of any way around it. I didn't want to leave any skin behind. But replacing the bodies, changing the dump sites to indicate a change in the killer's MO, I got a lot of that straight from Mr. Blanton's descriptions of the guy in Texas. Oh, and the Pacific Coast Highway guy. That was really the model, I suppose. And the killer's overall preparation of the bodies for discovery? Some of that I got from the job, of course, but the fingernails . . . I'm thinking it was the Pacific Coast Highway guy. Is Mr. Blanton coming back? I'd really like to clear some of this up with him.

SPIVEY: No. Mr. Blanton has . . . decided not to work on this case anymore.

KEVIN VERLOC: Oh. That's too bad. I suppose he'll see this transcript? Because I thought he'd be interested in the forty bucks. That was my own idea, my signature. You don't know anyone else who ever did that, do you? 'Cause I don't think I read it anywhere, I think it was all mine.

McDANIEL: No. I'd never seen that before. In fact we were wondering why you kept receipts for the money. Why you billed Landers for it.

KEVIN VERLOC: As a rule I keep exceptional records, Mr. McDaniel.

364

Always have. And I'm not a thief. I paid these women and I knew that detail might become important some day.

McDANIEL: I don't understand.

KEVIN VERLOC: Well, think about it. If you kill someone to cover up another crime, let's say felony robbery, that's aggravated murder. A capital crime. But if the killer doesn't steal the money back, if he leaves it on the victim—

McDANIEL: My God.

KEVIN VERLOC: No robbery. No aggravating circumstances. No death penalty. It's just plain murder. And I knew you would find psychological underpinnings for the money. That's why I put the money in the girl's mouth. Did you get that?

SPIVEY: Jeff? You okay?

KEVIN VERLOC: By the way, do you know what Mr. Blanton thought of the name? I just thought they could have come up with a much better name than Southbank Strangler, especially with the fingernails and the money and the moving of bodies . . . I just wished Mr. Blanton had been able to name me. He's really good at that, don't you think?

EPILOGUE

Caroline brought out the last box of clothing from her mother's house and found her father leaning against the trunk of her car, holding a long silk glove that had been white but was now a neglected gray. When Caroline set her box in the trunk, he looked up as if he'd just noticed her.

"She didn't still wear these?" He held the glove out for her to see.

"She was saving them for me," Caroline said. It was surprising how little her father knew sometimes, the way he could pretend that his life hadn't once been another life. She looked down at the open box, filled with slacks and sweaters and light blouses and on the top, the mate to this long, white glove, which her mother had worn at her wedding forty years ago.

Her father picked up the other glove. "Maybe we should save these," he said, his voice unsteady.

"Okay." Caroline looked up at his lined broadening face, his gray eyebrows. He was sixty. When he ran off to California he was thirty-six, Caroline's age. Somehow that fact seemed crucial to whatever they would make of this now.

"Are you coming, Dad?" she asked, and put a hand on his shoulder.

"You go ahead," he said. "I'd like to stay here for a while."

From the car she watched him walk back toward the house, the gray gloves dangling from his thick fingers. She drove slowly through her neighborhood and stopped at every intersection. She still wasn't used to the patch over her left eye, which limited her peripheral vision. It made her especially nervous when she drove.

She remembered waking up in the hospital after the surgery on her eye and seeing Dupree sitting by her bed, remembered him saying that he had moved back in with his family. "Anyway," he said, "I didn't get a chance to congratulate you."

"Oh?"

"You and Joel in the hall that day. I saw the ring."

In the hospital Caroline had felt the line of stitches for the first time, drawing her finger from her cheekbone across her eye to her hairline, along the four-inch gash that Lenny Ryan had given her. The doctor said she would have to wear the eyepatch for a month.

"So," Dupree said, "have you set a date?"

There was no catch or hesitation in her voice. "No," she said. "Not yet."

She parked in front of the Bright Shining Day treatment center, grabbed the boxes of her mother's clothes and carried them to the door. She leaned on the doorbell and a teenager wearing a Walkman answered, easing the earphones off her head. She stared at Caroline's eye. "I have some things for Rae-Lynn Pierce," Caroline said.

A few seconds later, the counselor she'd met before, Chris, came to the door and looked down at the boxes in her arms. "Rae-Lynn left," he said. "Last night."

Caroline nodded and wished she were more surprised. "Do you know where?"

The counselor just shrugged.

"Can I leave these anyway?" Caroline asked. "Maybe there's someone else . . . "

The counselor took the boxes, thanked her, and closed the door.

Preview Selection From

CITIZEN VINCE

On Sale April 2005

chapter 1

One day you know more dead people than live ones.

The thought greets Vince Camden as he sits up in bed, frantic, casting around a dark bedroom for proof of his existence and finding only props: nightstand, dresser, ashtray, clock. Vince breathes heavily. Sweats in the cool air. Rubs his eyes to shake the dust of these musings, not a dream exactly, this late-sleep panic—fine glass thin as paper, shattered and swirling, cutting as it blows away.

Vince Camden pops his jaw, leans over, and turns off the alarm just as the one, five, and nine begin their fall. Each morning at 1:59 he sits up like this and turns off the clock radio in the split second before two and the shrill blast of alarm. He wonders: How is a thing like that possible? And yet . . . if you can manage such a trick—every morning waking up a few ticks *before* your alarm goes off—why couldn't you count all the dead people you know?

START WITH GRANDPARENTS. Two sets. One grandfather had a second wife. That's five. Vince runs a toothbrush over his molars.

Mother and father. Seven. Does a stillborn sister count? No. A person has to have been alive to be dead. By the time he finishes his shower, blow-dries his hair, and gets dressed—gray slacks, long-sleeve black dress shirt, two buttons open—he's gone through family, neighbors, and former associates: already thirty-four people he knows to be dead. Wonders if that's high, if it's normal to know so many dead people.

Normal. That word tails him from a safe distance most days. He opens a drawer and pulls out a stack of forged credit cards, looks at the names on the cards: Thomas A. Spaulding. Lane Bailey. Margaret Gold. He imagines Margaret Gold's lovely *normal* life, a crocheted afghan tossed over the back of her sofa. How many dead people could Margaret Gold possibly know?

Vince counts out ten credit cards—including Margaret Gold's—and puts these in the pocket of his windbreaker. Fills the other pocket with Ziploc bags of marijuana. It's 2:16 in the morning when Vince slides his watch onto his wrist, careful not to catch the thick hair on his forearm. Oh yeah, Davie Lincoln—retarded kid used to carry money in his mouth while he ran errands for Coletti in the neighborhood. Choked on a half-dollar. Thirty-five.

Vince stands in the tiny foyer of his tiny house, if you can call a coatrack and a mail slot a foyer. Zips his windbreaker and snaps his cuffs out like a Vegas dealer leaving the table. Steps out into the world.

About Vince Camden: he is thirty-six and white. Single. Six feet tall, 160 pounds, broad-shouldered and thin, like a martini glass. Brown and blue, as the police reports have recorded his hair and eyes. His mouth curls at the right corner, thick eyebrows go their own way, and this casts his face in perpetual smirk, so that every woman who has ever been involved with him eventually arrives at the same expression, hands on hips, head cocked: *Please. Be serious.*

Vince is employed in midlevel management, food industry: baking division—donuts. Generally, there is less to making donuts than one might assume. But Vince likes it, likes getting to work at 4:30 in the morning and finishing before lunch. He feels as if he's gotten one over on the world, leaving his place of employment for lunch and simply not coming back. He's realizing this is a fixed part of his personality, this desire to get one over on the world. Maybe there is a hooky gene.

Outside, he pulls the collar of his windbreaker against his cheeks. Cold this morning: late October. Freezing, in fact—the steam leaks from his mouth and reminds him of an elementary school experiment with dry ice, which reminds him of Mr. Harlow, his fifth-grade teacher. Hanged himself after it became common knowledge that he was a bit too fond of his male students. Thirty-six.

It's a serene world from your front steps at 2:20 in the morning: dim porch lights on houses black with sleep; sidewalks split the dark dewed lawns. But the night has a grimmer hold on Vince's imagination, and he shivers with the creeping sensation—even as he reminds himself it's impossible—that he's on the menu tonight.

"SO, WHAT . . . YOU want me to do this thing or not?"

The two men stare across the bench seat of a burgundy Cadillac Seville. The driver asks: "How much would something like that cost?"

The bigger man, in the passenger seat, is impatient, restless, but he pauses to think. It's a fair question. After all, it is 1980, and the service industries are mired in this stagnant economy, too. Are the criminal sectors subject to the same sad market forces: inflation, deflation, stagflation? Recession? Do thugs suffer double-digit unemployment? Do criminals feel malaise?

"Gratis," quotes the passenger.

"Gratis?" repeats the driver, shifting in the leather seat.

"Yeah." And after a pause: "Means free."

"I know what it means. I was just surprised. That's all. You're saying you'll help me out with this guy for free?"

"I'm saying we'll work something out."

"But it won't cost me anything?"

"We'll work it out."

And it says something about the man driving the Cadillac that in addition to not knowing what the word *gratis* means, he also doesn't realize that nothing is free.

EIGHTY-SEVEN BARS in greater Spokane, serving three hundred thousand people. One taxicab company: eight cabs. So on a Tuesday morning just past two A.M., last call, the economics are clear: more drunks than the market can bear. They leach out onto the sidewalks and stagger and yawn to their cars—those who own them and remember where they're parked. The rest walk from downtown to the neighborhoods, scattering in all directions across bridges, through underpasses, beneath trestles, up hills to dark residential streets, solitary figures beneath thought bubbles of warm breath and cigarette smoke. Rehearsed lies.

Vince Camden concentrates on his own thoughts as he walks sober and rested among the drunk and tired. Stout downtown brick and brownstone give way to low-rent low-rise strips—karate dojos, waterbed liquidators, erotic bookstores, pawnshops, and Asian massage—then a neighborhood of empty warehouses, rail lines, vacant fields, and a solitary two-story Victorian house, an after-hours cards and rib joint called Sam's Pit. This is where Vince hangs out most nights before his shift begins at the donut shop.

Vince was only in town a few months when Sam died. Thirty-seven. The new owner is named Eddie, but everyone calls him

Sam—it being easier to change one's name to Sam than to change the faded Pepsi sign on the old house from SAM'S to EDDIE'S. Just as old Sam did, new Sam opens the Pit when the rest of the city closes, after Last Call. The place works like a drain for the city; every morning when the bars close, the drunks and hookers and lawyers and johns and addicts and thieves and cops and cardplayers—as old Sam used to say, "Evergodambody"—swirls around the streets and ends up here. It's why the cops don't sweat the gambling and undercounter booze. It's just nice to know that at three A.M., everyone will be gathered in one place, like the suspects in a seamy British drawing room.

The Pit lurks behind high, unkempt shrubs, the only thing on a block of vacant lots, like a last tooth. Behind, a rutted dirt field functions as a parking lot for Sam's and a factory showroom for the half-dozen professional women who gather here each night for last tricks. Inside, pimps play cards and wait for their cut.

Gravel cracks beneath Vince's shoes as he angles for Sam's Pit. Six cars are parked randomly in this weed-covered field, girls doing business in a couple. A car door opens fifty feet from Vince, and a woman's voice skitters across the weedy lot: "Let go!"

Vince stares straight ahead. *Not your business.*

"Vince! Tell this guy to let go of me!"

Beth's voice. At the door, Vince turns and walks back across the lot toward a tan Plymouth Duster. Inside, Beth Sherman is wrestling with a guy in a white turtleneck sweater and a navy sport coat. As he walks up to the car, Vince can see the guy's pants are open and that he's trying to keep Beth from getting out of the car. She swings at him with the frayed, dirty cast on her right forearm. Barely misses.

Vince leans down and opens the car door. "Hey, Beth. What's going on?"

The guy lets go and she pulls away, climbs out of the car and past Vince. He is amazed again how pretty she can be, triangular face and round eyes, bangs cut straight across them. She can't weigh a hundred pounds. Odd for a woman in her line of work to actually look younger than she is, but Beth could pass for a teenager—at least from a distance. Up close—well, the lifestyle is tough to hide. Beth points at the guy in the car with her cast. "He grabbed my ass."

The guy is incredulous. "You're a hooker!"

"I'm in real estate!"

"You were blowing me!"

Beth yells around Vince at the man: "Do you grab your plumber's ass when *he's* working?"

Vince steps between Beth and the john, and smiles disarmingly at the guy. "Look, she doesn't like to be touched."

"What kind of hooker doesn't like to be touched?"

Vince can't argue the premise. But he wishes the guy had just kept his mouth shut. He knows how this will go now, and in fact Beth steps around him, fishes around in her pocket, and throws a twenty-dollar bill in his face.

The guy holds up the twenty. "I gave you forty!"

"You got half," she says. "You get half your money back."

"Half? There's no such thing!" He looks up at Vince. "Is there such thing as half?"

Vince looks from Beth to the guy and opens his mouth without the slightest expectation that anything will come. He looks back at Beth and their eyes catch long enough for both of them to note.

About Beth Sherman: she is thirty-three, just leaving "cute," with brown hair and eyes that dart from attention. Her dislike of contact notwithstanding, Beth is well respected among the working women at Sam's, mostly for one big accomplishment—she quit heroin without methadone, cold fucking turkey, exactly nineteen months and two weeks ago, on the very day she found out she was pregnant. Her boy, Kenyon, is a little more than a year now and he seems fine, but everyone knows how she watches him breathlessly, constantly comparing him to the other kids in the park and at his day care, looking for any sign that he is slow or stunted, that her worst fears are realized, that the junk has ruined him, too. And while she is clearly on her way out of this life—she fired her pimp, *in writing*—Beth continues to turn tricks, maybe because there are so few ways for a high school dropout to support herself and her son. Anyway, she's not the only hooker at Sam's who introduces herself as something else. It's a place full of actresses and massage therapists, models, students, and social workers, but when Beth says she's in real estate, people actually seem to believe it.

When he first arrived, Vince purchased Beth's services (he tried a few of the girls) and found himself intrigued by her cool distance, the way she bristled under his hands. Then one night six months ago, she and Vince drank two bottles of wine and spent a night together *without* the exchange of money. And it was different—alarming and close. No bristle. But since then everything has been out of sorts—Beth not wanting to charge him, Vince wary of becoming involved with a woman with a kid. And so they haven't slept together in three months. The worst part is that it feels like cheating to be with the other women, and so Vince is in the midst of his longest stretch of celibacy that doesn't involve a jail cell. The whole thing has proven to him the old axiom among the professional class: *Free sex ruins everything.*

In the parking lot, Beth stalks away from the angry, unsated john—her tight jeans beneath a coat that stops midriff. Vince watches her go, then takes one of the bags of dope from his pocket, bends down, and holds it up to the window. The Bible says that even the peacemaker deserves a profit. Or it says something anyway.

After a second, the guy shrugs and holds up the twenty. "Yeah, okay," he says. As they exchange dope for money, the guy shakes his head. "Never heard of a hooker who didn't want to be touched."

Vince nods, although in his estimation the world is made of only such people, pot-smoking cops, thieves who tithe 10 percent, society women who wear garters, tramps who sleep with stuffed bears, criminal donut makers, real estate hookers. He remembers a firefighter in the old neighborhood named Alvin Dunphy who was claustrophobic. Died when a burning apartment building collapsed on him. Thirty-eight.

"YOU CAN'T HAVE half. You either get one or you don't."

"Bet a buck. I'm with Jacks. What good's the job if you don't get to blow?"

"I don't know, I think I got a half the first time."

"How old were you, Petey?"

"The first time? Thirteen. Bump a buck."

"Thirteen? No shit? Wish I had a sister."

"It *was* your sister."

"So what do you think, Vince?"

He has been quiet, lost in thought, hungover from a night of disquieting dreams. He sits perfectly still, leaning forward on his knees, staring off to the side, his cards stacked neatly in front of him. Sam's Pit is dark and carpeted—the old dining room and living room of the Victorian decorated with velvet wall hangings of men with mustaches and Afros screwing huge-hipped women. Light comes from a couple of bare bulbs hanging from the ceiling and a lamp behind the bar. There are six tables in two main rooms—poker games going on at two of the tables; at the other four, people are eating ribs. Four women, including Beth and her best friend, Angela, sit at the bar, swirling drinks made from the bottles Eddie keeps under the counter.

Vince sits up and pushes the hair out of his eyes. "I'm in." Snaps a five into the pot without looking at his cards. Eventually, they all know Vince will hold forth: "What do I think? I think you could reasonably have a half. Honestly, the first part is the best part anyway, and some people say that the end is the death of the thing. Or at least when it all goes downhill. No, I think the real value might be in those first few minutes . . . just getting someone's full attention."

The players look from their cards to Vince's, stacked neatly on the table, and try to remember if he's even looked at his hand. Vince looks up to the bar, where Beth is staring at him; she gives him a half smile, then looks to the ceiling, as if she's just let go of a nice thought and is watching it float away like a kid's balloon.

GAME OVER AND Vince is flush, counting a roll of bills as big as a pair of socks. The other guys exchange glances. Everyone has heard the whispered talk about Vince—the sudden appearance, the New York accent, the proficiency at cards, women, and crime. It is a reputation that Vince has been able to sustain without ever acknowledging—his past in winks and nods. "Where'd you learn to play like that?" Petey asks.

"Baking school." The guys laugh. Vince tosses two fives on the table for the drinks. Stands. Four-thirty A.M., and he's starting to get over whatever was gnawing at him this morning. "Fellas," he says, and taps the roll of bills.

Having finished their ribs and settled with their pimps, the hookers are standing in a clutch at the door. They know not to bother Vince until after he's either won or lost, but tonight, since he's won, they hit him hard. Arms trail his sleeves, lacquered nails riffle his hair. Vince moves through like an aging idol.

"Some a' this, Vince?"

"Got cards for us, Vinnie?"

"Take you 'round the world, baby."

"Smoke? You got any smoke?"

At the door, he exchanges lifted credit cards and lids of pot for cash and fleshy hugs. Although he rejects the offers of freebies and trade-outs, he'd be lying if he didn't admit this was his favorite part of each day, this bit of stage business outside Sam's, when the guys envy him and the women make their plays for him and he holds them off with pinched credit cards and at-cost dope.

When his cards and pot are gone, Vince continues out the door. Outside, he hears his name. He turns and sees Beth looking at her shoes. She glances up at Vince, all eyes, her chin still pointed down; it's a sweet, demure move, and the fact that she has no idea she's doing it makes it that much sweeter. "Thanks for earlier, Vince," she says. "I don't know why I get so . . ."

"It's okay," Vince says. "You been studying?" As long as Vince has known her, Beth has been studying to get her real estate license. She studies, but never actually signs up to take the test.

"Yeah." She shrugs. "I get to run an open house next week. Sort of a trial run. Larry's having three, and he needs someone to run one for him. If I sell it, he'll give me half a percent commission under the table."

"Yeah?" Vince asks. "I'll come by."

"Really?"

"Yeah. Maybe I'll even buy the house."

"Very funny." She squeezes his arm, does that thing with her eyes again—up and down, a flash of release—then turns to go back inside.

CARS LEER ON the street behind Vince; headlights trace his back. Who was that girl from junior high school? Got drunk with some older kids and stepped in front of a car. Angie Wolfe. Thirty-nine.

Vince's hands are in the pockets of his windbreaker, and his shoulders are hunched up around his ears. Only six blocks to the donut shop and he likes the walk fine in the crisp cold, sun still a rumor on the Idaho border, his shadow slowing up for him as he nears the next streetlight. What about old Danello, whose body was never technically found? Doesn't matter. That's forty.

The donut shop is regrettably named Donut Make You Hungry, and is owned by Ted and Marcie, an old gray couple who come in for a few minutes every day to smoke cigarettes and drink coffee with their old gray friends. It works fine for Vince; he gets to manage the place, and Ted and Marcie give him all the space he needs.

He approaches the building—fever-colored stucco on a busy corner a mile from downtown. Lights on inside. That's good. Vince walks down the alley to grab the newspaper, slides the rubber band off, and stands beneath a flickering streetlight to make out the front page: Carter and Reagan in a dead heat, with the debate tonight. The Iranian parliament is meeting to look for a solution to the hostage crisis. He glances at headlines but doesn't read stories, flips instead to the sports page. Alabama plus fifteen at Mississippi State. Seems heavy. Vince closes the paper and starts for the front door when something moves in his periphery.

He cocks his head and takes a step deeper into the alley, clutching the paper to his chest. A car starts. Cadillac. Its lights come on and Vince reflexively covers his eyes while the old voices tell him to run. But there is no place to dive in this alley, nowhere to hide, so he waits.

The burgundy Cadillac Seville inches toward him and the driver's window sinks with a mechanical whir.

Vince bends at the waist. "Jesus, Len. What are you doing here?"

Len Huggins's face is a conference of bad ideas: baby corn teeth, thin lips, broken nose, pocked cheeks, and two bushy black capital-*L* sideburns ("For Len, man! Get it? *L?* Len?"). Len runs a stereo store where Vince uses the phony credit cards to buy merchandise, and get cash advances. Len removes the aviator sunglasses he wears even at night, and slides them into his shirt pocket. "Vincers!" He extends his hand out the window.

"What are you doing here, Lenny?" Vince repeats.

"I came for my credit cards, man."

"It's Tuesday morning."

"I know that."

"We do this on Friday."

"I know that, too."

"Then why are you here on Tuesday?"

Finally, Len withdraws the unshaken hand. "So you ain't got my credit cards, that what you're saying?"

"I'm saying it doesn't matter what I have. We do this on Friday. I don't understand why you're even here."

"I just thought you might have cards today."

"Well, I don't."

"Okay." Len nods and checks his rearview mirror. "That's cool."

Vince straightens up and cranes his neck to see down the alley. "Why are you doing that?"

"Doing what?"

"Looking down the alley."

"What do you mean?"

"Is someone down there?"

"Where?"

Vince points down the alley. "Back there. You keep checking your rearview."

Len puts his sunglasses back on. "You're paranoid, Vince."

"Yeah. I'm paranoid." Vince starts to walk away. "I'll see you Friday."

"I won't be there Friday. That's what I had to tell you. I'm sending a new guy."

Vince turns back—cold. "What do you mean, a new guy?"

"I mean a guy who's new, as opposed to a guy who's old."

"Yeah, I got that part. Who is he?"

"Just a guy to help out on my end. His name is Ray. You'd like him."

Vince walks back to the open car window. "Since when do you have an *end*, Lenny? You buy shit with my credit cards. Since when is that an *end*?"

"Hell's the matter with you? Just meet with this guy, Vince. Relax." Len presses the button to roll up his window. "You're losing it, man." It's the last thing Vince hears before the Cadillac drives away. The car pauses at the corner—a wink from the brake lights—and turns, Vince alone in the alley, watching his own breath. He looks down the alley once more, then starts for the donut shop.

Vince hates alleys. Jimmy Plums got piped in an alley outside a strip club when he went off to piss. They made it look like a robbery, but everyone knew that Jimmy got taken off for a deep skim on some jukeboxes in Howard Beach. So what's that? Forty-one? Or forty-two? Oh, great. Now you've lost count.

MORE RIVETING NOVELS
BY JESS WALTER

CITIZEN VINCE
A Novel

ISBN 0-06-039441-2 (hardcover)

A story of witness protection, petty thievery, local politics, and murder—set against the turbulent backdrop of the 1980 presidential election.

"It's been a long time since I've read a book as compulsively, indeed greedily, as I read *Citizen Vince*. Here are characters who seem to live of their own volition, who talk out of a terrible inner need to make themselves known and understood, who reveal not just themselves but the yearning heart of our great flawed democracy."

—RICHARD RUSSO, author of *Empire Falls*

LAND OF THE BLIND
A Novel

ISBN 0-06-098928-9 (paperback)

Detective Caroline Mabry of the Spokane Police Department's homicide division is confronted with the arrival of an apparently unstable but somehow charming derelict—who proclaims that he has a murder he wants to confess to.

"Intelligently written, bittersweet, and thoroughly absorbing."
—*Seattle Times*

"Absorbing . . . Walter renders his blind land with a clear-eyed, compassionate vision."
—*Kirkus Reviews*

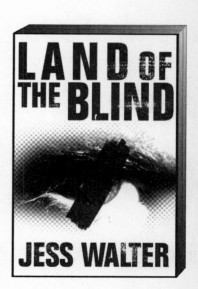